SECRETARIAL TRAINING
COLLEGE
4 Back Walk, Stirling.

PRESENTED

:: TO ::

MARGARET HUTCHISON

Completed Training
and
Higher Secretarial Diploma

1955 - 1956

Drummond Tract Depot, Stirling, Scotland.

BY THE ANGEL,
ISLINGTON

Jubilee week-end in London ! And Dr. Riberac's ten year search for a lost lady seems about to prosper. All doors open to this celebrated French archæologist, but he simply learns that the missing treasure has been thrown out as junk. And for this fatal error of judgment he himself is to blame. Yet how could he have guessed her full significance? Andra Hood was merely a sculptor's model. Beauty alone set her apart. And the world has many lovely women . . . Incredulously, he finds that the trail of the marble statue leads to the drudge's pail and scrubbing brush at Islington. But before he can claim his lost love— over-night she springs from obscurity to international fame. Dr. Riberac's breathless search outlines like a shadow the unforgettable story of Andra herself.

BY THE ANGEL, ISLINGTON

By
MARCH COST

COLLINS
ST JAMES'S PLACE, LONDON
1955

PRINTED IN GREAT BRITAIN
COLLINS CLEAR-TYPE PRESS: LONDON AND GLASGOW

"The way is not without danger . . .
the person must give himself to the
new way completely, for it is only
by means of his integrity that he can
go further, and only his integrity
can guarantee that his way does not
turn out to be an absurd adventure."

C. G. JUNG

"Fear not, little flock, for it is your
Father's good pleasure to give you
the Kingdom."

ST. LUKE'S GOSPEL

Contents

Principal Characters in Order
of Reference

DR. PHILIP RIBERAC (*a Frenchman*)	An Archaeologist
MADAME FRANZ ORTH (*an Englishwoman*)	His Aunt
ALDERMAN HURRUP	A Connoisseur
SIR AMOS STANDISH	A Sculptor
ANDRA HOOD	An Artist's Model
MR. JOE BAXTER	A Builder's Workman
MISS PANDORA QUINN	Alderman Hurrup's Sister-in-Law
MISS EDITH HOOD (*Andra's Aunt*)	A Music Teacher
MISS ZOË HOOD (*Andra's unmarried Mother*) Governess to the family of Prince Essling, Count of Landeck	
MADAME MOFFAT	Family friend of the Hoods
BLANCHE MOFFAT (*her daughter*)	Another Model
MAJOR TREVES	Family friend of the Hoods
MR. BURROWES	*Daily Clarion* Reporter
LETTY GALBRAITH (*friend of Andra's*)	A Young Author
MR. PIGGOTT	Andra's Lawyer
PUNCHIE COBURG	Supervisor at Lombard's Factory
MR. ENOCH TUCKER (*friend of Andra's*)	A Furniture Dealer
MRS. ROSE (*Punchie's Aunt*)	Suburban Landlady
MR. LUDLOW	Suburban Lodger
CONNIE (*Andra's first miracle*)	A Machinist at Lombard's Factory
GERDA RUSH (*friend of Andra's*)	An Actress

MR. MOTT   Attendant at the Victoria and Albert Museum

FRANCIE SEDGE (*Andra's second miracle*)

A Hospital Case, aged twelve

MRS. ELLIS   Andra's Islington Landlady

MR. & MRS. O'NEILL and the REIDS   Andra's Islington

MR. and MISS GOODGE   Neighbours

MISS LEECH   Registry Office Manageress

MRS. ST. ALBYN   London Landlady

CAPTAIN BOYD   Proprietor of the True-Blue Café, Bloomsbury

RUBY   A Charwoman

MIJNHEER and MEVROUW VAN BAERLE and PASTOR FRICK

Members of the Prayer Circle and friends of Andra's

MR. and MRS. BUSK   Later Islington Arrivals

SERGEANT MUSGROVE   A Detective

MONSIGNOR CAIUS   A Visitor

MRS. WILLOUGHBY   A wealthy Widow

PRINCESS ZILLER, COUNTESS OF GERLOS

An impoverished Austrian

MR. CUTHBERT   A Surgeon

Author's Note

I am again indebted to the Staff of
the Victoria and Albert Museum for
invaluable data. Once more names
and dates have been altered so that
no actual individual can be implied.
Two fascinating books have also
been most helpful—*The Romance of
Archaeology* by W. H. Boulton
(Sampson Low) and *The Literature
of the Ancient Egyptians* by Adolf
Herman (Methuen).

Friday Afternoon . . . four o'clock

His wild-goose chase could not have led him to an unlikelier spot! He was forced to admit this now, but some of his exasperation eased as he passed from the blazing June sunshine into the twittering green gloom of Cadogan Manor's trees.

It was incredible that in the year 1935 anyone could vanish off the map like this. Had he been able to call in the police, it would have been a very different matter. In the past he had spent considerable sums on private-detective agencies. These had simply resulted in the preposterous annoyance of having an entirely wrong woman fished out.

The nightmare element in the situation was that twice in the past ten years, he had actually been in the same room with her for a brief space.

Ten years of search? After his first fruitless efforts, the search had certainly flagged. The staggering thing was the way his determination had lately increased.

He was, despite his rancour, fascinated by the fact that he was still in love with her. He could not have believed it possible. It lent a reality to their relationship that appeared almost miraculous in the light of other experiences.

He glanced around him. The beech trees of the entrance had given place to giant oaks, more sparsely set on sloping lawns. These grounds were now a public park, but the Jubilee celebrations elsewhere at this Spa seemed to have emptied it.

Possibly it was always thus, as it stood some miles from

the centre of a town already rich in public gardens. An almost empty bus had deposited him here, in answer to a request for a ticket to the top of the hill.

As soon as he stepped from the London train, he had realised the futility of his visit. The forty thousand occupiers of a staid borough appeared to be out in force on the hilly, brick paveways fronting their Georgian mansions, their old-fashioned Victorian hotels and Edwardian villas—pushing, shoving, exulting in a variety of excitements which included open-air concerts, treasure hunts, a drum-head service at the Monument, and the jungle-like tattoo of the distant fair upon the Common.

A blessing that the British did not often let themselves go! Their stamina in such festivities was an affront to any Frenchman. They had a disconcerting genius too for pageantry, quite out of keeping with the label affixed to them, for convenience sake, by the rest of the world. By all their enemies in fact. What other nation would have launched itself on an eleven-week gala at such a time? A Royal Occasion no doubt, yet when all was said and done it was only a Silver Jubilee . . . twenty-five years achieved, survived—endured, put it how one would. But of course it included the War. It was the token that 1914-1918 had been assimilated, for no war was ever surmounted—least of all by the victors, saddled with the complex necessity of setting ruin to rights.

Abruptly Riberac seated himself on a wooden bench beneath a stunted oak which commanded the steep vista to a distant lake on which swans, serenely self-centred, drifted in their own snowy detachment. To the right, a nurse-maid with some children climbed the hill and disappeared. On his left two lovers, aimless rather than ardent, as if they'd found themselves in the wrong paradise, languidly vanished.

He was now alone, wasting more valuable time. There were at least four calls he should have made in London to-day, for he had learnt last night at the Club, on his arrival from Paris, that Baxter could not see him till Monday. But no sooner had he set foot in London than he was obsessed by the urge to find her again.

The 28th of June! Seven of the eleven gala weeks had gone with no lessening of the general hub-bub. The London streets still seethed with rejoicing crowds. Events were to culminate with a review of the Fleet at Spithead on the 16th July, when for the first time in history, the entire Fleet was to be floodlit. Reluctantly Riberac admitted that last night's illumination in the Capital had been unequalled. He attached no importance to his English blood. His mother had failed to make herself felt before an early death. Unlike her sister—his confounded Aunt now cooling herself in Bad Ischl no doubt! His Aunt, in the regrettable fashion of the outrageously wealthy was obdurately healthy. She had already seen the rest of their relatives out, and might end by surviving her nephew.

He removed his hat, and carelessly laid it aside. He was a tall, rather handsome man, with, surprisingly enough, a benevolent expression. He did not look more than forty. But in this also his looks belied him.

Now that it came to the bit, he scarcely cared whether the Franz Orth money came to him or not. Momentary defeatism of course, for he had only to consider what that wealth would have meant to the two most important archaeological expeditions of his career to come to attention again. The difference between semi-success and conclusive achievement.

His uncle by marriage, Franz Orth, of Austrian extraction, domiciled in France, had amassed this fortune through champagne. He had beaten the French at their own game, and had then proceeded to make his European reputation international by shrewd investment. There had been no children. One nephew only, the scholarly Dr. Riberac who had, to Orth chagrin, earlier adopted his distinguished but ineffectual calling.

At the age of twenty Philip Auguste Riberac had made his choice between the Sorbonne and his uncle's offices. His father, the highly intelligent, over-worked, under-paid editor of an important provincial newspaper had shrugged: "You have the right to your own decision. It's your bed. You will have to lie on it. But don't expect any padding from me." Nor had he. Not only had he done surprisingly well, he had done so fairly quickly. And now, in middle-age, he could count himself comfortably off . . . when he did not remember the Orth money.

Impatiently Riberac leant back on the unaccommodating public bench. Despite his Aunt's present animosity he had no doubt of her ultimate good faith. And, by heaven, the freedom that went with his profession, despite the drawback of comparative poverty, was infinitely preferable to the kind of existence he'd have led in a wine-merchant's shoes! His own work was everything to him. And it was intolerable that it should now be seriously affected. Earlier had he been told that such a state of mind could be possible for him, of all people, he would have laughed in derision. And indeed the position had become absurd—especially when marriage existed for the express purpose of meeting just such conditions!

The only clue that might lead to her present whereabouts was no clue at all. In his previous searches there had always been some method in his approach to the problem. Never before had he plunged into the void on the strength of a name he did not even remember. But the man had been connected with this place. That was all he had to go on.

There had, of course, been other friends of hers. He often heard her chattering of him and her . . . but frankly he had scarcely listened. He had had a vague idea that they lived in London, or thereabouts. It had come as a shock to him later that he could have been so utterly uninterested. Privacy had been essential, in their relationship, especially to him. Yet in his numerous absences abroad, he knew that she occasionally saw him or her . . . at some place other than the Kew house of course. Looking back now he realised afresh that her chatter of this one and that had gradually lessened.

"No, I haven't seen them recently," she admitted. "I never want to leave our lovely home. It's all I need now. The days don't drag as once they did. Each hour brings you nearer."

But leave she had, with a despatch that had been an affront. Returning from the Kelmscott Expedition he had found a note awaiting him in Paris:

Darling Philip,
I have gone, and will not be back. I shall love you always, but this is now good-bye. You will not be surprised.

Andra

Surprised! He was rocked to the foundations.

He did not deny—it would be futile to deny that he had behaved carelessly in cutting short that last visit of his, especially as the Kelmscott undertaking was bound to be a lengthy business. But that news about his Aunt had thoroughly alarmed him. At the time he could think of nothing but the importance of this issue—that he must by his return influence the old lady against the step she proposed. The fact was: he had panicked, and Andra had gone to the wall. His visit to his Aunt had achieved nothing—indeed from that date their relationship had steadily worsened.

The incredible, the inexcusable feature of Andra's defection was that nothing in her previous behaviour had prepared him for it. Two years earlier she had had a much more serious grievance which she had simply taken in her stride—in fact with a generosity that had redoubled devotion on both sides. It still made him slightly sick to think of that damned oversight of his, when during the Haversham Survey, Mesopotamia 1922, he had forgotten to despatch the money.

It certainly had not been her letters that had kept them together during the four years of their union, when he had been compulsorily absent. He did not understand why he kept the stilted things at the time—bald notes that were now, unfortunately, revelations. Understatements that to-day shouted disclosure. But the identical letters. Nothing had changed there—except in himself, the reader.

He was haunted too by a query she had ventured on one of his last visits to the Kew house: "You haven't changed towards me, have you?" "Don't be absurd," he had said tersely. If she began to be unreasonable (discreet description of suspicious) their situation would become impossible.

Yet when together, she was usually gaiety itself—which in itself justified the *ménage*. A trifle nervous of him at the start, he had enjoyed the way she rapidly gained confidence, and was in a few months daring him, as nightly she drummed on that empty salad bowl before supper . . . an elm bowl that after a year was mellow with olive oil, pungent with thyme, mint and chives, and finally bewitched by the flavour of paprika and pimentoes. She would enter his forbidden study, strumming on this wooden bowl as if it were a guitar, to inquire:

"Mild or strong?" And whichever he elected, she would intone: "Far be it from me to stand between any man and his garlic!"

What on earth had possessed her to ruin everything—to do what she had done? And in that cold-blooded way?

The last woman, he would have sworn—

Each year during their life together, their physical delight in one another had steadily grown. That men and women could respond in differing degrees, according to the types attracting them, he was well aware, and he knew enough to realise how rare was the contact with that other who held the maximum delight that love could offer. But he was astounded to discover, belatedly, that this influence extended to the mind, above all to the imagination. He had heard of such cases, and of course the centuries had recorded romantic examples but he had never seriously credited these. Poet's licence had been his explanation. He knew better to-day.

Moodily he now surveyed the park before him, the bleached lawns sloping steeply away. The June day's gathered warmth, murmurous as a hive, spun breathlessly —alive with dancing gnats, shining motes, all the frenzied activity of a minutiae so vast that it was usually unseen. Beyond the shadow of oak and sycamore, heat rose in a fume from the drowsy green-gold scene. Silence had become stupor above the lake, its water lustrous, its swans immobile.

The fact was that he had never really known her till she disappeared. Intelligent but not intellectual—he had earlier dismissed her claims upon his mind. Had he been deceived by what was actually a lack of formal education? He could remember now her delight in any kind of information—her wonder. But her equipment was so inadequate that he had scarcely troubled to enlighten her when tentatively she questioned.

He might as well face up to it. He had shown her no consideration whatsoever. All along he had adhered too rigidly to his own routine.

Well, he certainly could not be accused of that now—his whole day again disorganized. This search had become with years a kind of grim hobby. He was, he supposed, an obstinate man. A hobby, however, should not encroach on work.

He had no sooner put foot on these crowded streets below, than he had realized the futility of going to the Town Hall. What Information Bureau could be expected to deal with a conjecture that the man's missing name had begun with an H!

All she had said fourteen years ago was: "He used to come from Speldarch-Waters to the London studio. We never understood why. He didn't paint, or draw or model, and the others teased him terribly. But then he was always better dressed and a little prim. We prophesied that he'd be Mayor of Speldarch yet! That was where he lived. All the same, he was a dear. He coaxed his father, who'd made quite a lot of money quickly, to give the students one or two commissions for family portraits. It was really a great help. After a time we got quite accustomed to him dropping in when he came to London——"

Riberac arose from the seat, impatiently retrieved his hat, and turned back on his tracks. Possibly he could get out nearer the bus-stop, if he took the gate on the other side of the Mansion House——

Emerging from the trees, on to its terrace, he saw the derelict building fully, a hideous edifice, vast, Victorian—

a plethora of the worst from every known period. Its dimensions alone commanded respect. Blankly the empty windows stared due south.

Myrtle, in full bloom, brushed his shoulder as he drew near. There had been a great bush of myrtle in the garden of the house at Kew. Its perfume was sweeter than hawthorn, yet less cloying. Each summer since, this memory had revived sharply—as if she had already died. It was more shocking than if she had died. The needless waste of it all! When he thought of the time they'd lost——

Suddenly he stopped short. He was shaking with anger. Disturbed, he stared into the glassy shadows of a huge empty drawing-room.

To his amazement, twelve men, facing him, seated like a jury, were regarding him in cold appraisal, each with pen in hand. They appeared less startled to see him than he was to see them. Buttressed by filing cabinets and index-recorders they surveyed him. He was not alone after all.

Disconcerted he turned away. This colossal edifice apparently housed one of the Ministries in its Victorian *rococo*.

Hastily he descended the balustraded steps from the terrace, to regain the park.

What on earth had possessed him to come to this place in the first instance? Blind instinct . . . and he had humbled himself to this rather than reason!

Then turning to the left he saw the Moorish temple.

It stood beneath a towering Deodar, near a stone urn blazing with geraniums. The arches of this Moorish absurdity, which had a certain charm, had been glassed in by some barbarian, to prevent the depredations of other vandals no doubt!

Approaching he saw that the little temple contained a life-sized marble statue on a pedestal. The figure of an

Eastern dancing-girl, naked but for a brief kirtle, who faced the vagaries of these northern latitudes with a summery smile, a tambourine, and endless delight. What this enchantress thought of the Ministry on her right, he could not surmise. Her head slightly averted, she smiled instead with steadfast aplomb at the scarlet geraniums beyond. Yet she had clearly come to stay, for at those dancing feet there was a marble basket of fruit. A practical offering, for why give flowers to June? Amused, he walked round the tiny temple to study the statue more closely. It was the last sort of thing he would have connected with a public park in this staid Spa! The sculpture did not appeal to him—too suave, although the handling of the stone was competence itself. Precious little of the East about it though. The inspiration was Greek but sired by the Apollo Belvedere! This was no creation of a marble woman, but the reproduction of a human one in that medium. Yet the fellow could handle his chisel! The aesthetic vision alone was inadequate. A dismal fate for any sculptor—to miss doing something first-rate by a hair's breadth. But perhaps this man acquiesced in his destiny. After all, the public lapped up this kind of thing in most eras. He had probably made a big success financially.

At the centre glass arch Riberac paused, and read the inscription on the pedestal.

The Dancing Girl
by
Amos Standish
presented to the Corporation of Speldarch-Waters
by
Alderman Hurrup

He continued to stare at the last word as if he could

scarcely believe his eyes. Good God! that was the missing name. *Hurrup!* In the name of wonder, how could he have forgotten a name like Hurrup? Hurrup, Hurrup, Hurrup . . . he had found his man!

Amos Standish . . . that name echoed too, but more faintly . . . further off . . . less helpfully.

Startled, his gaze travelled from the Dancer's poised foot, across the lovely limbs, the smooth body, the firm delicate breasts to the full-throated neck which supported in graceful acquiescence the classical head with its serene features.

For a moment his heart missed a beat, his face paled. Without a shadow of doubt, it was Andra. Andra as he had first known her in 1921, when she was twenty-four and he was thirty-six. It was the actual woman. No marble interpretation, but the living body reproduced in another medium. A sheet of glass alone separated him from their endearing youth—invincible, evocative. Taken unawares by this joy, shaken to the heart he walked blindly towards the stone urn with the geraniums, and resting his hand upon it, turned his face due south towards the distant lake.

Suddenly, this summer scene bemused in light—the perfectly kept, deserted grounds, the silent Manor House, the odour of fresh-cut grass drying in the heat of the late afternoon, the statue in the temple behind him—all these facts outside shook themselves into life within him. He felt another man—for the way in which he had been led here, despite every obstacle that his nature presented, was surely more than a sign. It amounted to absolution.

His hard eyes tightened unexpectedly with moisture that he was incapable of shedding. Much affected, he walked quickly from the grounds. Prompted by the instinct of self-preservation, so strongly developed in him, he did not again glance at the *Dancing Girl*—obscurely aware that pain was closely akin to his new-found joy.

And was he not, in any case, now on his way to her—the reality? Every incident of this amazing experience confirmed it. To run Alderman Hurrup to earth was all that remained.

Friday Afternoon . . . five o'clock

Hurriedly he walked out of the Park. The bus was just leaving the stop—was already drawing past him. Fleetly he leapt on to the step. His luck had turned!

This bus, unlike the earlier one, was well-filled—country people, dressed for the evening's jubilee at Speldarch.

Four-forty-five already, but it might not be necessary to go to the Information Bureau. Any policeman should be able to direct him to the Alderman's house. This bus conductor himself might know it. He was fat, fresh-coloured, friendly.

Riberac, seated next the door, opened conversation.

"I'm a stranger here. Which Ministry works in the Manor House now?"

"Nosey Parker and Company!" the man winked.

"Pensions?" suggested Dr. Riberac.

"No. Inland Revenue. They're not allowed to use the Park though," said the man with satisfaction. "Not a foot beyond the terrace, and that's a fact."

His tone interested Riberac. Surely a bus-conductor did not suffer much from the Inland Revenue's depredations? But probably he disliked the Ministry on principle.

Aloud he said simply: "I believe Alderman Hurrup lives at Speldarch. Do you happen to know where his house is?"

"Everyone knows Alderman Hurrup's house," said the man. "Corunna Square. It faces west. You can't miss it. It's the only house with a stair outside."

A stair outside. It sounded a humble residence. Probably Hurrup had retained the parental roof. These self-made men often continued to live quite simply. This indicated a certain modesty in the Alderman not altogether displeasing. And from Andra's indications there was also the assurance of an accommodating personality. For the first time in ten years Riberac's search was prospering——

His mood mellowed upon him.

Things were speeding up!

Sir Amos Standish . . . at the wrong moment the name presented itself like an unwelcome visiting card. The Sculptor had acquired a title since that statue was presented to Speldarch. Yes, Riberac remembered now. There had been lengthy articles on his work some months ago in the Paris papers. Standish had died recently. Not that he would have been likely to help in tracing Andra. That connection had been brief. He was not the one that Andra had enlarged upon. Hurrup was his man. She had only mentioned Standish once or twice—with the sort of reverence that a young girl would naturally feel for a well-known man— in fact a celebrity. Standish had been a man of his own age—perhaps a trifle older. It was just possible that in those days Riberac had been a little jealous of him. Well, Standish had gone now, poor devil. A certain phrase that Riberac had not liked—forgotten till this moment—came back to him. Andra had exclaimed, of the Sculptor, eagerness abating shyness: "Oh, I wish you could meet him! He's not like anyone else." That had been enough.

Quite enough, Dr. Riberac decided afresh, and then dismissed this past unreason. What, he wondered was Alderman Hurrup's business or trade?

Abruptly the bus came to another halt on the country road. A dark little inn, with secretive windows, crouched beneath a gnarled oak, but this picturesque effect was completely spoiled by a large advertisement plastered on the gable of the building:

"*Have a Hurrup*," it commanded, "*the Ale for You.*"

Dr. Riberac was surprised at the Alderman. But his spirits rose again. Hurrup confirmed himself at each step. He knew where he was with Hurrup. Hurrup presented no difficulties. No *arrière-pensée* here!

Nevertheless, he was at a loss to understand why he had also forgotten Standish's name till to-day. As for Hurrup —how could anyone forget a name like Hurrup with its connotations on Hurrah! Not that Andra had left him anything to shout about.

The bus was now driving steeply down-hill between well-built houses, embowered in gardens that were dense with flowering shrubs—the blossom from these lying in frail drifts along the eighteenth-century side-walks—brick walks that undulated in places from the tremendous roots of the giant trees which so pleasantly shaded the town's many hills.

It was stiflingly hot in the bus. Riberac was thankful to get down in the High Street. And it was cooler still in Alma Road with its tall, Regency houses, which led directly to Corunna Square.

There he looked around him in astonishment. The crowds had deserted this place, but at any time these massive Georgian mansions would have imposed gravity. Seen for the first time Corunna Square was startling in its silence and distinction. From a formal garden in the centre some ancient trees straggled towards the light, with foliage that spread a thin canopy above their lurching boles. A few more storms would soon snap down these brittle boughs, but of course this walled enclosure was shelter against such. These sycamores might last another ten or even twenty years. At the moment they diffused a faint twittering from unseen birds. A plot of untrodden grass in the centre was green as the moss in a disused well. Corunna Square itself had something of the same stony silence. He felt a shout would echo here.

As instructed, he turned to the side that faced due west.

A momumental house confronted him, flanked by high walls, and approached by three flights of steps. Its columned doorway, its symmetrically disposed windows, its bold cornices, and dormered roof—its heraldic stone beasts at the entrance, now received the full oblation of the sun with the impassivity of a sphinx. The mansion suggested the palace of an eighteenth-century merchant prince. The Doge of Venice himself would have felt quite at home here.

Compressing his lips, Dr. Riberac walked rather more quickly than necessary up the three flights of steps.

The major-domo of his expectations did not, however, appear. The door was opened by a country girl in a starched apron, with blazing red cheeks. Scarcely aware of his courteous and tentative inquiry, and almost before he had time to present his card, she exclaimed:

"This way, if you please, Sir," and glancing at him side-ways, like a shying horse, she ushered him into a large cool hall, which again evoked Venetian comparisons.

Muttering to herself, "No, best come in here!" she hurried across the hall, and flung open the door of a long dim but, beautiful withdrawing room, and then retreated.

Dr. Riberac found himself alone. Seldom impressed, he looked around him with a feeling of incredulity. This was perfection inscribed by Adams! A medallioned ceiling, in egg-shell blues and greens; plaster cameos in ivory and faded gold upon the walls; and a sculptured fire-place with a formal design of garlands, nymphs and satyrs! Was it possible that these three landscapes were by Zuccarelli himself? Masterly the way in which the entire interior was dominated and yet integrated by the vaulted windows at the far end, from which were draped maize-coloured curtains in heavy, lustreless silk. A pier glass opposite reflected these windows and the garden beyond. On the Console table below this mirror, a crystal beaker bore some crimson roses, a trifle past their first splendour. But it was not only the *Directoire* furniture, thrown into admirable relief by the fawn carpet; the wedgwood urns in sentinel silence on each side of the recessed bookcase that compelled his homage. Such things could be bought, and assembled by an expert. But that costly carpet was much worn; the most comfortable of the tapestry chairs were shabby; the firescreen flaunted a frayed banner. Sun and shadow, heat and cold, wear and tear had throughout the years worked their slow havoc on sound craftmanship and the effect was irresistible. This was tradition—very much at home with time.

Hastily, Dr. Riberac was obliged to revise his suppositions upon Alderman Hurrup.

The door opened and a man of about forty entered. Dark, of medium height, spare—with a lean face and a wary eye. An astute, but dignified individual. His suit was of a careful cut which was not adequate to its excellent quality. His collar was irreproachable, his tie discreet, and he was shaved and barbered within an inch of his life.

"Mr. Hurrup?"

"That's the name," said the Alderman with finality. "What can I do for you?"

His brevity set the key.

With a word of apology first, Riberac said: "I have quite recently arrived from Paris. I live abroad. I have called to-day hoping to trace the whereabouts of a friend. I trust you can help me. Miss Alexandra Hood."

No expression whatsoever crossed Mr. Hurrup's face, but he remarked with interest. "Dr. Riberac . . . now you're the archaeologist, aren't you? The name rang a bell as soon as I saw your card. The Vaucluse Angel. I've just seen the early edition of the London evening paper—on the train from town. Congratulations."

Dr. Riberac's eyes narrowed. He could scarcely believe this misfortune. "May I ask on what?"

"The missing fragment of the Panel, which I understand has turned up at last."

"Indeed. I was not aware that the Press had discovered this possibility too."

"The notice makes it clear that nothing's definite yet. But a Mr. Joe Baxter has been interviewed after the news got round his Local. He states that he hopes he may be able to oblige you."

"Very good of him, I'm sure." Asperity concealed Riberac's apprehension. "May I ask if Mr. Baxter divulged the whereabouts of the alleged fragment?"

"No, he did not. When pressed he contented himself by remarking: 'That would be telling!' Two papers have it as front page news. *Vaucluse Angel Now Perfect* and the other headlines run: *Dr. Riberac Has A Clue*. Care to see the papers now?"

"Not at the moment, thank you. I have come on quite a different matter. Miss Alexandra Hood."

"Yes, of course. Sit down, won't you. Cigarette? Sorry to have let the cat out of the bag like this. But one always connects you with the Vaucluse Angel."

"A misfortune for which I have again to thank the Press."

"Oh, come now——"

With a bleak smile Dr. Riberac remarked, "I find it irritating to a degree that the Press cannot mention my name now, in any connection, without dragging in the Vaucluse discovery, 1920. An interesting find, but scarcely the event of a career."

"Hang it all," said Mr. Hurrup cheerfully, "it was a dashed fine bit of detective work on your part, and the newspapers hanker for a good story. You found the first half of the Panel in Vaucluse—yet recognized that it was English. You then started a search in Gloucestershire——"

"My dear Sir," protested Dr. Riberac, "typical British sandstones are Pennant stone and Forest of Dean—blue and grey. Any expert could have placed it. Luck served me when ten years later I ran the other half of the Panel to earth in the cellar of Burbage Abbey over here. Yet, it is a fact that—despite the odds against one—if one knows what one is looking for, one often finds it. But it is scarcely a feat initially to recognize a masterpiece when it falls into one's hands. Merely a matter of training."

The Alderman shook his head, "Which surely applies to every discovery!"

"I can only assure you," said Dr. Riberac briefly, "that any archaeological excavation extends its members considerably more than that."

A trifle waggishly Mr. Hurrup shook his head—his cordiality appeared to be growing. "You under-rate your Angel's importance you know. When we set out to be grateful as a nation, we don't let anyone forget it! And it was downright handsome of Madame Franz Orth to present it to this country. If Baxter's missing fragment turns out to be okay, the thing will be about perfect. And if that's not a miracle, after fifteen years investigation, you're hard to please."

Dr. Riberac's eyes had narrowed. "Mr. Hurrup," he said, "I am much less interested in miracles than the mundane. I am in search of facts at present. Am I right in thinking you are a friend of Miss Andra Hood?"

"Of many years standing," amplified Mr. Hurrup. "Yes, you're certainly right there."

"Andra spoke of you several times, in the past. This has

enabled me to find you to-day. She mentioned certain other friends of course too. But we—these friends and I—never met. Therefore I had no addresses to go by . . . or further knowledge."

Mr. Hurrup nodded amiably. "Is that the way of it?" he observed. "Yes, I met Andra in 1917. I had been invalided out of the Army with a leg wound. She was about twenty then. A model at the London Art School. At Kurragh's Studio I met her——" for the first time he hesitated. A look of diffidence crossed his face. "Of course, I was only on the fringe of the group——"

Courteously Dr. Riberac replied: "One has only to enter your remarkable home, Mr. Hurrup, to sense your appreciation of the Arts."

The other looked up quickly, "I've always been interested in the Arts," he said on a note of apology. "In a manner of speaking, they are my hobby. It was the chance of a lifetime to get this place five years ago when the Dowager Lady Dunorbyn died."

For the first time Dr. Riberac looked at him with the sympathy begot of humour. "You took it over then?"

"Lock, stock and barrel," said Mr. Hurrup tersely. "My wife's not interested in Art. Her hobby's gardening. She camps out—as she calls it—in the south wing, and so we both enjoy ourselves in our own way. She is my second wife," he added rather unnecessarily.

"I congratulate you on the sanity of your arrangements," said Dr. Riberac. "Immensely civilized."

The Alderman shot him a swift glance, but the fellow was quite sincere.

"I have just come from Cadogan Park," Dr. Riberac pursued smoothly, "where I saw the *Dancing Girl* which you have presented to the Corporation."

A perceptible shadow crossed the other's face. "And no

man ever regretted a benefaction more! I secured that fine
marble many years ago. Unfortunately my wife—my first
wife didn't care for statuary. And it wasn't altogether
suitable for the garden of the villa we had at that time.
I got rid of it, temporarily, before her death. The Turkish
Baths took it—up at the Spa. But I'm sorry to say the
members abused it. The British public has even less respect
for public property than for private. Our parks after each
Bank Holiday are in a state unknown abroad."

"As an Alderman," said Riberac pleasantly, "you can no
doubt speak with authority there."

But not to be wooed, the other retorted: "I speak as a
Councillor, and any other can bear me out. As I was
saying: the *hoi-polloi* at the Baths defaced it . . . stuck on
a false moustache, wrote rude jokes across the tambourine.
The Committee asked me to remove the figure. And had
the impudence to say that it had now impaired the dignity
of the entrance hall. It cost me pounds sterling getting the
mess cleaned off the marble. After that I put it in store,
until I presented it to the Corporation. Six months," he said
regretfully, "before I secured this place."

"A pity," Dr. Riberac condoled. "And now about Andra
herself—Miss Hood."

"Miss Hood," repeated Mr. Hurrup methodically. "In
what way can I help you there?"

"As I explained earlier. I am anxious to trace her
address."

Mr. Hurrup shook his head thoughtfully. "I don't know,"
he said carefully, "whether it's quite the thing to pass a
lady's address around."

"I appreciate that, and as an old friend of Miss Hood's,
I respect your reticence," Riberac said stiffly.

"Oh, well," an unexpected glimmer of humour showed
in Mr. Hurrup's eye, "the Vaucluse Angel, in a manner of

speaking, vouches for you. But I'm sorry to say I can't oblige."

"Do I understand that you have not got her address."

"That's a fact," agreed Mr. Hurrup. "It's years since I saw Andra. I've an idea that she had troubles she wasn't willing to share. And when that's the way of it, you don't intrude."

"But someone must know where she is——" protested Dr. Riberac.

"You don't know yourself," said the Alderman coolly. "And you're an old friend too. It's my belief that Andra cut away for her own good reasons. She's probably made new friends now."

Dr. Riberac rose, and then sat down again abruptly. Mr. Hurrup watched him with some curiosity.

"It's a pity, Dr. Riberac," he observed, "that Sir Amos Standish is dead. It's years since he met Andra, of course. But he might have been able to help. Better than most."

"I cannot for the life of me see how Sir Amos Standish could help," Riberac began coldly, "when on your own showing they had not met for years."

The Alderman continued to watch him with curiosity. "Then you haven't read Sir Amos' book?"

"Book! What book!" demanded Dr. Riberac. "I've only just arrived over here. I understood that Standish was a sculptor."

"That's right," said Mr. Hurrup. "But he wrote a book before he died. And it's been published posthumously. It's only been out three weeks, but it's caused a sensation. Everybody's reading it."

"I daresay," Dr. Riberac looked his impatience. "Standish was a well-known man. I believe he travelled widely. He had certainly met many notable people at close quarters. A book by such a celebrity is bound to be of interest. The public revels in exalted gossip. Such memoirs usually follow an accepted pattern."

"These memoirs," said Mr. Hurrup cautiously, "are a bit different. You must read them for yourself."

Dr. Riberac rose.

"The book," pursued his host, "is called *Armature*."

Dr. Riberac paused, arrested in spite of himself. "Rather an unlikely name surely for a best-seller?"

"A sculptor's best seller," corrected Mr. Hurrup. "He's put the dictionary definition in the front of the book. *Arms, armour; defensive covering of animals or plants; the support for a clay model in sculpture.* Of course a sculptor in marble doesn't need an armature—he hews out of the living block. A case of subtraction! But in this book on his life, Sir Amos looks on himself as dealing with clay. A question of addition—of summing up."

"Unusual modesty," commented Dr. Riberac.

"Nothing modest about his claims for Andra however," said Mr. Hurrup briskly. "In the old days, at a Studio birthday party, when he gave the toast of her health he once said she was bound for important places. And in his book, he's at it again. He calls her Thursday's Child."

"Thursday's Child?" Dr. Riberac frowned.

"It's a rhyme we have over here: ' *Monday's Child is fair of face, Tuesday's Child is full of grace, Wednesday's Child is full of woe, Thursday's Child has far to go——* '"

"In that case I should have thought that both Monday and Tuesday could just as appropriately have been her name day."

Mr. Hurrup made an odd little gesture of resignation. "She was the best part of any man's week, so it scarcely matters. But Standish should have the casting vote. You must read his book. He knew her better than anyone——"

"I must apologize," Dr. Riberac interrupted, "for trespassing on your time. I believe there is a train back to town about six——"

"Five-fifty-five," said Mr. Hurrup with precision. "You'll just about do it. Sorry not to oblige you on the other matter. However, here's an address at Hampstead——" he took out a card and scribbled some words across it. "This belongs to Miss Pandora Quinn—my first wife's sister. She used to know Miss Hood well. In fact, they went to the same school as girls. Old friends. She might be able to assist——"

Rapidly he escorted his visitor through the palatial hall, to the front door.

"Going to take you all your time," he warned as the other went down that imposing flight of steps. "Hope you'll manage!"

"Thank you," Dr. Riberac called across his shoulder. "Make no mistake about that. I shall!"

Friday Evening . . . six o'clock

He caught the train with seconds only to spare. A frowsty, first-class, non-corridor carriage—but empty. No chance now of a newspaper till London as the train was also non-stop.

He slammed down both windows, and sat back alertly.

That fellow doesn't know a thing, he decided. And he's determined I shall not either—

More charitably, the address in his pocket prompted second thoughts.

But the first conviction remained.

Miss Pandora Quinn!

Andra had never mentioned her. Yet they had been at school together. Old friends. Odd.

Miss Pandora Quinn. The Irish element tended to confuse the classical. It sounded elaborate—even devious!

Perhaps this accounted for his growing sense of insecurity?

But if an answer were to be had, he would have it to-night —whatever happened.

He had always been pretty certain that Andra was still in London.

Thursday's Child has far to go! No, she was still there. *Bound for important places*—that well might be. When she had made that first devastating reappearance in 1930 after six years separation, he had realized the folly of his earlier estimation. In that smart gathering she had been the shabbiest person present. He noticed that her hands were swollen, and that her ankles had also thickened. He couldn't imagine what she'd been up to—her figure was a little heavier too, but her face, calm and sweet, was still young enough to bear fatigue as a shadow. Exhaustion had not yet hollowed beauty. Yet her mild retorts to every angry demand he made below his breath had been formidable in finality. She was now more than a match for him. Not that anything she said mattered. The appalling thing was that she had simply walked out of the house ten minutes later, and that the only person who might have given him her address was the last woman who would ever do so. Four years had to pass before there had been another comet-like appearance. Who, in God's name, would ever have looked for her *there*? If he had even had half an hour's warning, he would have been equal to the occasion, despite his incredible predicament then——

Brooding, he summoned that final image of her. Weight had dropped from her in these last four years—almost alarmingly. She was slim as a girl again, but now it was a brittle grace that told its own story.

Miss Pandora Quinn—this woman at Hampstead might very well know her whereabouts. It was quite plain to him that for some reason or other Hurrup had not wished to intrude upon Andra. That first wife might have been jealous . . . so too might the second. Women could be the very devil. It was even possible that Miss Quinn might have withheld the address from her brother-in-law. Every solicitor knew that a relationship-in-law could be the most rancorous of all——

He raised his head, and gazed out at the flying landscape. The cloudless heat-wave blue of the sky had thickened in a sultry, smoky way. It was banking up for thunder! Rain would be a relief, he decided. And the optimism born of that moment of revelation in Cadogan Park once more flooded back. He was on the way to her. It was simply a matter of time. It might only be hours——

Now that he was cooling down, he realized that that fellow Hurrup had deflected him in the most successful way by wasting time over the Vaucluse Angel!

But what the Alderman did not know, confound him, was the curious way in which Andra had coincided with each stage of the Angel's history since its discovery. Coincidence of course, but none the less remarkable.

It had been during that visit, in connection with its presentation to the Museum in London, that he had first met her. Later he had taken her to see the Panel—the morning before it had been photographed for the Press.

Side by side, they had surveyed it, alone in the empty gallery.

It had all those ideal qualities that enrich the finest 13th Century work, with something of the grave simplicity of the earlier century. The British experts had at first considered the figure to be an angel of annunciation. But Dr. Riberac would not subscribe to this. That forearm had a curious turn—as if the lost hand were presenting an object rather than indicating an occasion, and the Press had seconded his views with an enthusiasm that embarrassed him!

The stone had crumbled in places round the life-sized figure in its bold relief, but from the ruin of the Angel's sleeve, the left arm was thrust forth in full vitality, as if its grasp on life defied the stone. The energy of the entire figure was so dynamic in its swirling draperies that the lost left hand, severed at out-stretched wrist, became a kind of obsession with the observer. An angel was a messenger, after all. What had been the mission of this heroic form? The brow was blank, his sightless eyes dispassionate, but although the right hand was raised in blameless benediction there was a sardonic rather than an indulgent curve to those mediaeval lips. An irony which was never lost on any beholder and which invariably whetted curiosity. What had the Angel borne in this imperative hand? Scarcely a flower . . . and hardly laurels—too much derision would be misplaced in a heavenly visitant, and there was no doubt as to the figure's divinity. Possibly a scroll, Riberac had mused, yet the turn of that wrist suggested a weightier object. The thing remained a mystery.

That morning when first she saw the Angel, the look of wonder on her face had been almost that of recognition.

"Why it's a gray Angel!" she had exclaimed. "And that was the very quotation on to-day's *Daily Thought Calendar:* ' *Drudgery, the gray angel of success.*'"

"Well," he had retorted dryly, "the missing hand *may* hold a broom or brush for all we know——"

She turned quickly at that, but laughed almost instantly. Although rather over-earnest, she mercifully had some humour. Pointing to the Latin inscription at the foot of the Panel she asked:

"What does it say there?"

" *The Strength of every mind that seeks Thee,*" he translated. "My friend Eldersley informs me that it is a quotation from a prayer by St. Augustine, and it may be a useful clue in assembling the complete Panel, should the missing portion ever turn up. You notice that across the top there is the start of the inscription: *O God, the Light of every heart that sees Thee.* The phrase that is missing, and that falls between these two, is almost certain to be somewhere on the lost half of the Panel."

"How strange," she said softly. "Did Mr. Eldersley tell you the missing words?"

For the first time he had a feeling of embarrassment. A trifle curtly he replied: " *The Life of every soul that loves Thee.*"

She shook her head compassionately. "Of course it's love

that's missing. No wonder it's the gray Angel," she said.
"What a search . . . what a *work*."

Unexpectedly he sighed. "Yes," he agreed, "to track down
the missing half is going to be a devil of a job . . . especially
as it may no longer be in existence——" abstractedly he had
shepherded her out of the Museum.

But looking back now he perceived that they had been
talking of two very different things. Both, however, elusive
as a needle in a haystack.

Andra's of course was a case apart. She had been born
happy. An idiotic expression, as of course it described but
did not explain her. She had invariably behaved as if
heaven on earth were feasible. A seeker also, but of a very
different kind——

Yet, he supposed now, she had gone forward on her
search, pretty much as he went forward on his. He was,
after all a professional seeker—when it came to his work.
And no matter what the objective, the procedure—to be
effective—was ever the same. First, one selected the likeliest
site, and after appropriate preparation—often the work of
years—one began quite simply to dig. And having found—
if that miracle occurred—the heaviest part of one's labours
often lay ahead: the tabulating, cataloguing, assessing—
with finally the climax—a living restoration of the truths
rescued, to the stream of history. And the operative words
were these three: *a living restoration.*

What a labour of Hercules any excavation was, when one
remembered the weight of opposition in public and private
life, the massive obstructions in the physical field. And yet
this very hindrance was essential, up to a point, if the
foundations of discovery were to be well and truly laid.
Only those with a vocation would ever see it through, of
course.

Just how would it apply to a single-minded soul in search

of heaven? She was, he knew, genuinely devout—yet the irregular nature of their union never appeared to worry her unduly. Or had he been deceived in this also?

Suddenly he frowned where he sat, in the rocking railway carriage. Some words from a commentary by Professor Jung had revived in memory. "*Whether a person receives his fate from without or within, the experiences and events of the way remain the same. . . . The way is not without danger. Everything good is costly, and the development of the personality is one of the most costly of all things. . . . The step to higher consciousness leads away from all shelter and safety. The person must give himself to the new way completely, for it is only by means of his integrity that he can go farther, and only his integrity can guarantee that his way does not turn out to be an absurd adventure.*"

Again Riberac glanced from the window. The outlying suburbs of London had darkened with incredible speed. Already in the distance he could see a thunder-down-pour issuing from a sulphur sky. He was rushing right into it.

The way is not without danger . . .

Was it possible that in her search after the celestial she had also suffered? At the hands of angels, as well as of men?

Disturbed, he thrust his hand into his jacket, and drew out his pocket-book. Like the ostrich of old, he would bury himself in Mr. Baxter's letters.

The first letter was headed *27 Forest Row, Sevenoaks, Kent*, and was dated simply *Sunday*, but the postmark confirmed postage Monday 3rd June.

It began:

Dear Sir,
Seeing your advertisement with Address regular in Wilts and

*Gloucestershire Standard every quarter for some years past Think
have something for your advantage but don't put yourself to no
expense as any time will do as may be Dud. But do not think
so with good Reasons. Measures are same as given in Paper
allowing for improvements me and Wife has been forced to add
to Relick since same has become our door-stop. Mrs. Baxter
fixing up a tidy job by sewing whole into a bit of baize. Coming
to my suspicions why same might be to your Advantage, Self was
present when cript of Burbage Abbey was cleared out. A proper
dirty job and can remember Panel man in bed the Half belonging
to your Angel. Not dead as Papers said for eyes was open looking
up. But nobody thought this Figure great shakes before shunting
to Museum. And when it fell on getting out this was no wonder
as a heavy job for all concerned Most of it useless anyway and
bound for the quarry Tip. One bit left behind in cart was picked
out as a handy wedge for door-stop. Weighing one thing and
another and being no way responsible for any breakages thought
you might like a squint at said wedge. Seeing that it has a man's
hand carved across it large as you like, I had to laugh and said
Here's how do you do or Goodbye. But Mrs. Baxter saying that
this gave her the creeps I covered same around with a bit of clay
which had handy for testing drains my Boss being a sub-
contracting mason to the Builder here. Hoping same will
now come off in water to your liking. Removing from Marlborough Mrs. Baxter and me took the Wedge along, for working in the back garden You don't hear the Front door unless back
is open . . .*

This epistle forwarded from his London Club had reached
Riberac in Paris. Without exciting the man unduly, he had
written ordering him to remove the wedge from the back
door, and had arranged with his bank to have a money-
order sent Baxter at once. This, he explained, would pay
the cost of a new door-stop—and defray any other expenses

till they met. The letter also made it plain that if wedge proved to be the find that Dr. Riberac hoped, Mr. Baxter would receive an additional sum for his trouble.

He had warned Baxter quite sternly of the necessity for silence—not only as to Baxter's views on the wedge's importance, but also as to the present arrangements. The wedge (absurd term but door-stop was ludicrous) to be stored meantime in the safest possible place known to Mr. Baxter.

In fact, his letter had been almost as lengthy as Baxter's own, but he didn't want the Press ferreting around at this stage. Journalists, like most opportunists, had a genius for jumping to the right conclusions before officialdom had staked its legitimate claim.

Mr. Baxter's second letter was again headed Sunday. It was much warmer and a great deal shorter.

Dear Doctor,

Anything you say and mums the word from Both alright. You-know-what is now under the Bed. If you say the word willing to oblige by trying to get Clay off Myself——

Riberac had said the word with explosive speed. He had telegraphed Baxter from Paris to do nothing whatsoever with the remains till his arrival.

An hour or so after despatch, it occurred to him that the word *remains* might have stirred local curiosity, or have other unfortunate connotations for Mr. Baxter. It was too late then for morbid speculation on his own part, but from that hour he too adopted the title of the wedge for this (presumed) relic. He had been throughout as irrationally convinced that this was the final missing section as he was that Baxter (damn him) was responsible for the accident to the second half of the Panel.

He had counted upon claiming the wedge first thing this morning, but to his chagrin a third message from Mr. Baxter had been handed to him at the Club on arrival yesterday. This also was headed Sunday, but the postmark on the card—for such it was—showed that it had been posted on Monday 24th.

The postcard simply said: *Owing to happy Event for my Son's wife, Mrs. Baxter and me will be going Friday to Surrey till late Sunday. You are welcome Monday next any time convenient* . . .

Now he had to kick his heels till Monday—in continued anxiety over this too! Not only as to its being the missing section, but as to its present safety.

Would the Baxters have taken it with them—or would it still be under that bed?

He could imagine the safety arrangements at *27 Forest Row* only too well. It would be the sort of place one could get into with a tin-opener.

And now the imbecile had let the news of its existence leak out.

Exasperated he leant back in his corner.

Suddenly, his attention quickened. In the rack opposite he had just caught sight of a discarded newspaper.

Seizing it, he flicked it over—a London evening paper. And there was the article—front page news. *The Vaucluse Angel Again*, with a sub-title: *Dr. Riberac Has A Clue.* They had certainly splashed it—confound the lot of them!

His eye raked the column.

Hurrup was right. Baxter had talked but had given no details. In fact the article read as if the wedge were already in Riberac's own hands! He hadn't suspected Baxter of as much intelligence!

The article was padded out in the way now so familiar

to him. Impatiently he read it through. Each time his name appeared the Angel tagged along. He had been resident in Vaucluse at the time he despatched the first detailed description of the find. The Angel had thenceforward appropriated his address. "*Dr. Riberac, who, as it will be remembered*" . . . or as now "*The unique Wall Panel discovered by Dr. Riberac, known as the Vaucluse Angel, lends weight to more recent discoveries of his——*" the patronage of it! There had actually been one occasion, too, when during the catastrophe to the Eldersley Excavation in Egypt his own death had been presumed and a preliminary obituary notice had laid him to rest in the Angel's company. '*Dr. Riberac, the distinguished archaeologist and noted excavator, who has conducted these recent researches, has also perished, it is feared, from this tragic fire in Pharaoh's Catacomb. A compulsory entombment that is a forcible reminder of his own dramatic rescue of the Vaucluse Angel from oblivion. The Vaucluse Angel, it will be remembered——*' and so on for the rest of the column, in which the Angel not only stole his final thunder, but made off with the major portion of the space allotted him by a thankless community.

A tissue of inaccuracies from start to finish, as usual. The Panel had not been unearthed. He had discovered it in broad daylight, stowed away at the back of a lot of 16th Century junk in the gallery-warehouse at Carpentras.

The train storming through London Bridge, had taken Waterloo in its stride.

Already Dr. Riberac was on his feet, as it swung over Hungerford Bridge. The Thames and Westminster flashed their beauty through tropical rain, but he scarcely noticed.

Miss Pandora Quinn of the Towers, Madeira Park Road, Hampstead, might be on holiday?

Or she might not!

He would give her time to have dinner, but not a minute longer.

And he would not telephone in advance.

He would arrive unheralded. Very much safer!

No . . . she would be there.

It was essential.

Friday Evening . . . seven o'clock

The Tube roared, raced and rattled him to Hampstead as if it had one object only—to disgorge him.

He emerged on that precipitous street, blinking, to find the rain over, and the soaking scene ablaze from the westering sun—the cleansed air momentarily fresh as water.

A newspaper lad directed him to Madeira Park Road.

"Top of the hill, Guv—across by the pond, then bear to the left, and down the road. Spanking ten minutes yet——"

Dr. Riberac walked on. Although he did not acknowledge it, he was tired. Physically as hard as nails, he decided that his need was food, and turned in at a likely tavern. A modest, yet self-respecting hostelry which in France would offer excellent fare.

He had earlier realized that Miss Pandora Quinn must be allowed to dine in peace. One hour and a quarter she should have for this purpose.

The coffee-room of the *Barley Belle* was clean and neat. Only two couples occupied tables, seated at some distance from each other.

Dr. Riberac, like many bachelors, attached considerable importance to his food. He therefore ordered his present meal with care. The elderly waiter departed—his silence might have been resignation or apathy, and Dr. Riberac was free to glance briefly at his neighbours.

An unattractive middle-aged couple, who looked as if they'd quarrelled, and two young people, completely engrossed . . . the girl, elbows on table, hands clasped beneath her chin, had her gaze fixed on the young man.

The youth was obviously talking about himself—at great length. Her attitude was dedicated rather than delighted.

Dr. Riberac decided that his soup was late.

Critically he observed the middle-aged couple . . . the man was almost servile in his attentions—placating her at every turn. Were they living on her money, or did he hope to? In a supercilious indifference that appeared to be habitual, she barely registered a reaction to these efforts.

What the devil had happened to his meal?

The waiter, lumbering across the room, set it down with a sigh which Riberac found surprising until he began upon it.

The soup was hot, but on a cold plate. No rolls. Instead a slice of stale white bread, on a tinsel doiley, was presented with such politeness that he accepted it.

Briefly he requested water.

A glass of tepid liquid was brought him, with a flawless impression of the waiter's thumb along the drinking edge. The hot roast beef that followed turned out to be remarkably good, but the greens were sodden, the potatoes hard. Butter, at this stage, was served separately. Mustard also made a belated appearance. By this time Dr. Riberac was unnerved. Gloomily he noted that the young people at the next table were finishing their meal with a banana. This confirmed the dictum that a banana at the close of dinner is an insult to the Chef. This cook deserved to be insulted.

By the time the sweet arrived, he regarded it with aversion. Amazing to relate, the raspberry and apple pie amounted to perfection. His spirits rose, then wavered. Was it too much to hope that the coffee would be drinkable? No, it was hot, strong, and good. Served in a chipped cup that caught his lower lip. Annoyed he paid the bill. It proved pathetically cheap. Rancour again defeated, he left a larger tip than necessary, and went out fuming. Had he had a meal, or had he not? Uncertainty prevailed. Was he satisfied? Definitely not!

Conflict thus resolved, he climbed the remainder of the hill, crossed by the pond, bore to the left, and entered Madeira Park Road.

At first he scarcely noticed where he was going, assailed afresh by the remembrance of past delectable meals at the Kew house. Andra had not been a chef in any ambitious sense of the word—but what she could cook, she cooked extraordinarily well. He appreciated that he was inclined to be critical. But she had improved remarkably. Her scope too had extended, and her salads had been memorable. The cleanliness and order of their home forced him to realize that he had been living in squalor ever since. "I may not be a startling cook," she used to boast, "but you will admit I am a perfect housemaid!" And she had actually begun to bake bread astonishingly well—just before she left.

Why on earth had she done this crazy thing?

Through this folly of hers the best years of their life had gone . . . were going——

Madeira Park Road, deserted in late sunshine, presented itself. As an answer to his query, it did not look promising. At one time quite a prosperous street, this was true of it no longer. He saw that at a glance—although flowering shrubs in their summer freshness concealed the shabbiness of the houses. As the street progressed, however, deterioration lessened—the windows looked cleaner, the curtains fresher and the gardens tidier. The names also grew more ambitious. *Avalon* and *Treetops* gave way to *Montrose* and *Sandringham*—ludicrous really! The district in its deterioration still drew its own distinctions apparently.

He had reached the end of the road, which proved a cul de sac without discovering Miss Quinn's house, when he noticed, between two stone pillars, a fair-sized drive taking quite an important curve between trim lawns sparsely set with dwarf rhododendron bushes. It looked exactly like the entrance to a well-kept cemetery, but both pillars in Gothic gold-leaf lettering proclaimed it to be The Towers.

He had arrived.

The Towers.

Friday Night . . . eight-thirty

The next turn upon the drive disclosed a large, luxuriant
garden, fronting an elaborate brick house. The Towers had
only one tower, but as this was crenellated, with a flag-staff,
the visitor was relieved rather than disappointed, for each
angle of the building had its individual turret commanding
varied views on every approach. The dim, still hour was
heavy with the scent of stock. Dr. Riberac, passing beneath
innumerable honeysuckle arches, felt slightly self-conscious
by the time he reached the front door. One side of the
building was dominated by a massive copper-beech, and,
glancing up as it flamed against the sunset, he reflected that
there was no depths so dark as its shadows. It did not
belong to the vegetable kingdom at all. It was a tree of
bronze.

Somewhat peremptorily he rang the bell.

An elderly maid, in impeccable uniform opened the door.
She regarded him with close attention as he presented his
card, and made his inquiry. Then quietly she invited him
to enter. A very different type of servant from the Alderman's! Madam was at home, she informed him——

Crossing the pleasant hall, bright with brass and bowls
of roses, he caught a vanishing whiff of mayonnaise,
cucumber, and freshly ground coffee. Miss Pandora Quinn
he was confident had dined a great deal better than he
had.

He found himself, solitary, in a large, square, blue velvet
drawing room, glossy with white enamel, and oriental china
—its interior pleasantly drowsy with the scent of summer.

No faded splendour here, as at the Alderman's, to pave the way, meditatively, to the gods! This was luxurious comfort in perfect order. The best that money could buy in dignified but commonplace taste. The flowers, like the golden June evening alone lent charm.

Expectancy had quickened almost painfully within him.

As he stood alertly there, nerves on edge, he saw immediately before him on a walnut sofa-table, a handsomely produced book. The title consisted of one word in Roman lettering: "*Armature.*"

The Standish book, and within his grasp!

At that instant Miss Pandora Quinn entered, a Pomeranian yapping at her heels.

Miss Quinn in a flowered foulard was both younger and larger than he had expected. A tall, dark, plump woman of forty-five, with strongly marked brows, bright brown eyes, and full lips, her manner was at once authoritative and arch. Her flawless, creamy skin was ruined by too high a colouring and an undeniable moustache. She held out a dimpled hand with very good grace, for curiosity had enlived her.

"Dr. Riberac, this is an unexpected pleasure. No, please don't apologise. The Vaucluse Angel has already introduced us. I was thrilled to see the evening paper. Now, before we start to chat—have you dined? Some coffee then? You are just in time to join me."

The entrance of coffee was the signal for renewed yapping on the part of the Pomeranian—a breed Dr. Riberac had always detested.

"Quiet Oscar!" commanded Miss Quinn, on a note appropriate for a bull mastiff. "Basket!"

Oscar, old, obese, irritable, the only possession present that was not in apple-pie order, stepped into a cushioned receptacle with a resentful snarl.

His mistress and her guest, coffee-cups in hand, were once more alone and in comparative quiet.

"Mr. Hurrup gave me your address, yet I really must apologize . . ." Dr. Riberac began, when again Miss Quinn overwhelmed him with understanding——

"I assure you that this is the greatest pleasure. It is not every evening, by any means, that one has the opportunity of entertaining such a distinguished guest. Positively, Dr. Riberac, one would never guess that you were French. Such perfect English——" her blandishments flowed on.

Riberac, as a Frenchman, attached no importance to verbal flatteries—these were legitimate gambits, but when his hostess added cosily:

"I have told Alice we are not to be interrupted. The Corbetts sometimes drop in for a rubber——" the male in him raised a wary head, much as a stag when the wind changes senses that the hunt is up.

"I welcome the Corbetts as a rule," pursued Miss Quinn. "So few of one's own kind now remain. You must see sad changes in London on your return to us? The fact is: money has just changed hands. I trust your coffee is as you like it?"

His coffee was perfection, and he said so with finality. He had now decided on his line of country.

"I have called this evening in the hope that you might assist me with a personal inquiry."

"But of course, Dr. Riberac. And if it's got anything to do with the Vaucluse Angel, I'd be fascinated to help——"

"No, Miss Quinn. I simply wish to trace a friend—an old friend, whom I believe you also know. Miss Hood."

A look of genuine pleasure crossed her face. "Miss Hood?" she exclaimed in wonder. "But how amazing that you should know Miss Hood, although of course she had foriegn connections!"

"It's a number of years since I've been in this country," said Dr. Riberac glibly, "for any length of time. One sometimes loses touch inadvertently. We bachelors are often careless——"

"Of course, of course!" Miss Quinn soothed him. "And you could not have come to anyone closer, if I may say so. Miss Hood dates right back to childhood. This really is the most romantic thing. It's as if you had been sent me from the past. I shall do anything I can to help you."

"Very kind of you, I'm sure. May I have her present address?"

"But, Dr. Riberac," Miss Quinn leant forward, her plump face animated by an absurd but eager solicitude, "I can hardly do that. Give you her address I mean. I don't know how best to break the news. You see—Miss Hood is dead."

"*Dead!*" exclaimed Dr. Riberac harshly, and paused, like a man incensed. "When did she die?" he demanded.

Miss Quinn stared at him. She scarcely recognized her sauve stranger in this peremptory personage.

"When did she die?" she repeated uneasily, and during her hesitation he aged ten years. "Let me see . . . it must have been in nineteen-eighteen."

"Nineteen-eighteen—preposterous!" he scoffed. "I've seen her repeatedly since then!" His relief intoxicated him.

But Pandora Quinn had also recovered. "Dr. Riberac," she said on a note of reproof, "you're not referring to Andra, are you?"

Instantly he saw his mistake. "I am referring to Andra, but naturally this news startled me. I had no idea that Andra's Aunt was also your friend."

"My mother's friend," corrected Miss Quinn. "I told you that she dated back to childhood. Miss Edith Hood gave me my first lessons in *pianoforte*. Everyone had the greatest respect for Miss Edith Hood in Madeira Park Road. Number nine it is now, but in those days her house was named *Lochinvar* . . . after the ballad, of course. But as a family friend, you know all this."

"As a family friend," said Dr. Riberac with some severity, "I cannot hear too much about Miss Edith Hood. Every detail is welcome. You must forgive my brusqueness, but your good-nature tempted me to feel at home for a moment! If you will be kind enough to tell me all you can of Miss Edith Hood, this will refresh my own memories, and I shall be doubly in your debt."

Miss Quinn dimpled. This elegant stranger had resented her imputation that he was solely concerned with Andra. And no wonder. The evening was retrieving itself——

"Well, Dr. Riberac, I need not tell you what a perfect pet Miss Edith was in her own prim, dry way. And quite a lady in spite of the penury in which she latterly lived." Miss Quinn shook her head tenderly. "Yes, we discovered later that it amounted to penury. Poor Miss Edith. Not that she ever complained. Such spirit. But of course it explained the daily drudgery of those music lessons. Her father had been a clergyman—some small parish in Somerset, I believe. Both daughters had been well-educated, as you probably know. And I'm certain it must have been a big blow to Miss Edith when Miss Zoë elected to teach Languages abroad. Miss Edith had put up that brass plate on the gate: *Music and Languages*, in full expectation. But apparently Miss Zoë was determined upon a continental career. I never met Miss Zoë myself, but my mother said she was a very different type from Miss Edith. Years younger too of course."

"Of course," Dr. Riberac nodded sympathetically. He could scarcely contain his impatience. "And Miss Zoë now . . . what of her to-day?"

Miss Quinn put down her coffee-cup, "I hardly know what to tell you, as I don't know how much you've heard already. At the same time, I am afraid it is already common knowledge—Miss Zoë's sad story."

"But you hesitate?" prompted Dr. Riberac.

"Andra"—she said slowly and again his heart leapt, "was once my best friend. Of course, I was a little older than she was, but I cannot forget those girlhood days. You will wonder how it was we came to attend the same school? But an epidemic at Miss Latour's Academy forced me into High School for the best part of a year. Every drain had to come up. Andra and I became fast friends——" again she hesitated.

"And once a friend, always a friend?" suggested Dr. Riberac. "I fear I have embarrassed you."

"No, no, *please!*" his hostess begged him. "It's simply that I always think it better to speak openly, or keep silent. Frankness," added Miss Quinn more robustly, "is perhaps a fault in me."

"Not in my eyes, I do assure you!" again Dr. Riberac bowed with distinction.

"Then I will admit, Dr. Riberac, that Andra's weakness was noticeable—even in childhood. And of course this accounted for everything that followed. No ambition whatsoever. Always so pleased with everything as it was, that she practically made no effort."

"Some people might find that restful, of course?" Dr. Riberac ventured.

"For a little. But one can't go on indefinitely lotus-eating in this life. Of course one could forgive her anything at the time——" Miss Quinn laughed generously, "for she *was* so good natured. Yet, I will confess that later there were times when this easy-osyness in the face of stern

necessity seemed almost simple-minded. At least to me——"
she paused.

"As her best friend,' he smiled inscrutably, "you should
know."

"Well," agreed Miss Quinn, "I admit it worried me. I
was a little older than she was. And perhaps more mature
in other ways. Possibly I foresaw that a girl like that
would be an easy mark for the wrong kind of man."

"Ah!" said Dr. Riberac, and he too paused significantly.

"Yet, I want to assure you," said Miss Quinn earnestly,
"that Andra had excellent early influences, as far as environ-
ment was concerned. Miss Edith Hood was a true Christian,
and a staunch adherent. Not C. of E. of course," Miss
Quinn amplified tolerantly. "Methodist. But although
background counts, and Andra's was certainly sound,
heredity is a strong force. Sometimes, I fear, a fatal one.
And this takes us back to Miss Zoë. At school, of course,
we understood that Andra was some connection of the Hood
family. The story went that both her parents had been
killed in 1906—the San Francisco earthquake. People
accepted this fantastic tale as everyone had a genuine respect
for poor Miss Edith, who was saddled with the child. But
later my mother told me that she could remember Andra
arriving at Miss Hood's—a little girl of six in 1903, speaking
the most *fluent* German! She was brought over here from
Austria by Miss Zoë—I hope this isn't boring you, Dr.
Riberac?"

"On the contrary, I am deeply interested."

"But many of these details you may already know?"

"I assure you," said Dr. Riberac with perfect sincerity,
"that all this is news to me."

"Then perhaps I should explain that Miss Zoë Hood held
for years the post of English governess to one of the most
important families in Austria—Prince Essling's, Count of

Landeck. They had great estates I believe, bordering on the region known as Venetia Tridentina. But once Miss Zoë had deposited Andra here, she did not again return to this country. Why, I do not know. My mother noticed that Miss Edith became increasingly reticent about her movements. This was only too obvious as earlier Miss Zoë had been one of Miss Edith's chief topics of conversation. So natural, don't you think? Miss Zoë was the travelled sister, the one who had ventured further afield. In the early days, so my mother said, Miss Edith almost idolized her sister. Miss Zoë was unusually good looking, I believe, but in a statuesque, dignified way. The *last* person, my mother said —but who are we to judge? And as I say, we all respected Miss Hood, and were quite devoted to Andra—who, oddly enough, never seemed to take the slightest interest in her antecedents . . . even when pressed for information. You know what children are?"

"I certainly do!" blandly Dr. Riberac agreed. "Devils incarnate. It would be interesting to know what became of Miss Zoë."

But Miss Quinn had raised a monitory finger, even as she lowered her voice. "There was one curious feature of the story, which in a sense confirmed it only too regrettably. During the ten years after Andra's arrival here, Miss Hood appeared to be much better off. One could understand her having an extra pint of milk a day for the child, but it was common knowledge that she could now afford meat three times a week. Her grocery order was not simply doubled, it was trebled. And twice in ten years she had the house painted outside. Her clothes also smartened. Not that Miss Hood was ever ostentatious. The last thing I want to do is to give an impression of extravagance. But her straitened means definitely passed into something that approached comfort. Then came 1914——" she broke off dramatically.

"And the return of Miss Zoë?"

"Nothing of the sort!" For the first time Miss Quinn showed signs of impatience. Her bright brown eyes snapped with zest. "The cat was out of the bag in a *very* different way. Abruptly the money came to an end, Dr. Riberac, which confirmed its source as enemy territory. There was only one conclusion any of us could draw. By this time Andra was seventeen. Things could not have been worse for them as through advancing years and more up-to-date techniques Miss Hood had lost many pupils. Nothing was *said* by Aunt and niece, but everyone saw that things were critical. Actually Miss Hood herself did not know till after the Armistice that her sister had died abroad *during* the war. Long before that, however, Miss Zoë had ceased to teach. Instead she had gone into business in Budapest—of all places. Millinery," again Miss Quinn paused significantly, "it would appear."

"*Quite!*" This time her guest bowed with becoming brevity, and Miss Quinn, confident that they were now in complete concurrence, continued expansively:

"No doubt the failure of funds forced Miss Hood's hand. Don't think I blame her. As Andra's best friend I knew better than anyone that she had no intellectual aptitude whatsoever. But still, Andra had pleasant, pretty manners —she had been quietly brought up, almost like a little nun by Miss Hood—she could easily have gone as companion-help to some elderly or infirm person. We proposed a bed-ridden cousin of our own, in this connection—a Miss Meg Patch and a most sterling personality. Instead of which Miss Hood took a fatal step for Andra. One so totally out of keeping with Miss Hood's whole character that it left her friends in Madeira Park Road literally aghast. I refer to Andra's engagement at the London Art School. Were you aware, Dr. Riberac, that for a time Andra was a model there?"

"I had heard that in 1917-1918 Andra was there for a little. The School has an international reputation and, I believe, is run on exemplary lines."

Gravely Miss Quinn shook her head. "For a period of two years, Dr. Riberac, and I am confident that it was this unnatural and unsuitable employment that killed Miss Edith by December 1918. After all, she had had influenza repeatedly during the war, and had not succumbed till then."

Sustained by more than her own eloquence, Miss Quinn next leant forward imperiously: "Tell me, Dr. Riberac, did you ever meet their friend, Madame Moffat? I thought not. Then let me tell you *she* was the woman responsible for that misguided entrance into the Art School. Unhappily Madame Moffat was an old and intimate associate of Miss Hood's— although had you heard them in acrimonious conversation you would scarcely have credited *affection*. But I can assure you that her influence over Miss Hood was unbounded. The fact that Madame Moffat was better-born than Miss Hood probably accounted for this—it gives a certain authority. And Madame Moffat was a Blythborough before marriage. In a big, breezy way she just swept people before her. But to no purpose, for she herself had made a wretched marriage —an impecunious Lecturer in Classics."

"As a fellow-professor," her visitor's smile glittered, "I sympathize."

"You misunderstand me, Dr. Riberac. The marriage was not wretched because Professor Moffat lectured, but because he died, and Bess Blythborough had to launch into that hat shop off Marylebone High Street which she named so absurdly *Madame Moffat*—a venture as erratic as herself, and which repaid her so capriciously that Blanche, her daughter, had already been three years a model in the Life School, when she suggested to Miss Hood that Andra should follow suit. So you see how the path was paved. Blanche was a tall, dark girl—handsome in a Spanish way, but hopelessly indolent. The worst possible influence. And into that bohemian home—if one can call a flat in Marylebone a home —Andra went upon Miss Hood's death. A short-lived experience—but probably enough to unsettle her—as Madame Moffat and her daughter later left for the United States. Blanche, to everyone's surprise, having made quite a good marriage with some American. But, of course, as far as Andra was concerned, the deed was done——"

"Now, why?" said Dr. Riberac smoothly. "The state of affairs which you describe so graphically leaves me with a feeling that a paragon like Miss Hood might have been rather difficult to live with?"

"Oh, no! Andra was devoted to her Aunt. If she had lived—one feels that Andra would never have lost grip as she did."

"Grip?" his emphasis was sinewy, arresting.

"On her old friends," fleetly Miss Quinn amended. "I assure you she did not simply lose *touch*. She deliberately broke off contact. Miss Hood was an educated woman, accustomed to mixing with the best people—some even beyond her own station—all of which makes Andra's subsequent behaviour unforgivable to say the least. I can but tell you the truth—unpalatable as it may be. But we here have reason to believe that Andra later became involved with some undesirable man—I know you'll treat this as confidential?"

"Entirely," he said grimly.

"No one knows exactly where they lived. But it went on for some years. She was seen at various times in the West End—extremely well-dressed. I myself saw her in 1923 from the top of a bus. She was walking down Regent Street.

Tripping along in a tailored suit which might have been one of Bradleys. Worn with a dear little fur jacket. Squirrel I admit, but dyed and worked like summer ermine—and that costs something these days."

"Your powers of observation," Dr. Riberac commented, "are certainly exceptional."

Miss Quinn's expression softened. She was delighted with the tribute. Encouraged she proceeded:

"Not only was the man moneyed, and, I understand, a distasteful type, but we have reason to believe that he was also married. And indeed everything—Andra's secrecy included—pointed to this."

Dr. Riberac's eyes narrowed: "You cannot be too sure of that. He might easily have been a selfish bachelor."

"Which only makes his behaviour more insulting," retorted Miss Quinn. "No, whichever way you look at it, the story is deplorable—for of course he left her. They always do. The next we heard of *her* was in the Police news."

"*What?*" Dr. Riberac could scarcely credit his ears.

"Yes—some time later. A most unsavoury case. It was in all the evening papers. Alexandra Hood, aged twenty-nine, a charwoman, living near the Angel, Islington, was charged with receiving stolen goods. Her story was that she had kept the parcel to oblige a neighbour, not knowing the contents, and as it was a first offence, the Magistrate released her."

"You mean she was exonerated?"

"Yes. And as her address was given in the papers, of course I wrote at once. What friend would not? There was no reply, and so Mother wrote a second time. That letter came back stamped: *Not known*. She had gone away."

"A charwoman," repeated Dr. Riberac icily. "I find this quite incredible."

"No wonder! Andra ought to have been ashamed."

"Ashamed of *work*?"

"Of course not. But ashamed of that type of work. So *lazy*, Dr. Riberac. After all, Andra had had quite a good education, and was really nice looking . . . yet she let herself sink to char-ing."

"Your point of view is certainly salutary," again Dr. Riberac's cold smile glinted. He resisted the temptation to demolish her at this stage . . . he was out for information —not to score points. "May I ask if that was the last you heard of Andra?"

"Oh, no, far from it! About three years ago, an extra-ordinary thing occurred. She cropped up again in the news. This time in the morning papers and in quite a different fashion! I have the cutting somewhere in my bureau. It was during Pastor Emanuel Frick's last visit to this country. Of course everyone knows he is quite a saintly person. He proved that by being willing to die for his enemies at the hands of his own people. And of course it's almost a miracle that he survived. People were especially anxious to see him over here, after his adventures in the Chinese Mission field as well. Particularly as there has recently been quite a revival of interest in spiritual healing. Huge crowds attended his meetings—many were invalids desperate that he should lay his hands on them. One just couldn't get tickets—although he was at pains to point out that prayer itself was more important than personal contact. Surpris-ingly enough, it was here that Andra came in! At his farewell meeting, he told the public that for years *his* work, if you please, had been sustained by a small prayer circle, the members of which were scattered all over the world. ' One devoted member belongs to the people of London,' he announced. ' I refer to Miss Andra Hood whose address may truly be said to be by the Angel, Islington, although she has long since left that district.' Such a peculiar thing to say, Dr. Riberac, as he at once added: ' *Who would true valour see, Let him come hither. One here will constant be, Come wind, come weather.*' And the meeting wound up with all singing Bunyan's hymn. My mother wondered if he'd done it to take the sting from that earlier police report from Islington."

"Alternately," Dr. Riberac's smile glittered again, "it is just possible that Pastor Frick did not *know* of that *contretemps*. His tribute may have been spontaneous."

"It was still a very odd one, Dr. Riberac. People talked about it a great deal in this neighbourhood. In any case, it didn't explain how she came to be mixed up in that movement. And I must say that the idea of Andra as a *healer* appears to me quite fantastic. But then I know her very well—perhaps better than anyone. However, I at once wrote the Pastor, care of *The Daily Clarion*, and explained that I was an old friend of Andra's who was most anxious to have her present address. You will scarcely credit it—but although I registered and expressed the letter, I received no reply whatsoever."

"And so," said Dr. Riberac shortly, "you do not possess this address—even now?"

"I do not," she exclaimed. "But you cannot say that this is through lack of effort on my part. Still . . . I do feel a little guilty about another matter. I fear now that I may have given you rather a biased impression of Madame Moffat. I'm sure she did what she could for Andra. It was just a pity that Madame Moffat *was* one of those breezy, boisterous people with no respect for the conventions. A good enough heart, of course, although it worked freakishly. She and Blanche once kept a Lascar for a week on the divan in the room behind the hat shop, because they found him weeping in the street—after missing his ship through a drunken bout. Yet drink was almost the only subject on which Madame Moffat held conventional views. Not for the usual reasons, however—but because spirits rotted the stomach. She was a health crank, *and* a food faddist. So for a week this Lascar made tea for the customers, and delivered hats to the wrong addresses. Yet London is full of people she might well have befriended. As President of the *Women's League of Pity* for the North-West Area, I could tell you some tragic stories. Especially of middle-aged or elderly women. It is almost impossible for an uneducated woman to-day to find employment. Since the war, Dr. Riberac, many hostels open to women have been transferred to men. The powers-that-be consider it unsuitable that our heroes be found homeless in the street—so as usual the woman goes to the wall. But it was quite impossible to interest the Moffats in the W.L.O.P. The truth is they were only interested in men or the young. They liked to be in the swim——"

"As Miss Hood lived here until she died—perhaps some of her neighbours have Andra's address?"

"In sixteen years not one remains, with the exception of Major Treves at *Kidderpore*."

"Possibly he might know?"

"The last person, I assure you. Of course I know that for a time people thought he and Miss Edith might make a match of it. Especially when he began to cut back the virginia creeper for her, and to wash down the outside paint. Miss Edith kept things very spick and span, and Major Treves thought it unsuitable that she should mount a ladder to the upper windows. In spite of his testy temper I really believe that he was fond of her. But nothing came of it. And now he's practically in his dotage and mixes with *no one*."

"Nevertheless——" and Dr. Riberac rose.

From his basket by the wall, Oscar yapped in warning.

Hurriedly Miss Quinn interposed: "In any case, he's not

at home at present. Each year he shuts the house for a month and goes to Bournemouth. Please don't hurry away . . . I wish I could help you——"

Suddenly she seemed to tire. "Mother used to be very fond of Andra," she added irrelevantly.

"But now no longer?" he queried, his mind instantly alert to possibilities through Mrs. Quinn.

Unexpectedly a look of pain passed over the plump face opposite, refining it for an instant. With brief dignity she replied: "Mother died last year."

"Forgive me," he said quietly, and to amend his *gaucherie* sat down again. "I see you have Sir Amos Standish's book here."

Instantly she recovered. "Would you believe it—I actually had to buy it to-day! I am a Class A Subscriber at the Library, but already every copy is out. So tiresome. If I had not heard the salesman say they were down to their last four copies in the shop, I would have waited. But these early editions will be valuable one day. He's had the most surprising press. The critics for once quite fulsome. But then a posthumous appearance is almost bound to disarm judgment."

"I have not seen it yet. May I——?"

"Of course. I've just glanced at it myself. The illustrations are well produced, but it's such a pity that the marble of Andra as an eastern *Dancing Girl* has been included. It does not do him justice . . . I would scarcely call Andra pretty, would you?"

"No, I certainly would not."

Miss Quinn nodded. "She was too pale—with that opaque skin. Colourless. But at the same time, there was something——"

"She was beauty itself," said Dr. Riberac briefly.

Rather hurriedly Miss Quinn continued: "There are only

two pictures of her in the book. But then she did not often pose for Sir Amos."

For the first time Dr. Riberac warmed slightly to his hostess. "I only know the *Dancing Girl*," he opened the book. "Which other is included?"

"The bust known as *La Pleureuse*. Many think it is his best work. The fact that she's smiling as well as weeping piques curiosity. No, it's not in the body of the book—it's the frontispiece. There . . . you see——"

And Dr. Riberac did indeed see.

Andra's face, upturned but with closed eyes, broke upon him with the full force of a masterpiece.

"The bust is unfinished," said Miss Quinn, "and of course that's saved it. It might as easily be said of Standish as it was of the painter Carlo Dolci: ' *he polished masterpieces into inanities.*'"

Dr. Riberac looked up. "I see that you understand sculpture?"

Miss Quinn shrugged. Her whole demeanour had changed —become more remote with this question. "I won an open scholarship for it at the age of seventeen. But my parents wouldn't hear of me taking it up. The Award went to the second-prize winner. I've never done anything since. I suppose I was too much annoyed at the time——" She spoke almost indifferently.

"Understandably," said Dr. Riberac shortly. A faculty full-fed on theory and unexercised in the creative field might well explain the critical spirit that consumed her. Her frustration now amounted to venom.

"I consulted the index," said Miss Quinn, "and the letter-press states that the bust of Andra was executed mainly from memory. I myself think that it would have been better named *La Dormeuse*. In spite of its erect posture, the subject is fast asleep, and there for once Standish has excelled himself. It's almost impossible to reproduce sleep without suggesting death. But he's managed it."

This was only too true. Impassively Riberac stared at the picture, his emotions a ferment. How often had he not seen that head asleep upon its pillow, or his arm. But how had Standish known that so exactly thus she was—the lower lip more prominent than by day, and slightly to one side . . . an irregularity that lent a curious stability to the sweet face from its emphasis on the jaw-bone?

Abruptly he closed the book, and stood up to take his leave —Oscar in frenzy yapping at his heels.

Miss Quinn had completely recovered her vivacity.

"Well, if you really must—but I do hope that one day you will call again. I just can't forgive myself for gossiping about Andra when we might have been talking about the Vaucluse Angel and something really important . . ."

Not until she saw his tall figure disappear down the drive did a certain contingency occur to her—most disturbing in its implications!

"She was beauty itself . . ."

Was it possible that *he* had been the unknown man in Andra's life?

What an embarrassment! The *things* she had said——

No, it was quite impossible. Not that dignified personage! She knew correctitude when she saw it. That man was in a class by himself. He looked like a stickler for everything—

Nevertheless, she was left in a state of uncertainty the reverse of agreeable.

As she turned back into her empty room, the dog, sensing her disorder, yelped his sympathy.

"*Basket*, Oscar!" angrily she denounced him . . .

Friday Night . . . nine-thirty

Dr. Riberac turned angrily out of The Towers' gate.

Portrait of a friend! he thought derisively. My God, commend me to the enemy where one can see the knife. What a poisonous woman——

But a relief to dwell on her rather than the doubts now seething in his mind.

It was lighter in Madeira Park Road than it had been in that confounded room. There were now some people on the pavement—abstractedly taking their dogs for the last stroll, the animals dejectedly aware that this enterprise would be short-lived. Two neighbours exchanged greetings from their gardens—their voices curiously muted by the growing silence of the night. A hose hissed its water through the warm air on to the rose bed next door——

Riberac looked hungrily around. The odd numbers were on the left. *Number Nine*, her old home, would be at the far end—among the small houses.

It was. A tiny Tudoresque villa with one rowan tree, four rose bushes, and a minute rickety balcony at the upper, side window. A child would probably enjoy that wooden cage—if his own youth were anything to go by. The name *Lochinvar* was still limned on the glass transom of the front door.

He put out his hand and touched the iron gate in the thickening dusk.

As he did so, he noticed a blank square there, painted green like the railings.

Miss Edith Hood's brass plate! It had been found easier to obliterate it than to remove it.

He glanced at the suburban villas on either side.

Music and Languages, he muttered. God help her—what a hope!

Miss Zoë had had more sense—but her woman's destiny had caught her out. Too bad. Yet if this had not happened —and he was startled by the revelation—Andra would not have existed, and he himself would not now be standing on this breathless June night outside the gate of her childhood. Life might not be some *rêve enchanté* as the poets sang, but its reality was ten times more mysterious.

Above his head, a light flashed on in the small balcony room, convicting him of homelessness. Mechanically he moved on. But at *Number Seven* he stopped short again—

The glass transom of this door bore the legend: *Kidderpore.* Both house and garden were larger than at *Number Nine,* and compared with the other villas at this end, remarkably spruce. It did not look like the home of a man in his dotage. *Kidderpore* had six acacia trees—three on each side of the house, separating front from back, and an arrangement of four holly bushes and a bird-bath on the front lawn. Stark yet adequate. Riberac conceived the idea that Major Treves would prove likewise, and again his spirits rose. But despite the heat of the night, every window was shut . . . and there was actually a padlock on the gate. Major Treves was clearly not at home. Yet this was Friday, the 28th. If Major Treves had gone for a month, as Riberac had been told, it was just possible that June was the one chosen. In which case Monday was the first of July and might mark the return of a methodical man.

Thoughtfully Riberac walked on. If the worst came to the worst, he too would return here.

Once out of Madeira Park Road, he skirted the Heath itself —its grassy hills olive green in the dun shadow of this stifling night—stretching to an infinity that by day was

Hendon. He raised his face to the vast, pale sky diminishing this blurred prospect. Across the moon, now in its last quarter, a small cloud sailed in isolation, slow as a century.

Andra, a charwoman! The facts suggested by her fate were quite hideous. But he did not mean to contemplate them at this stage. He intended to find her, and put a stop to them.

A charwoman. . . . No, it scarcely tallied with that exclusive circle in which he had last surprised her! That Quinn woman was the very devil——

His impassive face for once careworn, he strode downhill, towards the red-brick congestion of Frognal, and his speediest way to town.

Not a hope now of finding the Standish book to-night in the Club library. Other members would already have its few copies out!

And his deep dissatisfaction next proceeded to yield up its appropriate dead—strewing his mind with previously unconsidered trifles.

That incident of the four-guinea dress, for instance, struck him as significant when he remembered that Andra rarely spoke of her appearance.

On his last visit to the Kew house, she had for once interrupted him in his study, her face apprehensive.

"I've bought a new dress. It cost four guineas, and it's a complete flop."

"Can't you give it away then?" a little amused, slightly irritated he turned back to his work.

"Won't you have a look at it first? Daylight will soon be gone, and it's even worse in artificial light. I've got it in the hall."

At the unusual anxiety in her voice, he had smiled—for her dress-sense was exceptional.

"Bring in the body then!"

And she had brought in over her arm a trim, stone-coloured frock of fine wool.

"What's the matter with it?" he demanded. "It looks quite *chic* to me!"

"It's cold-looking on. Institutional. I feel unloved and unwanted in it," said the charming creature mournfully—at which he had laughed outright.

Instantly she had brightened. "Oh, Philip—I've got it! Yes, that might be the very thing. . . . I'll give it a velvet collar and cuffs. Would you rather have blue or aqua-marine? Blue will turn my eyes green. Green will make them blue. Choose."

"Get both," he exclaimed promptly. "Solomon himself could not come to terms with irresistibles."

"Oh, *darling!*" she gasped, between laughter and tears, "sometimes I think you *do* love me——" and she had run from the room before he could demand an explanation.

But of course he ought to have followed her. Followed her out. Followed this up. The whole episode was so unlike her that he might have known that something was amiss.

Was it conceivable that events might have taken a different course, had he done so? Did destiny sometimes hang on such trifles?

This he would never know—for all he had done was to go on writing, as if nothing had happened. The scene had ended on his own note as usual. And echoes were all that he now had to go on.

Perhaps the merry ones were the most disconcerting as her capacity for enjoyment never failed to astonish him. The simplest pleasure awoke a glad response.

Had this been the secret of her gift of relaxation?

In bed, if left to herself, she would stir about with a little moan of pleasure and then fall instantly asleep. He had been a trifle hipped, at first, by the ease with which she fell asleep. Almost at will. Yet looking back now, he well knew that never had he slept as he had then beside her. The temperature might be sultry as to-night's, but with midnight invading their darkened room, summer at full tide would immerse them both in deepest slumber. An owl hooting from the great Gardens beyond, together with the bosky scents and twittering sounds, all the plashing, lowlying liquid murmurs that were Richmond by the river, and they would vanish in each other's arms to some separate kingdom that yet remained identical! Awaking in the early hours as do those accustomed to the East, he had sometimes thought himself alone—until beneath his hand he felt her exposed shoulder, cool as marble in the growing dawn, and had thankfully drawn her to him once again. She was the answer to each unspoken need, his every desire.

An empty taxi cruising along Finchley Road caught his attention.

He hailed it—giving the address of his Club, got in and slammed the door.

Nothing further could be done to-night. He must keep his mind off Andra meantime. Let his other anxiety have its chance! Well, by Monday he would know the best or the worst there—if Mr. Baxter deigned to reappear at Sevenoaks. And if in this interval Mrs. Baxter's door-stop had not been stolen from *Number 27 Forest Row!* Baxter would scarcely take the wedge with him to Surrey. It must be weighty. And to a certain extent, it would be friable. Baxter, as a builder's mate would know this danger. Unless of course the man was a damned fool?

Uneasily Riberac continued to conjecture.

Between Andra and the Vaucluse Angel he had had a wretched day. In fact a nerve-racking one—apart from that revelatory moment in Cadogan Park when the certainty of guidance had informed him.

And in the glancing lights and shadows of the taxi as it swung through St. John's Wood, his face softened.

That experience to-day was akin to one other only in his life that might be called mystical.

Fifteen years ago he had had a curious dream the night before he met her for the first time.

In the dream he was on the site of an extensive excavation, and appeared to be on the eve of some momentous discovery. An instinctive recapitulation of surveying instruments, contour plan, earthworks, selected site told him that not only was all in order, but in advanced order . . . he was, in fact, on his way along the tunnel. Burial Chamber, untouched Tomb lay beyond. Endless seasons' digging had brought him to this critical point. And now, electric torch in hand, he was walking down steps which became a staircase into the bowels of the earth. Along a passage then, and down further steps to where the upper part of a doorway showed. On the door were set seals—with the usual Egyptian Tomb impressions.

Someone drilled a hole in the upper part of the door for him.

Widening this aperture, he introduced a candle as so often he had done on other occasions. And as always happened, the hot air released from the Burial Chamber made the flame flicker. There was also a strong scent of sycamore wood, used exclusively in ancient Egyptian funeral rites. From varied objects already found in other rooms around this Burial Chamber, he had reason to believe that this was the Tomb of a nobleman of the First Dynasty, and so a discovery of the first magnitude.

Therefore, with no sense of incongruity he now heard funerary priests of that period chanting formulae from the Pyramid Texts: *He is this that ascendeth, ascendeth, is hidden, hidden . . . the place of his choosing is among the living in this land for ever and ever.* It confirmed that he was indeed on the right track, after a lifetime of research. But due possibly to excitement he had difficulty in steadying his vision, although in a moment when this cleared, he would peer into the darkness of five thousand years to discover the antique animals, the be-jewelled statues, the inlaid caskets, alabaster vases and sepulchral Shrine itself . . . the fruits of his labour.

To his exasperation, with success at hand, the blurred moment prolonged itself. Was this to be his achievement, his own Tomb—or was it not!

Again the distant voices chanted! *He layeth hold on Command, Eternity is brought to him. Discernment is placed for him at his feet. Cry aloud to him in joy, he hath captured the horizon.*

On these words he peered through the door and saw—

Saw, to his stupefaction, with the detailed clarity of a view through a long-distance telescope, no Burial Chamber but a tiny scene vignetted in broad daylight. Beneath a young sycamore tree, brilliant in first foliage, stood the small Greek figure of a woman in a muslin chiton. But the singular thing about the sunlit tree, the Attic woman, was that around their charmed circle rain poured in torrents— but left them both untouched by storm.

Despite this enchanting picture, Riberac could not contain his chagrin. It was not his Tomb after all! This was no fabulous find of the First Dynasty, but a Greek maiden of the time of Pericles . . . quite a modern upstart—crowning his labours!

Mortified beyond expression—he awoke. Nor did he remember his odd dream until later that day—after he had met Andra for the first time. Then he was startled by the appositeness of the sycamore tree, the thunder shower, and the sheltering nymph. The very details of the dream which were dissimilar held a symbolic indication that confirmed the occasion as identical. Yet no thought of his dream was present as he looked upon her through the rain—with that peculiar awareness that amounts to recognition.

The taxi jerked him to attention. It had drawn up in a traffic block near Baker Street.

Somewhere a clock struck the half-hour. Ten-thirty!

Again by some dire affinity, another bygone night at the same hour flew like a cuckoo from the clock, and then snapped him outside again . . .

A deep dusk flittering with moths—June once more at Kew, and their upper windows faintly gilded by what appeared to be a quenchless after-glow, in which there shook the hot spangle of a solitary star. In the deepening silence, both had nonsensically sworn that they could hear it jangle! The hour prolonged its spell . . . the while their modest garden below assumed vast proportions in a summer gloom stolen from Hesperides . . .

More vividly now than then, he saw her face again, framed by her honey-coloured hair. Her eyes were large— of a pale blue tone that in some lights showed sea-green, yet with no hint of coldness, so serene was their habitual expression. But in animation, a look of wonderment lent a certain vagueness to the cameo clarity of her features. Her face was undoubtedly more impressive in repose—although then its calm withdrew it from any but a meditative regard. Yet once fully perceived, she dwelt in mind with the persistence of an echo.

As a realist, he had concluded that the romantic nature of their association which had lasted for years was due to the fact that they only met at intervals—that their whole relationship was heightened by a constant hail and farewell. But he had been duped by his own common sense. A unique bond had indeed been concealed from him by the emotional upheaval that was part and parcel of their irregular union. And yet he might have known that any such union could only have persisted year in, year out, if there were genuine affinity. He was after all, twelve years and more older than she.

In the name of the incongruous what was the meaning of Pastor Frick's reference to Andra's help in prayer? How could Riberac's unassuming darling, who had lived like a recluse for him, have become a healer connected with a world-wide movement?

As at *Number Nine* Madeira Park Road to-night, a light went on in her empty room with this report that left him farther off than ever . . .

Through the taxi window, "*All Rights Reserved*" flashed its defiance in coloured lights from the Criterion. He was now in the thick of Piccadilly. An idiotic title for a play anyway! The theatre traffic was not yet in motion, but the streets were again congested with Jubilee crowds . . . the pavements packed with people, all out and about and enjoying themselves . . .

The car was now out of the worst of it—drawing into the sombre atmosphere of Pall Mall. Yet here too unwonted intimacy prevailed. Many of the Clubs had opened wide their massive windows to the lulling heat of the night. In the gray, half-light of the street, members could be dimly distinguished standing, or seated, in silent contemplation, like shades on either side of the Styx.

The august entrance of his own Club conjured again his earlier annoyance with Mr. Baxter. Beneath that oppressive Roman portico he had read the unwelcome postcard: *Owing to happy Event for my Son's wife, Mrs Baxter and me will be going Friday to Surrey till late Sunday next. You are welcome Monday any time convenient.*

Passing the porter's box now, a quantity of mail was handed to him.

"This came by the last post, Sir," and on top of the pile, the Head Porter laid yet another card from Mr. Baxter.

A sense of impending misfortune forced him to read the flimsy card where he stood—the first communication that Mr. Baxter had not written on a Sunday. The postmark was Sevenoaks of that morning's date. The address was simply: *Post Office.* The message read: *Mrs. Baxter and me fancying you might fret along of house being empty has made You-know-what into Parcel meaning to register but Clerk says sealing Wax esenshul so been obliged send ordnory post as bus leaving no time for Wax. Hoping sturdy Packet will set your mind easy Saturday morning certain. All the Best J. Baxter. P.S. Parcel as like a bomb as two peas had to laugh when Clerk said now whats this.*

Dr. Riberac raised his head. Haggardly he stared into the attentive eyes of the Head Porter. Then in French he swore violently.

"I beg your pardon, Sir?" The Porter, who with mild interest had also studied this illiterate communication, was startled by the excitement of its recipient.

But abruptly Dr. Riberac turned away. Blindly he made his way to the seclusion of the Library—empty now but for two other members, engrossed at different ends of the wide room.

Exhausted he sank upon the couch.

With Latin impetuosity he had already decided that the wedge was as good as lost. The Post Office, the Press, might even now be closing around the package . . . that was to say if it had not previously been tossed aside as a joke, upon examination—not worth delivery. Sans string, sans paper—an old bit of stone.

Indeed his chance of finding Andra now seemed to him the likelier of two random events.

At any rate, he alone was in search of her. That somehow made her a degree more secure.

Mercifully, for his remaining peace of mind, he was unaware that at that actual moment, another, with similar determination, was on her track. A man backed by one of the most powerful organisations in the world—trading under that by-word: *The Daily Clarion.* Unknown to Dr. Riberac this investigator was already one move ahead of him. He had, in fact, that evening discovered the desired address, and as an ace reporter is scarcely to be deflected by a trifle like bedtime—his own or an other's—he was even now en route . . . a copy of Sir Amos Standish's book beneath his arm.

Involuntarily in the Club Library, someone groaned aloud.

Riberac glanced up startled. The two other men were staring in his direction.

Haughtily he out-faced them.

Instantly they glanced away.

All three had decided to disbelieve their ears—and a damned good thing too.

Friday Night . . . ten o'clock

The underground train on the Northern District Line was fairly full despite the hour. With expense no object in this case, any other reporter would have taken a taxi. But Mr. Fred Burrowes, ace reporter on *The Daily Clarion*, was not as others. Not only would a taxi cause an unwelcome stir at his destination, but he also foresaw the need of an immediate article on the heroine's daily journey to and from work. Authentic atmosphere could only be conveyed by hard facts. Mr. Burrowes, conscientious to a degree in atmospheric research, was now down to brass tacks—with his usual flair for killing two birds with the same stone. A pale thin man, much younger than he looked, the powerful lenses of his spectacles disguised the exceptional intelligence of his glance, and a sensitive, suffering smile further disarmed his prey. Mr. Burrowes' voice unlike that of most reporters was shy, as well as pleasant, and gave an impression that anything entering one ear would never reach the other. Thus encouraged, the interviewed invariably relaxed—sometimes to the point of volubility. Unobtrusive but impenetrably adequate, Mr. Burrowes was perfectly equipped for his job.

As the train swung through its tunnels he noted the type of passenger who would be likely to accompany the talk of the town on her nightly return—for the *personnel* of these trains altered almost hourly. On Friday night, he had been informed, she worked late, and at quite a different place of business. A West-End Nursing Home. His informant had then taken panic, and Mr. Burrowes had failed to discover the nature of this work. Probably something to do with that healing stunt that the Press had earlier noted. Equally cagey, too, the fellow had been about her work by day! Not that this mattered at the present stage. Mr. Burrowes disliked cornering his quarry at their place of business. It was the one thing that the pursued never forgave. They would sooner be discovered in their bath. But he hardly thought Miss Hood would be in bed by the time he got there. Home at ten each Friday—so he had been assured. That allowed nearly half-an-hour to take off her shoes, have a cup of tea and simmer down generally instead of surprising her, all hot, bothered and resentful immediately after her journey back.

Blankly his spectacles gazed around in their quest for local colour, and instantly recorded the haul. All these, and the inevitable city-office cleaner herself, immediately opposite Burrowes—pale, nondescript, with her black beret, black coat, black oilcloth bag, belatedly getting home.

In the steady glare of the electric light, as the train vehemently shook its passengers to and fro, these individuals, young and old alike, looked oddly shop-worn under the bright, shadowless advertisements above their heads—the garish haloes set by their civilization. Existence had already left its dejected mark—even on a tear-stained baby. It was not a cheering prospect, and Mr. Burrowes having briefly noted it, opened the Standish book as a get-away.

The letterpress he already knew, but the illustrations repaid scrutiny. *The Dancing Girl* was his favourite. No wonder one critic had referred to the book as *a study in inspiration*! A model like that would be a fillip to any fellow. She was just what Burrowes himself would have fancied. Flowers, fruit and a tambourine! Luscious but not loose. Some chaps had all the luck. Some women too— skipping through life with a figure like that. Classic was the word for that chassis! When you thought of the other girls——

He glanced up, and saw the pale, meagre cleaner opposite. Nobody's darling now or ever. A joyless sister.

Cataclysmically the train roared into Camden Town. The cleaner rose—more alertly than he'd expected of her—and vanished.

Mr. Burrowes, whose destination was Kentish Town, returned to his *Dancing Girl*—completely unaware that not only had the original model for this work of art just disappeared under his very nose, with her oilcloth bag, but that this colourless female was supremely happy in the deplorable state to which Providence had called her.

The only discovery he was to make that night was that, contrary to her custom, the latest celebrity was not home by ten, or ten-thirty.

He had, in fact, drawn a blank—but to-morrow was another day. He'd have to make it bright and early. With the big Event set for Monday—it was now or never. No escape this time . . .

Friday Night . . . eleven o'clock

Andra walked pleasurably up Park Street, away from Camden Town.

A deep blue night dappled by lamp-light—so still that she might be pacing the stone corridors of some vast building open to the sky! Yet despite its intimacy, the visible was a mysterious world which one could never make one's own, for one could never know the truth of it. It belonged, in part, to so many others. Yes . . . she decided happily, it didn't do to be misled by the events of existence, fortunate or otherwise. The real life was the inner experience. That was the true occasion.

The night was now cooler, and she could already feel the freshness from the trees ahead. She must, however, stop short of these, for Letty Galbraith lived on the wrong side of the canal bridge—just within back-firing distance of the big garage.

Letty, however, was luckier than most of the tenants in the seedy old Victorian mansion. Attic though hers was, it luxuriated in the soundlessness of some cellar, and was indeed almost as dark—a drawback that was discounted by the fact that Letty spent her days as assistant in a Baker Street flower-shop. Silence was its supreme charm—paramount for a struggling author, who had evenings and week-ends only for creative effort.

Crossing the road now, Andra had a shrewd idea what to-day's S.O.S. from Letty meant. Probably a new frock to be run up for the party that Letty was throwing next week. A celebration twice postponed till funds should accumulate

—for Letty, to the intense relief of her friends, had at last found a publisher.

"*Bitter*," she had told Andra, "to be congratulated on the acceptance of my first book at the age of twenty-four when its the hellish *third*. My stamina must be prodigious to have survived so much. What a life! I really enjoy writing, but literature is a *tragic* career. From the moment you try to find a publisher it's unending suspense. And when you remember the fate of Keats and Shelley, who had genius to sustain them, it's no wonder I'm a nervous wreck. Oh, yes, I know it's a godsend that *Home Comes the Heart* has been accepted. But I went through such agonies with *Zebra's Stripe* that now it's almost too late. Then the iron has entered another way, for I've got to admit that, here and there, *Home Comes the Heart* is definitely commercial. But what can you do? I made positively no concessions in *Zebra's Stripe*, I put my very soul into it—and no publisher would look at it!"

Yes, it was probably a new frock, or possibly help with the distempering of the flat before the party took place. That would explain Letty's urgency by post this morning. They'd have to get it done this week, to be rid of the smell in time——

Andra glanced up at the dark façade of the house ahead. It was getting late. She rather hoped that Letty would not want to begin anything structural to-night. Not that it would matter seriously if she did. It was now as easy for Andra to come as to go, and so her strength stood up amazingly to any demand upon it. And of course Letty herself was always a lively pleasure.

Industriously she began to climb the six flights to Letty's attic. Authors must live on top. Unlike painters, no writer could endure people's feet pounding to and fro above their heads. Noise drove them crazy. So different from the theatrical profession!

Pausing for breath on the fifth floor, Andra suddenly realized that Letty had compensated for the loss of Gerda—although, alas, never could she feel as deeply for her. Gerda had had such airy charm! Freedom was in her wake. Intensity had been reserved for her stage career. But Letty, poor darling, brought this force to bear on each event and any person who crossed her path. Gerda had made an instinctive selection. Possibly this explained a certain indifference in Gerda? Letty was warmer, worthier, no doubt. But Gerda had had glamour.

Letty's front door was painted chrome-yellow. Andra herself had helped to strip the original railway-station brown from its fibres—a feat that had permanently estranged Letty's landlord. Above the door-bell was the familiar typed card: *Do not ring unless essential.*

Andra rang.

Letty opened the door instantly, and Andra was somewhat astonished by her modish appearance at that hour of the night. She wore a cherry coloured muslin frock with the latest thing in puff-sleeves, which festively enhanced her brunette beauty—blunt features, vivid eyes and lips.

"Thank God you've come!" Letty's relief was quite emotional, and it was now noticeable that she was paler than usual. But perhaps the heat . . . .?

Andra quickly removed her beret, deftly folded her dust coat and left both on top of her oilcloth bag in the minute hall. In this way the appearance of Letty's room was preserved.

Without the shapeless coat, the grace of her figure in its plain black dress was at once apparent. Without the hat, it could be seen that her pale brown hair sprang with a certain distinction from an open brow, but fatigue had lent its own lack-lustre to an habitually still face.

"The flat's stifling," Letty led the way into a large, low-roofed room, sparsely furnished, but in undoubted taste. Letty was a perfectionist who contrived much from little. "I've had a frantic business keeping your butter cool, and your egg-mayonnaise fresh."

Andra felt a little dazed. A cup of china tea and a Marie biscuit was the extent of Letty's hospitality as a rule.

"I managed to get three country eggs at the greengrocer's", she went on. "I put two in your salad. Eat up."

"Well, I must say . . ." said Andra, more impressed than ever, and fell to with a will. "I'm always hungry in hot weather. I know I shouldn't be, but I am."

"You eat well in any weather," retorted Letty. "Thermostatically controlled no doubt."

She sounded heated, harassed.

Tactfully Andra said: "That frock is sweet. What news this week?"

For a second Letty looked hunted. Her manner softened. "No, no, finish your meal," she urged. "I want you to enjoy it. You'll feel better when you've eaten. There's a small cream cheese too. The milk goes sour so quickly that it's the only thing to do with it."

Uneasily she rattled on till the brief meal was finished, and she could lift aside the table.

"I certainly do feel better," the guest began cheerfully. "Food is a major miracle——" but Letty had turned back abruptly:

"Andra," her voice trembled. "I need your help—urgently. It's terribly serious. I've got bad news."

Andra's mind flashed to Inverness.

"Oh, Letty . . . is it your family?"

"No, no, of course not. How could you help them? It's

—it's about myself," Letty gulped, and sat down violently hugging her elbows.

Alarmed Andra exclaimed: "The Publishers haven't failed you?"

"That's absurd," said Letty sharply. "The contract was signed two months ago. How could they fail me? I get my advance royalties in September on publication day——" again her voice trailed off.

This time Andra sat silent. There was no denying it—writers were irascible . . . almost on principle.

"The fact is," Letty continued with ponderous, painful deliberation, "that something quite frightful has happened to me, and as you are my best friend—yes, I realize that now —I must tell you. I've hung on, hoping against hope, but now three months have passed and I can't doubt any longer. It has to be faced. Now, whatever you do—don't get in a panic. I just couldn't bear that. I've been almost demented. I had to tell Solange—about a month ago. I've just come from her flat now. You won't have to do anything *personal* —so for God's sake relax on that score. Solange has fixed everything up—with a doctor in Bayswater."

"Letty," breathed Andra, "what are you trying to tell me?"

"I'd better begin at the beginning," muttered Letty, still hugging her knees, and staring into space. "And you needn't think I'm not ashamed, because I am. But this is no time to lick the dust. Do you remember Caird Ellis, Solange's cousin from Canada?"

"I remember you spoke of him quite often, when he was over here last spring. You saw a good deal of him," heavily Andra was recapitulating.

"I did. I liked him tremendously. I'm sick to death of half-baked boys—all full of themselves. Caird was mature. He was really interested in other people. Oh yes, at the moment then—chiefly in me! Vanity if you like. I know quite well that the serpent was just an alibi for Adam and Eve. But I swear to you that *this* was the last thing either of us dreamt of. I never thought of falling in love with him. I knew from the start that he was married. He was just an exciting, unusual companion. And I'm dead certain, Andra, that he never intended anything either. The fact that it only happened *once* proves it. But we both lost our heads the night before he sailed."

"Letty!"

"I know," Letty nodded grimly. "It's ghastly. If anyone had said that such a thing could happen to me, I would have pole-axed them. But the fact is we both got tight after the Kingsway Fancy Dress Ball."

"Tight," repeated Andra stupidly. "But you don't like wine or spirits."

"I quite like champagne," said Letty sombrely. "And I'd been steeped in depression as six weeks had passed since I sent out *Home Comes the Heart.* The champagne cheered me up. Even Caird's departure didn't seem so dismal. After the dance we all went back to Caird's hotel. He had a suite —complete with sitting room, as his firm was paying. There was more champagne. Then Solange and the others left, as Caird was to see me home. . . . You can imagine the rest."

"*Darling*," whispered Andra.

At this endearment, Letty's hardihood cracked. Her head upon her hands, she briefly wept.

"The very next morning," she sobbed, "I got the news that the book was taken."

Silently Andra stared around the orderly room. At this agonizing point Letty would resent any further expression of sympathy—she must await her cue.

Almost at once, Letty recovered. "As I was saying—you

haven't got to do anything. Anything *personal*, I mean. Solange has fixed everything."

"But Letty—think of the dangers. You must face facts. For one thing, it's illegal."

Letty wiped her face. "Andra, you make me tired," she said soberly. "There's only one thing to be done, and you know it. You won't be mixed up in *that*—so for God's sake don't preach. I thought I had at least two friends."

Andra considered her for a moment. "You know you have. What do you want me to do?"

Tear-stained, Letty faced her at last. "Bless you for that. You don't know how it helps. I've got to raise a loan of fifty pounds at once. The money is as safe as houses. I can repay it in September from my advance royalties. Andra, I wondered——"

"You want me to write to Mr. Ellis?"

"Good lord no!" Letty looked inexpressibly shocked. "What an unspeakable idea. That sort of thing went out with East Lynne. I told you he was tight, or else it could never have happened. I'd feel like a common blackmailer if I asked him——"

Andra glanced away. A very different reaction from Gerda's! Had times changed, or was this simply a different character at bay?

"What about Solange—her people are wealthy, aren't they?"

"Not a chance. Solange is up to the ears in debt. Her father has threatened to stop her allowance if she can't live within it. This would mean losing her flat. She'd have to go home, which she says is *death*. Solange is so short of cash that she actually sold me this dress for next to nothing last month. What I *hoped*," suddenly Letty swallowed, "was that perhaps you would lend me the money?"

"I?" Andra was stupefied. "What on earth made you think that I had fifty pounds?"

It was now Letty's turn to glance away. "I feel awful— asking you such a favour. I know you work frightfully hard—and it can't be well-paid or you'd never do evening over-time. But you do look wonderful in your better clothes. And . . . and I thought you'd probably have some hundreds saved. After all, most people have something saved in their thirties——" now she sounded almost aggrieved.

Andra strangled an hysterical impulse to laugh.

Doggedly Letty pursued: "The money's dead safe, Andra. You know that. I shall have it by September——"

"I know, I know! It isn't that. Couldn't the Publishers let you have it now?"

Bitterly Letty replied, "I sounded them last week. But it was made quite plain that they had a policy in such matters. Especially with a new author. Do you think I would ask you if I hadn't tried everything? The Doctor's fee is sixty pounds—and I can only scrape ten towards it."

"And your own people?"

"*Andra!*" She blenched as if she had been stung.

Andra looked guiltily down, "I didn't mean your parents. I know they're not well off. But I wondered if there wasn't some other relation——"

"Look, Andra," said Letty making a tremendous effort to speak reasonably to a lunatic, "you must get this straight once and for all. My relations just don't come into this. The whole connection look on me as the soul of reliability. That was why I was allowed to come south. And I thought I was—oh, my God!"

Handkerchief to mouth, she turned and bolted from the room. Andra could hear her being sick in the kitchenette. Almost at once she returned, looking very pale, but quite composed.

"Darling," said Andra, "try not to worry. We'll find this money somehow. Believe me, if I had it—you should have it, right away. But I haven't got it."

"You haven't got fifty pounds?" repeated Letty dully. "Why apart from savings, I thought you'd have made twice that sum when you were holiday companion to that rich woman."

"No dear. I looked upon her as a friend. I only cost her my expenses."

Again Letty glanced away. "I'm sorry," she said faintly. "Excuse me."

For a moment there was a busy silence in the low-roofed room. Then Andra spoke again, and for the first time with a note of authority.

"There's no chance then of you turning to your own people?"

In a small, thin voice Letty replied malignly: "I'd kill myself sooner."

There was another pause, but a limp one this time. An ultimatum had gone forth.

"What's more, Andra, I've got to find the money by to-morrow—Saturday night at latest. I must deposit it at the right address on Sunday. He's agreed to help me on Monday. The time factor's got me by the throat. That's why I'm—I'm desperate. But I never dreamt you wouldn't have the money——" her voice petered out.

"Don't worry, darling," said Andra softly. "I'll find the money."

Letty looked up more alertly. "But how can you? Fifty pounds is a big sum. And in a hurry too."

"I shall call in an outstanding loan."

"A bad debt—oh, Andra, do you think you'll get it?"

"Yes, dear, I shall get it. But before you have the money,

I must know more about this doctor. How do you know he's qualified for this work?"

"Because Solange told me. She knows him quite well. That isn't his only address. He daren't be careless. After all, Solange's father is a peer. She says he's a doctor who's often called in for society women. And I must say he couldn't have treated me with more courtesy if I had been a—a normal patient. I've absolutely no anxiety on this score. For reasons I'm not at liberty to divulge I know for a fact that he's only too anxious to put himself out for Solange. It's an operation that's done every day. It's the law that makes it all so shady."

Andra remained silent.

"I hate to hector," Letty went on. "But if I'm not emphatic, you won't realize that there's nothing to worry about. Except the money. And I'm terribly sorry that you've got to round-up a debt. That's ghastly I know. Borrowers have literally no compunction when you come back for your own. They behave like nightmares. Not the same people at all. Do you really think I can have it to-morrow?"

"Yes, yes," said Andra, almost absently. "I'll bring it along to-morrow night. I may be late."

"That doesn't matter. I'll sit up all night, if need be. And don't think, Andra, that this hasn't sobered Solange too. She's really been frightfully good. It's an awful lesson to us all."

"Except perhaps the Doctor," said Andra rather oddly— obviously *distrait*. "I think I must go now."

"Oh, I *am* a selfish beast! What about your bus back?"

"I can still get the last tram to Kentish Town—but I must leave right away."

As she rose, she saw propped up prominently on the mantelpiece, a paper-bound book.

"Oh, Letty," she cried, "is that *Home Comes the Heart*?"

A look of intense pleasure flashed across the girl's face.

"The page-proof copy," she handed it down, displaying its points. "Rather marvellous the way they've set it up. They're a first-class firm. I like the title-page, don't you? Of course, the published copy will have superior paper. But, oh, Andra, I wish you could see the coloured design for the jacket! It's perfection. A Victorian valentine— but done in a delicate, sophisticated style. It really is attractive——"

She broke off, relinquishing the book with rather a sickly smile. "Till this anxiety's over—it's like a happiness that belongs to someone else."

Andra hesitated. "Letty," she said diffidently, "I know there would be difficulties—but you wouldn't think of going through with the child, would you?"

Letty stared at her, outraged. "Are you out of your mind, or what?" she demanded.

At the moral indignation in her tone, her visitor, shame-faced, turned away. "Good night, darling," she said. "I do understand."

Exasperated the girl shook her head. "Andra, you're hopeless. You're not simply out of date. You're just not *in* this world. That's the trouble."

Affectionately they kissed. Subdued they parted.

As Letty opened the door, she remembered something. A trifle apologetically she added: "Oh, there's one thing I forgot to mention—it's about the money, and it's very important——"

"It's all right, dear." Andra nodded reassurance from the top of the stairs. "The notes must be clean. I know."

Rather taken aback, Letty shut the door.

Friday . . . midnight

As Andra stepped into the street, she heard the slamming of the steel doors at the garage, with a feeling of finality.

This was how it always happened, she was remembering. You walked in unaware, and later left, bound hand and foot.

Letty's hardihood did not deceive her. It was dangerously brittle. Letty was at the end of her tether. She had not the slightest doubt that unless the girl were assisted in the fashion she had decided on, that she would take some other drastic way out.

She herself had gone up those stairs to-night, rejoicing that it was now as easy for her to come as to go. How swiftly life took one at one's word, in its ruthless need of integrity!

The first step would be in Letty's own words—to call in the bad debt. The prospect sickened her. But that was neither here nor there. The recovery of this money must be made at once.

Busily she thought for a few minutes. She would leave a letter at the theatre to-morrow, before the *matinée*, and "collect" either during, or after the evening performance. Even the famous did not carry fifty pounds around with them, as a rule! Yes, this would mean booking a seat for the evening performance . . . its number would have to be included in the letter earlier sent.

Letty would be all right—of course—and yet——

A shadow of a very different sort passed across her mind. But instantly she rejected its tidings. At least she knew the difference, nowadays, between psychic and spiritual awareness. This was no time to play the seer!

And agitation fell away as deliberately she turned towards home.

Out of the blue, the small narrow Regency house had come to her on Parliament Hill Fields. Not that it was her own, of course. She was just its caretaker. But in rather a special sense. The Professor's sister had written again last week from Florida: *Unlikely as it now is that we shall return in my Brother's lifetime, he is determined that I retain the house against my own return at some future date, as Florida without him would be quite unthinkable. How thankful we are that you can help us in this way . . .*

Help the Bairds—when there she sat rent free in clover!

The fact that drab streets paved the way to paradise only made both more remarkable. She had simply to live in a place to grow attached as any limpet. . . . Even to Islington. It had not been the *place* that betrayed her.

But this was blessed Kentish Town, where everything had come right. Or almost!

The station and the underground railway now behind, she walked on—along Highgate Road, where for a mile deserted shops, tall tenements and gaunt warehouses stared blankly down at her in this midnight silence.

With solitary precision her footsteps rang behind her.

Once under the Bridge, *The Southampton Arms* announced *Courage* in capitals, and, miracle of miracles, trees—full-grown, ancient trees formed the vista as far as eye could see!

Thirstily she drank in the scene, as she left the Bridge behind——

Crossing Highgate Road now, she began to climb the short incline that led to Grove Terrace, and the graceful little row of Regency houses that faced Parliament Hill Fields.

The freshness of the Heath opposite reached Andra as she stood fumbling as usual for her key. Here was her own little front door in its elegant moulding awaiting her—the whole building as intimate, as exquisite as a Georgian doll's house!

Yet a trifle uneasily she fitted the key. In fact, she experienced now a curious sense of wariness—as if someone were awaiting her in the empty house . . . which of course was absurd! Unless someone had called in her absence, and left a message?

She snapped on the electric light in the tiny hall.

Only a catalogue lay on the maroon carpet, shot there by the postman, on his last round probably. But a large catalogue, in an impressive envelope—from a first-class store. For Miss Baird, the Professor's sister——

She turned it over to read the address, and for a second stared—then almost fainted.

Recovering, she walked through to the kitchen—turned on the light, opened the window, and sat down close to this. The heat, and the fact that she was probably exhausted, no doubt accounted for weakness!

But her hands trembled as she lifted the large envelope, and again studied the many addresses with which it was covered.

The catalogue was from *Debenham & Freebody* and three weeks ago had been despatched to the typed address of Miss Alexandra Hood at the house at Kew. From there the post office had forwarded it to the address at Islington—she recognized the official blunt pencil script. That the Kew post-office should have forwarded any mail after ten years absence was strange enough—for at no time had she left any address with that office. True, her Islington address had been made public at the time of the Court case. But would any sorter make a note of that, and take this trouble for a catalogue? Yet, this was not the inexplicable thing. The incredible thing was that someone at Islington—in that tenement—had readdressed it correctly to her *next* address, which none at Islington could possibly have known. Thereafter, it had passed from address to address quite reasonably, taking its own time, until to-night it had discovered her here. But it was this bridging of the gap at Islington (despite every precaution taken) that had startled her.

Closely she examined the Islington handwriting. It was written in ink, with a scratchy pen, but quite legibly. Every detail of her next address was there, down to the correct district number.

Abruptly she rose, and drank some water.

Now she felt better!

She had simply had a touch of the old *clairvoyance* before she opened the door to-night . . . felt that some unwelcome visitor had recently been there—even that Philip himself was in the offing! No wonder that the *Debenham & Freebody* catalogue had unnerved her. Such foolishness! By now he had probably shelved her with the past—once and for all. He was safely in Paris, engrossed in his work. All was well——

She began to unpack her oilcloth bag.

On top was the evening paper which she had not yet opened. For a second, she hesitated—and then laid it aside. The news could wait! But bath and bed could not, for she was really tired now.

As she raised her arm to hang the bag on the back of the kitchen door, she paused again. She had just remembered her earliest resolve when she started out on this career: *One thing was certain, she'd never use an oilcloth bag. A small attaché-case instead——*

Grasping the small *attaché*-case, she had duly clocked-in

next day, with the good Samaritan who had found her that first job—one of six cleaners at the cigarette factory.

"Whatever's bitten you?" Ruby demanded. "Wasting a good case like that! Swank . . . that's what *they'll* think. It doesn't do to be different. They get offended."

"I had it by me anyway," she mumbled.

"Well, after this, you leave that posh case at home. I've got a spare bag that's just your ticket. You'll 'ave it to-morrow. No need to thank me. Welcome, I'm sure——"

The oilcloth bag was hers. She adopted it with loathing, but in a little was surprised to find how admirable it was —light, rain-proof, easy to clean. The cleaner's boon and blessing. The charwoman's badge. She had been, at one fell swoop, launched and branded by this kindly benefaction.

Smiling now, Andra went upstairs . . .

Saturday Morning . . . one o'clock

Exhaustion had passed off with her bath, and she sat down
in her dressing-gown by her open bedroom window—
rejoicing in the silence of the summer night. She need no
longer hurry. The whole night was hers——

First, she went briefly back over the day's events, until she
found herself at morning intercession again.

But now her prayer was one of gratitude, followed by a
silent admission of such failure as the day had discovered
in her.

Unusually wide-awake now, she sat on by the window.

This upper room was small and rather warm, but she
found it wholly pleasing. The two pictures on the wall
opposite were actually her own—the print of Venice that
had once belonged to Aunt Zoë (for thus through habit she
still thought of her) and the laborious Sampler, sewn so
mutinously by a youthful Andra for Aunt Edith!

Her sole-surviving household gods!

Yet each contained a universe. Who would wish for
more?

Venice had been undiscovered country until last year.

The Sampler, on the other hand, charted to a stitch, was
an open map. Childhood at a glance.

This ambitious undertaking, begun in wild enthusiasm,
continued in endless *ennui*, had been finally completed in a
grim determination that had emanated solely from Miss
Hood!

Even then she had recognised a very important thing
about Miss Hood. Fussy and consequential her Aunt might

be, yet greater even than her sense of personal dignity was an integrity that could on occasion leave her defenceless. Self-contained to a fault, Miss Hood had yet admitted quite openly to Andra, aged thirteen, that she blamed herself for retaining the unaltered brass-plate on the gate.

"But, Aunt Edith, you *do* speak French and German, so *Languages* is quite accurate—even although Aunt Zoë has gone."

Miss Hood, readjusting her *pince-nez*, had hurriedly, testily admitted: "My German is by no means as extensive as my French. By no means. My French is adequate, but with lack of practice, only just. I live in yearly apprehension that one of these days I shall be called to account."

And two nights later the recording angel's bill had been rendered. A peppery business-man, from the important end of the street, had arrived with a German letter from a firm in Hamburg, concerning hydraulic machinery. The only phrase that Miss Hood had been able to follow had been a threat relating to legal proceedings—which had sent Mr. Sandeman, sweating with fury and anxiety from their gate, banging the brass-plate behind him.

Oddly enough Miss Hood's attitude to the brass-plate had hardened after that. Never again did she speak of changing it. Like a flag beneath which she had experienced a baptism of fire, she had continued, tight-lipped, behind its auspices, to the end.

Yet, Andra remembered now, her rigidity had only existed in matters of principle. In those of personal prejudice she had sometimes shown a surprising—even a touching flexibility. The financial crisis which had precipitated Andra's Art School engagement was a striking instance of this. Never would Andra forget that August evening in her Aunt's back parlour, with Madame Moffat massively in the chair—Blanche lolling on the sofa.

Madame Moffat, despite her French corsets, tight kid gloves, and hideously smart hat, had a guileless habit when deep in device, of abstractedly chewing her veil, tied trimly under her second chin—a feat that never failed to fascinate the onlooker.

Waspishly Miss Hood was reiterating: "I don't say that the London Art School isn't the acme of respectability. I don't doubt that the arrangements for the models are beyond reproach. But it's the idea of Andra, or any woman, being stripped naked before strangers——"

Madame Moffat's eye gleamed dangerously. "She'd be stripped before strangers, and so would you, in the case of illness, or an operation."

"That's emergency, Bess."

"And what's the present predicament, may I ask? Andra, like Blanche, has no business ability whatsoever. They have no gifts, no aptitudes, and both just sidled through school. You've admitted that the L.A.S. is above reproach—yet you still shilly-shally. The explanation can be given in two words: petty parochialism."

"One thing leads to another," said Miss Hood obscurely, and Blanche, dark as Carmen, but affable as Doodles, had winked to Andra.

"Does it indeed?" Madame Moffat drew herself up. "Are you suggesting that it has done so with Blanche—after three years there?"

"No, of course not. Don't be ridiculous, Bess."

"Then why should it do so with someone *you've* trained?" There was nothing that Madame Moffat enjoyed more than a fight, and a fight with moral indignation presiding was a walk-over. "But, of course, if you'd rather ruin Andra's health in an office—for which work she has neither training nor talent—or lose her as a paid companion to a she-devil like Pandora Quinn's cousin, that's your affair. I can only assure you from personal experience that the Fine Arts represent a very different *milieu*. And that the vestal virgins of ancient Rome were not more highly prized than are the models at the L.A.S. The great Fra Blondel himself made this quite plain only last term when Blanche, in her slap-dash way, stepped out from the dressing-cubicle, and advanced for once in her red slippers but without her dressing-gown to the front of the platform:

"' Miss Moffat,' he said with *inimitable* courtesy, ' be good enough to return to your cubicle for your wrap. Ladies and gentlemen,' he addressed the class, ' I have asked the Model to go back these few paces for her wrap as usual. Until she takes up her position, she is a woman. Thereafter, she is a goddess.'"

"S'true!" nodded Blanche. "I'd got so accustomed to the blinking performance, I forgot my gown. I felt a complete idiot—dressing up again for a few steps I'd already taken. But I had to do it—dropping the wrap as usual on the dais, which the Master always picks up himself, until such time as I step down again. From start to finish in class, you haven't anything to do with the students."

In the ensuing pause, these certainties had settled themselves unanswerably. Tension eased.

"But don't you feel any embarrassment?" Andra ventured.

"Plenty—the first time I took my things off in that cubicle. But once I stepped out on to the platform, I didn't feel a thing. Fra Blondel was talking. Nobody looked at me till I took up the position. There they were as solemn as judges—ruling me in, rubbing me out! I was a problem, not a person. Believe it or not—I just didn't exist. It was all so different from what I expected, I almost burst out laughing. And it's no joke, I can tell you, being caught mother-naked in a gale of giggles. In fact, after *that* I could think of nothing except how best to keep sober.

"But don't you feel cold?" persisted Andra.

"Of course not. The place is properly heated. If they ever let the furnace down—you can always raise Cain. I've only had to do this once," said Blanche with the assurance of four years seniority.

"Andra!" expostulated her Aunt, "is the *temperature* all that worries you?" but the reproach was irritably made. Miss Hood was weakening.

Madame Moffta ceased to chew her veil. Judicially she declared: "Why agonize like this, Edith? We don't even know yet that Andra has a chance. The position is a plum —and the vacancy may already be filled."

Thereafter panic swung the pendulum. Madame Moffat and Blanche were pressed to stay to supper in the hope that confidence might yet be established.

Comically enough, it had been the nonchalant Blanche who had had the last word with Miss Hood. Blanche in her close-fitting fawn suit, with a white jabot stiffly starched, a saucy summer boater, and white gauntlet gloves, was in Andra's eyes superb—herself only too limply attired in home-laundered linen. The Moffats were guaranteed to sweep all before them. Style itself! A welcome commotion wherever they went.

"If it's Andra's honour with a capital H that you're worried about," Blanche volunteered, "don't give it another thought—either at Art School or the Studios. Artists are whole hoggers. You always know what they're up to. It's the half and half fry—business men on the suburban trains and anywhere else, with their silly jokes and sly pinches that make me sick. As for the Underground—now that's where you'll really have to take out Andra's safety insurance! The something-for-nothing merchants strap-hang there in swarms. I always ignore the preliminary nip (even a dog gets his first bite free) but at the second I let fly: ' Why don't

you *pay* for your pleasure—somewhere else?' That loosens
their grip. Nothing, if not respectable, these gents."

"Good gracious," muttered Miss Hood, "what's this
country coming to?"

"A bad end," Blanche assured her. "But Andra will be
all right with me. Not that I'm narrow. I don't mind any
good story, even if it's broad. But I just can't stand this
idiotic sniggering at sex. What's comic about sex anyway?
The Art crowd are completely decent in that respect."

Again Miss Hood shuddered. "I had no idea that such
things went on in public conveyances. Not once have I had
an experience like that."

"Be your age, Edith," retorted Madame Moffat. "What
Blanche says is a fact, but it is also rubbish. No refined
girl is in the slightest danger from a vulgar approach. The
real temptations meet us always on higher levels. And there
Andra will have to fend for herself, like anyone else."

Blanche, for once determined to have the last word, added:
"And if anyone tells you that a model's life is a lazy way
of making money, Andra, you'll soon be able to enlighten
them. You should see the varicose veins that some of the
old stagers have! But then—the students get these too.
After all—those keen on their work are standing most of
the day, and often part of the night at their easels. But it
isn't so bad once you get the hang of it. And though none
of the students have much money, there's always some
jollification hatching at the School itself. That's why I like
artists. They're festive at the drop of a hat. And the models
are always included. Why, I actually won the Fra Blondel
prize at the last Fancy Dress Ball, as the Queen of Sheba,
and my oriental robes, including jewellery and the Camel,
cost exactly twelve shillings and threepence! But the
sensation of the evening came when Mr. Amos Standish
(and he's world-famous already, Miss Hood) awarded the

second prize to my Camel which he said was the most convincing creature since Noah launched the Ark. Everyone
howled with laughter at my Camel. The platform party
were hysterical. And you won't be surprised when I explain
that Kurragh, an Irishman, was the hind legs, Stirling—a
Scot, the front, and the whole outfit was led on by an
Englishman, Vyse, constantly kicked in the rear by every
available leg the Camel had. Crickhowel, a Welshman, was
Solomon got up like a Bard. And the Interpreter, between
the front and back of the Camel was Paolo, an Italian, who
whipped both ends with equal gusto. Fra Blondel, who
knew the anatomy of the beast, said the group amounted
to a European parable, with myself as the current load of
mischief——"

The Moffats between them had carried the day!

Until that December night, more than two years later,
when, on a mounting pleurisy, Miss Hood had deliriously
besought her:

"Andra—if anything happens to me, try to get other
work. There's no future in posing. There must be something more suitable. . . . *Promise* you'll try——"

After the funeral, this sacrifice of a tolerable job in
pleasant surroundings and agreeable company had been
expedited by two facts: that the Moffats, on Blanche's
engagement to Jefferson Jebb, left unexpectedly for the
United States at the end of the current term at the Art
School, and that Andra herself had no idea how lucky she
had hitherto been. In any case, a death-bed promise was a
death-bed promise.

Very much the junior still, Andra watched Madame
Moffat organize Miss Hood's funeral. Thankfully she heard
Madame Moffat insist that she made her home with them,
till they sailed for San Francisco at Easter.

The only ordeal which Andra faced alone was the meeting

with Miss Hood's Solicitor. On this point, however, Madame Moffat was adamant.

Mr. Piggott of *Piggott, Pierce and Pembury* (known locally, and irreverently, as Pig-it, Pinch and Penury), was short, fat, kind and conscientious, but he was also very busy. Andra found herself disposed of before she had mustered! Briskly Mr. Piggott came to each point. And Andra who was susceptible to authority, reverently followed all he said—then went out and obeyed him literally.

The situation, Mr. Piggott affirmed, was regrettable, but by no means hopeless if she kept her head. She was young and healthy and could work. Work she must, as Miss Hood's annuity had died with her. Nevertheless, Andra was not entirely penniless. Miss Hood had effected certain savings which by the terms of her Will would result in yet another annuity. This would bring in for Andra a sum approximating to one pound a week. Mr. Piggott would arrange for the money to be paid in monthly, or quarterly instalments. Mr. Piggott strongly advised a quarterly dispensation, as it was essential that this sum should be saved from the word go! *Together*, emphasized Mr. Piggott, with the sums which Andra would receive from the sale of Miss Hood's furniture. He understood that Madame Moffat had found a reliable firm for this purpose. Very well then, that was that. And by these means a nest-egg would accrue for Andra's old age.

At this point Andra achieved lucidity for the first and only time.

"But what," she asked, "am I to live on meantime?"

"On what you earn," said Mr. Piggott crisply. "I appreciate that when Madame Moffat leaves for the States your expenses will rise. You will then have to find inexpensive board and lodging. But it can be done. And you will of course secure this with some respectable family.

The one essential that you must bear in mind, the issue of paramount importance is never to touch your capital. As you will be unable to save much of your salary at the start, it is not only your bounden duty to leave your capital intact —it is the one course open to anyone in your circumstances."

"My capital?" Andra was bewildered.

"Your annuity payments. To tamper with capital before middle-life—indeed at any age—is nothing short of lunacy. I hope I make myself plain?"

"Oh, yes, very," Andra dutifully agreed, and hurriedly shook his outstretched hand.

She had found this brief interview surprisingly exhausting. It confirmed her suspicions of the business world. All sorts of pressure appeared to converge on her with Mr. Piggott's emphasis. The weightiness of Mr. Piggott was almost more than she could bear. Escape was imperative. Fervently she hoped that she would never have to see him again.

And it was precisely this weakness that prompted the acceptance of Punchie Coburg's offer of work. Punchie's mother had been an early pupil of Miss Hood's, who had, unfortunately, fallen from grace by marrying considerably beneath her. An ice-cream trader at Thornton Heath. But the friendship had persisted, although Miss Hood also disapproved of Punchie's mania for the theatre—which took the form of a pit-seat for every available London first night. Punchie, who was five years older than Andra, was a plain girl with a frizz of red hair and a pepper-pot powdering of freckles on a high-bridged nose. She had no personal stage ambitions—the theatre itself was a passion with her, and although Miss Hood might condemn this infatuation, she was, nevertheless much impressed by the money that Punchie earned at Messrs. Lombards—the well-known furnishing establishment in Tottenham Court Road. The exact nature of Punchie's work was never defined, and Miss Hood had been far too refined to frame the curiosity that consumed her. Therefore, it was not until after her Aunt's death that Andra discovered Punchie to be overseer of the machinists' room in the Lombard factory.

"But you'd be all right there, Andra. I'd see to that. And the salary is thirty shillings more than you're getting as a model. Then there's all the extra you can make on overtime. And Lombards treat you splendidly. As you're educated, you're bound to become an overseer in no time. Although the war is officially over, our Workroom's schedule will run on for another year—then automatically you'll be graded into peace-products . . . and something better."

"But, Punchie, if I weren't able for that?"

"Don't worry. Tents, bandoliers and kit-bags are always needed for the regular army. You'll never be out of a job —and of course it's only the tent doors and windows *you'd* be working on. Nothing really heavy. But I must know now, as one of the girls is leaving at Easter—and I *could* keep the job for you. Father's widowed sister at Selhurst, the next station to us, will give you a nice room with breakfast and supper, far cheaper than you'd get in town. Selhurst is almost as good as the country. You've only to say the word."

Andra said it. Everything was settled in a sentence— without a single interview.

"A machinist in a factory!" Madame Moffat exploded. "Have you gone crazy? Life in a sweat-shop! You'd be out in a week, and by then we'd be on the other side of the Atlantic, unable to help."

"Oh, no," insisted Andra, "for this is Lombards . . . all the latest gadgets. And they treat you splendidly—— Think of the money! And Punchie's aunt has promised a really nice room in her country cottage."

"Lombards!" Madame Moffat was temporarily deflated. Lombards was a household word—the best on furniture vans as well as on furniture polish—in furnishings, as in real estate. Lombards represented universal benefit. To doubt Lombards was to discredit daylight.

"In no time," pursued Andra, "I shall be an overseer like Punchie."

But this Madame Moffat refused to swallow. Punchie's incisive profile had made a definite impression at Miss Hood's funeral.

"There's three months still to go," she warned, "let us hope something better will turn up meantime."

But nothing did, and Andra scarcely cared—so happy were these short weeks with the Moffats. A somewhat shocking admission she realized, each time she remembered Aunt Edith's death. In the hilarity and freedom of the Marylebone flat she was expanding for the first time in her life— a fledgling jubilantly discovering its wings.

And the enjoyable encounter with Mr. Enoch Tucker hadn't been like business at all. *En route* Madame Moffat had said: "He's unique—the only loan of money made by my husband that has ever paid dividends! Now, don't be disappointed by the look of his sale-room. There is a great deal of money in that furniture store. Mr. Tucker has made good in quite a big way. He's going to be invaluable to you."

Prophetic words! And there was Mr. Tucker that first day, small, rosy, resolute—smiling as if he'd known Andra always, as if an introduction were really rather a joke. Addressing Madame Moffat as Mrs. Moffat, another feature that set him apart, he quietly showed the list of items which he thought Miss Andra should not sell. A day might come——

"But what about storage?" Madame Moffat queried.

Bowing with just a touch of ceremony Mr. Tucker announced: "Storage in this case will be a pleasure."

One month later the proceeds of the sale had reached her. Quite a useful sum to add to Mr. Piggott's nest-egg. Andra was, in fact, slightly intoxicated by this cheque, although not for an instant did she dream of affecting the total in any way!

February that year was one of the coldest on record. The soil was frost-bound to the depths of a foot and later came drenching rains. But Andra scarcely noticed—so much went on in this particular home-circle. Every detail was of dramatic importance. Madame Moffat had pronounced ideas on food like everything else, and although she had no sooner adopted one diet for them than she changed it, she religiously adhered to what she termed the theory of compatibles. Andra learnt to make a salad that would not disgrace a French woman, and how to cook vegetables. Madame Moffat took her clothes in hand. The anatomy of style was vigorously demonstrated. The essential principles absorbed. And the hat shop itself proved a constant excitement. Periodically Madame would become bored with one particular customer, or hats in general. At such times, alarmingly, she ceased to play *vendeuse* and acted as nature dictated. An order would be a complete fiasco, Madame's point of view a revelation. After this outrageous event, the customer would desert, rumour would riot, disaffection spread. Then one week later, the window downstairs would again be a sight for the gods, the dark little show-room sunning itself in Madame's expansive smile with all its expensive connotations. The public (often the outraged also) would pause on the other side of the plate-glass, consider, covet, crave—then enter and be lost to every consideration but millinery.

At home Madame Moffat would work Blanche and Andra

B.A.I.   H like galley-slaves (so Blanche averred) then as suddenly they would down-tools, and be off to a theatre. Or another week-end she would drag the girls after her through the London museums to increase culture. At all hours, friends would descend on the Moffat flat. But Madame made short work of any young man who still hankered for Blanche. Such troubled her more than they bothered Blanche, placidly pleased with her solitaire diamond and her distant Jefferson Jebb.

And late each night, into early morning, the two girls would lie awake in the bedroom they shared, endlessly talking. In the darkness, the drowsy monotone of their voices hummed like a hidden hive. Both of them so much in love with life that they re-lived every day before they slept! Youth, inseparable in sympathy.

So the Moffat days flew by, until the departure for San Francisco. At Victoria Madame Moffat had wept, convulsively clasping Andra.

"Blanche, it's all wrong . . . we ought to have taken her with us. I can't bear this."

"Well, I told you so all along. But you worried about the money—which is just idiotic. Something always turns up. Jeff would have been delighted. What's to stop Andra coming later, when we're in and the flag's run up?"

And on the strength of this bright idea, they found courage to part. The engine bayed, the coach jerked back, then smoothly, stealthily drew away, gathering speed inexorably. Vehemently the Moffats waved till steam wiped them out——

Speechless, Andra turned to leave the platform.

Stepping on to the pavement outside, spring sunshine after weeks of dismal weather transformed the town. Her tears dried. She walked on, invigorated by a perfect April day. She felt a little guilty about this sudden soaring of spirits. She was alone . . . alone in the world for the first time—but this too had its own wonder. She wasn't frightened after all. She felt ready for anything!

Selhurst, the specific, was about to take her at her word . . .

Five o'clock found her in Nelson Road.

If this were Punchie's idea of a rural district, it certainly had not been Andra's.

Horatio Cottage, one of a row of two-storied workmen's cottages, in red and ginger brick, gave some reassurance from its obvious trimness, and a front patch bright with crocuses.

But with the opening of the front door by Mrs. Rose, an over-powering odour met Andra, enveloping her at each step within the small, bare, plaintively clean dwelling—a smell that was now to alternate like an invisible tide throughout all her days and nights there—advancing, retreating in waves according to the state of the larder: cats' meat cooking. And for four cats. Mrs. Rose was an animal lover whose charity in this respect was out of all proportion to her means or accommodation. There was also an elderly Cairn, belonging to Mr. Ludlow, the other lodger—which led a morose existence under the kitchen table, awaiting his master's return each night.

Punchie had said nothing of this menagerie, and of course the spotless cleanliness of the box-like rooms defied criticism.

"As you're a friend of Punchie's," Mrs. Rose announced, "you'll 'ave your meals with me and Mr. Ludlow. And this will save the stairs."

Mrs. Rose was thin, with an anxious expression, and a preoccupied manner. Andra soon discovered that she herself only had actuality for Mrs. Rose in advance or retrospect—so inveterately did her hostess assay her difficulties out of season.

Andra glancing around her tiny bedroom that first evening had timidly asked:

"Where do I hang my clothes?"

Mrs. Rose looked astonished. "On the back of your door of course—you've got three pegs. Mr. Ludlow's kindly settled to keep your trunk in his bedroom across the passage. Trunks," added Mrs. Rose in afterthought, "is a nuisance." Precipitately she plunged downstairs.

Mr. Ludlow, Andra remembered—nauseated and homesick in this cupboard of a room that did not even have its own key—Mr. Ludlow was the other boarder. Punchie had mentioned him at a time when he was an airy-fairy figment of a man to Andra. "We did hope," Punchie had mysteriously nodded, "that something might come of Mr. Ludlow. But now it never will. Aunt Ella's let it drift on too long. It's fatal to let a man go past a certain point. Then you're after him with the boat-hook—and there's no disguising *that*!"

Almost in tears, Andra shut the door and opened the window. Fresh air poured in. Salvation! No doubt any new place must seem strange at first——

Barely, however, had she registered gratitude than another aroma assailed her. Someone, to an outbreak of rapturous barking below, was smoking a pipe—and a tobacco unknown to her before. Heavy and sweet it penetrated the close door, its sickly eddies laying waste the air around her.

Mr. Ludlow had regained the home he shared with her! Was he even now enquiring for the trunk that would shortly enter his possession?

Hysterically Andra began to laugh—but as she smoothed her hair, she wondered uneasily if her sense of smell were abnormal. Staring at her pretty nose in the Woolworth mirror on the wall, she little knew that through this perceptive organ, her Waterloo in life awaited her.

Meantime Mr. Ludlow had settled in for the night. An elderly man, with a thick mane of hair, heavily lidded eyes, a set smile and averted gaze, he had that expression of smug nobility to be found in the lion of royal armorial bearings. Ever aware of the unicorn's prancing proximity, he steadfastly gazed beyond. Endurance, Andra felt, would be his strong suit.

"Pleased to meet you," his glance skated off Andra's brow and vanished aloft to the plush parlour chimneypiece. "Chilly for April. Come in to the fire. . . . Nice district this, you'll find. Nobody ever begrudges the train journey. Yes, we're certainly well-placed here."

Something in the sincerity of the last phrase went to Andra's heart. She felt ashamed of her earlier discontent.

"And I'm told you have a park," she began.

"Well, it's more of a recreation ground. But very welcome none the less . . ."

And Selhurst's defection as a rural retreat was scarcely to matter in the months ahead, as Selhurst she hardly saw.

She rose at quarter to six each morning, ate a hurried breakfast, then dashed for the 6.50 workmen's train to Victoria.

Punchie joined the train at Thornton Heath.

At eight o'clock each morning they clocked-in.

Lombard's warehouse was so vast that it amounted to one roundsman's daily delivery—the man passing with his milk bottles from machine to machine in 1919.

The first sight and sound of her own Workroom almost winded Andra. The noise of a hundred sewing machines driven by power made a din so deafening that once when there was an explosion in a neighbouring factory, the machinists knew nothing of it, until the Electrician walked round announcing: "It's all right, girls. That was only Lyles!"

Andra began on red and white signals. She had used a treadle-machine before, and quite quickly learnt to put her foot forward and catch the power, while she fed the material to the needle. The simplicity of the operation soothed, and her growing efficiency pleased her. In a month's time she had passed to sleeping-bags. These were the best paid item of all, but as they made the hands raw, the workers were only permitted to earn on those for three days at a time. Lombards looked after its own! Lombards also insured its employees against any accident. But horrors such as a needle through the finger were unknown in Punchie's room. "Because why?" she explained to Andra. "I won't have hustle. Smart and steady is my motto. Accidents bring the management on to the scene, and then you get *dislocation*!" Nervously Andra perceived that calamity here would amount to a personal affront.

The women themselves were a sombre sight. Dressed in black Italian-cloth overalls, they looked as if they were in perpetual mourning. Through the pressure at which they worked, they scarcely knew one another—with the exception of the woman on either side. Andra, seated next a window, had only one neighbour. She and this girl worked their material in lots of a dozen, and were obliged to take an empty spool for each new reel of thread. Every detail was under control—except for the fact that Andra's scissors were twice stolen, and Connie's footrule once. Tools were considered fair game. But nothing else was ever touched.

Happily for Andra the monotony of the work did not affect her. Accustomed from childhood to a groove, from which rut the Moffats had briefly shaken her, she soon adapted herself to this jog-trot day. But by six o'clock she was exhausted, and as they did not clock-out till eight, it was after nine when she regained Selhurst. Next morning the treadmill started at quarter to six again.

But Saturday was gala—at least to Punchie, and Andra was swept along in her wake. They knocked off work at one o'clock and then plunged for places in the pit queue decreed by Punchie for that week . . . a relaxation which in its varied stimulus stunned Andra afresh, Punchie often electing for an evening Show as well. No man ever accompanied them, Punchie explaining that she went to the theatre to concentrate. Much better, wasn't it? Supinely Andra agreed.

The Moffats . . . the Art School . . . the gaiety of an occasional studio-party . . . the fascinating hours in Mr. Amos Standish's spectacular studio now belonged to another world. It was as if she had died abruptly, and gone pell-mell to purgatory.

That she continued to endure this existence for almost a year was readily explained. Bludgeoned by exhaustion, a docile mind had ceased to reason. Weakness was still disguised as amiability. And Mr. Piggott's nest-egg, growing steadily in importance lent its own sanction to these melancholy proceedings.

But when the end came, it did so with lightning speed.

The long bleak Workroom wavered in March sunshine. Connie, the girl on Andra's left, cheered by this break in the weather, called hopefully across her shoulder—then screamed in anguish.

This shriek, indescribably shrill, unspeakably prolonged, brought Andra in one leap upon her.

"It's all right, Connie!" she shouted, and the ringing power of her cry pierced the din. Every machinist heard it. With one arm round Connie's shoulder, and her right hand hooding the trapped finger, Andra was unrecognizable, her face and eyes blazing with light.

The tortured girl stared up at her, and in that interminable minute before the power was turned off, felt her strength passing—then knew it transformed. Later she said: "It was like being hypnotized. I thought I was going to die, and then I just didn't feel any more. I seemed to be out of myself. But safe, safe, safe——"

On the way home, Punchie, much worried admitted: "I can't think why she didn't faint. They always do. It was the craziest thing I ever saw—the two of you staring into each other's eyes. As if you were in a trance."

But echo did not answer for once.

Andra remained silent. She was shaken to the soul by the sense of that power that had been instantly available for Connie and herself. In her passion to help—this force had sprung into being, like an angel supporting them both.

The episode not only awakened her confidence, but when next day reaction set in, this too had changed its course.

Hastening down Nelson Road in the rain, for the inevitable supper of tinned beans, she noticed rising from her coat (Madame Moffat's farewell gift) a peculiar odour.

This coat in wet weather Mrs. Rose permitted her to hang on the kitchen door. Now, soaked through, it reeked of stale cooking.

Quite suddenly this revolting smell took charge of her destiny. In sixty seconds she became adult.

She entered Horatio Cottage knowing she was about to leave it for ever!

One week's notice would see her through at Lombards. And—oh, wild relief—she would also escape a summer holiday with Punchie at Brighton, and a further orgy of theatre-going. Thank God, thank God, it was all over at last!

Once in her bedroom, pencil and paper would be needed to work out figures.

She could hardly wait for freedom now!

And midnight found her plan fully hatched—together with Mr. Piggott's nest-egg.

She would take an unfurnished room in London, install her own furniture, as Mr. Tucker had earlier suggested. The rental of this room, and its upkeep would mean the weekly sacrifice of her annuity, but she no longer cared. Why save for an old age that might never come? And before she looked for accommodation, before she removed her furniture from store, before she searched for work, she would take a week's holiday in some beautiful place. She could well afford this, and she knew exactly where she would go.

To Buxleigh-on-Sea.

An elderly cousin of Madame Moffat's had written after a month at the Winter Garden Hotel: "This house is ideal. Cosmopolitan in the best sense. And *so* quiet. Any lady alone may safely relax here." The notepaper had had a picture of a tiny empty table, set invitingly under palms in a conservatory through which the sea beckoned. At Buxleigh Andra would recover her courage and some desire for life. There she would sleep herself out. In that quiet conservatory, she would sit up and begin to take notice again.

But no one must know where she was going . . . nor her future plans till these were accomplished facts. Mr. Piggott had left no doubt in her mind that to go into capital (the annuity) amounted to lunacy. She was therefore cutting herself off from Mr. Piggott, but this too would have its brighter side. The privacy known at Aunt Edith's was something she could no longer exist without. It was essential. Basic.

Her life was her own, after all.

Exhilarated by this discovery, she met Punchie's protests unmoved.

"But you've never made any complaint? It just doesn't make sense . . ."

Nor could she wait for Carter Paterson. Her trunk ten days later, reclaimed from Mr. Ludlow, was set on a taxi. Re-united with it, and in a coat successfully purged by Messrs. Eastman, she rattled triumphantly out of Nelson Road. Her sense of deliverance was overwhelming. It amounted to rebirth . . .

Seated now fifteen years later in the upper room overlooking Parliament Hill Fields, Andra almost laughed.

But how inevitably every step of the way had led to Philip —Buxleigh-on-Sea was still lyrical in memory. So too was the Kew house. That was the disconcerting feature of the case!

The June night was growing cooler now.

She rose, crossed to the bed and wound her clock.

Setting the alarum for quarter to five, she got into bed and closed her eyes.

But as she drowsed, the drudge within proceeded to recite a curious litany—a sequence anticipated from the coming day's events, which for her would lie, remarkably enough, among the heirlooms of the nation:

Out of the locker (dark as a cell) and up the marble stairs to *Seventy-Four*. Then through the *Illustrated and Design* into the *Jones Bequest*. . . . Pass over the *French Furniture*. (This always takes more time than it should). Out into the *Picture Gallery* . . . then over the bridge into the *Saltoun Collection*. Down the stairs to *Sixty-Two, Sixty-Three, Sixty-Four—Sixty-Four* and her heart again missed a beat. Quite absurd . . . only the Italian marriage-coffers! She must be dreaming. . . . No, she must be dusting—and she must look alive. The *William Morris Room* is still to come. Then through to the *Students' Court*—the old coaches and sedan chairs swallow time too. From there into *Forty-Five Court* and the *Musical Instruments.* . . . All to be done before ten a.m.

Specialized work . . . an undertaking of great responsibility
—for which the highest credentials had been required——
Her breath wavered for a second. The *highest credentials*.
. . . Then oblivion absolved her. Soundly she slept.

The sky was closely shrouded when she arose, for by summer-time reckoning dawn was still an hour ahead.

Dressing, she crossed the passage, opened the door of a small study used by Professor Baird, and vanished for that period.

Emerging at six o'clock, as was her custom, she made her bed, swept, and dusted before preparing breakfast.

To-day, however, she had an extra task.

The rounding-up of the bad debt.

Seated in the silent drawing-room she wrote a letter on a sheet of paper, without address. It was not an easy letter, but she wrote it quite quickly.

Only at the envelope did she pause. Yet everyone in London knew that address. The morning papers advertised it, the evening papers emphasized it, and the night-sky blazoned it. Gerda Rush starring at the Regency Theatre in *My Love, My Lady* . . . London's Jubilee musical comedy now playing to capacity——

Would she be able to get a seat?

She must trust——

Breakfast, eaten in the early sunshine of a perfect June morning, was invariably a hearty meal—with the table at the open kitchen window dappled by the chestnut tree. But to-day she found that she was less hungry than usual.

Barely had she finished clearing up than, to her surprise, the front door bell rang. Still too early for the postman——

Puzzled, she opened the door.

Hat in hand, a young man stood there—perhaps not so

young. He had a sensitive face and spectacles, and was quietly but well-dressed.

"Good morning, Miss Hood," he said. "Please forgive an early call. I came last night, but think you got back later than usual."

"Much later," she echoed, astonished.

"My name is Burrowes," he began. "This is my card. I shall be grateful if you can spare me a few minutes——"

"I'm very sorry," she said swiftly, without glancing at his card, "but I must leave this house in quarter of an hour. I have to be at South Kensington by eight-twenty."

"I realize that. But please let me explain my business, for I have a car outside, and shall be delighted to motor you direct to Kensington. This will give us longer here. The matter is urgent, Miss Hood. Connected with an old friend of yours—whom you recently lost through death—a notable personality, who has figured much in the Press."

Blood drained from her face and lips. White-faced she stared at him.

Apologetically Mr. Burrowes stammered: "I thought you must already know of Sir Amos Standish's death."

"Sir Amos Standish," she repeated slowly. "Sir Amos Standish. Yes . . . I know of his death. Please come in."

Blindly she led the way to the kitchen.

Abruptly she sat down at the empty table.

Silently Mr. Burrowes took the other chair. It was obvious that he had given her some kind of shock—but *not* through Sir Amos Standish. He cursed his clumsiness.

Quietly he said: "I represent *The Daily Clarion*, Miss Hood."

"*The Daily Clarion!*" she drew back involuntarily. "Please tell me how you got this address?"

"We canvassed every person who was present on the

platform at Pastor Frick's farewell meeting. Mr. Enoch Tucker alone knew it."

"And he gave it?"

"Only when he heard of the issues involved."

"What has happened?" she asked a little huskily.

Mr. Burrowes laid a copy of Sir Amos Standish's book upon the table.

"You have seen this posthumous publication, no doubt."

"No. No, I have not."

"But you have heard of it, of course?"

Somehat apologetically she said: "I'm afraid not."

"You haven't heard of Sir Amos Standish's Memoirs? But Miss Hood, newspapers and radio alike have been full of it. Already it has broken all the usual records. Before six months are up, it will probably have been translated into every living language."

"I'm so sorry . . ." she began. "I'm afraid I'm very much out of things. My hours, for one thing, are rather unusual. Often I miss the newspapers. Days may also pass without my listening to the radio."

By this time Mr. Burrowes was completely in charge. He tapped the volume between them with authority:

"This book has made you famous, Miss Hood."

"The sculptures for which I posed——"

"No, no! What the public is interested in is the woman behind the marble. This book has greatly excited public imagination—through Sir Amos Standish's hidden vigil, the selfless devotion with which he followed every step of your career."

"My *what*?"

"Your career. Your deliberately sought obscurity."

She stifled a laugh: "That was certainly thrust upon me!"

"Well, I assure you that you are obscure no longer. His

book has made your story a unique romance. Here is a great artist, one of the wealthiest bachelors in town, the friend of princes, fêted abroad, lauded at home, watching over this unknown woman in all her vicissitudes. And what a woman——"

"In all my *what*?"

"In all your troubles. And what a time you've clearly had! He makes that clear—in the most delicate way. Step by step he followed, yet never intruded on you. But was always ready to do so, had extremity occurred."

"One moment," her colourless cheek had flushed painfully. "Is my name mentioned in this account?"

"Not once. That's why it's been so difficult to trace you. Sir Amos simply said that you were *La Pleureuse*."

"That is true," she interrupted, "but it does not make me the woman you describe, whose career he followed step by step."

"Miss Hood," said Mr. Burrowes, a trifle crisply, "I have read this book, and you have not. I have also confirmed that the place names given by Sir Amos are correct where you are concerned: Hampstead, Selhurst, Buxleigh-on-Sea, Kew. On leaving Kew you disappeared, but ultimately he traced you to an address which he gives simply as by the Angel, Islington. It was there that the worst—and yet in some ways the best period of your life was spent."

"This——" she stammered, "is almost unbearable. I cannot believe that anyone has the right to—to——"

"Now, Miss Hood, your name doesn't come into this once. Public interest has been stirred by the fact that this great artist could so simply record his indebtedness, and the steps he took to keep watch over you."

"*Watch!*" she could scarcely contain her impatience.

"Oh, he makes it plain that he did nothing of any practical

sort. Always you won through on your own. It's a portrait of fortitude."

"May I ask," and her voice trembled slightly, "if he gives any reason for this unusual interest?"

"Yes, he makes that quite clear too. After all, a man like Sir Amos Standish sees numberless gifted or beautiful women. There you were simply one among many. But the secret of your fascination for him was your fidelity in intercession."

"Mr. Burrowes, it is almost useless to continue this conversation. I cannot be the woman to whom he refers. Although I knew Sir Amos well, never once did I mention such an undertaking."

"But he knew of it, Miss Hood. Long before Pastor Frick made any reference to your healing powers through prayer. Sir Amost states that he owed recovery from his own grave illness in 1930 to this. You were back in the west-end by then——" he broke off.

The woman was staring at him as if she'd seen a ghost. Her lips had parted slightly, and her hand went to her throat.

"Does he say how he knew that I—that I was constant in prayer?"

"No," Mr. Burrowes was momentarily non-plussed, "no, he doesn't mention that. I've studied the book carefully. But one can tell from the way he writes that he was completely *en rapport* with you. He has left no doubt in the reader's mind that he was an adept in telepathy. He calls it an invincible affinity. Space and time could not prevail against it. Why, when you left that address at Islington after that unpleasant case was decided in your favour—he knew in no time where you'd gone. A small flat above an antique shop in London, west-one! No actual street is mentioned. Come, Miss Hood, you've nothing to worry about. Sir Amos' discretion has been all that anyone could wish. You'll discover for yourself that it's not only a moving tribute, but a highly unusual story. And to-day's *Clarion* publishes the news that Hollywood has applied to the Trustees for the film rights of a picture, based on the book, to be named provisionally: ' *Hidden Vigil*'."

To his intense relief, she began to shake weakly with laughter. "Mr. Burrowes," she said, "I'm quite certain that you have not called to break this fantastic news in advance. Why have you come?"

Mr. Burrowes liked her voice. It was deeper than that of most English women. Almost continental. She didn't look particularly English for that matter—Danish? A more subtle, less explicit type. Austrian perhaps? No trace of accent, foreign or otherwise. He could not place her. And why on earth were they sitting in the kitchen?

Aloud he said: "Monday, first of July, is the day appointed for the opening of the Standish Club. Sir Amos has made a bequest of his mansion in Regent's Park, fully furnished with many of his treasures, and a number of his own sculptures to the nation. Or rather, to the poor of the borough. Adolescents will have their own recreation rooms, so too will adults. But on certain nights, each will entertain the other—exactly as you planned that day he met you by the lake in Regent's Park. Another instance of his second sight! Discovering you on the seat there."

"Scarcely clairvoyance," she protested. "After all the lake was close to his house. He must often have walked in the park."

"But you did not, Miss Hood. No, you had travelled from Kew that day—intending to call on him; had changed your mind; and sat there to rest. And Sir Amos in his studio, walked straight out and found you. Listen to this," and Mr. Burrowes opened the book:

I

*She had thought better, or rather, worse of confiding in me!
But in a little we began to plan her ideal club, which I was
amused to find closely resembled my own home—with the owner
absent.*

Involuntarily Andra laughed. "How strange to record
that! Everyone who saw Sir Amos' house must have been
inspired by it. Our plans that day for the Standish Club
were drawn up in fun. The whole thing was a joke."

"Only at the start, Miss Hood. Remember I have read
this book! Finally he insisted that you too should con-
tribute to the good work—make some small sacrifice for
the benefits you were ordaining. Don't you remember Sir
Amos' pun? ' *And you shall open it— Venus shall be vocal for
once . . . marble wax eloquent.*' When you protested: ' *I shouldn't
know what to say,*' he replied: ' *You could tell them how
wonderful I was, as a start. In fact you might continue indefinitely
in that strain. I should always see you through!* ' In short, Miss
Hood, the Trustees want you to open the Standish Club on
Monday."

Andra's smile faded. "Mr. Burrowes—I can't believe
you're serious! Of course, it's quite impossible. No one
could be more unsuitable. I'm the last person——"

"Don't say that," he interrupted. "You're the most
widely discussed personality in town, at the moment.
Excitement will mount, if you agree. I assure you that the
occasion must prove memorable. In tribute to Sir Amos,
various embassies will also be represented—an international
event."

"It is out of the question for me."

"You mean to break your promise?"

Exasperated, she laughed again. "This Club may have
arisen for the reasons you give, but Sir Amos never intended
to keep me to any embarrassing bargain."

"That's where you're mistaken, Miss Hood. The book

reports that you laughed so heartily that Sir Amos warned you: '*Remember I shall hold you to this—from the other side of Jordan. And I shall not wait for the Last Trump, I shall summon you by Clarion!*' And here I am," said Mr. Burrowes, laying his rejected visiting-card before her.

Silently she gazed at the small white piece of pasteboard on which, in funereal black, these words: *The Daily Clarion*, confronted her.

Then she glanced up. Between smiles and tears she said: "You're undeniable. And so is he. I'll do it."

"Good!" said Mr. Burrowes heartily. "My paper is administering this endowment fund. No one could teach Sir Amos anything about publicity. He hoped for a chain of such clubs across the country. And the *Clarion*'s opening its own fund for this purpose next week. Clubs that are not merely hostels, but centres of beauty. That's what you said the poor needed——"

He was studying her as he spoke. Not much colour, but the nearer you got to her, the better she became. She was not striking, yet she stood out. And her eyes had an astonishing clarity in the morning light. The white of each orb was still delicately washed with what was popularly known as baby blue! Yet she must be thirty-five if she were a day. Catching sight of her profile, he saw how suavely chiselled this was. But her hands were a shock— the skin roughened, the nails bluntly cut, the knuckles discoloured . . . as if she'd recently been working in some laboratory.

"Wouldn't be surprised," he announced, "if you took a stunning photograph."

"One moment," she said fleetly. "I must have your assurance that this address will be kept private. In a sense it isn't mine at all. I look after this house for friends who are abroad. I am only the caretaker."

"Miss Hood, your privacy will be as much respected as if you were royalty. Throughout, I shall handle all arrangements myself. And you needn't worry about your speech either. One of our Editors will turn you out a little posy for the occasion. Won't take you more than ten minutes to memorize it."

A slight frown appeared on the smooth brow opposite. Surprisingly she said:

"But if I speak, I shall want to use my own words."

"You would, would you?" adroitly Mr. Burrowes concealed his misgiving. "You think you could manage that? Well, so much the better. I'm all for a spontaneous approach myself. It gets the public every time—as long as you remember to speak out. Possibly some personal recollections of the great man? Perhaps you'd give me an idea in advance what you'll be likely to say?"

"No," said Andra slowly, "I don't think I could give you any idea beforehand. I always wait for guidance."

Hastily Mr. Burrowes swallowed his qualm. "Details can wait. Meantime the Committee wish to put the procedure before you. Our Chairman, Lord Fortdevon himself will introduce you. If it's fine, and of course it's going to be fine, the opening ceremony will take place on the terrace to accommodate the large numbers expected. Two of Sir Amos' servants remain as permanent caretakers, Mr. and Mrs. Ash—very reliable people."

"Mr. and Mrs. Ash?"

"You know them?"

For a second she covered her eyes, and he had a moment of consternation. Was she going to weep?

But a second later, it was clear that she was only shielding herself from too much sunshine.

"Years ago," she said, "when I was in more prosperous circumstances, I recommended Mr. and Mrs. Ash to Sir

Amos. They are old friends. I'm glad that they have been a success."

"Well, there you are! What could be better? The Club staff has already been chosen by the Committee. They too will be there to welcome you. And of course a car will be placed at your disposal that day." He rose. "Sorry we'll have to hurry now, if I'm to get you to Kensington on time."

Almost at once she rejoined him in the hall—wearing a black beret and dust coat that eclipsed all charm, with an atrocious oilcloth bag, such as cleaners use, slung over her arm.

His dismay was ludicrous, but as he put on his own hat, she suddenly laughed:

"Now, I recognize you! We've met before. In the tube last night. Don't you remember? We sat opposite—until I got out at Camden Town."

It was only too true, and as they drove off, his anxiety increased. Yet smoothly enough he broached the difficulty, after a decent interval:

"And of course, Miss Hood, any expenses for the Opening Ceremony, we shall gladly meet. In fact, such expenses will be essential for Monday. We appreciate that few people these days can have outfits for such unique occasions. I'm afraid this doesn't leave you much time for shopping. But don't hesitate to get the necessary outfit."

"Thank you very much," Andra smiled faintly. "You are very kind. But I think I have something that will answer the occasion, important as this is."

Relieved, Mr. Burrowes took refuge in gossip as they cut across the park. "Sir Amos did too many things too well for people to remain generous. Now they're saying he ought to have been a writer instead of a sculptor. Grudging."

"Even in death?"

"I'm afraid so. It usually takes fifty years to establish

an able man, and one hundred to confirm a genius. Dispensation in a way, of course, as it saves the artist, though not the man, from the clutches of his contemporaries. By the way, am I to know where to set you down?"

"Of course, Mr. Burrowes. I realize I've no secrets from you! I'm due at the Victoria and Albert Museum at eight-thirty. And I enter by the Secretariat Gate in Cromwell Road."

There was a little pause.

"We shall just do it," Mr. Burrowes said. "And talking of secrets, there's one I'd like to know. Don't, of course, answer, if you'd rather not—although I assure you that this reply of yours won't go further. But *did* you and Sir Amos ever meet again—after your ways parted that time in Regent's Park?"

"Didn't Sir Amos tell that too in the book?"

"Unhappily he did not."

He shot a glance at her and saw merriment flash.

"Too bad," she said softly. "Especially as you've guessed that my reply won't go further!"

"Ah well," Mr. Burrowes nodded good-naturedly, "it was perhaps too much to expect an answer. But what beats me is how any man could follow a woman's destiny as closely as he did yours, without her knowing a thing about it. And I gather you didn't?"

"I certainly did not."

"Well, please forget my question. Just an idea of mine that you might have bumped into each other again in the last ten years. And that's what the Public's bound to think, you'll find . . ."

The Victoria and Albert Museum slid past the car, imposing its own vast calm in the midst of uproar, with the figure of Fame aloft the lantern-crown, dazzled by sunshine, and shimmering unsteadily in the tender blue sky.

Quickly Andra walked through the Secretariat Gate.

Her heart was beating much too fast. Not for a moment, though, did she believe that fantastic tale of the Film Rights' application. It just could not be true. It was the sort of story that newspapers *would* exploit!

The hidden vigil itself was responsible for her quickened pulse. It was a vindication of all she believed might be possible in personal communion. Yet what she felt now was agitation and a sort of sick disappointment . . . for the wrong man had worked the miracle for her.

How small, how paltry! What did preference matter, when the feat had again been proven? How could she still deplore that this affinity had not been hers with Philip? Time and again the thought of Sir Amos had sustained her. Yet never once had she suspected that there might be a mutual contact! Why did people pass like sleep-walkers through the very wonder they desired?

Passing the glass and brick sentry-box now, the warder briskly nodded her on . . . and in the passage she overtook the Housekeeper.

Apologetically, Andra made her request, for she had barely been eight months at the Museum: might she have Monday off? And well aware that the Press would use her name, she thought it wise to add:

"It's rather a special do. I've been invited to the opening of the Standish Club."

The Housekeeper's alert face brightened. "Saw quite a bit about that in yesterday's *Clarion*. It said his old staff would be present. It's not often they remember *us*, is it? Of course you must go. I didn't know you'd worked there too."

Feebly Andra smiled. Well, if it came to that, she had worked there. Hastily she thanked her superior.

"Not often *you* ask any favour," said that lady graciously. "See and enjoy yourself. We'll be looking for your photo in the papers on Monday. Ha—ha!"

"Ha—ha!" echoed Andra with misgiving, as she turned away. Complications had already begun.

In the work-room, a small, square cell of a room with a towering ceiling, a borrowed light, and a sink, which she shared with Mr. Mott, the chief attendant, she took off her coat and hat and collected her dusters.

Thankfully she remembered that to-day was Saturday. She would later eat her meal alone here. Every other day she and Mr. Mott solemnly shared this monastic gloom. Mr. Mott's luncheon was an ambitious affair, prepared by a landlady who clearly thought the world of him, and was carried on enamel plates in a gladstone bag. This tier of dishes, which was finally placed above a saucepan of boiling water, in which Andra cooked an egg for herself, had become part of a rite that appeared to link them in an increasingly significant way. Mr. Mott was a man of few words but his silences had recently become pregnant. Andra drew a breath of relief each time she found the room empty.

Dressed in his navy blue uniform, with a gold crown on each lapel, he nodded curtly to her now as she re-entered the corridor. But his eyes followed her unhappily. Yet at first he had not liked her, which had been almost as uncomfortable. "What's *your* sort doing here?" he had asked resentfully.

Taking her key, she unlocked the door before her, and entered the Museum.

At once she breathed an ampler air. The contrast between secretariat and treasure-house was that of two worlds and a step separated them.

Marble stairs, vaulted courts, grandiose galleries rose soundlessly around her, for the great doors were not opened to the public until ten. This vast sanctuary, with its fabulous *objets d'art* was hers alone. Freely she passed to and fro, touching, tending with deft and reverent hands.

So high were those great rooms that even when hushed, as now, they still held fugitive echoes. As one attendant, and then another, patrolled his gallery, their discreet movements touched-off a rumbling movement like distant thunder. Bright though the June day was, the brilliant courts were dominated by a shadow of another sort—an overpowering significance . . . as if the various exhibits still reverberated with their past history, as well as their own intrinsic worth.

Gazing into the Quadrangle garden now, this momentous effect was heightened by that cloistered silence in the midst of London's din. As Andra dusted, she could feel the centuries congregating in peace here, glimpse sun-lit statuary, hear the mild twittering of to-day's birds.

She loved this work. Fervently she hoped that Monday's events would not affect her life here. To-day, for the first time she realised, with some pride and a certain amusement, that in the Victoria and Albert she had now achieved the summit in her own profession! She could only hope that she would be left in peace——

A notable personality whom you recently lost through death——

If her heart had beat too fast over Sir Amos Standish's hidden vigil—it had almost stopped with the Reporter's first announcement.

Involuntarily her duster paused. She stared at the *Painted Pinewood Table*. Its medallion in *grisaille* showed a romantic lady seated solitary in the eighteenth century.

In the twentieth, at the Winter Garden Hotel, Buxleigh-on-Sea, quite as romantically she too had awaited the unknown.

That cosmopolitan hotel, which according to Madame Moffat's cousin was yet so quiet that any lady, alone, could safely relax there, had terrified Andra at sight! But the luxurious bedroom facing the sea had restored her nerve. Blanche's simple but smart clothes had also helped when unpacked from Mr. Ludlow's trunk, for Blanche's American trousseau had released Blanche's earlier outfit for Andra. But confidence had only been established by an accident— that glimpse into the hotel's Beauty *Salon*.

Monsieur Henri prowling at his door had bowed her in. The great man had attended in person. A free hour for him, he explained, was her opportunity.

"Shampoo," faltered Andra.

"After re-styling, of course, Madame."

"Something simple," Andra pleaded.

"The essential!" Swiftly Monsieur Henri flashed first his comb, and then his scissors through her hair. "From present confusion, I shall rescue a beautiful Grecian lady. Of classical distinction."

Two hours later, Andra emerged, spell-bound by her own appearance. Monsieur Henri had been as good as his word. The bill was likewise revolutionary. Mr. Piggott would have had a stroke. But Andra, transformed, wildly, wickedly knew that it was worth it.

That night, with shy dignity in Blanche's black taffetas,

she braved the resplendent restaurant. The Head-Waiter, impressed by Monsieur Henri's handiwork, Blanche's frock, and her obvious timidity had with infinite tact, placed her in a tiny, velvet alcove. From this retreat, which was raised by one step, she could see the room without the room observing her—unless she changed her chair. All his beautiful patrons did this at the second meal. Andra proved the exception.

In a dream of delight she had eaten her excellent dinner, then like a sleep-walker made her way to the winter garden, and seated at just such a table, on just such a chair, been lulled by the palm-court orchestra.

Next morning, after a night of incredible comfort, breakfast proved a further felicity.

Following so closely upon the rigours of Nelson Road, Selhurst, these varied blessings, enjoyed in solitary state (for many looked, but none spoke) occasioned such a welling-up of gratitude, so much unexpressed zest, that Andra found herself as often in thanksgiving as in the outward occasion.

Gradually this struck her as odd.

Instead of relaxing and lapping it up as she should, for this would probably be the last time on earth that such a thing would happen to her, she found she was beginning to think as well as to thank.

The weather was wet, which favoured introspection, and seated alone in the palm-court, or her expensive bedroom, she found herself returning time and again to that miraculous minute in Lombards' workroom, when she and Connie had leapt outside danger into perfect safety.

Dwelling on this, the wonder again beckoned—but from afar. She could no longer inhabit it. Sometimes it drew nearer, like a landmark on the horizon. But that was as near as she got. Yet by the serenity it dispelled, she knew that the region still existed. Present pleasure, like past difficulties, would, she suspected, matter little, if she could regain that foothold.

Methods of again securing this boon next absorbed her, for Andra was not a reader, and rain continued. To start any book was an undertaking with her that required care and a deep breath. But faithful to Miss Hood's teaching, she still read a portion of the Scriptures each night. Only a verse or two. It really was no trouble—although Aunt Edith would certainly not have approved of that attitude! Sometimes it was quite a pleasure, for, reading slowly as she did, the Biblical people would now and then emerge for a second, or a landscape slide smoothly between her and the printed page. But of course that was at night. This was long, lovely, empty day-time!

Tirelessly Miss Hood had taught that happiness was unreliable as the weather! Andra, reinforced by Scriptural verses, speciously selected, continued to believe in the possibility of joy everlasting. It amounted to an instinct with her. And Lombards had conclusively proved it. In that moment she and Connie had known a freedom so great that it was power—or power so great that it was joy.

Seated in the seclusion of the palm-court, exotic also with the whiff of an occasional Corona Corona—Andra continued to ponder cautiously, comfortably. Perhaps if she were patient . . . kept a confident look-out, the lost region would reappear. She had an idea that it might not be long——

But on the second night, Dr. Philip Auguste Riberac walked with authority across the imposing restaurant, and abruptly Andra ceased to dwell on the invisible.

The concrete had become all-important. The corporeal took command.

Concealed in her alcove, Andra studied him with awe. She had always thought Amos Standish the handsomest man in the world till now. But in sixty seconds this stranger had become the only one. He was exactly like the plaster-cast in the Standish studio of the Roman Augustus. The resemblance was uncanny—except that the living version looked definitely more amiable. Aloof but benign. Like Andra he too sat alone. Fascinated, she watched his every movement. The sight of him both frightened and exhilarated her.

Alas, there was no sign of him at breakfast!

But April sunshine now raced across the sky on a wet breeze, and she turned inland for her first walk.

The hotel and grounds, which lay a mile from Buxleigh, adjoined some wooded country, with, beyond that, open farmland. The wind behind her, she skipped into this deserted landscape like a blown leaf. The odour of earth, of fresh foliage was a revelation after a year at Lombards. Forgotten was the lordly stranger, the luxurious hotel, and the fact that Blanche's heather tweed was most becoming. A pale yet intense blue sky wavered almost within reach. Into the wood, out across scampering green hills she went, the grass thick with primroses . . . and, here and there, a cluster of dark violets! Filling her hands with those soaking flowers, she failed to notice a solitary rain-cloud, dove-grey, imminent, despite the sunshine. A blinding shower was over-due.

The down-pour chased her to the only tree at hand. Stray drops pattered on her, the rock on which she sat was hard, but she drank in every moment. Last year's leaves and moss; to-day's grass and flowers; to-morrow's fruit and nuts welled to her on this warm wet air.

Then turning, startled, she saw him . . . completely equipped for the occasion, for Riberac, as a Frenchman had no false shame about an umbrella in the country. As well, he wore a double-breasted weather coat, of the type favoured by the fishing-fleet, which was at any period of the year, a permanent part of his British wardrobe. Andra had never seen anyone so thoroughly forearmed. He looked as resolute as one about to launch a life-boat, and appeared to have materialized from nowhere.

"Can I help you?" he enquired with so much benevolence, advancing with such firmness, that inevitability went hand in hand with him. She had yet to learn that his benignity was as constant as his facial contour, yet to discover how devastating irony could be—delivered with this same bland address.

For the next five minutes she simply chirruped spasmodic thanks as, seated together on the rock, the rain redoubling its fury, the umbrella hooded them both as closely as a mushroom its roots, and proved to be salvation.

Their astonishing yet compulsory proximity disposed of any shyness. And when he next inquired, as naturally as if they had spent their life there: "A penny for your thoughts?" she answered quite frankly:

"I had been wondering again about joy . . . joy ever-lasting. Do *you* believe in heaven on earth?"

Dr. Riberac took a moment to reply. He might have been answering by telephone—long distance.

"Many have believed in that," he said cautiously. "As far back as five thousand years ago the Pyramid texts declare: '*He layeth hold on Command, Eternity is brought to him. Discernment is placed for him at his feet. Cry aloud to him in joy, he hath captured the horizon*'."

"But do *you* believe it?" she persisted.

"At a moment like this," the Frenchman's eye was calm, his smile light, "I might believe in anything."

At a much later date he had admitted: "Positively I could not place you at that first meeting. I indexed you as: *Ingenuous Angel—perhaps!* You piqued my curiosity. And of course I was enchanted by your appearance."

By the time the shower was spent, Dr. Riberac was in command. Had Miss Hood seen the memorial tablets at Chantrey Abbey? Would Miss Hood care to drive there this afternoon. These tablets were the reason of Dr. Riberac's visit to Buxleigh. To-morrow he returned to London.

But to-morrow Dr. Riberac did not return to London. There proved to be other notable tablets in the district. And Andra who had come to breathe ozone, spent her time in cathedral crypts, and only glimpsed the sea with Dr. Riberac, over morning coffee or late tea, in the warm palm-court.

On Friday night, her third last in paradise, Dr. Riberac proposed a theatre at Buxleigh.

"Oh no, please!" Andra besought him. "I dread the theatre—already I've seen everything. Your conversation," she hesitated, "is much more of a treat."

Dr. Riberac, flattered but sceptical, queried this. Andra found herself explaining about Punchie.

Punchie led to Lombards, and Lombards to Aunt Edith's death . . . and the Moffats' departure. Dr. Riberac who had hitherto talked almost exclusively now proved himself a listener in a thousand. An adroit query here, a sympathetic aside there, and Andra's story released itself in detail . . . which included the misappropriation of her own annuity! But over this, and her escape from Mr. Piggott, Dr. Riberac shook his head. Piggott struck him as particularly sound. Money was a serious matter. And he next read her a lecture on economy that astonished her. For the first time he addressed her as Andra, and seemed slightly irritated. She might have been a relative—of the tiresome type. Her attitude to finance, he affirmed, simply would not do. Everything that Dr. Riverac said confirmed his own reliability. Andra's admiration became veneration. She had a fleeting vision of pillowing on this strength for ever. One could leave everything to such a man, and what a lot of effort this would save! Devoutly she listened, but when asperity clinched his point, a tear stole down her cheek.

Dr. Riberac, catching sight of this frail token, was horrified by his own brusquery. In words that were warmer than he intended, he besought pardon. He even took her hand . . . enabling Andra to take heart again. But in her own time. The relationship advanced by leaps and bounds.

A gala dance, advertised by the hotel for Saturday night, prompted an arrangement to dine and dance together. Andra, elated, planned to wear Blanche's white lace ball frock, which Dr. Riberac had yet to see in all its glory. So eager was her anticipation that when on Saturday morning a telegram summoned Dr. Riberac to the next county, the news came as a personal bereavement!

"Strictly speaking," said Dr. Riberac, "I ought to have seen the fellow in town on Thursday. But I hope to get back for late dinner. Just go ahead." He was sorry but by no means stricken.

Feverishly Andra dressed on Saturday night, yet intuitively knew that she would once more be alone.

Her small table was festive with favours, bright as a baby bonfire with scarlet candles and flame flowers—gay details that would earlier have delighted her, but Dr. Riberac's absence had laid waste the night for her.

This was the second last night of her wonder week.

With a sinking heart she realized that on Monday they would part. He would return to France—to the work that often took him right across the world. His work, he had earlier explained, was one of the reasons why he had not married. Yes . . . quite early he had made it plain that marriage did not enter his scheme of things! His work was all-demanding. His aunt, Madame Franz Orth had not been mentioned at this stage.

With dismal clarity over dinner, Andra began to see how

foolish was the importance she had attached to his pleasant attentions. These had just been a holiday excitement. With time to reflect, for the first time since they'd met, she knew that now!

Sobered, but steadied by these conclusions, she finished her solitary meal and left the crowded restaurant. She would spend the rest of the evening writing her monthly letter to the Moffats——

Crossing the vestibule, she suddenly heard a voice exclaim: "Andra Hood!"

A fair man, of medium height but undeniable elegance was smiling down at her. His face was quiet, self-contained, the eyes a trifle abstracted in expression—the calm mouth beautifully cut. A haunting rather than an impressive personality—Mr. Amos Standish.

All gaiety now, she greeted him.

Enthusiastically they exchanged news . . . moving inevitably towards the palm-court, where over coffee and liqueurs she learnt that Mr. Standish was here for one night only. To-morrow he would leave early for Monoux Manor where he was engaged upon a portrait bust of the invalid Lord Delme. Did Andra think of posing again, once her holiday was over? Well . . . if she ever did, she knew where to find him. And if there was anything that he could do at any time——

A sense of security stole over her, a feeling of continuity, of recovered peace. Soon, she assured him, she would look up the others. She was returning shortly to London. How were Kurragh, Stirling, Vyse and Crickhowel . . . not of course forgetting Paolo? Was their studio still as untidy, the gas as liable to be cut off?

Laughing together, Mr. Standish had charming things to say about Blanche's frock and the new hair style. Never had he seen her look so well——

An hour later found them on the dance floor. There Mr. Standish proved a superb performer. Following his steps with the effortless ease he induced in every partner, the night became an increasing delight.

For the first time in days, she had forgotten Dr. Riberac.

Shortly before midnight, floating with Mr. Standish to the nostalgic strains of the Blue Danube, she was in fact startled to see Dr. Riberac watching them from a distant pillar. He had changed into evening clothes and, smoking a cigar, wore a sombre expression. His Havana prompted the conclusion that he did not mean to dance, and from a safe distance she exclaimed:

"That is Dr. Riberac, the famous archaeologist."

"Ah . . ." said Mr. Standish, and then a second later, "a particularly interesting head. Know him well?"

"Yes and no," Andra hesitated.

"I imagine one might always say that with him," Mr. Standish observed. "A heavily masked personality. He has his difficulties like the rest of us, however—although these may be almost the only link!"

But such niceties were beyond Andra. With zest she had finished the evening on the dance floor.

The last waltz and final gallop found Dr. Riberac gone.

Festive but breathless, she had regained her bedroom, where the long mirror flung back the vision of a flower-like nymph, radiant with life.

Next morning eagerly, almost anxiously she had explained that that had been Mr. Amos Standish, the sculptor, for whom she had sometimes posed. Dr. Riberac would remember—she had first met him at the London School of Art.

Dr. Riberac listened quite courteously. But his reply appeared to cut her short. He did not seem to be interested in Mr. Standish. Instead he said:

"I have a suggestion to make——"

And Dr. Riberac's suggestion, so amazing, so amiable, so generous completely dazed her!

He must, he explained, now return to France. But there was no need for Andra to terminate her holiday yet. What was a week? Nothing, and less than nothing. He would be charmed if she cared to make use of a small house of his at Kew Gardens, in his absence. This would cost her simply her food, and she would be doing him a favour by keeping the place aired. The house in question, although quite attractive had proved a white elephant—but he could not get rid of it till autumn. His aunt's governess had had this place, but as she was simply life-rented in it, it had returned to Madame Franz Orth on her death.

"My aunt (English like my mother) made the house over to me as a useful *pied à terre* in London for my work. In this way she escapes rates and taxes! Wealthy people delight in those frivolous economies. Actually, it has been little or no use to me. I invariably stay at my club."

One thing only caused him some concern, he continued. Would Andra be nervous of living there alone? Perhaps she had some friend who could join her? There were, of course. adjoining villas.

Spell-bound, Andra assured him that she had sometimes stayed alone at *Lochinvar*. She would definitely not be nervous. The idea of continuing her holiday bereft her of words——

In that case, stated Dr. Riberac, they would have a look at the place on Monday. Andra would see for herself . . .

Andra saw for herself. A tiny villa, an early Victorian bird-cage of a house, with a wrought-iron porch fronting the street, and a trelissed veranda above an over-grown garden at the back? The veranda was a tangle of ancient wisteria, the garden a riot of ramblers. The small rooms held the faint melancholy of a past era, furnished in Edwardian taste, with a number of expensive trifles from various country houses, tributes from bygone pupils. One french window of the little drawing-room was darkened by a pink hawthorn, the other danced with light into a diminutive conservatory.

"This is heaven!" Andra the girl said . . .

In the Victoria and Albert Museum, Andra the woman spun a *Celestial Sphere* beneath her duster. A skeleton globe, executed in brass, mounted on mahogany, and now an open secret, for in six months at Kew, the inevitable had happened.

And how simply! No difficult decision appeared to have been made. Everything seemed to be the most natural thing in the world—which indeed it was, granted those particular circumstances.

That first year in heaven—and everything was known afresh! Philip included . . . a man in a million, the lover in a thousand. Spring, summer, autumn, winter conspired to enshrine them. Wild wet winter weather held as much poetry as October's frost, June's windless calm or April's sun. The now became forever.

Four years in heaven, yet all the time she had been moving steadily out of it! She saw that now. And what agonizing periods there had later been in paradise! Surely these might earlier have instructed her?

Yet in the beginning Philip's remarkable personality had justified this step she had taken, their intense happiness sanctioned it. She might be winded at times by a certain blunt reminder: you are living in sin. But of course *their* case was different! Philip was a man apart. She even continued to go to Church—without too much sense of guilt. The evening service only as this somehow seemed less rigorous for a sinner. Her prayers of gratitude were offered at St. Anselm's over a mile away—a Church of England edifice from which, obscurely, she hoped for more latitude than from the Society of the People called Methodists to which, strictly speaking, she belonged. Not to have gone to Church would have been as unthinkable as not to have washed—so conclusively had Miss Edith Hood had the first and last word with another woman's child. And besides . . . Andra enjoyed Church, despite the fact that now she had no right to do so. To Church she went. In Church she remained—although Church could be no more than background music to the daily wonder that life had been at first with Philip. True she had found it wiser to move from Church to Church at frequent intervals. Clergymen of all denominations showed a marked tendency to follow up their flock. Inconspicuous souls who sat at the back, or concealed themselves behind pillars were deftly rounded up. And this led to ministerial visits, and ensuing embarrassments—such as Philip's startling experience with the Vicar of St. Anselm's. Of which the less said the better. As Philip pointed out, it ought never to have happened. People in their position did not attend Church—unless as sightseers. It was asking for trouble. The Church had its rules. One ought to observe these—or keep out. He was surprised at Andra. And extremely annoyed with the Vicar. Apart from which, he added, Church in their circumstances indicated muddled thinking, which he detested. An untidy moral code was the very devil. Andra, suitably silenced, had thereafter, on Sunday evenings when alone, withdrawn to Chiswick and its environs. There were not as many Protestant Churches as she had imagined. She too was surprised. In no time she had reached Shepherds Bush. . . .

Ten years later now, her duster paused on the adjoining *Terrestrial Globe*. Philip's journeys flew again below her fingers—Egypt . . . Greece . . . Mesopotamia. Infinite distances, perpetual separations from which she miraculously recovered him. Yet these had been in key, and so were bearable. The ordeal of the Eldersley Excavation, his obituary notice in the papers, had been a thing apart. Calamity. But death could not separate them. Life had been needed for that. And Madame Franz Orth.

With a slight shiver Andra moved on to the next gallery. *Embroideries* in *petit-point*.

Lightly she flicked the first *Pole Screen* . . . its three figures stitched as finely as if the work were painted: two lovers comically concealed in an arbour, with a wary old lady biding her time outside.

Madame Franz Orth did not need to watch Andra. Andra had never seen her enemy. Madame Orth rarely visited London. Yet there too her power was absolute. Philip might curse, but he trimmed to his aunt's every wish like a weather-cock. Her caprice could cut short their happiness on any visit, or precipitate a surprise reappearance of Philip at a time that he had taught was impossible—if Madame Franz Orth needed help with her London solicitors, her London brokers, her London agents. Latterly, Philip would come on a cable, or leave on a telegram if Madame Orth decreed it. Sometimes he scarcely troubled to make an excuse . . . was barely aware of the need.

And money had been the magnet. This was the fact that had made his defection fatal. Once when challenged by Andra he had quite lightly admitted:

"My aunt can leave her fortune as she pleases. But of course the essential thing is that she leaves it to her nearest relative—my not unworthy self—for there are other relations, and above all, other friends."

"But you have your own money," Andra urged. "I mean . . . you have your work. It seems a pity to set your mind on something that you may never get."

"You have the British attitude to family finance," he informed her, "sentimental . . . ineffectual."

Frequently he protested that Madame Orth's claims exhausted his patience, bored him stiff. It was abundantly clear to Andra that Philip could meet those or not as he chose. This liberty, therefore, relieved the situation for him. But Andra, in every instance, was wholly dependent on Philip's decision, on Philip's will. And in her heart a hunger for freedom was building up—recklessly, because un-acknowledged . . .

At the Victoria and Albert, on the early round, Andra had come full circle.

She glanced out of the great side windows to where, in the still June sunshine, through trees, Cromwell Road ran swiftly. Close to the kerb, a small red milk van, with a shaggy pony trundled by, slow as a country lane.

It had taken a miracle to clear her out of Lombards and Nelson Road. A second miracle had failed to sever her from Philip, despite secret despair. Humiliation, abject but absolute, had been needed for that.

But the second miracle had occurred.

And the milkman at Kew, with his small red van had paved the way for it. A meek little man, prompt to please. She had at once noticed his absent air that day——

It was Francie, he explained. She was twelve, and her Mum couldn't get to Hospital to see her. Mrs. Sedge was down with asthma. Francie was creating in consequence.

At once Andra had volunteered to go. "What is the matter with Francie?" she asked.

"Asthma too," said Mr. Sedge. "Francie's by way of being hereditary. But *her* asthma's developed something horrible." Francie, he added, wasn't on the visiting list. He would telephone Ward Sister to say Miss Hood was on her way, instead of Mum.

Three o'clock found her at St. Margarets, dressed in myrtle green, with a Russian squirrel jacket—Philip's last Christmas present—looking as pretty as a picture.

A new building, bright, bare, sterile—she hesitated for a second. It was her first visit to any hospital. Aunt Edith had disapproved of hospitals much as she disapproved of Bank Holiday Fairs on Hampstead Heath. At both one picked up things—although of a different sort. An attitude that had reinforced Andra's own pet phobia. Skin diseases.

Following the porter now, she was happy to reflect that asthma was certainly the safest illness one could hope to visit!

On either hand, she saw open wards—with rows of beds, an invalid to each, and here and there a visitor in muted conversation, or a nurse hurrying by. Cold, clean, and fresh, but Andra's infallible nose detected another odour, fugitive, frightening, foreign . . . yet doctors and nurses gave up their lives to share this smell——

Francie's Ward Sister had stepped out of a cubicle, with gray hair, keen blue eyes, and a bow of frosted muslin under her angular chin.

She led the way down another corridor.

" We've had to move her out of the children's ward, of course. This has upset her. She's a difficult child. These asthma patients are far too intelligent."

"I hope she's not worse," Andra began.

" Well, since the eczema started, the asthma has subsided. That does sometimes happen, but it's unusual."

" Eczema!" exclaimed Andra. " But isn't that infectious? What sort of eczema is it?"

" An acute vesicular eczema," said Sister briskly. " Of course it's contagious. She's a glove case. And short of visitors, poor little thing. However, you'll cheer her up.

Here you are—that bed in the corner, with the screen. Francie . . . this is Miss Hood . . . a visitor for you!"

Andra was left alone with the patient.

At that first sickening glance, she scarcely recognized the object on the pillow as a face. The entire surface of the little girl's skin was a mass of blisters. Most of the larger bubbles were pustular. Francie's asthma, in the words of her father, had certainly developed "something horrible."

Shakily Andra sat down.

The sullen child did not look at her. Mercifully she had not yet met Andra's eyes. Instead she fixed her gaze on Andra's jacket, and, when her visitor sat down, turned her head away—a gesture of defeat that smote Andra.

"Francie," she said with something like anguish, and drew her chair closer, "Francie, don't go away."

Furiously the girl said: "Nurse wears gloves to dress my skin, as if something nasty were wrong with me. Nurses oughtn't to be afraid. It's what they're here for."

Basely Andra echoed: "No one should be afraid. Forget the lot. Look what I've brought you."

Hurriedly she opened the parcel, which held books, a jigsaw puzzle, crayons, and some hot house grapes.

Startled, Francie sat up. Rapidly she examined her gifts, and then gave a hoot of laughter . . . a hoot of good-natured contempt. Andra could scarcely credit her ears.

"You'll have to change the books," said Francie. "What do you think I am? A baby? I finished with school-girl tripe at nine. Change these at once. Anything by Dickens is okay with me. Except the *Christmas Carol*. I know it by heart. I got it as a prize. Come to-morrow with Dickens. 'Tisn't a visiting day but they're glad to keep me quiet." She lay back exhausted, and said irritably: "I want a straight answer quick. There was a lot about spirits in the *Christmas Carol*. Spirits are angels, aren't they? Not ghosts."

Astonished, Andra said yes.

"I can believe in bad spirits easier than good," said Francie. "But that's not my fault. After the *Christmas Carol* I prayed to have my asthma lifted. And just look what I got instead."

Swiftly Andra said: "You should have kept on praying."

"And got a dermatitis? No thank *you*," said Francie with professional bitterness. Turning on her elbow, she added more confidentially, indeed with a certain nervousness: "It was letting the Nun pray for me that did me in. She used to pass my bed in the other ward. A Roman Catholic. Mum says they can do any wickedness as long as they confess it. The night before my eczema started the Nun said: 'I'll offer prayers for you.' It was the Nun's prayers——"

"Rubbish!" said Andra indignantly. "No one can harm you but yourself with such ideas. Fear is a bogy that we make ourselves."

Francie in growing agitation sat up. "But I can't stop myself."

"Yes, you can. When you get frightened thoughts that you can't manage, you can trust in your guardian angel, through Jesus Christ, our Lord."

Sullenly Francie lay back again. Then her eye quickened. Alertly she said:

"But sometimes the fright's really there—like when I was nearly run over."

"Well, you weren't. You ought to be grateful. Do stop brooding. A real fear can always be dealt with. But the fears you make for yourself, only your angel can cure. When you treat that kind Nun as if she were some sort of witch, it's nothing but suspicion. Think of *her* angel and feel ashamed."

"Miss Hood," said Francie coldly, "my Mum says all Roman Catholics is in league with the Pope."

Tartly the Methodist retorted, "I'm thankful to hear it."
Andra was already tired of Mum.

"And my Mum says that Roman Catholics pay to get to heaven."

"But we Protestants," said Andra, "hope to get in for nothing."

Francie, after a second's reflection gave a further honk of laughter. Another idea had been sown, but loyally she still clung to her crutches.

"Well, my Mum says this world would be all right, if it weren't for everybody in it."

"Then see the funny side of that, for goodness sake! Even the unpleasantest person has a guardian angel. Try to link up with their angel when they disturb your high and mightiness."

"Is that true?" the child again sat up. "Sister going down the ward . . . that beastly Nurse Brown . . . Dr. Nairn and all the patients here?"

"Yes," said Andra calmly, "I'm quite certain of it. I've always known it, really."

"Have you ever seen an angel?"

"No, but once during a desperate experience I felt one—full of love and power."

"Gosh!" said Francie incredulously. "You did?"

"I did."

The girl stared at her for a second, perceived the truth, and then lay back spent. Tears of relief began to trickle from her eyes, to lie rigid between the blisters.

"I didn't know, Miss Hood," she began. "I didn't know for sure."

"That's all right, darling. Now, do you know. We both know." Andra stared down at the broken skin of the little hand which she had been unconsciously nursing for some time—her own sore now healed by this poor child. "I'll be praying for you too. This illness will pass like a cloud. Don't be frightened any more."

"No, I won't be frightened any more, Miss Hood. I'll remember the Angel . . . *and keep quiet like you say*——"

Already Francie had divined her uncompleted thought.

At ten o'clock next morning, the house-man making his rounds was astonished to find that the purulent discharge from the eczema case in ward eleven had ceased over-night. Loose skin was flaking off. Beneath this rough powder, sound flesh could be seen. The patient's temperature was normal, and she was very hungry.

"Almost a miracle!" said Sister indulgently.

Andra and Francie, hugging their sweet secret, were launched on a life-long friendship.

Alone at Kew, Andra that day had later sat lost in thought.

For a timeless period the night before, the petition for Francie had exhaled from her heart. Assurance had reached her with each returning breath . . .

In those early days prayer had prospered with beginner's ease. All had gone well. Supremely well. To pray for herself she perhaps had no right, but to pray for others was still clearly possible. Her prayer for Francie had been the Prodigal's return in peace.

Yet even at Kew, uneasiness stirred.

If prayer could heal, or help to heal, why was she not devoting herself to this task? To use it at random was surely to snatch a blessing in passing—scarcely a grateful or seemly thing.

Prayer had then been a lovely lure beckoning her on the hidden way.

Ruefully she had decided against it. Prayer might lead her further than she could go. Already she had begun to sense the massive reserves of egotism bulwarking her frail soul—defences that were so alarmingly her only strength.

To pray might not only be to heal. To pray might be *to know*. And she who was not fit to be a channel, was certainly quite unfit to know.

To know what?

She shied away from definition.

Besides there was Philip! Dominating every dream and each desire, there was Philip. Philip came first and foremost. Prayer might lead her further than she was prepared to go.

No, no, no, these two miracles, at Lombards and now at St. Margarets, were just two wonders that God had divinely shown her, to prove that He was there. God was love. He wouldn't expect too much of her. No one as inadequate as herself could be expected to launch out. These two miracles would last a lifetime. They were all she needed to go on with——

She . . . she . . . she! Was she never to get away from herself—that anchor or millstone on this chartless ocean of discovery that Kew had become?

She was growing morbid! This would never do. She needed Philip. Philip her Eden upon earth . . . and due at Kew to-morrow! For a whole week this time—Bliss!

But Philip could not stay a week. Only two nights this time. There was a sale he must attend in Ireland for his aunt. Blankly, benevolently he lit his cigar.

He had quite forgotten that a week had been arranged. And after such an absence.

There was only one thing to conclude. He no longer cared! Andra, incapable of acting on this conclusion, now issued a fiat of her own. Things had come to such a pass that she warned him: "If this happens next time, Philip, I won't be able to bear it."

"It won't," rashly he declared. "I'm as tired of her as you are."

Two months later, on his return, the cataclysm occurred —almost on reunion.

A letter from Monte Carlo arrested Philip at the Club. Brevity itself, the note gave no details. It merely announced the fact that Madame Orth (at sixty) was contemplating marriage.

Philip, beside himself with fury, had broken the news.

Silently Andra had hailed it as an order of release . . . the brightest idea Madame Franz Orth had yet had.

Aloud she ventured to suggest: "Why shouldn't she marry again if she wants to? She's probably lonely——"

Philip, incensed, had begun to pack his bags.

Andra could scarcely believe her eyes.

"Philip, you can't go . . . it's not possible. . . . You've only just come! I've got a pheasant for dinner——" she added idiotically.

But Philip could go . . . it was quite possible, and they'd had one night together!

Acidly he declared this.

And if there was one thing he would not tolerate, he added, it was a scene. She might as well realize this. There were few men, he informed her, who could, or would, have made those lengthy journeys throughout years, so often. Instead of realizing how damned lucky they were to meet at all, in view of his difficulties, Andra was behaving like a spoilt child. Moreover, they could not always expect to meet as freely as they had done in the past.

"Not meet . . ." she began.

"What I mean to say," he rasped irritably, "is that it's quite possible we may, on occasion, have to meet at longer intervals."

The blood drained from her heart. Its very structure seemed to alter.

"And if the present crisis clarifies our situation," Philip concluded, "it will not have been in vain."

Twenty minutes later he had left the house—a man of one idea: the Night Ferry. It would take him all his time——

Andra sat on, stunned, in the deserted drawing-room.

He had always been perfectly frank. From the start everything had been on a cut-and-dried basis. She knew that. But they had lived together for years. Made memories of an inescapable kind. Daily they had grown closer—or so she had thought. Now through those last words of his, she realized that things were basically as at the start. Life together had done nothing. She could no longer conceal the truth from herself. Their relationship had been quite a different experience for him.

The shock was terrible.

In the pretty little Edwardian drawing-room with its genial English *bric-à-brac*, its French and Italian travel trophies, the golden September evening imperceptibly faded. Quite suddenly it grew cold among those bygone souvenirs, but she did not notice. The room was heavily over-hung by the hawthorn tree. They had always meant to cut it back, but each spring the pink blossom was so fabulous that they had borne with the shadow every summer. Now through the approaching dark, an autumnal robin piped in warning. Sunk in the faded chintz armchair, Andra did not stir. Soon she could not see across the room. The telephone rang violently—twice in ten minutes, for prolonged periods. She made no movement to answer it. Dully she listened. Philip —with some time to spare after all. The racket of the bell, shattering in the empty house, subsided into silence. It was all over . . .

Soundlessly Andra Hood, cleaner, crossed the Victoria and Albert corridor. There was only the clock to face now. *Clocks, clocks, clocks*—carved, japanned, veneered. Hanging clocks; long-case clocks; barometer, thermometer and bracket clocks . . . all at different times, but all declaring it was time to go . . .

At ten the doors would be open, and the public in upon her. She must be out of sight by then! And she always was.

Beneath the marquetry clock at Kew she had paused that last day, her luggage packed, the taxi at the gate, and faced the final issue:

Was she taking this step in anger and indignation—cutting off her nose to spite her face?

Nothing so spirited!

She was simply forestalling the inevitable. That she now knew. This agonizing step was simply the best, the quickest way out . . .

In the vast, sunny gallery, duster and feather brush gathered together, quietly she turned on her heel.

Dispassionately the great Museum Clock struck ten.

She was through again—and to the minute.

Abruptly her swift step halted—Mr. Mott's sentinel figure blocked the way.

Cynically he indicated the Entrance. "Take a look at that."

Andra turned round.

To her surprise a stream of people was flowing in. A queue must have awaited the opening of the doors. Quickly these persons—a varied assortment—crossed the Loan Court. They were all heading in the same direction.

"What is it?" she asked, mystified.

"The Vaucluse Angel, of course. A blinking set of silly sheep. Not one of them's been near it for years."

"The Vaucluse Angel," she echoed, then said nervously, "But why?"

"Didn't you see the papers last night? The missing section's turned up. Found at Marlborough by a man in Kent. Don't ask me how! Fellow called Joe Baxter. And although the missing portion's not *in situ* yet, the great British Public's rushing in to-day to see if the hole still looks the same."

Andra steadied her voice. "Did the papers say anything else about it?"

"Usual build-up for the big-shot who discovered the Panel. That Doctor chap. He's expected next week from Paris."

Mechanically Andra enquired: "Will you have your tea now?"

"On a Saturday," said Mr. Mott stiffly, "you know I never do. I check out at twelve, and have for ten years."

"Sorry," she muttered, hurriedly turning the Secretariat key.

And not until she reached the empty, cell-like work-room did she draw breath again.

Next week was not this week!

Flushed of cheek she watched the kettle boil.

Forewarned was forearmed.

Why these platitudes . . . this panic?

She had simply to avoid the front entrance, and keep out of the Vaucluse gallery.

She was as safe at the Victoria and Albert as a needle in a hay-stack.

Abstractedly she set out cup and saucer, and poured the water into the teapot. But was a needle so safe in a hay-stack? After all, it was the only one——

This was sheer hysteria.

She had quarter of an hour for tea.

How had that phrase first originated—*a bad quarter of an hour?*

Why ruin fifteen minutes of much needed rest? Years ago had she not learnt to subdue fear by facing it as evil in itself, and not simply as an ordeal to which she was martyr?

Had the very mention of the Vaucluse Angel the power to overwhelm still? Of course not. She was behaving like a guilty person.

Decisively she sat down in the small, high, gloomy room, and glanced up at the borrowed light, distantly washed with the undefeated blue of June.

She was quite safe—even if she and Philip did meet.

Too much lay between them!

She took the coarse white cup, and raised it to her lips——

Islington . . .

Saturday Morning . . . *ten-ten*

Mr. Tucker had disapproved of Islington from the start. But it was at his showroom that she first saw the tempting advertisement in the *Gazette*. A self-contained flat—and at such a price! No harm in *seeing*, Andra had persisted.

She had taken the Underground, and with a sense of astonishment arrived at a station called Angel.

Islington was another world from Kew. Utterly different too from Hampstead. Rather terrible, but full of life.

The Angel milled with activity, blared with noise, its streets whirling like a circus with buses, trams, lorries, vans, pedestrians. Its tall tenements teemed with industry—of a variety that left Andra dazed, for in the street leading to her destination there were *Dental Laboratories*, *Costume and Jacket Manufacturers*, *Metal Workers and Electric Platers*, *Heating and Ventilating Specialists*. In fact, the headquarters of the *National Society of Retention of Corporal Punishment* alone evinced a note of informality—it had a pot of geraniums dying on the window-sill. No—there *was* an office labelled *London and New York Exporters* that likewise gave a feeling of escape——

So startled was Andra by the Angel, Islington, that by the time Bollard's Court was reached, its silent *cul de sac* seemed an oasis of desirability. Hemmed in by brick buildings on three sides, two of which were warehouses, and the third a block of artisans' flats, Bollard's Hold itself was a well-built three-storied building, painted battle-ship grey, with white window-sockets, which gave the barn-like place a staring sea-gull look. But it was not the cleanliness of the stone paved court, or its comparative quiet that conquered Andra, but two ancient birch trees, soaring as one, some thirty feet into the air, their yellowing leaves dipping delicately against the bald top windows of Bollard's Hold. If that were her attic-flat, it was practically a nest in those trees!

Mrs. Ellis, an elderly angular widow in a rusty black dress, had a certain dignity, and was indeed a woman of some property. Her pale business-like eye summed up her prospective tenant at a glance. Miss Hood, despite her youth, would be up to no fancy tricks. She had, moreover, the satisfactorily subdued look of a person recently bereaved. If her references were in order, she couldn't be more suitable.

Yes, Mrs. Ellis admitted, her unfurnished top flat was still to let. Self-contained and approached by an outer staircase on the gable. It had two rooms facing south, with a kitchenette and a bathroom. Mrs. Ellis was not so much interested in a large rent as a quiet tenant.

The white freshly distempered rooms trembled with sunshine and the gold of the birch leaves. Andra exclaimed with pleasure.

"But as you think of moving in," said Mrs. Ellis sharply, "I'd like to make one thing plain. I keep myself to myself here. And you'll be well advised to do the same. Friendliness always ends in friction. We live in a difficult neighbourhood. It doesn't do to know anyone, if you can help it. Old Mr. and Mrs. O'Neill and the Reids in the tenement are quite respectable, but one thing leads to another. And if you're sociable, before you know where you are—you've got an enemy. No one in Bollard's Hold itself will trouble you. My other tenants are very respectable. Father and daughter. Name of Goodge. She's been in service with the Dowager Lady Lutrell, but left to keep house for the old man, who's night porter at the Channing,

Holborn. They're very much ones to keep themselves to themselves——"

That seemed to be the hall-mark of refinement by the Angel, Islington!

In the hustle of removal, there was no time to dwell on such oddities. The Selhurst plan, four years late, was about to go into operation with an individual softened by four years of comfort, and with a heart that turned over each time she remembered Kew.

That first Saturday, in her new home, with Aunt Edith's furniture familiarly arranged in the bare clean rooms, and the birch boughs dancing in October sunshine—screening out the tenement opposite, her numbed spirits rose a little. I'm recovering, she thought. I've been weak. I go on standing things too long. But when I'm finished, I'm finished.

Later that night, before she drew the blinds, she paused again. Philip would have her letter by now. But she realized this dully. She did not dwell upon it. She was indeed finished . . . and so exhausted that she slept like the dead.

But she had counted without youth.

She awoke that first morning surprisingly refreshed, if a little dazed.

The geyser actually struck her as comical! Steam had apparently banked-up overnight. It was as noisy as an engine in a railway station, panting to go! Even when she turned it off, it still refused to die, but gasped stertorously—

Clapham Junction, she decided as she opened the window. That would amuse Philip . . . she must save it for him——

Her eyes dilated. She found herself clinging to the ledge.

This was not one of Philip's absences. How could she have forgotten?

Was she going crazy . . or what?

But Monday had introduced Miss Leech, and ended introspection.

In her inexperience she had chosen a west-end registry-office. Before she could speak, Miss Leech snapped:

"This is the *domestic* agency. Upstairs for the secretarial offices."

"It's domestic work I want——" Andra clutched Mr. Tucker's personal reference tightly. "I've only worked for friends before, but I enjoy almost any kind of housework."

Miss Leech, impatient and incredulous, scanned Mr. Tucker's letter.

"Can you cook?"

"I can manage something for one or two people but I've never done anything on a bigger scale. Even in this small way, I'm always a little nervous as to how it will turn out."

"That's no use at all," said Miss Leech irritably. "A pity you can't cook. A cook usually commands a good salary. However, I've several house or parlour posts on my books."

"But I don't want to live in," Andra began.

"Then the position's hopeless. Never in known memory has there been so much female unemployment. This is 1924, you know. You'd be well advised to reconsider——"

"I'm sorry," said Andra faintly. "I must live at home."

"Then it'll have to be a post as waitress."

"No, no!" Andra pleaded. "Not that, please! Among food. . . . I'm not smart enough for that."

"But you've quite a good appearance," protested Miss Leech, who had, in fact, been rather taken aback by it.

"Oh, no, *please*. Can't you offer me a position as a daily Help somewhere?"

"Please yourself," said Miss Leech shortly. It was patent she was dealing with an imbecile. "I suppose you know what you're in for." She turned a page, and wrote down some particulars. "Mrs. St. Albyn needs someone again at her boarding-house, Swiss Cottage. Islington's a mistake. It's going to mean a lot of travelling. Eight o'clock to-morrow morning. One shilling an hour and all your meals."

"Won't Mrs. St. Albyn want to see me first?"

"Mrs. St. Albyn takes what I send her," retorted Miss Leech, "and glad to get it. But see you're punctual. I don't want her on the phone each time you miss the bus. Good afternoon."

Ascot House was a monster five-storied red brick house with yellow keystone facings, and an outside frieze of Moorish tiles clasping that dubious gem in architectural history, the date 1878.

The door was opened by Mrs. St. Albyn herself—a large, ebullient person in a soiled, bead-trimmed cocktail frock, wearing pendant ear-rings. To Andra's surprise it was a refined accent that exclaimed:

"Such a relief to see you! I always do my utmost to get a gentlewoman. They don't mind *what* they do. It's not that the working-classes won't work to-day. They can't. Effete. But a lady will tackle anything. Even the front door steps—always such a problem. Blood tells. I always say that the Royal Family wouldn't be ashamed to wash a floor if It had to . . ."

One floor? There were six a day including four Victorian bathrooms, one kitchen and scullery. And all the stairs to sweep. Five stories of them.

From the first day, Andra had been persuaded to wait on and help to cook the dinner. On this scene of frenzied activity and mounting temperature, she had discovered how swiftly Mrs. St. Albyn could pass from blandishment to abuse.

Mulligatawny Soup had opened hostilities, when Andra reported that there was no stock, no ham, and, oddly enough, no onions.

"Stuff and nonsense!" Mrs. St. Albyn expostulated. "Yesterday's Brown Windsor thickened by those cold potatoes makes an admirable Mulligatawny."

"But there's not even curry powder," persisted Andra.

"Then add that tablespoonful of rice over from the kedgeree and extra pepper. Use your head, Miss Hood. Any chef, worth his salt, will tell you that cooking is nine-tenth imagination. But see that the soup is *hot*."

Andra stood Mrs. St. Albyn for a month, solely because of Gerda Rush, the young actress on the top floor. Gerda was out of work, and had now moved to the cheapest bedroom in the house.

Gerda at nineteen was the loveliest creature Andra had yet seen, with her red-gold hair, and the transparent skin that so often accompanies this, her tawny eyes, proud little nose, passionate mouth, and that fastidious air which set her beauty at arm's length. Indeed, it was a curious fact that off-stage Gerda piqued rather than allured the opposite sex. She could not only dance and sing with verve but with the finish of the fully trained.

"Not that Father could really afford it. But he's always had faith in me. Periodically he gets qualms about my being alone in London. Luckily he's absent-minded, and rarely follows up presentiments!"

Father, it transpired, was a middle-aged widower, with a second-hand book shop in Cambridge.

"Quite a famous shop in its way, Andra. Mail orders from all over the country. But money fluctuates. People *will* browse instead of buying."

It had been love at first sight with Andra and Gerda— so completely at home were they with one another. Gerda's struggle to get a foothold in the suburbs, let alone the west-end continued to leave Andra at a loss—when she remembered present stars.

"But these ladies often oblige in other ways," Gerda affirmed. "I mean to get there on my own. You wait. I'll have you in the stage-box yet!"

In no time Gerda had spent a week-end at Islington, transforming the flat with her gaiety and her guitar— borrowing extra glasses or a corkscrew from Mrs. Ellis with as little ceremony as if Mrs. Ellis were her own age. Yet Mrs. Ellis didn't seem to mind these depredations, or the hasty hug that rewarded her. "That girl will go far," she told Andra. "She's got command." And Andra who was eight years Gerda's senior felt almost a maternal pride.

Within a month Gerda had organised their departure from Ascot House. "Why should I pay that harpy for another fortnight before I leave on my midlands tour, when I might pay *you*?"

Andra, broaching Mr. Piggott's nest-egg once again had bought a camp-bed and blankets, for, as Gerda pointed out: this was simply an investment. Gerda might often need that bed.

The day that Gerda left for Bradford, Andra returned to Miss Leech.

Without a word of explanation sought or given, Miss Leech suggested that Miss Hood might like a post with a gentleman for a change.

"A small restaurant in Bloomsbury. Recently opened by a Scotsman—Captain Boyd. Wounded in the war. Place is called the *True Blue Café*. Captain Boyd needs an assistant to keep an eye on two waitresses, the cook, and char. Also his stores—there have been disappearances recently."

Captain Boyd, jocularly known as the Skull to his employees was a cadaverous man, with wide-winged nostrils above a slit-like mouth. His restaurant, in which the last of his money was literally sunk, stood in a listless side street behind a frosted-glass window. The walls within were rough-cast, and had been painted crimson to give an impression of comfort, but were perpetually blurred by humidity except where the customers on their blue chairs rubbed a clear wet spot at the slightest touch.

To Andra, who was engaged at sight, Captain Boyd explained that she would simply have to watch the cook, the waitresses, and the char. The disappearances had gone beyond a joke——

Next morning Andra discovered the sum of these to be complete. With the exception of the char, Captain Boyd's staff failed to materialize. Andra found she was expected to deputize for all. Frantically Captain Boyd assured her:

"I'll do every other blasted thing—if you'll cook. Only a skunk," he added, almost lyrical in agony, "would see me sunk."

By the end of the week, Andra's cooking had doubled embarrassment by increasing the *clientèle*. Dripping with sweat, she grappled with dishing and washing as well. At the end of three weeks, in self-defence she was forced to emulate the skunk. And the fact that Captain Boyd abruptly proposed marriage expedited departure.

Worn out, she scanned newsagents' boards at Islington.

She couldn't face further travelling at present.

Should she try as a shop assistant?

A local newsagent took her in.

Short on her cash sales that first week, she was promptly fired—having made good the loss herself.

Business was clearly not for her. Yet other vacancies were almost as hard to secure. No matter how plainly she dressed, she seemed to inspire respect without the essential confidence.

Mr. Piggott's nest-egg which had gained weight at Kew, was again unhappily raided.

In desperation she began to take any job she could get.

A series of Islington situations followed—third-rate

restaurants in Holloway, fourth-rate hotels at Highbury. The food in their dining rooms was wretched, the dirt in their basements incredible. The January cold in the last of those cellars felt like a damp shawl round her shoulders.

She contracted pleurisy, and collapsed on her own stairs.

Mrs. Ellis appeared once only on this scene—to send for a doctor, who called in a nurse.

Protesting wildly, Andra passed into delirium with a vision of the last of her savings vanishing at the double.

Upon recovery, when she could scarcely drag herself across the room, Mrs. Ellis had again made an oracular appearance.

"You have been very foolish, Miss Hood. No one can afford to be ill these days. Now you will have to have a holiday—or go under."

Terrified, Andra agreed, and went for a week to Worthing, where Mrs. Ellis knew of a reasonable boarding-house.

Mr. Piggott's nest-egg, on her return, had received such a fright that tensely she vowed: I won't touch the rest of it—ever. If I need money again I'll sell the bow-fronted wardrobe!

Mr. Tucker had promised fifty pounds for it any day of the week. Anything rather than give up her home. If she had to become a domestic servant in someone else's house, she'd sooner be dead.

She had awakened next morning in her attic, to the sound of rain purring upon the pane. February was again washing winter away, but the elements had ceased to restore her. She was utterly spent.

Six months since she had parted from Philip! Six months and still she had not found her feet in this demented struggle for life.

Gerda had been a distraction, but Gerda was still on tour. Postcards alone linked them. To-day would see Andra once more in Miss Leech's bad books——

But to-day did not!

Rescue was at hand—and over a cup of tea that was nothing but extravagance!

The Marylebone A.B.C. was rather crowded. She was obliged to share a table with another woman—middle-aged, neatly but stodgily dressed in green corduroy, with a black cloche hat, and a patent-leather handbag . . . a woman with beady eyes, sallow skin and an impassive manner.

"Ruby!" Andra exclaimed.

"My!" said Ruby. "I hardly knew you. Haven't you lost weight and no mistake? You look all-in!"

"I've been ill," said Andra. "Are you still at Lombards?"

"No fear. I struck out independent, and I've struck lucky. Never looked back since."

"I wish I could say the same," Andra hesitated. "But then I'm only casual labour, because I won't sleep in. Domestic assistant. And it's nearly killed me. I'm on my way to the registry office now."

"Slave markets," said Ruby. "Never go near them. At Lombards I was a hundred and one. Now I'm one in a hundred," she winked. "People are desperate to get me. I can pick and choose. I've taken to char-ing. Life of a lady —if you work it the right way. Yes, I'm an early-morning char! Six hours at top pay, and I'm done for the day—two at the Cigarette Factory, two at the City Offices, two at the Cinema. All three places near each other. I'm through for the day by 11.15 a.m. *And* I never work Saturdays."

"*What!*"

"Fact. I'm on the look-out for a new hand. I could fix you up along of me, if you don't mind early rising. This way you get the best of the day to yourself. And if you're in bed by nine you manage more sleep than most. Into the bargain—wherever we go, *we're* in charge, for we're always two hours ahead of what's coming in. I like my freedom," said Ruby.

"But do you think I could manage?"

Ruby looked at her beadily. "I use my judgment," she said.

Two days later, Andra had taken the plunge.

The refined calling of Lady Assistant or Home Help knew her no more—on Miss Leech's books, or elsewhere. She had now burned her boats. She was consigned to the wilderness, and the improvement was amazing.

She had become an early-morning charwoman, queening it over a sleeping world!

Although it meant rising at 3.15 a.m. to catch the night-service bus, she found the life all that Ruby had boasted, and the silent nocturnal journey comfort itself after day-time crowds. Moreover, she was now working on self-respecting premises. True, her work was of the humblest sort, scrubbing, dusting, polishing—but she had always enjoyed cleaning. This was something at which she shone! She delighted in the reappearance of order, and now, apart from the taciturn Ruby, she laboured in healing silence. An hour's rest once she knocked off duty, and she could forget that these hidden services had actually taken place. She was once more at large in daylight, free to enjoy leisure.

Ten days after this work started, she had an odd experience.

The early evening papers had given front page prominence to the news of a violent murder in Islington, together with the fact that this homicidal maniac was still at large.

Somewhat gingerly Andra set off for the 4.12 a.m. bus. There were dark shadows always under the archway of Bollard's tenement and the garishly lit Angel was subdued by its own lifelessness, an echoing melancholy at this hour —like a town overtaken by sudden paralysis.

Hurrying through the archway, on to the main street, she glanced across the road and was surprised to see there, at a deserted bus stop, a well-dressed man—apparently watching Bollard's Court. This elegant figure, so unlike any other in Islington, moved off at once, in the opposite direction.

Involuntarily, she glanced back over her shoulder——

It was Mr. Standish—yes, she could almost swear to it! For a second she hesitated. She might be wrong, and she dare not miss the bus.

As she took her seat, doubt resolved itself. She could only wonder what Mr. Standish had been doing at the Angel, of all places, at that hour in the morning. *Sir Amos Standish* —since the last Honour's List. She was vain enough to be thankful that he had not recognized her in her old water-proof and black beret, with this abject oilcloth bag!

But somehow, it had been comforting to see him—a reminder that Islington could have distinguished as well as undesirable visitors!

Existence now settled into a healthy jog-trot rhythm. She had leisurely afternoons to spend as she pleased in London parks. But fresh air and sunlight also restored her strength to suffer. There was the unexpected betrayal of moist spring days; the lonely caress of hot summer ones; and in the sedate west-end the fugitive whiff of a good cigar; all evocative of Philip, and each a sightless arrow that winged her as she went.

In solitude the past now threatened to overwhelm her. Yet she was incapable of looking-up old friends. From time to time at Kew she had seen Kurragh, Vyse, Crickhowel. James Hurrup she was bound to avoid for his had been her first proposal. She had not even told Aunt Edith—for Hurrup was the answer to any relation's prayer. Dreamily interested in Mr. Amos Standish, as she had been then, the sculptor had set an unusual standard for her. She admired and liked James Hurrup, but she was incapable of marrying him. And almost at once he had married Pandora Quinn's sister Sybil—of all people! But Andra had visited old Major Treves during the Kew years, and she knew that this present shrinking from friends was weakness.

When her position improved she would no longer postpone——

She was still young enough to hope for a change of luck to-morrow! And after all, things had gone badly for the Moffats too out there . . . but at last Jefferson Jebb was heading out of the slump.

Thus the months went by . . .

In her solitary walks through this park, or that, with thoughts of Philip taboo, she dwelt increasingly on those long hours in the Standish studio.

As she had posed: "Now you've gone lumpish," would be his occasional complaint. And in those early days as he worked clay or marble, he would relate anecdotes of the great artists, past and present, to beguile monotony for her. She enjoyed these continuous tales and stood longer without tiring.

Later, there had followed easy, endless conversations on almost every subject.

The genial sympathy of Sir Amos had been very different from the magnetism, the nervous vitality of Philip.

Once when she timidly spoke of her longing for just one glimpse of the celestial, Sir Amos had humorously replied: "But we'd need this miracle regularly to convince! The intellect is a citadel that must be retaken daily. Thought is of little use, Andra, in that voyage of discovery. We enter the kingdom only when the mind is still, and by way of the noble present."

Hungrily now she remembered these words.

The noble present!

Her own was desolation. She was gradually sinking under the sense of her own unimportance.

She stared down at the Caenwood sparrows greedily picking the crumbs she had brought them. What were the words again? *Ye are of more value than many sparrows. The very hairs of your head are numbered.*

I *will* be joyful—she thought suddenly, even without Philip!

But this defiance winded her. Exhausted, she leant back on the park seat.

How did one begin again—especially with a confused, despairing heart?

One had begun with one's catechism as a child: *What is the chief end of man?* And the answer of old had been: *Man's chief end is to glorify God, and to enjoy him for ever.*

Clearly the start had been a belief in joy. But now it seemed that deprivation would always threaten, whether one loved God or man—because of one's own nature.

Then she must change her nature, for this misery was no longer bearable.

But how?

Closing her eyes, she prayed briefly, weakly for guidance, but with the last of her strength.

Then, rising, she began to walk beneath the trees, through the old Duelling Ground, down the shallow, turf steps——

The noble present, she repeated, the noble present. She must stop thinking of the sad past and the anxious future. Between them, they were unbalancing her. She must dwell solely on the present.

Yes, she would try to go from minute to minute being guided by God—accepting the clues as they came along, and not in any way imposing her own plan ahead of time.

She halted. With the trees of Caenwood behind her, she looked downhill across the open expanse of Hampstead

Heath, its rounded green hills buoyant in sunshine, and saw far away the blurred skyline of London, clarified by an indissoluble bubble that was St. Paul's, in a May-time sky.

By a deliberate act of will she absorbed this scene in itself, divorcing it from every memory and any hope except its own. As far as possible she ceased to be. She did not so much think as watch in humble awareness. And, imperceptibly, the fever of the self passed from her like an illness. It was then that the third miracle of her life occurred.

Momently, the scene before her yielded a beauty and repose never known before. Her very breathing deepened to accommodate the experience in perfect security. The little lakes, bearing so lightly the sombre image of Millfield Lane's ancient trees, became oracles on their own. Wherever her gaze rested, on grassy hill, still water, or vast sky, revelation lay in classical calm. Through tranquility she approached intuition itself. The passing moment had become her sanctuary. This was indeed the noble present. And it restored her as a masterpiece might have done—an environment of increasing significance in which she yet enjoyed complete detachment. Detachment was, in fact, the key to it. She must remain a watcher well-aware, and nothing else, or the commonplace again clouded perception . . .

From that afternoon a remarkable steadying took place in her. The very attempt each day to see the world around her on its own, apart from petty or important problems, had an immediate and salutary effect.

Encouraged, she took heart, for suffering had reinforced her will, and shortly she achieved a detachment that surprised her.

A dismal street, a squalid courtyard, a crowded escalator were now imbued with that heightened existence to be found in art . . . as if this selected approach had mysteriously endowed each with fresh meaning.

People also, considered apart from any personal motive or reaction, and detached from all past or future reference, took on an enlightening aspect. There were times when she could scarcely contain the joy of this experience. But the moment any sense of her own past or future intruded, the spell was broken—almost comically.

Gaining confidence, the experience strengthened, and ushered in another revelation.

During some moment of detachment, when the present alone existed for her in its own strength, she would find herself, amusingly enough, back in remote childhood, enjoying some forgotten memory . . . for of course in childhood there was no past worth mentioning, and the future scarcely counted! These forgotten but now vivid glimpses gave not only a glad sense of continuity, but restored a zest that had belonged to early health. Yet in this new-found lease of life, each episode was clearly isolated in its own period. She had simply learned to travel in a new way. The movement was one of the greatest delicacy, but surety. After a certain stage it seemed to need fidelity rather than vigilance.

And with this discipline, a further wonder was disclosed that crowned the experience, for in renouncing the immediate future, or any image of it, she would be aware, again and yet again, of an unseen presence approaching in celestial peace—and knew this to be some future state in advance upon her.

For a few weeks only, and at intervals, this ultimate joy existed. Then as quietly as it had come, bliss was withdrawn.

For a brief space her boundaries had been divinely extended, and this was her sweet solace. But that other country, nearer than breathing though it was, she had not made her own. She was still on the road, alone.

Yet things were never again as they had been before. The

personal past that had haunted her, the individual future that had threatened, had both received quietus. She had definitely taken up residence in a present that possessed its own calm and a certain virtue. She had, in fact, achieved an unusual degree of freedom.

And that summer, strangers, from varied walks of life, began silently to attach themselves to her—as if resuming some earlier relationship.

Now began a charmed and memorable period—brief only as regards time, when each step of the way with others, was secured.

A street accident precipitated a unique encounter one summer Sunday, when she helped to carry a stunned child into the home of Mijnheer and Mevrouw Van Baerle in Egerton Crescent.

After the ambulance left, they insisted that she remain to supper. And while the child's bloodstains were washed from her dress, she had changed into a voluminous wrap of Mevrouw's, an elderly lady who might have made two of her! This metamorphosis had caused much merriment for from the first Andra had felt completely at ease with her amiable host and hostess. To-night, they assured her, one guest only was expected. Usually more attended a small, informal concert which they held on Sunday evenings as, during the few months in which they rented this house, in preference to an hotel, they liked to keep open house for other travellers of like mind. However Miss Hood need not feel shy in her borrowed magnitude! The other guest was an old friend. At present on an unofficial visit to this country.

Such had been her introduction to the Prayer Circle, and almost at once Pastor Frick had been announced.

With awe Andra gazed at this hero of wartime days.

He was a thickset, rock-like man with a deep vibrant

voice, as rich in register as an organ, but with a slight German accent.

At his first sight of Andra in her trailing gown, he had burst out laughing: "'And some have greatness thrust upon them!'"

"If you only knew how true that is!" Andra began.

"Give me time," he urged, shaking both her hands, "give me time!"

That evening, Mevrouw, a professional pianist before marriage, played for them in the garden room, as the July sunset died into dusk.

At a later date, when Andra exclaimed that never had she known such serenity in another, Mevrouw, much amused, admitted: "Melancholy, my dear child, is my besetting weakness. For many years I suffered from a peculiar form of clairvoyance. Where calamity was concerned, I was so often ahead of time that life became unendurable. Then I met my beloved husband, and through prayer I was enabled to control fear. Gradually my clock kept better time!"

But that first night it was Mijnheer and Pastor Frick who talked.

"Where do you live?" the Pastor asked.

"By the Angel, Islington."

"What an address—most wonderful!"

"So different from these parts that I can hardly credit this chance meeting."

"There's no such thing as chance," he smiled. "Some contacts have a greater reality than others—that's all."

"For occasionally," said Mijnheer teasingly, "we recognize each other. That is important to remember."

"True," Pastor Frick agreed. "And the worst of the Van Baerle oasis is that we never wish to leave it. Yet leave it we all shall."

"But not for two months yet," said Mevrouw quickly, glancing at Andra. "It might be three——"

And so it proved.

All Andra's spare time was now spent with the Van Baerles. She became almost a daughter of the house. And on her second visit she found six other guests—some poor, some well-to-do—all visitors to this country. But despite dissimilarity, each had, in different degree, something of the Van Baerle tranquillity. In the course of weeks, this group grew to twelve. Two or three of these people proved to be accomplished musicians, and often played or sang to the circle. Some were highly educated, others of humble learning. There was also an Irishman, whom Andra later discovered to be a celebrated poet, and an elderly Italian actress, on her way to Rome, who read aloud to them in a legendary voice. The experiences of this brief period held a wealth, a diversity that ever afterwards appeared dream-like to Andra.

But there were also many hours alone with Mijnheer and Mevrouw—Mevrouw's large white hands flashing dextrously among the bobbins of her pillow-lace while Mijnheer returned again and yet again to the subject that absorbed them. Prayer.

As once she had learned from Sir Amos of the great artists, past and present, so now she heard the story of prayer through Mijnheer—of private and public, of monastic and secular prayer . . . together with legends of the desert Fathers, the hermits, priests, and churchmen of tradition. And time and again Mijnheer spoke of the hesychast method, reciting for her benefit the definitions of St. John of the Ladder. Delicately he indicated the disciplines of prayer, its dangers, its delights for the beginner—those emotions and ideas which were the weather, he declared, through which the all-important journey of the soul must be made.

He dwelt on intercession, meditation, contemplation. In intercession, for instance, there were occasions when beginners chafed beneath this burden——

"How strange!" Andra exclaimed, round-eyed. "To me all prayer is pure pleasure."

For the fraction of a second Mijnheer Van Baerle paused, but fleetly Mevrouw had said:

"Cornelius, every approach differs. You, yourself, have often said this."

"It is true," he answered in his measured way, "that every approach differs. In spiritual matters none dare generalize. But it is well to husband joy against the day when the sky may cloud. The continuance of the journey in any weather is the vital matter."

Many remarkable cases of healing through prayer were now brought to her notice, both by absent treatment or personal contact, yet she did not mention her own three miracles. But indeed there was no need, as the joyous token of the third still streamed from her at a glance. She had become an embodiment of belief.

On their last Sunday together, Mijnheer told her: "To-night Pastor Frick is bringing a countryman of yours to see us, after supper. But it is unlikely that he will remain for prayer. To-morrow he leaves for Egypt—the doctors recommend a winter abroad. So he, like us, is also a bird of passage——"

But Andra scarcely heard for Mijnheer had then added: "Wherever we go, Andra, we leave one member of the circle behind who will continue with us at the appointed hour. Three months ago Pastor Frick, my wife and I recognized you at a glance."

She seemed to be moving in a sphere where every moment prospered, and happiness chimed with its most fruitful occasion.

It was almost with a sense of inevitability, therefore, that an hour later she saw the door open, and Sir Amos Standish, among others, cross the floor.

"You are less of a surprise to me than I think I am to you," he admitted. "Yesterday I heard that you would be here to-night."

He had never looked better. Egypt for health reasons seemed so unlikely that she did not mention it. Nor did he ask a single question of her. He might have been in daily touch since their last meeting. His high spirits were contagious, and she noticed that his light touch set a key that was entirely English in that cosmopolitan group. The very music that night was of sparkling rather than sober persuasion, Mozart for once ousting Bach.

Only at goodbye did any personal note emerge. Andra who was remaining overnight found herself alone with him at the front door. In the shadows there, she noticed for the first time a certain translucence in him, as if night brought him nearer—no, made him clearer.

"Letters will be forwarded, of course," he said, "but happily between friends there is often a closer communion —if they would but use it."

Next day she had a further surprise. Mijnheer had inquired before departure: "That first Sunday, three months ago—may we ask how you came to be in this neighbourhood . . . so far from home? It's often helpful to trace events to their source."

"I had been to the Victoria and Albert Museum, to look at the Vaucluse Angel again. And then I took a walk which led me past your door."

"Interesting—very!" Mijnheer smiled across his coffee cup.

And Mevrouw added, "Then we may thank the Vaucluse Angel for this introduction!"

"The Vaucluse Angel . . ." Mijnheer repeated. "I

remember its discovery some five years ago. Dr. Riberac, the archaeologist, has that, with much else, to his credit."

There was a clean-cut little silence.

"Do you know him?" faltered Andra.

"No," replied Mijnheer, "only by reputation."

Both her friends had turned towards her. They seemed to be watching—no, they seemed to be waiting.

Andra's voice trembled slightly, but she made her declaration. "I used to know him well. He once meant a great deal to me."

Mevrouw looked up startled. "And not now?" she protested.

"We no longer meet," said Andra faintly.

Mevrouw set down her coffee-cup. She was still looking at Andra, but almost wistfully now. Firmly she said:

"I shall pray for Dr. Riberac's happiness."

Across Mijnheer's face amusement flickered as he changed the subject:

"Between the Angels Islington and Vaucluse, I feel that we leave you in good hands, my child . . ."

She was once more alone at Islington.

There, reverently she held to the Prayer Circle's methods. Always she rose one hour earlier, to give the first strength of her day to intercession—although this meant bed at eight each night to meet night-shift demands.

Nothing could exhaust Andra at this time. Ardour had come with the knowledge that the spiritual interpenetrated the material, that the celestial was a region as actual as Islington, and that it could, in fact, dominate Islington, without altering one stone or street. Islington's unchanged slums might still rear around her, but each tenement was now endowed with another significance. Thus she breathed another air, abiding on a longer, easier respiration. Hurry had passed from her with anxiety.

She could, of course, deviate from this state by careless-ness, annoyance, indolence, as one could lose one's way in any city through want of watchfulness. But, such was her distress, her sense of separation, when this happened that instantly she would repair her error. All was well!

And then, quite suddenly, Gerda returned——

Jubilant, on the crest of the wave! A west-end engage-ment as one of Mother Goose's eight gold eggs, dressed in swansdown and a smile! The provinces who knew a good thing—the provinces had done the trick! Gerda, promoted from one line to ten in their press, was inch-ing her way up! Now, it only remained, secretly, to understudy both principals, and to pray for an accident. Mercifully panto-mime was prolific in accident!

They had met for a snack in Oxford Street.

Gerda had matured in charm—her velvety beauty was now that of a golden dahlia. Yet as well as glamour, she possessed a dignity that might one day prove the core of an outstanding personality.

Andra felt very proud of her.

And she in turn still clung to Andra with flattering affection. She needed a confidant—a woman older than herself, yet not too old.

Andra had a sense of rekindling her own youth in this companionship. Yet Gerda's laughter now seemed merry rather than infectious. Humour, in fact, she lacked—a defect not so noticeable when one is young and high-spirited.

Gerda was full of news. Islington was out of the question, for the moment. Gerda was living rent-free with Margot MacBride. Margot MacBride had a studio flat. Margot MacBride was a perfect pet—full of poise . . . a concert pianist. Margot MacBride had also private means and a fiancé. Drummond Hesketh. He was the only snag. A stiff stick who didn't approve of Gerda. The strong, silent type

—full of his own importance, which truly amounted to *nothing*. A nondescript job in some publishing house with practically no salary. But might Gerda come to Andra for Christmas? The idea of Drummond under the mistletoe was more than Gerda could bear. Andra would understand that this didn't apply to Margot MacB. who remained, rain or shine, a downright dear.

Four weeks later Gerda arrived for Christmas. Vibrant but pale. Margot MacB. was no longer a perfect pet or even a downright dear.

"She practically ordered me *out*. Luckily," added Gerda, "I've found a flatlet in Paddington, not too far from the theatre. Rather a hole. But it will see me through. Drummond carried everything over—in six journeys . . . which saved a taxi."

"Drummond?"

"Yes, he's been *tremendous*. Of course he realized before I did what was at the bottom of Margot's moods. Jealousy, pure and simple. Not that jealousy's ever either. Life's so *complicated*, Andra. It's heaven to be back here. You're fundamentally sane, which is so rare with women. For, of course, it's just as bad for poor Drummond, as for Margot MacB.—to discover it's *me* he really loves. Actually, he feared this from the start, he says. His coldness was just a defence-mechanism. And, of course, I will admit it piqued my interest. In fact at first we were quite hideous to each other! Then, all at once, there was the eternal triangle defining the three of us. Two weeks ago I *had* to go."

Even then, although Andra certainly saw more than Gerda stated, she had nothing but praise for Gerda's speedy departure.

"I just will *not* meet him," Gerda declared. "He's in despair, but I'm adamant. And, in any case, Andra, there's my work. I simply must concentrate now. Believe it or not,

I move out on tour as second lead with the Number One Company end of March——"

But it had been the beginning of March when Gerda moved out—and into Dr. Fuller's hands.

Andra, at the eleventh hour, appalled, had been left to make the arrangements . . . at an address supplied by a stage friend, for in extremity, Gerda proved suicidal.

Andra, who had expected the doctor's rooms to be shabby —even shoddy, in keeping with a shady transaction, was dazed to discover that these were sunny chambers, indeed almost sumptuous—with the first daffodils on view, and a sleek secretary with a candid smile.

"But you do realize don't you," her voice had become almost plaintive, "that this is *not* a nursing home. If the patient needs a little rest afterwards, there's a nice room upstairs where she may remain overnight. But next day it is essential to complete convalescence elsewhere. At an hour agreed, the friend usually comes in a taxi——"

Gerda might have been entering these chambers for a fashionable rest-cure. In fact, the smug ease of the place bore no relation to the gravity of the occasion. And it was not until Gerda was returned, drained of vitality and colour, the bloom of her first youth gone for ever, that the situation had been fully declared. But Gerda, who had collapsed on discovery, now showed remarkable tenacity in recovery.

After ten days at Islington, a wraith of her former self, she answered rehearsal-call, and by the end of March was on the road restored. Manchester, Liverpool, Edinburgh, Glasgow ushering in her first important part . . .

A devastating experience had come and gone.

The only visible sign was a gap in the bedroom at the Angel, where Andra's bow-fronted wardrobe had been.

But inwardly Gerda had left an altered Andra behind. An Andra with a dragging sadness. An Andra of two-minds.

True, the Fuller decision had been Gerda's, but Andra had found the money for this rescue, and in complicity her peace had gone.

One month later Gerda had posted back ten pounds with her undying gratitude. The remaining fifty would follow by instalment . . . another five in May as she could manage.

In May there came instead a bombshell. One of Gerda's postcards, but this time in an envelope.

Just heard from Elsie that Drummond and Margot MacBride were married last week. Even more than I despise him, do I despise myself.

A silence of five weeks left Andra anxious. Then came a sheaf of laudatory press-notices from the provinces, with a pencil scrawl: *Keep these, darling, till my return. A west-end engagement is now only a matter of time.*

It was a summer of moody, uncertain weather. From a newspaper report she learnt that Sir Amos Standish was still abroad. It was some time since she had had a letter from Mevrouw; and Madame Moffat was behind with hers also——

Repeatedly that summer Andra had to remind herself of Islington's advantages. The Angel was so cheap! When any of its drawbacks chafed, she dwelt on this redeeming feature.

And how thankless to forget her double Birch Tree! Now that September was here again, the tiny leaves which in spring had hung like giant bunches of green grapes, were once more golden globes, and a gaiety to behold—dipping and swaying before her windows. Or petrified by hard frost, they shone in a banner of beaten brass. The blue and yellow tits which, despite sparrows and soot, hid their nests in mossy holes known only to herself, were old friends now. So too were the spiders and caterpillars, the profusion of minute insects that, at the appropriate season, launched themselves on her window-sill. And spring, summer, and autumn she would find, in turn, her floors sprinkled by a delicate confetti from the winged seeds and rusty tassels of the tree. There were anchored winter hours as well, when the sky flowing far beyond those living masts held an illusion of the sea at ebb on some distant beach. While on dull December days the leafless boles would slide like spotted snakes through their cloud of purple twigs, which in wild weather swept a witch's broom against the glass. A tree of perpetual delight.

Mrs. Ellis' fears about enemy neighbours had proved groundless. Andra knew them all by sight now, and many in daily greeting. Mr. and Mrs. O'Neill went out of their way to be helpful, and the Reids often carried her dustbin upstairs. The timid Miss Goodge sometimes brought her two fresh eggs and a few flowers when she came back from a day at the country-seat where once she had been lady's maid. Old Mr. Goodge, a small, clean little man with the face of a melancholy monkey, had knocked up a new shelf for Andra, across the corner of her bedroom, where behind a cretonne curtain her clothes now hung.

Andra had been luckier than many—as strenuously she reminded herself that year and next. In the redoubled earnestness with which she now addressed herself to prayer, she missed the fact that ardour had become urgency, and was only aware at times of an unusual exhaustion. This, plausibly enough, she put down to broken sleep for reasons that were not far to seek——

By June, 1927, a misfortune had overtaken Bollard's Hold.

Mrs. Ellis announced her departure. She had a bit of property in Wales that needed an eye kept on it for a year. Mrs. Busk, her niece, from Nottingham, would take over in her absence.

"Blood," said Mrs. Ellis, almost as if she regretted the fact, "is thicker than water."

Andra and the Goodges were shortly to regret this too,
Mr. and Mrs. Busk, with two strident children moved in.
Mr. Busk spent more time than most at the *Duke's Head*,
and when these hospitable doors closed, he brought home
company. The noisy days were nothing to the rowdy nights,
with the radio blaring, undefeated by quarrels and hilarity
alike. The tenement children of Bollards Close, hitherto
dominated by Mrs. Ellis, now swarmed shrilly into the court.
There were constant fights, in which a deafening din
volleyed between the narrow walls. For the first time
children assaulted the Birch Tree, and in attempting to
climb higher, a mossy limb broke off amid yells.

"Dinegerous!" shouted Mrs. Busk to such of the tenement
as leant on elbows from their window-sills. "You keep your
brats off, and so will I!"

A large, stout woman with hot brown eyes, mobile mouth
and heavy chin, Mrs. Busk had jocularly rallied Andra from
the start: "For I won't make no bones about it, Miss Hood,
I don't know as I ought to feel too friendly to you—seeing
as there you are, in the very flat I'd 'oped to 'ave for Mother.
But Mrs. Ellis says you won't be parted from your birch
tree. Mustn't grumble, I suppose!"

Mrs. Busk was shortly on terms of such noisy fellowship
with the tenement that the Reids and the O'Neills were
openly mutinous, and the mild Goodges, resentful. No one
could now rest or work in peace.

"Lowering! that's what it is," Miss Goodge had declared
when she handed in the last bunch of country flowers—a
misty tangle of asters and michaelmas daisies with a few
frosted roses.

As Andra took them in through the twilight, a moth
flew out of the bouquet which added to its enchantment.
She felt that the October night had flown in too with the
flowers.

As long as some beauty remained, Mrs. Busk, she decided was bearable!

Next day was October second, summer-time ended, and she returned later than usual, for it was Saturday afternoon and she was at leisure.

Passing under the tenement arch, the clock struck five.

At the entrance to Bollard Court, she stopped short——

For an instant she thought she had come to the wrong address. The blank walls of the court were splashed by fast-fading sunlight. And this revealed a stark, angular place of dismal outlook.

She stared again, incredulously.

The Birch Tree had gone.

No, it had not gone——

Sawn down and dismembered it lay in a monster mass, stacked among its own branches at the side of Bollards Hold. The paving stones were slippery with trodden leaves, and the ruin of various bird-nests. Already a large pile of winter wood waited at Mrs. Busk's door.

Trembling, Andra walked up the denuded iron stairs.

Outside her door, someone had left a present. Half a dozen birch logs——

An hour later her bell rang.

Dully she opened it . . . and then was surprised to see two tall men, well-dressed, and of unusual solemnity. One politely produced a Warrant Card; Detective Sergeant Musgrove of that county's constabulary.

For a moment she imagined that they had come about the felling of the Birch Tree.

"Are you the occupier of these premises?" the older asked.

"Yes."

"Well, miss, as you see, I'm a police-officer. I'd like a word with you."

"Certainly. What is it?"

"Perhaps," he said cautiously, "it might be as well if I came in. That's to say, if you've no objection?"

"None at all," she said sharply, and led the way into the sitting room. "Please be seated."

"It's been suggested that you might be able to help us, miss, with an inquiry."

"By whom?"

"That I'm not at liberty to say."

"You're certainly guarded," she smiled wryly.

"Well, miss, we're not always in a position to say all we'd like. But perhaps you'd help us now with some straight answers on quite a nasty business."

"Am I obliged to answer?" she said slowly, fumbling for some clue.

"In your own interests. There would be no point, would there, in trying to hide something that was really no concern of yours? I'm sure you'll give us every assistance. The fact is that two of your neighbours were arrested to-day on a serious charge. Theft. Known locally by the name of Goodge."

"But that's impossible!" Andra stared. "The Goodges . . . why it's ridiculous!" She was stammering in her embarrassment. "Old Mr. Goodge is a porter at the Channing Hotel, Holborn. His daughter gave up an excellent post at the Dowager Lady Lutrell's to keep house for him——"

Detective Sergeant Musgrove listened politely, his companion in stolid silence.

"Mr. Goodge, so-called, hasn't got a daughter, miss, but he has got an accomplice, female of the name of Figg. And what we're after is their latest haul—a mink coat and some jewellery. Would you be able to suggest where they might have stored this?"

Bewildered, she stared: "I? How could I?"

"It was suggested to us that the woman might have left a parcel here."

The blood rushed to Andra's face, then drained, leaving it ashen. Weakly she said:

"Miss Goodge did leave a parcel with me this week. A winter coat she'd bought for her father's birthday. She didn't want to keep it at their flat in case he saw it beforehand. She wanted it to be a surprise——"

"Did you see the coat?"

"No, of course not. The parcel is still tied up—just as she left it. It's quite a big dress-box. I've got it under my bed."

"Then we'll have a look at it right away."

And from its wrappings, Detective Sergeant Musgrove had drawn a full-length mink coat, of such superb appearance that the dumb colleague whistled. "Father's winter coat and no mistake!"

His senior shot him a blighting look, and addressed Andra with growing gravity:

"Now, miss, would you care to tell me all you know about this coat?"

Dazed, she stood silent.

"First," he said, "I must caution you. It is my duty to tell you that you are not obliged to say anything at this stage unless you wish to do so. But whatever you say, will be taken down in writing, and may at some future date be given in evidence."

Still Andra did not answer.

"In view of the fact," pursued Detective Sergeant Musgrove, "that you are in possession of property which is undoubtedly the proceeds of a criminal offence, it will be in your own interest if you are perfectly frank with me."

Andra moistened her dry lips.

Sergeant Musgrove waited patiently for a minute, then quietly motioning Andra to be seated, he drew up a chair for himself and said persuasively:

"Now, please be sensible. I know you think that you are in a difficult position, but you really must tell me all you know. Begin at the beginning, and I shall write it down——"

Hoarsely she said: "I can only repeat what I have already told you . . ."

Half an hour later, as she showed them out, she managed to ask: "What will happen now?"

The Detective Sergeant glanced away. "The facts will have to be reported, miss. And I cannot tell you, at this stage, what action, if any, will be taken against you. These matters take time to investigate. It will be at least two or three weeks before the case is brought into Court."

It was three weeks—with the Busks invisible; the Reids cutting her dead; the O'Neills scuttling out of the way; the other tenants staring askance; and the children shouting "Copper's Nark!" each time she crossed the courtyard.

On her door, chalked notices now appeared—obscene epithets, foul abuse. These tokens of disfavour she had at first obliterated, before the postman saw them. But later, she learnt to let them stand, as with the need for repetition, the scribe redoubled virulence.

Returning with Mr. Tucker, after the Court case, they found together with these inscriptions, an unstamped letter in her box. It ran:

Mr. Busk and me is instructing you to vacate premises this day week prompt.

(Signed) E. BUSK LANDLORD.

"Now, Miss Andra," said Mr. Tucker grimly, "I mean to show you less consideration than Mrs. Busk, for I insist that you leave this place to-morrow. In fact, arrangements were completed yesterday in London, with this end in view. I have found a pleasant two-roomed flat for you, above an antique shop in Wigmore Street. This client of mine does not live above his shop, and he is more interested in finding a reliable tenant than in making profit from the flat. It has one drawback only. When the shop changes hands, as it may in a year or so, the flat must be vacated then. But it will help you out meantime. It is a good address. The rooms are large and unfurnished but have fine fittings and expensive curtains in the front windows, for it is important to the shop that the place looks well from the street. You're going to be happy there."

Huskily Andra said: "You've been busy."

"I've been deeply distressed. Anxious, too, lest you fail to make a clean sweep of a nightmare experience."

She smiled wanly. "I did that yesterday—in case the newspapers report the case. The factory, the city-offices, the cinema have all been told I won't be back."

"Excellent!" Mr. Tucker had become his hearty self again. "And I have spoken with two other friends of mine, on your behalf. One is the manager of the Wigmore Hotel, the other the matron of the Henrietta Nursing Home. Both assure me they will be delighted to give you as much work as you can undertake. These two places are almost on your doorstep —another advantage!"

The first tears she had shed welled into her eyes. "Mr. Tucker," she began, " I have no words——"

"But you have many friends, Miss Andra, although they don't happen to live at Islington! Now, I'm going downstairs to secure a receipt for your rent from Mrs. Busk. You must have no further contact with that lady. And there is another point: I'd like you to leave here as soon as my van arrives to-morrow. The men will bring your luggage later with the furniture. Just walk out, as if you were going round the corner, and might be back."

At the door he paused again. "I attach so much importance to your cutting clear of this place, that I shall not give your new address to my men until they reach my warehouse with your goods to-morrow."

The following night, Mr. Tucker had been able to relate the last news from the Angel, over a quiet dinner in Baker Street.

"It was as I expected. Both the removal men and the driver were questioned as to your destination. Cigarettes and beer were handed out. The men, previously cautioned by me, and anxious to avoid unpleasantness, promised to look up the address on their consignment-sheet before departure. And as they finally pulled out, with the Busks at attention, they shouted as they accelerated: 'Buckingham Palace—best regards!' Nothing, my dear, like a good address if you want to cut a dash . . .!"

Soundlessly Andra set down an empty cup in the Victoria and Albert work-room.

Time with the speed of light had telescoped three years in four minutes.

Islington lay once more behind her.

Saturday Morning . . . eleven o'clock

At ten-twenty prompt she passed into the galleries again.

To polish the glass and wood-work cases was the only labour permitted with the public present, and now, in her dark overall, she moved as inconspicuously as possible through the collection.

The place was unusually busy for the hour. No doubt the Vaucluse Angel visitors were finding their way through other galleries. With them trailed the usual casuals off the street, who had come in simply from boredom!

Two old men, shabbily dressed cronies, with time to kill, passed the monastic textiles with hauteur.

"Wot I say is: if we'd been meant to live in monastries, we'd 'ave been born in them."

"Yah!" said his friend in disgust.

Remarks such as these were a commonplace. How uneasy the dedicated life made many!

An elderly well-dressed couple passed next. Unlike most visitors, both noticed Andra as they went by.

With a cold stare the lady said: "Rather odd, don't you think—a cleaner in the galleries at this hour?"

"Bad management," pronounced the gentleman, moving on.

Silently Andra continued to brighten the glass-case that recent fingers had blurred. A critical sort of day despite the sunshine! She hoped it wasn't an omen with Gerda ahead of her——

Two girls were lagging behind their teacher, and the rest of the class. They frowned at the Good Friday Shroud, dedicated by that servant of God, Nicholas, in the year 1407.

"Of course the detail's something," the first admitted with adolescent patronage.

"They'd nothing else to do," the second said impatiently. "You don't call saying prayers work."

"Don't you?" said Andra suddenly.

The two girls stopped, stared, and then—startled—made off.

The censorious day had affected her too! Andra had ceased to behave like a cipher. How outrageous of her—but for once she scarcely cared.

The measured tread of Mr. Mott passed, re-passed, then paused beside her. Notwithstanding his leisurely patrol, he was breathing hard.

Andra, alarmed, continued to polish.

"Sorry I spoke so sharp about my cup of tea. Anyone can forget it's Saturday."

"Please don't give it another thought."

Eagerness had mollified his expression, softened it deplorably. "I tell you what," said Mr. Mott, weightily, "you're too good for any man!"

That was how Captain Boyd's proposal had begun, at the *True-blue Café*. And his next sentence had precipitately run: *if you'll only let me take care of you*——

"If you'll only let me take care——" began Mr. Mott, but at that moment the Curator walked briskly through the gallery.

Mr. Mott with dignity resumed his measured tread. He might never have paused.

Abruptly Andra decided to change her circuit. Less chance of him dawdling beside her in Pottery and Glass.

For twenty minutes she worked in peace among the ceramics—intrigued afresh by the Fulham Stoneware

Figure. For the first time she saw the skull at the bare feet of the girl more clearly than the strewn memorial flowers. Yet the skull had always been there, discreetly in the background. Now it seemed the most significant feature of the portrait.

One so rarely saw what was at one's own feet!

Sir Amos had adopted this device of a telling symbol with his full length figures. As the *Dancing Girl* she had had a basket of fruit at hers. And when the marble basket was completed, he had sent her a gilt basket of hot-house fruit—its perfume as penetrating, as delicate as that of lilies.

Since then at her solitary feet there had been instead the Scrubber's pail of water . . . or the oilcloth bag!

No . . . for four years there had also been Philip's shoes beside her own at Kew!

Involuntarily now, she glanced down.

Barely a yard away, to the right, the shoes of a large, expensively shod man were advancing towards her——

Terrified, she looked up.

Philip, with a face of fury, was bearing down upon her. The next instant his fingers gripped her arm.

"*Got you!*" he exclaimed.

It might have been an arrest. Hysterically she laughed. He was breathing much more heavily than Mr. Mott, and his eyes were bloodshot.

"Come away, Andra," he said shortly. "It's all over. Let's get out of here."

"Philip . . ." aghast, she shook him off. "I work here. I can't."

"You what?"

"I work here. Can't you see . . ." anxiety of another sort invaded her. Was he ill . . . or out of his mind?

"Nonsense! We'll make your excuses right away. By God

—I can hardly realize it! *You at last*. Here, of all places. Come along!" Alarmingly his manner alternated between anger and triumph.

"Philip, I can't. I've told you—I'm on duty. I must finish my work."

"Then let's sit down somewhere——" his exhaustion was as noisy as his vigour. He had the unstable yet taut look of a man at breaking point. He was almost unrecognizable as Philip.

Hurriedly she said. "I must not sit down. I ought not to be talking with you at all. It's against the rules."

"Yours or the Museum's?" his smile was blighting. "Well, we've got the rest of our life to fight that out! But first of all, give me your address. I'm taking no chances this time."

Trembling she repeated: "We've been into that already."

Impatiently he swore. Then: "Hasn't there been enough suffering?" he enquired. "If you won't give me this now, I shall simply remain with you till the place shuts."

"You wouldn't, you couldn't do such a thing!"

"Wouldn't I, couldn't I? Don't be a fool, Andra. This has been a search of ten years. And twice in the last five you've given me the slip. I intend to be heard. Your obstinacy is as nothing to mine."

"I told you then that there are things from which one cannot recover."

"Things from which one doesn't wish to recover, my faith-healer! Things from which one doesn't mean to recover. As your Alderman would say: that's the way of it, is it?"

"Do lower your voice, Philip. Those people glanced over!"

"Behave yourself then!" he spoke almost humorously now. He was breathing more easily. He took out an immaculate handkerchief and wiped sweat from his brow.

Blindly she began to polish another case. He was thinner than of old. Bland was the last word for him now.

Stammering, she said: "I only heard of the Vaucluse find to-day. It's wonderful news!"

"Find!" he scoffed, "the damned thing's lost again. Baxter, that abject ass, has posted it, unregistered."

"Oh, *no*!" her consternation drew them briefly together.

"When it didn't turn up this morning, I knew it was hopeless. I came here simply to kill time till the next post. Not that there's any chance now——"

"Don't say that," she urged. "I'm sure it will turn up yet . . . although this suspense must be dreadful. Oh, I am so sorry——"

"Are you?" his voice was low, his face so intent that quickly she turned away. "Then at least go on talking to me— to relieve strain."

With a nervous laugh she moved on. "Pretend to be studying the things in the case. Don't stand so near me. I can hear you perfectly."

"Good God, what a situation! Am I to comment on the exhibits? I'd like to drown you in that Wedgewood Tureen —it's almost large enough?"

"Where are you staying?"

"At the Club, of course. It's something to find that you can still make a friendly inquiry."

"Oh, Philip—surely I'm not as bad as that?" Feverishly she added, "How—how is your Aunt?" the time-worn courtesy slipping out before she could weigh its suitability.

"Flourishing like the green bay tree—when last I heard. A matter of months ago. I've just returned from the United States. Where shall we lunch, Andra?" Again his spirits rose.

"Philip—it's useless. I mean what I say. But if you

insist on another meeting—then it must be later. I've certain appointments to-day that I just must keep."

Between his teeth he said: "Are you determined on this delay?"

"I can't help it."

He drew himself up. Stiffly he enunciated: "Of course I realize many things now. And have done so for long. Had it not been for your isolation—the death of your aunt, the removal of Mrs. Moffat and her daughter to San Francisco . . . you would probably never have taken that step with me."

Behind his clipped words, a torrent of interrogation was stemmed. She was terrified to find that she could not stop trembling. Mercifully, he was aware of nothing but his own agitation.

"Oh, *no*!" she exclaimed. "People who didn't know might think that. But had I had parents, brothers and sisters, an entire family around me—it would still have made no difference. I would have left everyone for you. It was love."

"Was?" he repeated harshly.

"I'm sorry," she said in a low voice, again moving away.

"One moment!" he said sharply. "You left this in the *escritoire* at Kew. It was the only thing you left behind. I've been carrying it around ever since——" he opened his pocket book. "Psychologists might say it denoted an unconscious desire on your part to return—as I cannot think that you really wished to be rid of *this*!"

And he handed her the printed card with the *Rules of the Society of the People Called Methodists*.

Silently she took it—and then saw that he was carrying quite a large volume.

Perturbed she exclaimed: "You've got Sir Amos' book—have you read it?"

"Not yet," he said acidly. "That is a pleasure still to come."

Nervously she said: "You do mean to read it then?"

"That's the idea of the purchase. Have you any objection?"

"Oh, no, not at all," she said unhappily. "It's yours to read if you wish, of course."

"I should say it is. Quite a costly item too!" his eyes snapped. "And when we're about it: may I ask how this study in sleep known as *La Pleureuse* was captured? Your critics (myself among them) are unanimous that this is not death but slumber. The authentic trance."

She smiled, despite herself. "I fell asleep one day in the Studio before posing. He was late in arriving. And I was tired. I did not even hear him come in. But now, Philip, I must ask you to go."

"When will you telephone the Club to-day?"

"It will have to be to-morrow."

"Then you *are* resolved on this attitude?"

"Yes, I am. But I promise to telephone. Do leave me now! People are watching. You *must* go away. It's endangering my position here."

"*Your* position here . . . as if that mattered now! 'Pon my soul you're as great an egoist as I am! But I shall get you out of this place—*by hook or by crook*. And permanently. That much is certain."

Appalled by his intensity, she stared at him, and again he gripped her arm——

"Stop that!" she exclaimed, panic-stricken.

"What's going on here?" said the voice of Mr. Mott at their elbow.

Quietly, but with precision, Dr. Riberac said: "You go to hell!"

Philip the conventional, the correct! She could scarcely credit present misfortune.

"If you'll come along with me, sir," said Mr. Mott in the

voice he considered suitable for border-line cases, "we can go together."

"Mr. Mott," said Andra hurriedly, "this gentleman is known to me. Everything is quite all right. But thank you all the same——"

Mr. Mott, resentful, suspicious, and reluctant, moved slowly off.

Flushed to the brow, Andra turned in the opposite direction, closely followed by Riberac.

"Evasion is useless," he said, "as you may as well realize, Andra. I insist that you telephone me by to-night—*I shall wait in till you do.*"

"It can't be to-night. I've told you that."

His eyes narrowed. Slowly and distinctly he said: "I am now on my way to the Director of this Museum. And I warn you, that if you have not telephoned me by nine o'clock to-morrow, Sunday morning, I shall then take steps you may regret."

"Philip . . . I can't believe it of you—This isn't a threat?"

"Indeed it is. Make no mistake about that!"

Incensed, he walked away, his steps ringing abruptly through the marble court.

Dazed, Andra gazed after him . . .

But at least she had till nine on Sunday morning——

Saturday Afternoon . . . four o'clock

"You're in luck!" the theatre box-office clerk announced, pushing the cancellation towards her at two o'clock . . . so quickly, so smoothly that it might have been pre-arranged!

Had Andra secretly hoped that the House would be sold out? That she would be spared this penalty meeting with Gerda, after that malign scene which had parted them five years ago?

But there was Letty—to-day living through every hour as if it were a life-time . . .

Hastily Andra drew aside from the *matinée* crowd, marked the seat-number in her letter, closed this, and walked round to the stage-door.

"Miss Rush need not receive this till after the *matinée*," she told the stage-door keeper. "But I'd like her to have it then. It is important."

"Certainly, miss," he said.

Kinder not to upset Gerda as she was going on . . .

The bus was full of Jubilee holiday-makers on her way home. She caught snatches of gossip. The R.A.F. display at Hendon was expected to draw enormous crowds. The King, recovered from his recent illness, would see the second test match at Lord's. The newspaper on her lap related that Mr. Eden, after conferring with Signor Mussolini, again discussed the situation with M. Laval. . . . That must be the Anglo-German naval agreement in Paris. There was also an article on a moratorium arising out of Germany's foreign obligations. . . The year 1935 was the year of Peace movements, of course . . . just as 1925 and 1928 had been notable for Pacts——

Guiltily Andra knew that she could not keep her attention fixed—despite the recent dangers of ignoring newspaper reports!

The startling events of her own day dominated.

As she opened her front door, the distant blare of the brass band from Parliament Hill Fields reached her in the pounding emphasis of *March Lorraine*. The drums were much in evidence, with ever and again the easy sentiment of the refrain. But at what speed it went! A French battalion on the march was almost at a run! Philip had once said no British regiment was equal to this pace——

But then the French did everything at the double—once they started.

On the maroon carpet lay an orange envelope.

She stared at this unusual sight. It was years since she had had a telegram.

Philip . . .

She tore it open, and barely took it in: *Safely through finals Honours in all subjects Hurrah Francie.*

Belatedly Andra smiled. Francie at twenty-two was already well on her way as a medical missionary!

The telephone bell rang sharply beside her.

A telephone-call was the rarest thing——

Nervously she lifted the receiver.

But it was only Mr. Tucker—to explain why he'd given the Reporter that information.

And, of course, she understood! But there was another odd matter—a catalogue forwarded from the Angel, Islington last night.

Across the line, Mr. Tucker surprised again: "Our van-man mentioned recently, when taking furniture to a flat in Bollard's Court that Mrs. Ellis was back, and Mrs. Busk gone. Mrs. Ellis told him she was sorry about the Goodge affair, and asked for your address. He told me he felt awkward, as she seemed genuine, so he gave the Wigmore Street address—knowing you had left! She'll probably be writing soon."

Andra laughed. A relief to know that Mrs. Busk was no longer on the war-path.

Telegram . . . telephone . . . what had she expected?

Philip, of course.

Quite terrifying that her passion could outlive love like this—for thus she identified the emotion now disturbing her.

But Saturday afternoon should be a period of relaxation. She must make the most of it. She had been up since quarter to five——

Lifting the Standish book, she went with it into the back garden, dense with its chestnut leaves, and cool as a well. Silence was a feature of those narrow high-walled retreats. On such a fine Saturday, sometimes the sound of voices or laughter in passing gave companionable pleasure. But to-day the terrace was profoundly still—as if every other inhabitant, intent on Jubilee festivity, were elsewhere. Andra, alone, was left in charge—to put the kettle on and make tea when the others got back——

The others?

What was she dreaming of? There were no others.

Resolutely she opened the book.

It was indeed a large one, and would certainly take some time to read. Ingenuously she marvelled at the amount he had written . . . pages and pages.

An adept in telepathy, the Reporter had said. But now Andra remembered something else. Something that might have escaped her—had it not been for Mr. Tucker's recent telephone call.

Two years ago, at the opening of Mr. Tucker's imposing

new show-rooms in Grosvenor Square, she had exclaimed on seeing the entrance murals by Sir Amos.

Complacently Mr. Tucker had said: "Yes, I've always been a great admirer of the man and his work."

"Then you know him too?"

"Oh, on and off," Mr. Tucker admitted. "Off and on! He first came into my shop, over an antique, about twenty years ago. But I didn't meet him again till 1918 when Mrs. Moffat gave me a ticket for the Art School Exhibition. There was a small marble of your head, with a wreath, which I tried to buy. But it was not for sale. Sir Amos, however, gave me a cast of this work."

Intently now, Andra stared back at the house. The address for the Reporter. The address for Mrs. Ellis. Mr. Tucker had always known her every address!

Had this been the extent of Sir Amos' telepathy? Had he traced her always through Mr. Tucker? Was Sir Amos' continued "distance," a condition imposed by Mr. Tucker, in his anxiety to respect her confidence?

It looked very like it.

So much for telepathy! Despite herself, she began to laugh again.

Then, as swiftly, her amusement died, for, of course, there was also Sir Amos' own reason for remaining apart——

It was inconceivable that he would mention *that* in his book.

And sympathy of a unique kind there had always been between them. She must not forget that. During his grave illness in 1930, she had had several dreams of him that were as vivid as visions. Never would she forget the perfect peace of the first one—for that had been its sightless environ-ment . . . or the thrilling contact of his presence, invisible though this was. Yet with what precision his words had reached her through sleep: "The world of every day is very important, but this other world is all-important. So one ceases to be impatient. *One awaits the provident hour.*"

But, of course, that was, after all, only a dream. And her own.

Absently, she went on turning the leaves.

Suddenly, she stopped. On the open page, she read these words:

"I regard my recovery in 1930 as a turning point in my life. And with this *La Pleureuse* was closely linked. Our invincible affinity was then fully declared—as although this world of everyday (with its privations and separations) is very important, we were then enabled to realize that that other world is all-important. . . . So one ceases to be impatient. *One awaits the provident hour.*"

Breathless . . . she gazed upwards.

It *had* happened after all! And during life—despite every disability. The wonder that was the desire of all. Communion in spirit.

Telepathy might not cover Sir Amos' knowledge of her addresses, but insight itself had recorded her dream.

Yet what could have been unlikelier than the events that led up to this experience—for in that pleasant little flat above the antique shop in Wigmore Street, with everything at last in order, and Islington safely behind her, the direst fate of all had overtaken her.

Prayer, which had been the joy and restoration of existence, quite suddenly died within her.

And the shock of the Court case, the Islington ordeal, was not to blame. Even then she was forced to recognize this.

Inexplicably, prayer had been dying for some time.

The lack of ardour in her approach, which she had noticed after the Gerda disaster, was now become apathy.

Stubbornly she had held to her daily intercession: the cases of illness or need brought to her notice; and those calamities in the news—for victims and bereaved she prayed alike . . . finally, in the case of crime, moving through the shadow of the assailant to beseech healing there as well.

But now she seemed to have identity with the misery she sought to alleviate . . . or to be implicated in the guilt. She had ceased to be a channel.

Exiled alike from past and future, the indifferent present had also rejected her—its nobility a memory that had then begun to suggest illusion.

Illusion?

In praying was she acting under some compulsion? And surely compulsion was an abnormal state?

"Well," she decided dully, "if I'm going to suffer from compulsion, it's better that it takes this form than another!"

Doggedly, she had continued to pray. But there was apparently no virtue in this. She became increasingly nervous . . . apprehensive.

At night her sleep was broken, by wreathing forms that might have been the minions of the principalities and powers of which St. Paul had preached. Was her reason going? Was it prayer that had brought this upon her? There was no one she could ask. Something deep-seated within her rejected the idea that prayer had opened this door. But perhaps she had been doing too much? She might do less at a time. Yet she must keep on. All her deepest joy had been centred in prayer, and there was evidence that it *had* availed. No, she must accept the situation—bear it patiently. The way would clear.

For the first time, pressure lifted slightly, as if an unseen adversary had been worsted.

Yet outwardly all was well enough.

Instead of Islington, this was the fashionable west-end—thanks to Mr. Tucker. Dignified squares, spacious streets, with limousines gliding by, and well-dressed people passing: patients and doctors en route to Harley Street; customers for the Times Book Club; Mayfair women shopping at ease. And during the week-end, those impressive buildings took on an added calm with emptiness. True, over all lay the shadow of town . . . mansions that stood in their own light; mansard roofs that blocked out the sky; tier upon tier of flats; luxury hotels. Yet although she was at last within a few minutes of Regent's Park, the witchery of early October twilights now meant nothing to her. At five o'clock, when the wind dropped in Wigmore Street, and above the gray, lamp-lit buildings the sky was full of a wan light between wild cloud—she could no longer soar.

Bewildered by the pall that had fallen on her, she redoubled her efforts in prayer, and had no idea that by this intensive process she was about to bring upon herself the grim experience of self-knowledge.

Instead she felt herself embroiled in a contesting, a clarifying, a dispersing of inimical forces.

An occasional victory, a brief respite brought self-consciousness only, with resultant depression.

"I must somehow be praying in the wrong way. I am so ignorant——" she realized afresh. Finally, "I believe I'm having a nervous break-down," she decided. "I ought to take advice."

At her new Church in that district, the Vicar preached a moving sermon the following Sunday evening.

Summoning all her courage, Andra followed two or three people to the vestry afterwards—future communicants registering now for instruction. She was the last to enter.

But the Vicar's methodical smile faded, when she explained that she had simply come for some advice.

"And what's the trouble?" he said pleasantly but briskly. He was already a little late.

"Prayer," said Andra, and he noticed with discomfort that her voice shook. "I feel I need help. I'm sorry to trouble you, but you'll see it's serious—for I've begun to wonder if I'm praying too much."

The Vicar shot her an attentive look, and his manner became brisker still. A lack of humour simplified the situation for him. He had had people who complained they couldn't pray, even that they didn't want to pray, but never before had his time been taken up by someone who complained of praying too much. At once he recognized an eccentric. And of course there was only one way to deal with those. Bluntly.

"Pitfalls in prayer do not exist," he said crisply. "Prayer simply reveals the pitfalls that exist in us. Prayer alone can get you out of any such hole."

Fervently he hoped that this would see her out. His wife, often irritable, didn't like supper delayed. And he was determined to fit in the visit to old Mrs. Bell before bedtime —for if this were postponed, Monday's heavy schedule would also be out of gear.

"Prayer is a great privilege," he added as make-weight, and to induce a more suitable humility he remarked as he rose, with a playful shake of the finger—"you are probably not praying enough."

Fear reinforced many of his difficulties, but, unlike Andra, he did not know this.

"Thank you," she said faintly.

Regaining the street in a matter of seconds, she felt that she had been struck—as indeed she had been, by the Vicar's schedule, which periodically knocked him sideways too.

But a moment later she was forced to admit: he was right, of course, as far as he went . . . but he didn't go far enough.

What a blessing she hadn't mentioned her spectral invasion! He would have been as frightened as she was——

For the first time, she began to laugh as she got out her latch key.

Turning it, she glanced into the side window of the antique shop, and saw that it had been re-set for Monday, with an old print of some Gothic cathedral prominently placed.

For a second she gazed at the grotesque figures projecting from the steep roof to carry water clear of the walls. Gargoyles stood for a surplus. Here too were strange beings, before one passed into the holy place . . . images like distorted creatures, outside a cathedral, frozen into stone. Was hers a common experience in the life of prayer? Was that why artists of old had placed these there? But that was where they remained—outside. One must pass through them, and on.

Now that she recognized them, there was almost a kind of humour about those bogys. Larger than life, here was one answer anyway! And the last verse of Pastor Frick's favourite hymn confirmed it

> *Hobgoblin nor foul fiend*
> *Can daunt his spirit,*
> *He knows he at the end*
> *Shall life inherit.*

Resolutely once more she took up her burden.

It's not enough to hold on, she told herself, I must hold out, for this may last some time.

Unaware that rescue was once more at hand, she had fully accepted the situation . . .

Evening work at the Henrietta Nursing Home was not immediately available when first she moved into the flat above the antique shop. Calling at the Registry Office, where Miss Leech was surprised but quite pleased to see her, Andra discovered she had a "short" vacancy. St. Dominic's char was off ill. Could Andra go to-night?

"I'm not a Roman Catholic, Andra pointed out.

"They must take what they can get," Miss Leech brushed non-essentials aside. "Your duties won't take you into the Church. But you'll have the choir-boys' cloakroom and an adjoining library, also an office and a small kitchen. Father Mayo will see you himself to-night. Here's the address, and the hour. The work should be easy."

It was, but Father Mayo had proved a fussy and consequential employer, and Andra was relieved when the second last night came round.

"I shall not be here to-morrow," he announced. "Monsignor Caius will have the uninterrupted use of this study. He is a guest of the greatest importance. And the cup of cocoa will, of course, come in as usual at nine sharp." He looked at her with some severity.

"Yes, Sir," said Andra. "I quite understand."

"You will, of course, go through your other duties as silently as possible. Monsignor Caius will be engaged on research. I have already spoken to Father Shannon about the scandalous noise the boys made yesterday when dismissing from choir practice."

Earnestly Andra assured him: "Everything will be in order."

"I trust so," he said doubtfully, as, reluctantly, he departed.

At nine the folowing night, cocoa in hand, she tapped at the study door.

There was no reply. Perhaps, like Father Mayo, Monsignor Caius had stepped into the adjoining room?

She had better do as she usually did.

She opened the door, and saw a second light on the desk. He had evidently been working there—so he must be about.

She crossed the floor, and laid the cup of cocoa on a small refectory table—drawing an open book nearer it, so that his supper should not escape his notice.

The book's title caught her attention.

Unseen Warfare, being the Spiritual Combat and Path to Paradise of Lorenzo Scupoli.

What a title! Never had she seen anything like this before. Eagerly she bent over it, and there on the printed page read these words:

Of the wiles of the enemy against those who have entered the right path:

Arrows from above are suggestions of excessive spiritual works, above his powers; arrows from below are suggestions to reduce or even completely abandon such works through self-pity, negligence and heedlessness.

Arrows from below! That was exactly what she was suffering from. This book knew about it. Oh, thank God—this was what she needed. This was help at hand——

She looked up.

A tall thin man in a black cassock was regarding her steadily. But she was beyond timidity, as she stood there with deliverance in her hand.

Her face shining, she exclaimed: "This is wonderful! It's the answer. Forgive me——"

"Scupoli has answered you?" He came forward smiling. "You are a reader then?"

"No—no, I'm not. But I pray. And recently there have

been many difficulties. Perhaps because I've been so much alone——"

"Difficulties in prayer?" he drew up a second chair. "Perhaps between us we might divide them. Won't you sit?"

"You're very kind," she began, a trifle apologetically. "Perhaps I should explain that I am a Protestant."

Amused he said: "Even Protestants have been known to unbend! You *do* sit, don't you? Then may I know Scupoli's answer?"

"The arrows from below," her gaze earnestly upon him, they sat down.

"Ah!" he answered.

"I haven't known what was the matter. I've been as dry as dust. Disinclined for any effort. And that was only the beginning of it."

Easily he began to read: "' *For when the soul is in this state of dryness, when it tastes this bitterness and suffers temptations and thoughts the mere memory of which makes one tremble, it poisons the heart, and almost kills the inner man. But when the soul finds itself in this state, it learns to distrust itself, and not to rely on its own good state, and so acquires true humility, which God so wishes us to have. . . . But since these good fruits are hidden from the sight of the soul, it is troubled and flees from this bitterness, for it does not wish to be deprived of its spiritual comforts even for a short time, and regards every spiritual exercise not accompanied by them as wasted time and useless labour.*' Is that also an answer?"

But Andra could not speak. Tears were pouring down her face.

"How good such tears are," he said tenderly. And his sympathy was part also of this strange yet inevitable occasion. "How healing!" he continued. "When prayer first turns its arc-light on oneself, revealing the nakedness of that land, it is a painful experience, but" he added lightly, "a commonplace and inescapable martyrdom."

As he spoke, she noticed for the first time that, had it not been for his humour and compassion, his aloof Spanish features would have seemed cold, disdainful. In fact, had she not been carried away by Scupoli, she would have been afraid of this aristocratic mask.

"Now," he continued, "how are you dealing with this present distress?"

"At first not at all, Monsignor," she hesitated. "But lately—as a last resort, by acceptance."

He laughed, and said softly, "Splendid, splendid! You are now on the way out then. There may be other difficulties, of course, until the end. But acquiescence puts a term to anxiety. Blair has described anxiety as: ' *the poison of human life: the parent of many sins and of more miseries*'."

"What I have found frightening," again she hesitated, "is that one has no sooner emerged, than there's another difficulty. The way seems to grow harder and harder. Why must it be so?"

"In over-coming, pride might steal in. Let us remember that each fresh day is also in the nature of a summation— of all that has gone before. In every past there is much secret sorrow. Stark truth is also concealed in that ground, for there is a sense in which our past is a grave. And although the stone conveniently seals it off from full consciousness—the Soul knows all about it, and anguishes. More so, if it does this unaware. Consciousness is liberation."

"The stone?" she faltered.

He nodded. "Our hardened heart. Until pride is over-come, the way must have its difficulties. But also its en-couragement. Let us hear Scupoli on this: ' *In an ordinary journey, the further the traveller proceeds, the more tired he becomes: but on the way of the spiritual life, the longer a man travels, the greater the strength and power he acquires for his further progress.'* Cheering, you see."

"Yes," she said soberly, "but now I see that I have not begun at all. This is a shock, for I thought I had! There were cases of healing——"

Again his eye gleamed, and rather tremulously she found herself smiling with him.

"Tell me about these," he said.

But she shook her head, the forgotten tears still running down her face.

"No, no," she said, "I begin to see more clearly. . . . I had proof of these cases, or I dare not have credited them. And of course they encouraged me to go on—I'm really quite lazy."

He listened attentively, and yet with the abstraction of one who has his eye on remembered country, a familiar landmark.

"Now I see," she said half sadly, "that the sick for whom I have been praying, have really been healing me."

. Raising his head, he looked at her directly. "Come," he said quietly, "it is something to secure one convert for Christ. As for the miracles, the cures—all such are hid with Christ in God. That must never be forgotten. Our efforts themselves sometimes need fresh scrutiny, for each step in the life of devotion is made with so much effort—or so much ease!—that we tend to cling to the beaten track. Our rut becomes snug. Having created one's routine with self discipline, one may harden in it. One must watch as well as pray. Habit can be a hindrance in prayer as in any other concern, once it has served its purpose of confirming fidelity. Then any free approach seems like a step into the void. Prayer may lay us open to this experience, among others, for the day comes when we must begin to climb. One must gain the strength to continue. The response is always there, by grace—but it is not always possible to claim it."

Silently she nodded.

"Hitherto," he suggested, "you have perhaps prayed for those who aroused your compassion, fear, or hope."

"Yes . . . that's true."

"But intercessors need preparation in mediating! What have you done for those sufferers who fail to touch our imaginations because they are unknown?"

Dubiously she shook her head. "They have always left me cold."

"These are the people you need then. Love is not simply something that befalls one through mutual attraction. It is a warmth, an activity one can induce, as one lights a fire. And it can grow—even for those inimical to one. You will be astonished." Again his eye glinted humorously. "Doesn't the sybarite himself admit that only the acquired tastes count? Above all, never be discouraged. By merciful dispensation, there is often a most fruitful opportunity after intense disappointment, or failure. Humility is its own insight." He paused. "What do you desire most?"

Her face brightened. "The hunger and thirst after righteousness—for then nothing is an effort. All is joy."

"As it should be. Scupoli himself bids us not be perturbed by impoverishment of spiritual feeling, or by other inner temptations. So with every wilderness experience, remember that you are a day's march nearer home—'for it is the Father's good pleasure to give you the Kingdom.'"

With a sigh of gratitude she arose—then, smiling, stopped. "And now your supper is cold! I'll bring you some more cocoa."

It was his turn to look up guiltily. Apologetically he said: "Please forget that benefaction! Cocoa subdues me as nothing else can! Here is a bribe——" he put his book into her hand. "Scupoli for the rest of the way! And you won't forget, will you, that in breaking down one's natural inertia one sometimes goes to the other extreme, and becomes over scrupulous. It is always easier to veer towards exaggeration, than to steer a middle course. We suspect the tranquil, balanced course, because we fail in trust. Sometimes too"— he glanced away, "we are punishing ourselves. This also should be left to God. We must forgive ourselves, as we forgive others—and be as happy as we can."

"That's true, that's true!" she cried. "Prayer began to die in me after Gerda left. I avoided happiness. It seemed too good to be true, too easy to be right. I didn't deserve it."

"Exactly. Your gratitude for what you felt was undeserved would have broken your heart. And when one's heart is broken by gratitude in this way—there is no pride left to protect one. One does not know what is going to rise within one, and walk off with one's life—as an offering."

"Ah, yes," she said, as she turned to go, "ah, yes!"

At the door, he called cheerfully across the empty corridor: "Remember: the next arrows might be from above. *Watch!*"

It was three years before she finally overcame languor in the prayer he had prescribed—the prayer that left her cold! The prayer that was so inevitably to reveal her aversion for the masses, and all that this implied in egoism.

As Monsignor had indicated, she veered first to one extreme, and then the other—in this painful retrieving of the particular in the general. In fact, it was almost comical to come through so much buffeting only to realize that moderation was best!

But as weather sometimes seems to clear permanently

after a storm, her days now went steadily by. Her work at the quiet, luxurious Wigmore Hotel was simply that of a cleaner, but she was well-paid, and the hours excellent. The evening tasks at the Henrietta Nursing Home were much less menial. Matron had become a friend.

Once more her health improved. She was better able to accept Gerda's continued silence, for the long-expected west-end work had again failed to materialize. And Gerda on successful tours in South Africa, and the Colonies had forgotten.

A dull, pedestrian period, for gone was all inner bliss. But she read Scupoli, and, in painstaking obedience tried to follow Monsignor's indications.

One step was consolidated, however. Acquiescence might be to suffer still—but it was to suffer without fear.

Early in 1930, Monsignor's prophecy came true:
You will be astonished——

One day in intercession, she had a sense of expansion that was like a breath bearing her beyond herself. Yet such yearning went with this, that she knew the unknown multitudes had at last become her promised land . . . their very number now the measure of her indebtedness. Her poor prayer, so blind, so full of effort, had finally returned, dove-like, with its olive leaf. Her cold heart knew itself to be at last near in far-ness. And in this dedication to the impersonal, she had her first warm inkling of infinity as a familiar fact. She was down to earth at last, and this too was holy ground.

Then almost before she had time to marvel—Gerda came back.

By accident . . . which might have been a warning!

On a late January afternoon, towards sunset, they met by chance in Regent Street. The day had rained itself out, and although heavy drops still scattered, the sky was now serene, and of a pale, transparent yellow, like a false dawn, as the last low cloudlets vanished in water.

"Gerda!"

"Andra——"

In the soft gloom of the street, both paled. There were further exclamations, a convulsive kiss, some tears, then a good deal of nervous laughter.

Would Andra, her own dear Sunshine, ever forgive her? Gerda felt a perfect swine. But she'd only been back two months, and positively had not sat down *once* . . . for in February she was opening as second-lead at the Regency in *Damask Rose*! The stage-box was at last at Andra's command! Had Andra had her postcard from Durban . . . or was it Sydney? Gerda was literally in sackcloth and ashes. Meantime Andra *must* come home to supper. To prove that Gerda was forgiven! Gerda had a flat in St. John's Wood. Looked better than it was, but quite a nice old hen went with it—to cook and look after Gerda. No rehearsal, as to-night was Saturday. They could talk, and talk, and talk——

And in Gerda's spacious but haphazard flat, Gerda talked.

Gerda was giving a birthday party next week. To celebrate *Damask Rose*. There would be at least thirty guests. Most of them *pros*. But Andra simply must come. A buffet-supper starting at nine. Andra would meet Gerda's young man—a bit of a bookworm this time, the poetical type (don't shriek) but Gerda had almost made up her mind to reach out a boarding-house arm, and hook him home! In fact there were several Desirables that Andra must vet!

Gerda continued to talk.

Sunshine must come back to lunch to-morrow. Gerda just couldn't wait to see her again and Gerda was then free.

Sunshine! The old pet name came pat as ever, but perhaps

with more precision. Gerda's poise was now the finished article. Every sentence shone—clear cut. She could not have been more cordial.

The street was regained before Andra discovered that Gerda had failed to ask for her new address—or to make any inquiry as to Sunshine's present state.

But perhaps to-morrow?

To-morrow . . . Gerda forgot again.

Was it possible that Gerda's own circle alone had any reality for her?

And on Tuesday Andra dressed with care, but a little less pleasure for Gerda's party.

Sighing, she told herself that her hands were to blame. No matter how carefully she washed, there was always now, ingrained, a definite grayness around her knuckles. They were certainly clean, but they didn't look it! Discouraging.

Happily her black, close-fitting afternoon frock still looked fresh, so rarely was it worn. Seven years old—but its perfect cut almost suggested a coming vogue! It had the decorous yet romantic air of a Victorian riding habit. Her hand hovering over her trinket box, she picked out Aunt Edith's cameo brooch. This was all it needed.

Heartened, she smiled into the mirror. Beneath her honey-coloured hair, her face was paler than usual, but her blue eyes in this light were dark as violets. Her face and figure, at least, were still presentable!

To-night, another servant opened Gerda's door.

The party was at its height, for Andra's work at the Nursing Home had kept her late.

Gerda had spoken of thirty guests. There seemed to be double that number milling in the large lounge, which, massed with spring flowers and with a log-fire blazing, was heavy with mimosa.

So long was it since Andra had been to a party that she

felt confused. She had no idea that these were now so noisy, so full of cigarette smoke. It was worse than any studio party. Could this be gaiety—new-style? The women were certainly fashionably dressed, and the men smart enough, but the dense atmosphere seemed about as festive as a saloon-bar on a heavy night. Or was she growing old?

At once Gerda, in white, lovely and lustreless as a gardenia, hailed her with open arms.

"Darling—at last! F.P. come here at once! Now Sunshine, you'll see why I've christened him F.P. Isn't he just utterly Father's Pride? No Mother's Darling about this hero!"

Gerda was ushering forward a formidably tall man.

Andra looked up at him. Her face stiffened. Her smile became grimace.

With sinister clarity she saw Philip Riberac glaring down at her.

"Our natural enemy, Sunshine! A man's man."

"Ha!" exclaimed Riberac, in cynical reprobation.

"Now, isn't this wonderful?" cried Gerda. "My two specials meet! You must get to know each other right away. F.P. this is Sunshine. I haven't had time yet to tell you how wonderful she is—but you can see for yourself! Andra, here he is! We met quite romantically in Father's bookshop at Cambridge. He picked me up, the wretch, with a volume of Latin Love Lyrics. Positively F.P. I don't believe you ever paid Father! Now, champagne for Andra—here you are, darling. And I leave you two—to pull me to pieces."

Andra raised the glass, and drank it like water.

A force, fierce as hate, but cold as ice had already come to her rescue.

Pride fully investing her, she heard herself say lightly: "How do you do? Gerda has talked so much about you——"

"For God's sake," he said hoarsely, "let's get out of this!"

"But I've only just come." To her own merciless ear she sounded almost arch. "May I have some more champagne?"

It took him several minutes to get this.

By the time he next reached her—at the window, where there was some air, she was completely master of the situation. The crowded guests, momently jostling them, were her greatest advantage.

"For six years," he began, his voice rasping with anger, as he edged another couple off, "I've been searching for you. This is not the place to tell you what I think of the scandalous way you've treated me."

"It certainly is not!" brightly she agreed.

Darkly he glowered, but in the press of people he had again to lower his voice.

"Almost incredible . . ." he muttered, "that it should be *here* I discover you!" Then in a more normal tone he added, "I first met Gerda a month ago—in Cambridge."

Politely she replied: "This is such a small world. Almost too small at times. Now, I first met Gerda over five years ago——"

But he had passed a hand of relief through his hair, as if he did not hear her. "Anyway . . . it's all over now!"

"It certainly is," glassily she smiled. She was managing so well that she suspected the champagne. In challenge to herself she looked full at him.

His wine was untouched, he was staring into space, his eyes snapping in derision. "I expected the usual ecstatic female friend, *Sunshine!* And I find you. My God—another of her banalities!"

Swiftly she said: "I prefer these to disloyalties."

"What the devil do you mean?" violently his mood veered. "I owe her no loyalty. In fact her father has my sympathy. You're completely at sea in these deductions."

Calmly she replied: "They are my own. I am quite satisfied."

"Then you're pathological . . . which I've suspected ever since you first ran off."

"What an odd reproach," said Andra in a small clear voice, "from one who never anchors!"

Hotly he stared—nonplussed for a second. Where had she learnt such unlikely slickness.

"I've never seen you glitter before. In you its meretricious."

"I'm sorry," she said indifferently. "All I can run to these days!"

"*God*!" he exclaimed, "what does anything matter now? *I've found you again.* Forgive my anger. I'm beside myself with relief——"

To her horror, he flung one arm convulsively around her shoulders. "Wait here," he ordered. "I'll see Gerda at once, and make our excuses——"

"One moment!" sharply she stopped him. "This is my secret that you're making off with! And unknown to any of my friends. I forbid you to tell Gerda one word."

For the first time in their experience, implacably she outfaced him.

Glaring at her, he hesitated.

"F.P.," called Gerda . . . "where on earth are you? Come and meet my favourite aunt!"

Precipitately Andra turned, and plunging into the party crowd was instantly lost.

In the cloakroom, she retrieved her coat, made a conventional excuse to the old maid—and was gone.

Swiftly she crossed the hall.

The hired man-servant politely opened the door.

Rather than wait for the elevator, she passed quickly down the stairs, and out of the building.

The present moment was her only danger, for no one had her address.

But the moment, like herself, passed unseen. So too did the exhilaration of the champagne.

She found herself walking foolishly fast in the direction of Regent's Park—alone with these ruinous words: *We met quite romantically. He picked me up, the wretch, with a volume of Latin Love Lyrics!*

Escape was again her only hope . . .

Now, five years later in the green twilight of this narrow town garden, the case against Philip wavered for the first time—in a disconcerting way.

It had not been his words that morning, although his incisive voice always managed to ransack her heart.

He had looked thin, and rather ill . . . yet somehow younger. Was this due to that new uncertainty in his eyes —a flinching expression at odds with his drastic manner?

No, that must have been some nervous spasm. He was both ruthless and acquisitive. It was simply her withdrawal that had again made her desirable.

But ten years was a long time for any man to persist— even at intervals? He too might have changed?

No, no, this was the old fascination working in her again —the excitement that left one senselessly longing for more and more of the disperser of one's peace! He had merely gone to her unaccustomed head again.

And to-night she had Gerda to face for the first time since that disastrous party . . . the party that was to have been Gerda's celebration.

Yet nothing had come of Gerda's romance with Philip . . . or as far as Andra knew.

Jubilee week-end! It was proving instead a penance, a scourge! And now the theatre loomed.

So still had she sat, and for so long, that, in rising a blackbird flew out of the bush below her hand, with the whirr of a fan flirted in open affront.

Not for nothing had the garden grown steadily cooler. The afternoon had passed only too quickly. Evening was already upon her.

It was almost time to go . . .

Saturday Evening . . . seven-fifteen

The Regency was packed to capacity. Andra's rejected ticket proved to have been an early booking—her seat was right in the centre of the front row of the dress-circle.

The theatre, re-decorated for the Jubilee festival wore an unfamiliar air. The old sulphur and gilt walls, draped by red velvet hangings had vanished in cream and gold, with delicate lilac curtains. The interior looked larger, more remote, and yet less mysterious. But the orchestra, in tuning-up, was the spark that set the tight-packed audience on fire.

In her varied experience with Punchie, Andra had never known a house as electric with excitement as this.

Suddenly, with a feeling of wonder, almost of incredulity, she realized that this was all for Gerda!

Gerda, after a gruelling struggle of years had at last enslaved London!

Andra's breath quickened, her eyes grew moist as she waited. Merely a musical comedy show *My Love, My Lady* might be, but more than gifts and ability fed this anticipation. Ten years ago at the Angel, Mrs. Ellis had summed it up: "That girl's got command!" Gerda was of the enduring stuff of which legends are made——

Oddly exhausted, Andra leant back in her seat.

A tuneful, challenging overture with nostalgia in discreet abeyance!

Insidiously the atmosphere of the expectant theatre—its restless vitality had begun to work upon her.

With something like dismay she realized how solitary her own life was, how austere in its loneliness.

Should she telephone Philip on her return to-night, instead of to-morrow, Sunday?

Sooner or later the call must be made. It might as well be sooner——

Alas, it must now depend on when she got back from Camden Town.

Oh, Letty, she breathed . . . Letty, Letty!

Hopelessly, it was now borne in upon her that she had not changed, and never would. The old dream of progress through virtue had, of course, died when she first aided Gerda. She had known then that if the demand were made, she must always respond. All she could hope for then, and since, was to hold on through prayer. But in prayer at least she still had a place—and a joyful one.

Yet whether or not her own salvation had hung on it, she would have had to help Letty—in the present misguided way.

Yet now there was no conflict, as there had been after Gerda's case. To-day her suffering was of a very different sort. A recognition that for her there could never be a short cut. Each day she began afresh. That was what it amounted to. The long way round was hers. Not the endearing approach through goodness or beauty. If she were ever to advance at all, it could only be through truth. And oh, how strange that this wry road was the very way to which her sentiment and weakness had laid her open!

Abruptly the house darkened. Its pastel prettiness vanished. Earlier mystery reclaimed it, as washed by shadow, flushed from the footlights, it stirred like a shell with the bodiless murmur of its own awe.

On this with-drawn breath, ageless as spent seas confined in memory, the curtain rose——

Rose to reveal the prologue of an enchanting operetta— with the romantic young man asleep after his glass-too-many, in open defiance of his parents' choice: Miss Penny

Plain, *Wholesome she may be, and homely she is, But not for me!*
Dream revealing, of course, his chase down the ages. In
Arcady first, for the shepherd's Nymph, then for the Sorceress
of the middle ages, and lastly for that costly modern jewel
—Miss Pearl of Paris—— ... the whole simply a vehicle for
Gerda's versatility, her voice, her grace, her loveliness.

One glance, and Gerda was again Andra's idol, and
Andra's alone. ... Not a jot did it matter either, that everyone in the audience shared the same illusion—for this was
recaptured youth.

The felicity of the first act, the witchery of the second,
and the comedy of the third held Andra spell-bound, for
Gerda who showed so little humour in daily life, abounded
with it on these boards! And the climax in which as the
homely maiden she appeared finally as Penny Plain to rescue
the hero from Twopence Coloured brought down the house
again. This was charm triumphant over beauty, banality
transformed, and the audience exulted in the miracle.

As the lights went up at the first interval, Andra saw,
with a sense of unreality, an attendant edging her way
towards her.

With the festive smile that the most ordinary theatre
attendant boasts, she said in a low voice:

"Miss Hood? Miss Rush will see you in her dressing-
room after the performance. She cannot make it before."

Andra sat gazing into the gray blank of the Safety
Curtain, which in dividing the front from the back of the
house bore that cryptic reminder in large letters: *For Thine
Especial Safety.*

Well, perhaps the encounter was better then, than at an
interval. Might cordiality be gleaned from this arrangement? Fervently she hoped so!

Abstractedly she glanced down into the dense gathering.
Few people had left their seats for this interval. Nearly all

had remained to enjoy the spectacle that they themselves presented, and, in this fevered buzzing of an over-turned hive, were noisily discussing the operetta, their own affairs.

Suddenly her heart seemed to draw up—and then bolt with her.

In the fourth row of the stalls, centre gangway, with an empty fauteuil beside him, sat Philip facing the empty stage.

Philip, who was even now anxiously awaiting her telephone call!

With a little gasp, as conclusive as laughter, she sat back out of sight, shading her eyes with her hand.

Her own pique was almost as much of a shock as his indifference!

Well, this left them both exactly where they had been all along.

How silent was the solitary life, but after all how safe!

Her racing heart slackened, flagged, and fell into a painful jog-trot.

Nor did she again glance into the stalls.

Where Philip spent the long interval was no business of hers, for in another sense she now knew exactly where the three of them were.

Stiffened by this shock, she felt, curiously enough, better able to face Gerda.

Yet when it came, the dressing-room door did so too abruptly.

A short, stout dresser with a bland smile and reticent eyes opened the door, and at once Andra heard Gerda announce:

"All right, Ellen—you can go now. I'll manage." A voice metallic in its precision—no, its impatience.

The limited floor-space was massed with floral baskets, the centre table banked by bouquets. Through yet another door

Gerda sat superbly before her toilet table, in a crisply tailored Shantung dressing gown, her face already freed of make-up.

In the mirror she watched Andra's hesitant approach.

"Sit down," she ordered, and then turned intolerantly upon her. "Well, what's all this about?"

Andra swallowed. "Fifty pounds," she said with an effort. "I'm sorry, but I have to ask for it now."

"And why, may I ask, should I be expected to hand out such a sum?"

"I thought you might help—as once you were helped."

"Thank you for nothing!" Gerda's neck flushed. "A damned tactless remark. I still don't see the obligation on my part."

"Well . . . you needed it once."

"Have you come back, after an absence of years, to break this sad news?"

"If I must. A friend of mine is now in the same terrible position—and I can do nothing this time."

"So you think *I* should?" irascibly Gerda picked up a puff and powdered her face and neck. "You certainly have some nerve. And when you remember that I paid you back at once——"

"You paid back ten pounds," said Andra in a small, thin voice. "I lent you sixty pounds."

Gerda ceased to powder, although she continued to stare at her own reflection. Animosity filtered from a face in which anxiety slowly dawned, like a sort of paralysis.

Incredible to relate, Gerda with time had duped herself that this debt was cancelled.

Hurriedly Andra averted her gaze.

Silently Gerda opened the dressing table drawer, and drew out an envelope.

Frigidly she said, "I had it for you in any case."

"I'm glad of that," said Andra more clearly, but her hand trembled as she took the money.

Strength had drained alarmingly from her in this punishing scene. We love each other, she told herself, that's why it's being so dreadful. Nothing we can say or do will ever alter that. Our love is indestructible, that's why it's almost finished us. We're too small for it.

"And when we're at it," pursued Gerda, "I'd like to tell you how damned peculiar I thought your disappearance from my party. You've such a good memory. That episode should be fresh."

"I simply took a leaf out of your book for once. And why not?"

"Because it didn't suit *me* at that time. You explode my friendship with Riberac, and then you vanish. I required an explanation. I still do."

"He could have given you that more suitably."

Gerda laughed shortly. "What self-importance! But you were always on the priggish side. Now, to hear you, one would think that there had been an *affaire* between you! However, I happen to know that whatever may have been the link, it certainly was not *that*!"

"Then there's no more to be said."

"Oh, yes, there is—don't be so smug! When I challenged Riberac he simply said that he had a considerable respect for you. That puts your past connection on an understandable basis—but it doesn't explain his dropping me like a hot brick from that date. Your disappearance, coupled with this, made me wonder how much you'd told him about *me*."

"What I told him?" Andra repeated dully, "it must have been plain to you that Philip and I had not met for years."

"That wouldn't prevent you seeing him again. Now, would it, my dear friend? You're the only person who knows my . . . my whole story. He wouldn't have flung me over for anything less than that. Without a word too——"

But Andra had risen. "If you believe me capable of that, Gerda, nothing I can say will reach you. I'll go before you break my heart."

Quickly she crossed the floor.

"Andra," called Gerda angrily, "come back at once! You can't go like that. You're behaving abominably."

Andra turned.

Gerda had faced round from the mirror, her cheeks flushed. "I'd completely forgotten about the money. Being a debt I mean. It upset me to be reminded. So I didn't care what I said——" she broke off, and added resentfully, "I've always been mean about money—well, *careful*. You know that."

Andra put out her hand. This painful avowal had bound them once more together.

Abruptly Gerda turned her head away—aloofly, distantly she began to weep.

Andra, holding her hand, stifled an impulse to put her arm round her. "It's all right, Gerda," she said gently, carefully, "we're through the worst now."

"We were that a long time ago. You were wonderful."

"No, Gerda, this has been the worst—for me, I mean. But it's over. Things will now clear between us."

"Yes, yes . . ." Gerda turned a recovered face. "It's been a kind of nightmare to-night. What does Riberac matter anyway? He's all over and done with—pompous ass. You're back again. For good this time."

"That's not important," said Andra rising. "But thank you, Gerda. Perhaps. One never knows."

"Of course you're back! I know it sounds ridiculous, for I really *am* fond of you, but the fact is, Sunshine, I don't think I've ever *realized* you till to-night. On your own, I mean. Now I know how much I've missed you. There's something *genuine* about you."

"Darling!" Andra turned to smile again. This time she had finally reached the door through its flowery avenue. She opened it, and went down the corridor, her eyes wet.

At the end of the passage, compelled, she glanced back.

Gerda's door flew open . . . Gerda was rushing along the corridor like a girl again, vehement, vibrant.

"Andra stop! You idiot, what a fright you've given me. . . . I've nearly lost you again! Only this instant did it dawn—*what the hell is your address?* Islington is all I can remember now . . ."

Saturday . . . midnight

Later than it should have been! Guiltily, Andra rang Letty's bell——

There was no answer.

She rang again, and yet again.

Was it possible that poor Letty, worn out with anxiety, had fallen asleep?

Andra lifted the letter-box flap and peered within.

The flat was in darkness.

"Letty!" she called, and more loudly yet, "Letty . . . *Letty*!"

The hollow silence of an uninhabited dwelling spread vacantly towards her.

From the flat below footsteps could be heard padding upstairs. She had awakened the place!

With a sense of foreboding, Andra watched the tousled gray head of a woman emerge from below, a woman with an overcoat above pyjamas.

"Are you the friend?" this person said.

The familiar words struck a chill. For a moment Andra hesitated.

"Miss Hood?" insisted the newcomer, holding out an envelope. "Miss Galbraith left this for you before she went off—in case you got back first."

She padded downstairs again.

Hurriedly Andra tore open the envelope.

Letty's cursive script raced across the paper. Andra, by the light of one gas jet, had the greatest difficulty in deciphering this. Letty, it seemed, had gone unexpectedly to the Savoy, of all places. Solange's father had asked them both. Letty was taking the tube though it meant evening dress, but Solange had promised to drive her back. She would be home by eleven certain. It was only dinner and cabaret. But Letty had felt so utterly miserable, she knew this would cheer her up. Or at least pass the blasted time. Andra would understand.

Poor Letty indeed!

Andra stood till one o'clock on the upper landing, in the spectral light of the stair jet, which drearily suggested a third-class carriage passing through endless tunnels, except that the teaspoonful of condensation was missing from this globe.

At ten minutes past one, after a second's hesitation, she dropped Gerda's fifty pounds through the letter-box.

It was definitely too bad of Letty, she decided, as she went downstairs. To-night of all nights too!

But as she regained the street, she paused again, glancing up and down its length.

It was also very unlike Letty. She was invariably punctual.

Could anything have happened—or gone wrong? Solange's father, Lord Netley would know. His number must be in the telephone book. But he knew nothing of Letty's difficulties. Impossible to telephone there! And Andra had never known Solange's married name. Only that Solange, who had separated from her husband, lived in a flat in Kensington——

No, she must possess herself in patience.

What a day it had been! And now the last bus had gone——

With a sigh Andra prepared to walk the three miles, and more, from Camden Town home . . .

Sunday Morning . . . nine o'clock

She awoke with a violent start to hear the telephone bell ringing like an alarum downstairs.

The room was bathed in sunshine. She must have over-slept after that disabling walk last night——

Snatching a wrap, she ran downstairs.

But as she reached the telephone, the bell cascaded into silence.

The grandfather clock struck nine.

She stared at it in dismay. Philip's threat was tolling forth!

She must telephone the Club at once.

But even as she put out her hand, the telephone rang again.

Lifting the receiver, she heard a woman's voice exclaim: "Miss Hood! Miss Hood? Oh, thank God, I've made you hear at last! Solange speaking . . . yes, yes. Don't worry more than you can help—but a ghastly thing has happened! No, no, she never reached the Savoy. She was in evening dress, you know. Well, going down the escalator stairs, she tripped—the long skirt caught. There was quite a crowd behind her. All rushing down. They fell on top of her, and were swept to the bottom. Her dress was ripped right off, for nobody did the right thing till it was too late. If only the others had not fallen on her, it wouldn't have been quite so bad. But she was knocked senseless—and taken to St. Jude's Hospital. As soon as she came round, she gave my number, and I went at once. Miss Hood, she's had an awful night. But she's going to be all right, although she's

239

badly bruised. I've seen the doctor, and he's promised that. She'll have to be there for at least a week. Yes . . . yes, she'd like to see you. Three o'clock this afternoon. Hello, hello, can you hear me? I must not say too much . . . but perhaps you'll guess what's really happened when I say *it's all over*. Yes, yes . . . the money won't be needed after all. Poor Letty——"

Unsteadily Andra sat down by the telephone.

Poor Letty indeed! What a fierce rescue.

Irrelevantly, unsuitably, an old saying flashed across her mind: " *Take what you want, said God. But pay for it.*"

Letty had certainly paid.

She had a swift, satirical picture too of that costly fifty pounds sunk in an empty flat. Needless now.

Yet how much good that visit to the theatre had done—and how much damage!

She glanced at the clock—almost nine-fifteen.

Instantly she rang his Club.

The Head Porter himself replied, pontifical as ever. Dr. Riberac had left the Club at nine precisely. The Club regretted that it could not say when Dr. Riberac would be back. Was there any message?

Defeated she hung up.

Was he even now *en route* to the Director, as he had threatened?

Scarcely! The visit to *My Love, My Lady* on the very night that he expected an urgent call suggested a definite lessening of tension! Andra had nothing to fear——

Certainly no further softening of her own heart towards him, as yesterday in the garden.

Alone now in the drowsy house, Sunday calm marooning her with the inescapable, she knew why.

She was consumed by jealousy . . . and of Gerda whom she loved. Ever since that disastrous party five years ago this had been the case. Her own swift withdrawal from Philip then, had only been a means of fostering self-importance!

Realization faced her at last in her own image. A likeness transformed out of recognition. And she was horrified by its disclosure.

Abruptly she rose from the telephone.

She was once more back in her own life—safe, secure from him, but with this devastating knowledge, which now laid waste the day.

Sunday Morning . . . nine-forty-five

The Head Porter, with relief, saw Dr. Riberac depart at nine. Never before in his experience had there been panic over the parcel post in these precincts. Unashamed panic at that! Occasionally, an amorous Member might show anxiety over the letter-post. One or two had been known to become feverish over the non-arrival of a telegram. Cables were a rarer complication, during which temperatures might rise. But to pine for the parcel post in this bare-faced way was just plain childish. Yet he would not deny that the situation itself had livened up the week-end considerably. The Club tended to torpor on a Sunday. Already the kitchen had put a bit of money on Monday morning's possibilities. . . . At nine-fifteen there had been, unusually enough, a woman's voice on the phone, for the Doctor. The Head Porter couldn't place it . . . yet it rang a bell. No name left, either! Well, Dr. Riberac had now lost the lady too . . .

And with this fact well in mind, Riberac turned rapidly into Madeira Park Road, Hampstead—somnolent in the Sunday stillness that follows breakfast and precedes Church. Already the cloudless day threatened to be another scorcher —a smell of tar rising even now from the blistered road.

It was, of course, a chance in a hundred——

But *Kidderpore* stood open—the padlock off the gate, the windows wide upon the trim, green garden.

His luck had turned again! And on a morning so still, so hot that the crowing of a cock, the barking of a dog were twice as loud as on any week-day.

Beyond reason now, he hurried down the path, and rang the bell like an alarum.

It was opened at once, so speedily that Riberac, pale with hurry and heat, hesitated.

A small frail man stood there, transparent as some skeleton leaf that yet bears etched within its veins the total image of its tree.

"Dr. Riberac?" said the small man.

Astonished, Riberac replied, "You are expecting me?"

"For years," the other said. "Come in. You're late. I'm late . . . but possibly that gives more time for breakfast."

With a feeling, half dream, half delight, Riberac followed him through a shadowed hall, into a sun-flecked garden room at the back. There was a delectable aroma of coffee, and breakfast was already set.

"Bachelors," said Major Treves, "who have forgotten how to live, sometimes learn to eat." Almost absently he set down some extra china for his guest, and uncovered freshly made toast, cold ham, and french mustard. There was also a dish of lettuce, and a bowl of fruit upon the table. "Begin . . ." he said. "You're tired, and so am I. I got back late last night. This will restore us."

Amicably they ate and drank, exchanging the merest monosyllables—as if they'd spent a life-time, *vis à vis* . . . Riberac found that he was famished—much to his surprise.

Opposite sat his strange host, who did not seem surprised at all. A face inscrutable with calm. A man with a close-clipped moustache as sallow as his leathery skin, on which were harshly rutted lines of authority. But the eyes gazed mildly, as if a growing tolerance were at home there. Yet the hard-bitten features were less a mask than a guard. Tradition lent this visage familiarity, but discipline had barred and bolted it. Riberac looked at it with respect. Rectitude alone was apparent here.

"Yes," said Major Treves, as if in answer to an unspoken

query. "I didn't see Andra for years either. A complete cut-away. But I'm glad to say that for the past five, we've met regularly. So I know a certain amount about you both! As soon as she saw my collection, some years back, she told me you were very dear to her."

Dear to her! The words were balm to Riberac.

Aloud he said: "What collection, sir?"

"This," said the other. He led the way on to a small verandah where two deck chairs awaited them, and lifting what appeared to be an album from a side table, laid it before his guest.

Opening it, Riberac found to his astonishment that he had before him a formidable collection of his own press notices, starting from the outset of his career.

"Always been fascinated by archaeology," said Major Treves. "Cigarette? They're at your elbow. . . . In fact wanted to make a job of it. But my parents had different ideas—and I complied, for one reason and another. In an army career, my insignificant size was a certain disadvantage, so vanity——" he gave a short, bark-like laugh, "may have had something to do with filial obedience! We are fearfully and wonderfully constructed . . . or perhaps I should say *constricted*! Puns inevitable with my generation . . . but both will pass, ha ha!" Cheerfully he ran the extinguished match through his fingers. "I filed your first press notices, as notes on archaeology are my hobby. But I would scarcely have devoted a book to yours alone had it not been for one curious factor—I hope you will forgive a digression at this point. May I remind you of Isaiah's pithy words? *And though the Lord give you the bread of adversity and the water of affliction, yet shall not thy teachers be hidden any more, but thine eyes shall see thy teachers.* . . . With age, Dr. Riberac, most of us begin to perceive more——" he chuckled. "Adversity is a meticulous instructor. But it was another man's difficulties, tenaciously met, that proved to be my liberal education. Some careers," he tapped the press-cutting book, "are signal in this respect. Achievement time and again flawed by bad luck! Genius itself failing to come into its own in the possessor's lifetime. Success repeatedly falling short of its true meed, while lesser men romp home with the spoils," again he paused.

Dr. Riberac continued to sit silent.

"And yet it was your set-backs that first appealed to my imagination. These, and the way in which you have persisted. Gradually, very gradually, of course, the public are tumbling to this too. Your one bit of luck—if I may say so—when the Vaucluse Angel literally fell into your hands has ever since been hailed as your triumph! Interesting how these things sometimes speak for themselves. But take the Eldersley Excavation, almost the only one that was a sensational success for you: would it be an outrage to ask now for the true story of the final calamity, which nearly cost your life . . . the explanation that the newspapers didn't get?"

"Not at all," Dr. Riberac laughed softly, maliciously. "Eldersley financed the excavation. He's probably the ablest amateur on the field. But, as you know, it's the spade-work in any profession that is its foundation and its discipline. Patience in fact gives insight, judgment. At the last moment, with the find of the century within our grasp, Eldersley lost his head. The treasures of a kingdom lay around us, in the soundless dust of four thousand years. Eldersley advanced first with his candle, and before I could stop him, had bent over the royal coffin. In a flash, the bitumen was ablaze. Not only were the other objects wildly inflammable, but the chamber was fanned by the corridor draught. We were trapped by flame. If I hadn't had to drag Eldersley out, I believe I might have murdered him! As it was, I took a

wrong turning in the maze, which ultimately saved us—
although those who escaped first took long enough to
re-discover us."

Again Major Treves gave his brief bark—this time almost
soundlessly. "The last story for the popular press.
Assuredly."

"Talking of the popular press," said Riberac, "yesterday
I bought the Standish book, but find I can't face it . . . till
I've made my peace with Andra."

"Quite a sound decision," opined the other. "The book
might prove confusing. Romantic persons like Standish
are a source of bedevilment to purblind realists like us. We
suspect their fanfare. Yet they often go into action itself
without a single signal. In this way they steal a march—
sometimes the day itself. Artists like Standish, moreover,
understand women. And women appreciate this. Yet
happily for the rest of us some women cannot love them.
You have heard, have you not, of Andra's prevailing passion?"

Riberac stiffened. "No . . . I have not."

"Surely you can't have forgotten? Joy everlasting! This
is the dear girl's illusion. The aim and object of that ardent
creature is, of course, freedom. This may be the reason why
she never loved Standish. You assessed her too, just as he
did. But you, I imagine, were wider of the mark. With you
she could afford to be indulgent. With you she had room to
grow, for the sky is literally her limit."

"With me she starved."

"Oh, I know you quarrelled. I've heard no details, but I
gather more than she imagines. You hit her on the raw.
Standish would have been wiser."

"For an angel," said Riberac grimly, "she is extremely
unforgiving."

"You're telling me!" murmured Major Treves. "But she
wasn't always an angel. She was once a woman, and it may

take time to double the *rôle*. Quite an undertaking after all. We must remember she's been through a great deal. Much of which we can't even guess. That's where a fellow like Standish has the advantage. Would you say that you, personally, had much imagination?"

"So much," said Riberac sombrely, "that I scarcely ever use it. Too damned painful."

"Dear me," said Major Treves, "you're cleverer than I thought! Perhaps you've been too clever—it's only a suggestion. As to Andra—the explanation of her obstinacy is probably simpler than we guess. I feel pretty sure that the loving life is the good life, and in that sense a truly religious one. This being so, I can't help feeling it's a pity that you forfeited so much solicitude. I have your interest at heart!"

"'Pon my soul," Riberac exclaimed, "I believe you have—incredible as this is! Possibly then . . . you'll help me now? I warn you in advance that my request is highly improper. I want Andra's address, which she declines to give me."

"*So*," Major Treves intoned, his gaze reflective, "you propose that crime should now cement our friendship? Well, why not? Periodically, I confess, virtue palls upon me. I might have made a tolerable archaeologist, but I have never subscribed to the myth that I am cut out for the Trappist's vow of silence. Philip Riberac, I think it's high time that your luck changed. Don't forget my address. And here is hers——"

Sunday Morning . . . eleven-thirty

Buoyantly Riberac regained the crest of the hill, and set off downhill across the Heath, its rolling heights now sandily bleached by the sun. On his left, Caenwood's trees shimmered in their shade. All else was palpable blue sky, blurred like a pastel on the horizon where, to his right, the distant thread of the Thames glittered to vanish.

To-day those wide acres of dry grass bore a salt odour of the sea, but impervious to the midday blaze, he strode on victoriously.

He was, in fact, slightly intoxicated by his recent good fortune.

Again he sensed a pattern in these events, as when first he glimpsed the marble Dancing Girl. But that had been on Friday—a lifetime ago.

Now the design was settling smoothly into place. This was the authentic and triumphant present!

Andra was almost within reach again.

That was enough.

Major Treves had his blessing, now and henceforth! Indeed, his host had done more for him than he could well assess at present. And his respect for Treves was only equalled by the sense of compassion which the small, frail man had roused in him. The latter was an emotion so unusual in himself, that to-day for the first time he realized its novelty. Without the slightest invasion of privacy, he felt nearer this once-met man than he had yet been to another. He was at a loss to explain this curious experience, this strange sympathy. The old gentleman had awakened an understanding in him that he had never felt for Andra. But then, of course, woman was man's natural enemy——

Nevertheless, peace with this foe was an imperative.

He stopped short in his headlong pace——

Now he came to think of it, the only asperity Andra had ever shown was once when he had carelessly dismissed the subject of his mother. Quite early on, she had asked point-blank if he were a Protestant.

"My mother was Protestant," he replied. "I was brought up in her faith. My father was completely indifferent in such matters, my mother regrettably sentimental. I natur-ally remain critical."

Stiffly Andra had said: "You shouldn't speak of your mother like that! It's all wrong."

Startled he had admitted: "You are quite right. I apologize."

And her silence had aloofly confirmed the unusual occasion.

Again he quickened his pace—only to remember that she was probably still at morning service. The soft blue air above this arena of little green hills was distantly pierced by innumerable spires.

Well, she would find him on the doorstep on her return— as once so long ago on a hot June day he had found the Vicar at Kew . . .

His *second* visit, the Vicar had stressed.

Riberac, nonplussed, had bidden the stranger enter. The man who had a pleasant smile, seemed to expect it. His thin face had been pale with heat, his shoes thick with dust. Andra had gone to shop, and Riberac, secretly cursing, had brought iced coffee from the refrigerator.

"Most welcome," the Vicar assured him, adding that to-day he had missed luncheon!

To miss one's midday meal struck Riberac as madness, and he said so, leaving his guest in the cool little drawing-room.

An omelette was Riberac's only culinary accomplishment, but such was his ease with this *chef-d'oeuvre* that he found ample time to wonder what the devil a clergyman was doing in their house. Earlier, Andra had admitted that in his absence she sometimes went to Church on Sunday evenings—an odd, yet harmless foible for a modern miss. Ardently she had added: "If only you'd come *once*—then I could always picture you beside me." Agreeably enough he had complied on one occasion, much as he might have gone to a museum or any concert she selected. The only thing that had interested him in that particular service had been a hymn taken from 12th century Latin. But the translation was inadequate and so had slightly irritated him:

> *O come, Thou Key of David, come*
> *And open wide our heavenly home:*
> *Make safe the way that leads on high,*
> *And close the path to misery.*

Dishing the Vicar's omelette, he suddenly remembered that he *had* seen the man before. After that service he had stood in a white surplice at the Church door, and, to Riberac's surprise, had wrung his hand with these words: "Glad to welcome you."

At the time, this cordiality had disconcerted Riberac. Andra had been warned that there must be no further attendance. "We must avoid a false impression."

Hurriedly, guiltily, Andra had agreed.

And now here the man was, devouring Riberac's omelette as if he had not eaten for days.

The omelette, served on a kitchen tray, with the loaf beside it, and quarter of a pound of butter, was pronounced the finest in the Vicar's experience. Men, he ventured to think, were the only cooks! His own dear wife, a soul of rare spiritual quality, took no interest whatsoever in what she ate. Sometimes he thought this a pity.

Riberac forbore to say what he thought of such an un-natural female—but only just, for on the Vicar adding that they had no family, Riberac retorted "Ha!" with such acid attention that the Vicar was as startled as he was touched by this concentration on his needs.

At once he broached the reason of his call. He was here to throw himself on his kind host's mercy. In fact, a state of emergency existed at St. Anselm's!

By the time Andra had returned, it was to find that Riberac had agreed to accompany the Choir Boys' outing next day.

"I look upon it as my annual penance, Mrs. Hood, and as two other members have failed me on short notice, I am doubly in your husband's debt!"

Barely was the Vicar down the path, than Riberac, in-censed, had rounded upon Andra! "Your Church-going habits have now put us both in a confounded fix."

But he had gone to Wedbury Sands as arranged. And there had made, with dire results, Choir history. To their delight, the boys had been detailed to work upon a thorough-paced excavation, which yielded from its earthworks, after hours of digging: some ship's timber; one parrot cage; a pair of corsets; three old boots; a ginger-beer bottle; and a number of bones that the boys gleefully insisted must be human. The Vicar had dozed in the sun throughout, his panama across his face, but his day had been equally satisfactory. The train journey back, usually an occasion of outrageous devilry on the part of the Choir, had for once passed in professional silence, as on Riberac's instructions, the boys had busily tabulated the day's trove on sheets of foolscap supplied, and later scrutinized by him. The party ended with assurances that individually the Choir's career was now clear-cut, and in farewell, each boy had clamoured for his autograph.

Compressing his lips, Riberac had grimly scrawled his illustrious signature on the pink, blue, and yellow pages of various small grubby autograph books. Fortunately, the Vicar did not urge this on his own behalf——

But on his next visit to England, Riberac learned that the inevitable had happened——

Andra had ceased to attend St. Anselm's.

"The boys kept calling to see you. And then one night, as I left Church, I saw by the way the Vicar bowed that he knew the truth."

Tersely Riberac replied: "People must abide by their rules."

"Oh, yes," she agreed hastily, humbly, "of course." Then to his relief she had begun to laugh. "Philip, *you're* the lost sheep that he most regrets—that I know. Never mind . . . you're an undying memory to the Choir—and me . . ."

Engrossed in these remembrances, the Heath now lay behind him.

Again he crossed a tar-blistered road, and entered Andra's terrace.

The blue of the summer sky was graying with heat. The green lawns glared, as they sloped to the pavement. The terrace trees drooped sullenly. Thunder once more brooded.

Even as he rang, he knew she was not there.

Of course not! He must wait. She was at morning Church.

She would be back at any moment.

It was inevitable!

Yet even as he waited, an imperceptible uneasiness cooled his hot heart. As an excavator, he had just remembered that, having found, the heaviest part of labour often lay ahead.

Sunday Afternoon . . . twelve-thirty

He saw her first. Very differently attired to-day! It might have been the Andra of a decade ago approaching in that gray voile frock, patterned with white petals, and the bell-shaped hat which eclipsed every other woman to-day, but which she wore like a tiny helmet, on her small classical head. Unlike most fair women, her opaque skin never scorched, and every summer was, as now, a golden brown.

She came slowly, and she was smiling slightly, as if she enjoyed every step beneath the trees. He had no idea that although he was in a softened mood, she was in a hardened one.

Then as she turned in, she saw him, and stopped short.

"I have come direct from Major Treves," he said.

Transferring her prayer book, she politely shook hands, and remarked: "So you've undermined him too!"

This unchristian observation, so outrageously unfair, so totally uncharacteristic of the Church-goer, momentarily silenced him.

Smiling in the same unlikely way, she took out a latch-key and opened the door.

They entered, and stood confronted in the narrow but dignified hall.

"To whom does this house belong?" he demanded.

"Professor and Miss Baird. I met them in Mr. Tucker's show-room many years ago, when they bought a wardrobe of mine. They have now put me in as their caretaker."

"Very good of them, I'm sure!" he said satirically. "Where are they now?"

"Florida."

"Still considerate, I see! Where do we sit—the kitchen?"

"Usually . . ." her smile was now apologetic, "but of course——"

"Not at all! In Rome, I do as the Romans," and he stalked after her into the kitchen, a-flicker with green and gold from the chestnut tree.

"I'd suggest the garden," he said, "but you look as if you might quarrel with me. Perhaps we should have privacy."

"Perhaps we should!" Warily she sat down, then added with genuine anxiety, "Has the Vaucluse relic come?"

"No, and never will now."

"Oh, don't say that, Philip . . . I feel it will."

"I wish you were as hopeful on the score of my other losses. You didn't telephone."

"I did this morning, but you had just gone."

"Why didn't you telephone yesterday? I waited in."

"Did you?"

And he noticed that she had paled.

"All afternoon. Then as I felt excessively depressed I went to the theatre."

"Did you?" she said slowly, while swiftly she thought: *Why doesn't he say which one?*

"Yes. I left instructions at the Club where I could be found, if you rang. But in the end, I couldn't sit the show out."

Relentlessly she remembered: *but he stayed till nine.*

"Andra," he said, "it is useless to ask your forgiveness. I am too much in your debt. Nor can I say that I have changed in any way for the better. But at least I am now more aware. To-day, after seeing Treves, I realized for the first time the hardness of my heart. I must accept this repellent fact. I have not the faintest idea what I can do about it. I feel rather like a patient who awakens from an anaesthetic to find that a limb is missing. I'm a minus quantity. This leaves me, in a sense, outcast. Dead though not buried——" he broke off. "Remember the Pharaoh of Exodus? The one who hardened his heart? When the bandages were removed from the actual mummy, Professor Elliot Smith and Monsieur Maspero discovered a unique phenomenon—calcified patches on the aorta. His heart was literally hardened. Crossing the Heath to-day I felt that my heart like Menephthah's had also been exposed for what it was—sterile. In spite of all this, I beg you to have pity, and to end this separation."

"But, Philip, I cannot. I couldn't go through that again . . . our life at Kew."

Shocked, he exclaimed, "You misunderstand. Now I ask you to marry me."

Helplessly she sighed. "Philip, it was always a marriage to me. But now we've grown away from each other—in every way."

"Nonsense! Cease thinking of your own salvation for once—or that of the multitude. Be humble. Devote yourself to mine, for a change!"

"I tell you it's impossible."

"Hell and damnation!" he exclaimed. "I may not have altered much, but I tell you that I'm not the same. Do you think everyone but yourself has stood still? Your self-righteousness would paralyse any sinner. Now I'm losing my temper."

Ruefully she smiled. "We mustn't quarrel—especially as I'm no match for you. Let us at least part kindly."

"Kindly!" his eyes blazed. "What hypocrisy!" and with infallible but unforgivable insight, he added: "If it hadn't been for that damned Gerda, this separation would have been over and done with five years ago."

"If it hadn't been for Gerda, we'd never have met five years ago. That encounter we owe entirely to her."

"And one you've never got over, in consequence."

Again her face paled. "How can you say such a thing!"

"Quite easily for I know myself at last. I'm so resentful of Standish that I can't read his book in case he afflicts me more. Belatedly I recognize my own jealousy. This enlightens me as to yours."

In a low voice she said: "Some things may be thought, but should never be said."

"Confound it—if they can be thought, they're better out! Nothing has so effectively hardened *your* heart against me as the fact that I'd had a flirtation with Gerda. In the past I've had any number, with other Gerdas. They don't mean a damned thing. And I wish to God you didn't——" he stopped short. "I need water," he said hoarsely. "May I have a drink?"

"Oh, yes," shocked by his distress, she ran to the tap, and, in her anxiety to help, ran back with a brimming glass.

He rose, and the next moment had seized her in his arms, the wasted water soaking them both.

Rigid with fear, furiously she beat back his shoulders, but so absurd was her strength against his that, instantly, he desisted, his voice acid.

"This certainly is the end," he said, "as far as I am concerned. Till to-day I've always looked on you as a being apart. Now I know you for what you are—my grudging counterpart!"

He walked through the kitchen, into the hall, picked up his hat, and opened the front door.

Across his shoulder he called indifferently:

"Next time—*you* will come to me."

Andra in her crumpled, wet frock heard the door close decisively.

He had not even had his drink of water.

By some sly caprice of justice, this seemed the only heartbreak now.

Sunday Afternoon . . . five o'clock

Four o'clock found her in the west-end, a reassuring visit to Letty in hospital safely over.

Scarcely worth going home, she decided, for this was one of those Sundays on which she was due for night work at the Nursing Home. She might as well spend the time till six o'clock in Regent's Park.

The sulphur haze of midday had dissipated without thunder, yet the air had not cleared. Heat, like a fever, consumed the day. The parched town trees hung inertly, their leafy amplitude now a lack-lustre weight. These staid mansions and dignified squares which led to the Park, brought back at each step the six years spent here so peacefully, so pleasantly in the end.

She walked slowly on. There were more people than usual in the Sunday streets. Jubilee festivity had drawn them out. Those hatless young people to-day wore London like an old glove, or a summer sandal! It gave her a sense of freedom. In the past, people had dressed for London— even the office boys and girls. But now all that was changed. At the same time, it was perhaps a blessing that there were some smart people left—or London's glamour might vanish.

People like Mrs. Willoughby, for instance.

Passing the Wigmore Hotel at that moment, where once Andra had been the treasured Char, she marvelled yet again at the thought of fashionable Mrs. Willoughby.

But she sighed as she sat down on the first empty seat within the Park, as much for Mrs. Willoughby as from weariness.

Yet to dwell on Mrs. Willoughby always restored morale. The Queen of Hell had been the title bestowed by the Hotel staff on Andra's good angel, and a lurid picture drawn in the servants' hall of her temper and her tantrums. The Charlady had respectfully listened, as she listened to tales of wealthy Mr. Wex, the biscuit manufacturer, who lowered the tone of the dining room by wearing his napkin four-square under the lapels of his jacket, so that he looked like an artisan supping with the exclusive; or to the eccentricities of Lady Sybil; or the three shabby old ladies, worth quarter of a million, affectionately entitled by the staff Three Smart Girls. At that stage Mrs. Willoughby had simply been a newcomer to the Wigmore, whose lavishness in no way reconciled the management to the exacting way she later scrutinized each item of expenditure.

Andra had merely distant glimpses of the *clientèle*.

Her hours were seven till noon. Scrubbing was taboo after seven-thirty, and all public rooms had to be completed by eight-thirty.

Startling, now, to realize that she would never have met Mrs. Willoughby, who rejoiced in a suite, had the night-porter not upset a tray crossing the lounge-hall—a tray which destiny decreed should hold the lees of stout.

Hurriedly he wiped up the mess.

But these were stout stains!

Although the forbidden hour of seven-thirty had tolled, and it was precisely seven-forty-five, Andra was summoned with her pail and scrubbing brush.

Kneeling in the empty hall, she began to scrub the marble floor. The night-porter had left the carpet turned back for her, as etiquette ordained he should. There was some broken glass too. This was going to take time——

Suddenly the elevator descended with the buzz of a swarm of bees. She could only hope that it was not a guest.

Round the tub of hydrangeas, a stout, elderly lady hurried, walking with such angry decision towards Andra's sofa, that Andra at once recognized her from hearsay.

The lady, although it was August, wore a travelling coat and carried a jewel-case. She must be going away—as soon as her car came round. But why, oh why, had she chosen this sofa, when there were three other dry ones? Her shoes must be already wet.

Nervously Andra glanced up from her knees, and then paused.

Mrs. Willoughby, seating herself abruptly, was staring into space with such fierce blankness that Andra saw she was oblivious of her whereabouts. It was a square, resolute face, with pouched eyes and a frog-like mouth, but from this stout, rigidly groomed figure there emanated such an impression of anxiety and tension that Andra caught her breath.

Less nervously, as she knelt there, in fact, almost with commiseration, she stretched out her arm and dried the floor more closely round this afflicted person's feet.

As she did so, the lady groaned, and then said harshly, "This is the end . . ." with such finality that Andra involuntarily exclaimed:

"Oh, don't say that, *please*!"

Mrs. Willoughby started violently. She looked up and then down before she discovered Andra on the floor. Her reaction was characteristic:

"What on earth are you doing there? Get up . . . it's ridiculous."

But Andra continued to kneel. "I heard you groan. I couldn't bear it. I know what you're feeling, and it's dreadful."

Mrs. Willoughby glared. "So you've heard too? It's infamous!"

"No, no, I haven't heard a thing. Except your groan. And I recognized it."

" *Recognized* it?"

"Yes, it might have been my own—once. When I felt like death."

Mrs. Willoughby's hag-ridden face cleared slightly. She looked at Andra sharply. "Did you?" she demanded.

"Yes, but I got over it, and in an extraordinary way. I stopped thinking and began to *feel*."

"Feel? I'm almost demented with feeling."

Andra shook her head. Apologetically she said: "So you *think*. But I'm afraid you're only thinking. Thinking just whips you around. It's a frightful scourge. I almost went out of my mind. Now, if you could just *feel* yourself into calm——" she spoke coaxingly, caressingly. "You must remember being calm before . . . before this happened. Feel yourself into that. Don't think of anything else. Don't think of *anyone* else. That's specially important. People can be torture. And even if you don't succeed at once, the very effort to feel breaks the spell."

"The spell . . ." repeated Mrs. Willoughby with astonishment. "Then you *do* know!" but this time she stared without heat.

"Only what you're suffering," Andra amended.

"Well, you don't know half of that," exclaimed Mrs. Willoughby, again on a rising note of indignation.

From the vicinity of her smart patent leather shoes, Andra earnestly assured her: "But I know enough. I know your symptoms, and everyone was mine. And after all," she moved the wet cloth aside and said almost ingratiatingly, "you're bound to be equal to it, or it wouldn't have happened to you."

"Rubbish! You don't know what you're talking about.

I had an experience eight days ago that doesn't happen to one woman in ten thousand. Dire."

Andra nodded in an irritating way. "But it happened to you. It's been your portion."

"It certainly has!" gibed Mrs. Willoughby, "but that doesn't mean I'm going to accept it."

"You must," said Andra solemnly. Suddenly she began to laugh softly, but unsuitably. "You must take it—*and* leave it."

There was something so sane, so sound in her merriment that the older woman paused in spite of herself. "Take it *and* leave it?" she frowned.

"Yes, that's the secret of the whole thing, I found. If you take it—you can leave it. Not otherwise."

"Pick up that pail," said Mrs. Willoughby abruptly. "We're going upstairs. These are the first constructive words I've heard since the calamity. No, leave the pail where it is. I don't know what you're doing with the thing."

"Someone may trip over it," Andra objected, for now a few people were crossing the hall, and the hall-porter himself had come on duty.

"Porter!" commanded Mrs. Willoughby, "send up my luggage. I'm not travelling to-day. Page, get rid of this pail."

The second porter lifted the pail with hauteur, and the staff in the Reception office saw, with astonishment, Mrs. Willoughby prodding Andra towards the elevator.

Inside that gilt cage, Mrs. Willoughby subsided on to the seat, her pugnacious face pale with sweat.

For a second she closed her eyes, thankful that her companion had made no further fuss—in fact, her relief was so great that she felt almost light-headed, or was it light-hearted. She had dreaded that lonely journey as much as she abhorred that empty suite upstairs. But the present situation gave a curious sense of lessening tension—as if she were literally on her way out of the tunnel. Under guidance. The tunnel was, in fact, revealing itself as a channel of deliverance. No, no, she was surely light-headed—after too much suffering. But, *if it were so*, if this premonition proved itself intuition, then there was nothing further to fear in life. Nothing further to fear? Nothing further to fear. What a deliverance! Then life would be freedom. God *must* exist. And the bluff be called on the battle-field of the body!

Once inside the suite, the young woman said in her mild way, "May I please telephone the Housekeeper?"

"Of course . . . of course. And take off that ridiculous overall. It's wet through."

Mrs. Willoughby's luggage was once more stacked in Mrs. Willougby's dressing-room and vestibule. Her jewel-case was laid on the bureau of the sitting room, until such time as she restored it to the safe.

She, herself, was now removing her hat and gloves, a smile, unlikely as youth in age, wavering across her redoubtable face. She had definitely thrown in her lot with the angels. But by no act of faith. Premonition had become intuition as she re-entered her suite.

Bending stiffly, for she was thick-set rather than stout, she rang for the floor-waiter.

"Breakfast for two," she ordered.

Andra, relinquishing the telephone, announced: "The Housekeeper was quite pleasant, but I'm afraid *they* won't like it."

"*They*?"

"The Management."

"Don't be absurd. I represent the *clientèle*."

"If you had waited . . ." Andra ventured, "my time here finishes at noon."

Irritably Mrs. Willoughby said: "Why should I wait? I wish to talk to you now. Can't you see that this is important to me?"

And because Andra saw it was, she sat on in the pleasant but impersonal hotel sitting-room, after the waiter had wheeled away the remains of an excellent breakfast.

It was a sunless August day, the air tepid as milk, and for the first time it struck Andra as strange that Mrs. Willoughby, now impatiently fanning herself with the *Times*, should be in town at present.

"I have felt so ill," Mrs. Willoughby began, "that I feared my reason might be affected. One thinks of one's age, and all the rumours one has heard. Yet one fears to visit a doctor in case he names the affliction, clinches the symptoms."

Andra nodded, "I know . . . I know."

"Nothing of the sort!" retorted Mrs. Willoughby. "How can you possibly know? I have been involved in a unique set of circumstances, which has precipitated my nervous breakdown. Yet a wholly fortuitous set of circumstances. I stress that. These misfortunes had their climax in a suicide, for which I have been held responsible."

Andra gazed at her wide-eyed. "How terrible for you."

Mrs. Willoughby's voice shook slightly, "Incredible to relate, you're the first person to say so—though the Coroner himself indicated as much. But *his* relations and friends have been intolerable. He was," she added angrily, "madly in love with me."

Imperceptibly Andra's jaw dropped. Yet this astounding statement had an authentic ring. But then everything about Mrs. Willoughby seemed formidably genuine.

"I married Willoughby late in life," her hostess continued. "I have no children. When my husband died some years ago, I missed him. Naturally. But I was resolved not to marry again. I was well accustomed to fend for myself. Fond as I had been of Willoughby, I realized afresh after his death, that freedom has advantages. For one thing, I travelled more widely than I had done for years. My late husband had left me a small estate in the Lake country. Quite delightful. I still spent the summer months there. Mr. Simon Yule was an elderly neighbour and an old friend of my husband's. An historian and a bit of a recluse. When *his* sister died, I mistakenly took him in hand, as we were both by then alone. Not only did he dine regularly at my house, but we often met in London, for I entertain a great deal. His means were modest but sufficient, and these brief holidays acted as a tonic on him. He was a quiet man, but quite elegant. I found him a restful and agreeable escort. You may not credit this, but in spite of his erudition he was at first incapable of ordering a dinner. And he did not know the first thing about his wines. A man who has lived exclusively with his sister is often a minus quantity. But at the end of our mourning period, he could not only order a respectable meal, he could distinguish his wines. His wits had also sharpened conversationally. And I was pleased to find that he was dressing well. Even his Bridge improved, which at first I had feared was beyond hope. In fact, I was often complimented on him, although everyone was, of course, aware that all was strictly *de rigueur* between us. But he had become a definite asset, and I felt myself most happily placed, when, to my annoyance, he began to spend absurd sums on flowers for me. Knowing his limited means, I had always insured that we moved on a fifty-fifty basis. It was a friendship of mutual benefit, nothing more. When I protested about these flowers—to my alarm, he proposed marriage. At first I laughed it off as a joke. But in less than no time, stronger action was needed, as he began to haunt my house, or my hotels in London. On one occasion he actually followed me abroad, when my only need was my own company. Finally last May I had to insist that we did not meet again. By then he had got on my nerves so thoroughly, that when I opened my house for the summer season at Rendalsmere, I was exasperated to find a letter warning me that after years of constant companionship, the boredom of absence from me had made his existence insupportable. He had the effrontery to add that unless I could see my way to sharing his life, *he would be obliged to end it.* I contend that I did what any rational person would do in these circumstances. I ignored this absurd threat. And three days later, he committed suicide. I was obliged to give evidence in Court, where his married sister and a nephew openly stated that our deferred marriage had preyed on his mind. And his own doctor testified that from a man in renewed health and vigour, he had gone downhill in a matter of months. The Coroner alone appeared to think that I had any right to my single state. But in spite of his final remarks, the entire County holds me responsible. I left Rendalsmere as soon as the case was heard last week. Fortunately the London papers did not exploit it. But it can only be a matter of time before my entire circle knows."

"Did he . . ." Andra hesitated, "did he shoot himself?"

"Of course not. He knew nothing of firearms. He had led a sedentary, scholarly life. Violence of that sort would have been quite unthinkable for him. He simply jumped into the lake. But he walked a mile first—and did it from my garden. He was a Scotsman too, which made his behaviour more preposterous. The last man, one would have said."

"Terrible," Andra shook her head.

Abruptly Mrs. Willoughby said: "Do you know the *Dream of Gerontius?* No? There is a line in that which aptly describes my present condition. ' *I feel the ruin that is worse than death*'."

Andra looked up quickly. "Then it's only a matter of time. That's the extremity. You *must* hold on."

Mrs. Willoughby sighed. "You act on me like a sedative. I don't know what it is about you. But I believe you're what I need. What were you doing downstairs with that pail?"

"Washing the floor."

"I could see that. I'm not an imbecile. Why are you wasting your time and energy like that—an educated woman."

Andra hesitated. "Cleaning's my work," she said, "and I like it. I'm anything but highly educated."

"I didn't say highly educated, though I find you highly intelligent. Why hedge? You haven't hesitated to break into *my* privacy?"

Andra began to laugh, but hastened to add: "I promise to tell you later."

"I should think so!" scoffed Mrs. Willoughby, her mania for domination now getting the better of present misery. "I never heard of such absurdity. As if there wasn't enough waste in life without people making needless martyrs of themselves! And in any case, that hall is a man's work. The floor is marble. You can tell me your story later. When you feel like it. London's impossible in August. I came here simply because I knew it would be empty—after the Court case. Now we can leave together. You look as if you needed a holiday. We both do."

Andra looked at her almost stupidly. "You're not serious?"

"Of course I am. It's the only thing to do. Where would you like to go? A trip abroad?"

"*Abroad!*" breathed Andra, "I've never been abroad. It's like a dream!"

Even the calamitous Mrs. Willoughby was not proof against such transparent delight. She smiled. "Then choose."

"Are you sure *you* wouldn't rather do that?"

"Of course not," said the other testily. "I've been everywhere. I've done everything. I'm completely indifferent."

"Then," almost in trepidation Andra framed the fabled word, "may it be Venice? All my life I've longed to see Venice."

"Venice?" said Mrs. Willoughby reflectively. "Not a bad choice, though scarcely an ideal time—but Venice is always interesting. Dine with me to-night, and we'll fix our date."

Late that night before Andra left the hotel, her hostess said with finality. "And you must have a salary—but leave that to me."

"Oh, *no!*" protested Andra, "all I'll need will be the price of my rent, and that's quite reasonable."

Frowning, Mrs. Willoughby brushed this aside. She held out a cheque. "Meantime, this is a cheque for your outfit. And don't insult me by giving me change. You must be suitably clad for the Italian coast."

Blushing, Andra took the cheque. "I've scarcely anything left that would be suitable," she began. "I wouldn't like my appearance to embarrass you." Glancing down, she saw the sum upon the cheque. "But this is fantastic!"

"Don't be an idiot," said the other briskly. "It's a business proposition. No wonder you're reduced to a pail and scrubbing brush. I take back every word I said about your intelligence. We'll leave on Monday then. I needn't warn you that I may prove a moody companion at times. But I have an idea that we'll travel well together——"

And how right she'd been!

To Andra the journey had been an hourly enchantment—starting at Victoria where she had been astonished to hear her gloomy friend laugh outright.

The first sight of Andra in her new travelling outfit had occasioned this: "Good heavens!" roared Mrs. Willoughby, "you're elegant as well as charming. I never suspected that —you dark horse with fair hair! I now look like your housekeeper . . . tagging along!"

Together both had gone from strength to strength.

During the weeks that followed, Andra regained lost youth in the shelter of superior age. And Mrs. Willoughby, who had long estranged relatives and friends alike, and had drearily learnt her lesson too late, now knew Andra as the solitary sympathetic survivor on her shore—Man Friday.

Andra might sometimes be puzzled by that tart iteration: *I have no patience with . . . I have no use for . . . I refuse to truckle,* but in the sense that both plied an intrepid course, Mrs. Willoughby reminded her of Madame Moffat— although only as a steam-ship may evoke earlier sail. Mrs. Willoughby was not simply up to date. She was ahead of schedule. Her irony and vitality left Andra breathless. She was self-centred, but she knew it. In fact her unexampled awareness filled the younger woman with awe. Mrs. Willoughby evaded nothing. Her integrity was conclusive, and long before they reached Venice, Andra secretly adored her.

In the convivial French dining car that first night, its wicker baskets of fruit festively sprigged with leaves, its wine bottles winking, its tumblers dancing, Mrs. Willoughby learnt a great deal about Andra, her childhood, the scarce-seen mother who had once been governess to the children of Prince Essling, Count of Landeck, whose estates bordered Venetia Tridentina. "That's why it had to be Venice, you see. It will bring her nearer."

"Romantic creature," retorted Mrs. Willoughby, but not unkindly. "It strikes me that you had a better mother than most in that Aunt Edith . . ."

But it was not until Venice was achieved that Andra had told the rest of her story.

They came in on a tranquil golden evening, to the city that is as mysterious as a reflection in a mirror, and as elusive, and yet which welcomes the first footfall of the traveller with the solidity, the intimacy of a house—a vast and grandiose building with canals for corridors, and water clucking beneath its ornate balconies! A city where the sky is not simply part of the street, but lies like a garden at the end of it—as open as its ancient doors are secretive, its alleys tomb-like. A city encircled by the witchery of water: with the light of heaven drowned at the steps of its fabulous churches; the sea indolent around its prodigious palaces; or washing the basements of precipitous tenements with their remote, ghostly windows—all in such contrast to its gay, gregarious piazzas.

"Our hotel is not the largest," Mrs. Willoughby explained, "but it is the best. In fact it's unique—a period piece!"

The hotel, like Venice, was as silent as a dream, as strange as another century, as familiar as a welcome. Andra felt that she had left a life-time behind her, its failures fully forgiven, so powerful was her certainty that this had long awaited her, that Mrs. Willoughby and she had always been en route—for ever arriving in this perfect peace!

That night as they drank their coffee on the dim balcony, with the cry of a passing gondolier, and the pulsing of a distant *vaporetto* muted by the heat, Andra told Mrs. Willoughby the rest of her story, with the ease of reminiscence, the detachment of another existence. A confession never before made to another. Venice, becalmed yet intense, sanctioned confidence, restored trust. Philip's name alone she did not mention.

Mrs. Willoughby listened silently, and then said without any trace of her usual peremptoriness:

"You were a perfect fool. Even with marriage one can't always get a square deal, yet you thought you could carry off the other situation!"

"I'm afraid," Andra admitted apologetically, "I didn't think at all."

"Did he leave you?"

"No. I left him."

"Oh, well," said Mrs. Willoughby impatiently, "if *they* don't leave, they see *you* do. There are more ways of killing a dog than choking it with butter. Had you a settlement?"

Andra looked alarmed. "Oh, *no!* There was nothing like that about it—ever. I loved him."

"Tush!" said Mrs. Willoughby, "that's where we Britishers can learn much from any sensible Frenchwoman. There is positively no virtue in such haphazard arrangements. In fact they can lead to tragedy—or the next of kin footing the bill . . . another type of calamity! Disorderly, disastrous. Again, I take back every word I said about your intelligence."

Leniently they laughed, now linked indulgently by a mutual compassion.

Mrs. Willoughby's restoration to health had taken place surprisingly soon, but in a wholly unforeseen fashion.

Dining next night in her private suite, at a small refectory table in the 17th century room, its stolid stone mouldings tremulous by candle-light, Andra by chance held up her glass of hock, and delightedly exclaimed:

"Oh look! the room is twice as wonderful seen through the wine glass."

Mrs. Willoughby raised her glass, and shut one eye

professionally the better to view the miniature chamber tranced in hock.

"Delightful!" she agreed. "And the same room would be quite another place seen through claret, or chartreuse. It would make an attractive study for a still-life canvas—if one had the energy."

"But the glass?" objected Andra. "The glass would be the difficulty. It would have to be such a large glass and that would spoil the picture."

"Nonsense!" said Mrs. Willoughby. "There would be no glass shown. One would simply paint one's picture through it."

Andra gazed at her in admiration. "That's brilliant!"

"No, it's technical ability. In my youth I studied art—at the London Art School, which you later graced!"

"But you didn't go on with it?"

"Of course not. I wasn't good enough." Mrs. Willoughby was again considering the room through hock.

"What a pity!"

"Not at all. I became rich and too busy to repine!"

"But now that you have got time—at least while you're here, why don't you begin again? My Art School friends always sketched on holiday."

"Because," said Mrs. Willoughby impatiently, "it's useless to play at art."

"But this would be a private adventure. Think of the pictures you could get at every turn here! There are artists at home who would give anything for such a chance. Why, it's almost wicked to waste it. For once I'm going to put my foot down! We'll buy sketching material to-morrow. I know exactly what to get. And you'll begin . . ."

And one week later Mrs. Willoughby was admitting with a laugh:

"It's quite absurd . . . I haven't had a brush in my hand

for thirty years—yet I've improved beyond belief! Now I know exactly what I want to do. Plenty of misfires, but no fumbling nowadays."

Already her nervous tension was easing. This creative work had transformed her. And Andra, who as a model had seen hundreds of sketches at all stages, was amazed at the vigour and economy of this elderly woman's.

Delightedly she exclaimed: "Soon I won't be needed. You've come into your own."

"You'll always be needed," Mrs. Willoughby retorted. "But this hint alarms me, so lest you grow restless, I'll give some parties for you."

And that day, heedless of Andra's protests, she despatched invitations to various Venetian friends. "I held off till we were established, for now, of course," she chuckled maliciously, "they'll stir up my relations by post or encounter, which always makes for jealousy."

"Jealousy . . . how could they possibly be jealous of me?"

Mrs. Willoughby continued to look amused. "I've had favourites before. They never lasted, but my relations always feared they might."

Andra smiled, but felt a twinge of pain. She had forgotten the relations and friends—the assiduous and respectful retinue of a wealthy woman. She had become fonder of Mrs. Willoughy than she realized. It hurt her to realize that she too would not last in the natural order of things. But gamely enough she rallied:

"Well, I'm already due to fade-out."

"Don't be an imbecile," Mrs. Willoughby, placidly seated on the balcony, was confirming a measurement on the latest sketch. "I now look on you as a life-sentence. The Forlis and the Gozzanos are going to dote on you . . . so too will the Binches. But they'll spread the good news, and we'll have to move on, if I'm to get any painting done, and if you're to have your beauty sleep. Florence next I think. Not Rome at present: The *chauffage* there never goes on before a certain date, and it's death in a cold snap."

"But I must go home. And work. I can't let you do more for me. You've already done too much."

"I assure you, I'm thinking solely of myself. I've now grown accustomed to your peculiarities—so very different from my own! Henceforward, we'll follow the sun together—as soon as Venice becomes too sociable."

Coffee parties, water-picnics, concerts, theatres, balls—all Mrs. Willoughby's prophecies came true, in a riot of hospitality.

A quiet dinner became a luxury. Laughingly, they made their plans for departure.

On their second last night, Mrs. Willoughby announced: "This evening I shall dine in bed. But you go down, and decorate Signor Empoli's restaurant for him."

A mediaeval banqueting-hall, green as a glade with tapestries, and bewitched by candle-light! Andra sat alone at their usual table, happy that to-night there was no party, that she could placidly enjoy the gaiety around her—for the hotel was festively full.

The old lady in the far corner was the only sombre note. Upright as a Spartan in her high-necked black dress, she sat inscrutably at the least desirable table in the room, silently eating her meal alone.

Signor Empoli had told them her deplorable history—the Princess Ziller whose husband had been Count of Gerlos, one of the oldest names in Austria. "She lives now in one of our back bedrooms, having lost all. But I am able to give her a certain amount of work. She speaks six languages fluently, and is useful for translation—whether it be correspondence or conversation. Breakfast and luncheon she takes elsewhere, as these she pays for, but it is my good pleasure that she dines here nightly."

"Infamous!" Mrs. Willoughby had obscurely declared. "And at that age. . . . Has the Princess no relatives?"

"There indeed you have tragedy," Signor Empoli agreed. "Her son, the heir, married quite late in life. A marriage, it is said, that delighted no one but his mother. The Princess, you will perceive, is of an inflexibility! Three years later, the heir, Count of Gerlos, was obliged to divorce his wife. There are no children. The son became restless, and travelled incessantly. Then during the war, he died abroad. And the irony of this is: that then the estates passed to the next of kin—cousins for whom no love was felt. So that for lack of a grand-child, male or female, this old lady has become homeless. But Austria to-day has many such stories."

To-night Andra found it easier to look anywhere than at that solitary table with its spectre—a reminder that this brief Venetian dream held also its appointed despair.

Not for the first time had she a curious and uneasy impression that this impassive ghost was watching her. With lessening enjoyment, she finished dinner . . . relieved to make her way to a quiet withdrawing room, where she wrote her monthly letter to Madame Moffat——

A longer letter than usual, and she rose late from the writing-table, the empty room somnolent, its air exhausted—

As she did so, she started slightly.

The room was not empty after all.

The Princess Ziller sat opposite, her ebony stick in hand, confronting Andra who had not heard her enter.

"Miss Alexandra Hood?" she spoke coldly, with pedantic precision.

"Yes . . . yes, of course!" Andra hesitated. She strove not to sound apologetic. The face and hands were white and brittle as chalk, but the eyes were despotic, the carriage hauteur itself. "Princess Ziller?" she added, and then wondered if that were the correct way to address her.

The old lady bowed. "Forgive what must seem an intrusion," she said briefly, "but this is not an idle interruption. For the past three weeks I have hoped to speak with you, but you are never alone."

Again Andra hesitated—then drew up another chair. "That is true," she smiled. "Mrs. Willoughby and I are usually together."

"Miss Hood," said her *vis à vis*, in the same frigid way, "may I ask if you have a relative of the name of Miss Zoë Hood?"

Andra stared at her—her first reply, still-born.

Slowly, carefully she agreed, "Yes . . . I had a relative of that name."

"The Miss Zoë Hood to whom I refer was for years governess to the children of Prince Essling, Count of Landeck, whose estates marched with ours. You speak of her in the past tense?"

"Because she is dead."

"Indeed?" For some reason her interlocutor was disconcerted. She too paused. "When, may I ask, did she die?"

"In 1918. We did not hear till after the Armistice. She died in Budapest."

"Ah!" said Princess Ziller, gazing at the knotted hands clasped upon her ebony stick, and so prolonged was this pause, that Andra's anxiety grew. Then the heavily-lidded eyes were raised. Deliberately the old lady said:

"I am sorry to have out-lived her. That will mean little to you—which is another regret I have to add to my considerable store. But I should like to satisfy myself on one point. It would indeed be a relief to do so. You look happy. Are you?"

Andra caught her breath, bewildered by this astonishing inquiry from a total stranger. "Oh, yes," she said hastily, "and growing steadily happier."

For the first time a flicker of amusement passed over those frosty blue eyes. "I congratulate you."

"But how," Andra began, "did you connect me with—with Zoë. Hood is quite an ordinary name."

"By the resemblance of course," the old lady rose. "I then enquired at the office as to your name. After that I was certain."

"Resemblance?" echoed Andra. "You must forgive me—but this makes it stranger still, for I have seen photographs, and I in no way resemble her."

"Of course you don't," said the other shortly. "It would scarcely have been remarkable had you done so. But feature for feature you duplicate *mine*."

And with a sense of incredulity Andra found herself, at brow-level, gazing into her own features, seared by a lifetime's experience. The nostrils opposite were more keenly flared, the mouth more intrepid—that was the only difference.

"From the first glance, I saw the likeness," said the Princess, "but then it is easier for the old to recognize their youth, than for the young to envisage age—extreme age in this case. Goodnight Miss Hood."

"Goodnight," repeated Andra. She was stunned by this phantom of herself taking its desolate leave with complete calm. "Perhaps we shall meet again——"

"I scarcely think so," Princess Ziller was pacing her way to the door. Across her shoulder, she added with a glimmer of pleasure that further laid bare the bleakness of the prospect, "It has been a satisfaction to see you . . . Goodbye."

Wide awake in the darkness that night, Andra strove to

accustom herself to the fact that in this austere personage she had at last met her grandmother.

All next day, a sense of aftermath . . . no, a melancholy like the presage of misfortune dulled her. Hastily, she decided that this must be due to their departure to-morrow. Yet was she not invited to follow the sun? And did not at least a few weeks still remain with the one and only Mrs. Willoughby?

Evening found her once more in what Mrs. Willoughby described as her gala mood . . . eagerly donning her new petunia picture frock, for, on this their last night in Venice, her hostess had taken a box at the Opera.

All was as usual once again . . . with Mrs. Willoughby grumbling that the Gozzanos and the Binches would probably invade them at the first interval.

But it was shortly before the second interval that interruption occurred, with the stage still aglow, the house warm and dark and flooded with the music of *Don Giovanni*.

The door behind them opened into the box, and above the music she heard, with sickening shock, the words that meant the end:

"Well, my dear Aunt, this certainly is a great surprise!"

"Philip, you wretch, where have you sprung from?" Mrs. Willoughby was laughing bluffly.

"From the Padua Congress, but more instantly—the stalls at your feet! I was scarcely able to credit eyesight during the last interval, but you look remarkably well. Am I not to meet your charming companion?"

Frozen, Andra heard Mrs. Willoughby effect this introduction with a chuckle. Darkness mercifully concealed her own shock. But the scene would come to an end, the lights go up, and she be at the mercy of this deception which he had imposed upon her.

Low as their voices were, already she sensed the triumph,

the barely concealed excitement in his. Mrs. Willoughby
too had observed this, for she remarked *sotto-voce*: "You
sound as if you'd dined well . . . but let us give the singers
a chance now!"

The house sprang into light and applause.

Riberac had risen.

He was bending over Mrs. Willoughby, with one inquiry after another, the while he studied Andra's averted
profile.

Mrs. Willoughby said indulgently: "Turn round, my
child. There's no news you cannot share. I certainly have
no secrets from you."

Mrs. Willoughby—*Madame Franz Orth*!

Madame Franz Orth who, for a decade now must have
been Mrs. Willoughby . . . Madame Franz Orth, her enemy,
whose second marriage had synchronized with Andra's
break with Philip.

"*Turn round, my child*," repeated Mrs. Willoughby.

For one terrible moment, at the warmth in that brisk
voice, Andra almost burst into tears. But, instead, she
turned, her smile stiff on her face. And at that moment,
the Gozzanos appeared with the Binches. There was safety
in numbers! Hurriedly she accepted their invitation to
supper. Mrs. Willoughby meant to return early. He would
have to go back with her. Every moment the three of them
spent together, her sense of guilt grew.

It was two o'clock in the morning when Andra regained
the hotel alone. And as she crossed to the elevator, he rose
from a seat beside it. This she had not foreseen.

Coldly she said: "It's very late."

"It is indeed. The lounge on the next floor will be more
suitable now."

As always, his distinction invested him with authority.
His assurance sanctioned all he said.

Silently she followed him, and heard him order two iced drinks.

With these before them, and the waiter gone, he exclaimed: " Four years and seven months since you made your last get-away!" and again she was aware of his angry yet exultant mood.

Calmly she said, " Gerda has done great things since that party. I haven't seen her since, but of course I have followed her triumphs."

" Why tell me this?"

" At that time you were as good as engaged to her, were you not?"

" I neither was, nor am. There was little in me that would have held that young woman's interest. For my part, I found her appearance attractive, her ability unusual—but as a woman she failed to move me. She blew hot and cold on principle, my dear Andra. And coquetry has always bored me. Such an admission of inadequacy."

" Philip, I intend to go upstairs in a minute or two, so I must tell you right away that your Aunt is the only person now who causes me any concern. I am appalled that you have deliberately concealed the fact that we know each other."

" A most natural precaution! Can you imagine my amazement to see you seated there . . . or my confusion later to hear her eulogies on you?"

" Well, whatever happens next—I won't have her hurt."

" Hurt!" he scoffed. " My Aunt hurt?"

" Yes. I love her dearly, and she's as sensitive as she's noble."

" Sensitive, noble! She's intractable and dogmatic to a degree."

" I daresay . . . and with reason. She's almost always right."

"This is sheer infatuation."

"I don't think so. Of course I know she's got her little ways—like barnacles on a boat. But they're not important."

"All I can say is: either you or I are completely deluded."

Fleetly Andra retorted: "I think my delusions are pleasanter than yours—and they seem to work better. I've got to tell her the truth about us? Otherwise, I can't remain with her. It would mean deceiving her at every turn."

"How much does she already know about yourself?"

"Everything . . . except the name of the man I lived with for four years."

"Damnation!" he exclaimed.

"The truth's the only possible thing now."

"No," he said brooding. "No . . . it's impossible. It would never do. I must remind you that, first and last, she remains my Aunt. During the four years that we were together at Kew, I lied repeatedly to her—over my visits there. Then . . . she has grown attached to you. She's the possessive type. She'd never forgive my treatment of you."

Andra paled. "I think she should be given the chance to do so. We can't continue like this—deceiving her at every word."

"No. I refuse to risk it. Too much hangs on it. You and I must accept the position as it now is. And proceed from this point. In a sense, it could not be better—as now we meet with her blessing. It amounts to a dispensation. So get some sleep right away. We'll have another talk soon."

She rose. "The three of us?"

"No. You and I privately. We're powerless in this matter —so now be reasonable. Everything will turn out for the best this way. I'll make some excuse to see you alone. In any case, I'm travelling with you both to-day by the night-train to Florence. That's already fixed."

She looked at him for a moment, without a word. And then walked abruptly to the elevator.

Well enough satisfied, he rang the bell, and as the gold cage swept her out of sight, he left the hotel younger than he had felt for years.

Older than she had ever been, six hours later Andra had her first quarrel with Mrs. Willoughby.

"You say you must go, and refuse to say why? There is only one thing for me to conclude. You're bored. And have seized this chance to leave, while my nephew is here——"

Her voice shook with anger. It was the first time Andra had seen Mrs. Willoughby in one of her furies.

"Well then—as you're bored, I won't attempt to delay you. In fact, *the sooner you go the better*!"

But as Andra reached the sitting-room door, Mrs. Willoughby called out again:

"*Stop!* I'm convinced that there's some sort of idiocy behind this sudden decision. But if you won't be frank, I can do nothing to clear it up. Are you still determined to leave?"

"Yes," said Andra dully.

"Then" said Mrs. Willoughby, growing white, "better go before I say more. And I never want to see you again. You have behaved outrageously. I shall never forgive you."

For the first time Andra's own anger rose:

"You're quite right," she said passionately. "And I'll never forgive myself."

Blindly she ran out of the room.

Mrs. Willoughby, startled despite herself, stared after her. Then with a grunt of the gravest displeasure, she sat down heavily.

At midday, Andra had left the hotel, without seeing her hostess again.

That night Mrs. Willoughby and her nephew both departed

for Florence—each in a ferment neither cared to explain . . .

Back in London that winter . . . which had been last winter, the leafless trees stood stark most days in a black frost, and the misery of the sunless scene, after Italy, the starving cold, belonged peculiarly to childhood, set, as it seemed to be, in an iron eternity.

But spring had come, and now summer had discovered all too soon a languor that was oppressive.

Nothing would ever reconcile her to the loss of Mrs. Willoughby. And that too had to be faced.

Andra rose from her seat in the Park.

Over the bleached six o'clock Sunday sky, a thick gray gloom had again spread, and settled. It was ominously quiet.

It would be warm in the Nursing Home this evening, but no warmer than it was out here!

For once she was glad to leave the Park . . .

Matron was off-duty, but Sister greeted Andra cordially as she presented herself at the service-hatch, dressed now in a white overall, and as surgically presentable as Sister herself.

"A blessing you could come, Miss Hood. We're short-handed again. I'm afraid this means two floors to-night. Mr. Myers in Number Seven has his operation to-morrow at eight a.m. The cup of chicken soup for him, and only one thin piece of toast."

"Of course."

"I mention this, as he began to be troublesome about food at tea-time. It's childish, but he may try to persuade you to bring more——"

Andra smiled. "I'll pass the request at once to you."

"That's the thing. And the same meal for Number Fourteen. That operation is nine-thirty a.m. to-morrow. All the other dinners are quite straight-forward. Nurse Neil is taking in the Diabetic Trays as usual. We're leaving Seven and Fourteen to the last, as then the evening won't seem quite so long to them."

Fourteen was Andra's last journey. It certainly seemed a sparse little meal set out on the dainty tray. Number Seven had received his repast so resentfully that Andra could only hope that Number Fourteen would be more resigned.

She opened the door, and walked round the tall screen. Large as the dim room was, with its luxurious front view of the square, it also was airless to-night.

The patient, an elderly woman, lay back limply on her pillows, with her face turned towards the trees.

"Good evening," said Andra politely, and set down the tray on the bedside table. "Shall I put the bed-table up? I'm afraid it's only a cup of soup——" she stopped.

The woman turned her face.

Stupefied, they stared.

"*Darling!*" breathed Andra, "oh, darling, is it possible?" Mrs. Willoughby did not answer. Grimly she gazed. She appeared stunned.

But Andra, for once beyond timidity, had flung her arms around her, and with a wild, inexplicable rush of tears was kissing her, again and yet again.

"Oh, thank God," she wept, "thank God you're safely back. Nothing else matters now."

"If this," said Mrs. Willoughby, "is God's idea of safety, it certainly is not mine!" But her voice shook. Once again she was not proof against Andra's startling approach.

Kneeling by the bed now, incoherently Andra besought her: "Tell me what's happened! Why are you here? When did you come? Is it serious—oh, I pray not!" . . . totally remote from the calm creature that Mrs. Willoughby remembered.

Oddly mollified, the patient exclaimed: "Get off that floor at once! How can I converse with the top of your head. Sit on the bed—the chairs are hopeless. Of course it's serious. Do you imagine that I'm paying Mr. Cuthbert of St. Bride's two hundred guineas to-morrow for fun?"

"But what does he say? How has this happened?"

"He declines to commit himself till to-morrow. But he's optimistic—on the whole."

"To have met again—and like this!" Andra covered her face, tears pouring through her fingers. Never had she wept as she was weeping now. Her emotion was beyond control. Every event of the week-end, of her whole life, seemed to culminate in this deluge.

Silently Mrs. Willoughby surveyed her.

"This proves," Andra tried to dry her face, " this re-union proves we do belong."

"Thank you for nothing!" retorted Mrs. Willoughby. "I could have told you that without tempting providence, as you so thanklessly did."

"I couldn't help it. You'd never understand."

"Wouldn't I? You hadn't been gone twenty-four hours, before I tumbled to the whole thing. I challenged Philip, who admitted all. I not only understand, but find your desertion of *me* twice as unforgivable. I ought to have been your first consideration. Not a quixotic loyalty to *his* interests. The most selfish man since Adam. However, if I die to-morrow, I've double-crossed you both!"

Weakly Andra laughed, "Oh, it's wonderful, to hear you again! You're just the same."

"I'm nothing of the sort. You've confirmed me in every weakness—the pair of you. A couple of crashing egoists. You with your virtue, he with his worldliness. Enough to put anyone off heaven and earth. I'm looking forward to purgatory."

"Don't say such a thing! I loved Philip once—but I know now that I've *missed* you more than I've ever missed anyone!"

Mrs. Willoughby gave a sceptical snort. "You'll miss me more yet. In one way, I can hardly wait to die, when I think of the lesson I'm going to read you both! I only wish I might see your faces when my Will is declared. *I've left you every penny that Philip should have had.*"

Appalled, Andra stared at her. "You're not serious?"

Mrs. Willoughby shrugged. "That's one way of looking at it. You're welcome to any view you like. But after due consideration, it seemed to me that you two are the only people fitted to deal with each other. I propose in this way to effect the impossible. The more you think the matter over—the more convincing will the situation seem. I may add: that even if you disclaim the money, he still gets nothing."

Trembling, Andra whispered, "I don't believe it. You couldn't be so cruel. It's Philip's money. It's always been his money."

"What impudence!" Mrs. Willoughby laughed outright. Coolly she proceeded, "At no time did I intend to make Philip, or anyone else, my sole heir. But the very considerable sum he would have got, now goes to you."

"To *me*?" Andra stupidly repeated.

"To you." Mrs. Willoughby's smile was slightly feline.

Andra quailed. "But this is ghastly," she began.

There was a tap on the door, and Sister opened it.

"Miss Hood, what *has* happened?"

Briskly Mrs. Willoughby replied: "I've met an old friend, Sister. In fact an, er—distant relation. It's been quite a surprise . . . on what may prove my last night on earth."

"Mrs. Willoughby, Mrs. Willoughby!" laughingly Sister shook her head, "you will have your little joke."

"Glad you look on it so cheerfully. I always say you nurses have as much sentiment as a sergeant-major on parade. I know too that you don't approve of visitors sitting on beds—but the bed's so high, I enjoy the risk they run. So don't deprive me of what may also prove a final pleasure."

"But, Mrs. Willoughby, you haven't had your soup. It must be stone cold now."

"It ought to be iced on a night like this. However, I'm half way through it already. All that my relative and I now ask is to be left in peace—until the end."

Mrs. Willoughby gave a ferocious wink.

Sister, considerably astonished, closed the door.

"Peace," pursued Mrs. Willoughby, "is perhaps a euphemism for our present hostility! To resume controversy: be good enough to restrain your resentment at the generosity of any future bequest. I am, after all, an invalid, and I intend to get such consideration to-night as this thankless state demands."

"I'm sorry," muttered Andra guiltily. She stared in a hunted way around the room, as if seeking some solution of her present extremity.

In an aura of martyrdom, Mrs. Willoughby finished the soup.

"Aren't you going to eat the toast?"

"I am not. I'm leaving you that also!"

Andra stifled a laugh. Then hurriedly she said:

"Did you know that Philip is in London—at his Club?"

Mrs. Willoughby started. "I did not. But then I'm not in touch with either of you!"

"I didn't know till yesterday myself. We met by accident. But I believe the news was in Friday's *Clarion*—over the Vaucluse Angel."

"I only read the *Times* in London. Never penny dreadfuls like the *Clarion*, with which Philip seems permanently involved . . . ever since they handled the Vaucluse discovery as if the Angel were a film star."

"Dearest," said Andra earnestly, "I must let him know that you're here—and why."

"Sweetheart," said Mrs. Willoughby sarcastically, "you and he always come to what arrangements seem best for *you*. But, let me remind you that here I'm not obliged to see either of you—unless I feel so inclined."

Helplessly, Andra gazed at her. This was only too true.

Distantly Mrs. Willoughby added: "I told myself I must come back to England. Like a sheep seeking pasture. Abroad one is always lured by its greenness. It's a form of nostalgia"

Eagerly Andra nodded. "That's what Major Treves always says. He too would rather live abroad, but he declares the Thames is his undoing."

"And who may Major Treves be?"

"A martinet left over from childhood! He keeps Madeira Park Road in order—to its discomfort. Yet once a year, he returns to Hampstead from holiday, to find himself a hero. In his absence there's been no one to report the Dustman's carelessness; the Postman's omission of the time-check on the pillar-box; the water-cuts without notice; or additional gas and electricity fluctuations. ' I return,' he says, ' to find my neighbours almost as irascible as myself—nettled also by the discovery that their own amiability is only skin deep when *they* have to make an effort! '"

Mrs. Willoughby chuckled, "He sounds invigorating! You may bring Major Treves along, as soon as I'm through the worst."

"Oh, *yes*!" beaming now, Andra leant forward, ever ready to bask in the pleasurable. "And tell me about your painting? How has it gone?"

"Beginner's luck! I exhibited in Monte Carlo last spring under another name, and had some amusing notices. As a newcomer, my youth is the only thing to be held against me at present! One picture was actually bought by a distant cousin, Telfer Mace, who informs me that I'm a man of thirty, of whom a great deal may yet be expected. He'll never recover, of course, when he discovers he's had it! Yes, I have to admit that my painting is something I still owe to you . . . one thing you couldn't remove," and Mrs. Willoughby sniffed.

Andra put out her hand. "At least see Philip once—before the operation. I beg you to believe that there's no one so constantly in his mind as you."

"I daresay! He always dances attendance when it suits

himself. But only when. My interests have simply to clash with his for me to go to the wall."

"No, no!" cried Andra, "that I can vouch for. Only if his work is affected. And you know as well as I do, that he and his work are one."

Mrs. Willoughby gave a satirical laugh. "Is he still at that stage?"

Andra was silent, as she rose to go.

"If a man can't get his work into perspective with life by the time he's forty," said Mrs. Willoughby, "it's a rigid look-out that I, for one, decline to share. But the biggest grudge I owe him is that he deprived me of you. You took panic—silly creature—and I was the loser." She lay back, much paler and grayer than usual. "Everyone involved with Philip is stiff with selfishness. I'm a ramrod with it —where he is concerned. It's . . . it's a form of defence!"

"I wish I hadn't to go——" again Andra looked round the blurred room with a feeling of helplessness. The oppressive gloom of the hour was now almost tangible. "Shall I turn on the light? It's growing dark."

"Yes, you may as well," the reply was indifferent.

And as the pillow leapt into radiance, Andra saw for the first time that the patient's skin had the leaden look of the pent-up day itself.

Her heart sank.

Mrs. Willoughby was indeed an ill woman.

Sunday Night . . . nine o'clock

As she hurried from the Nursing Home, on her way to a telephone-box, she heard the first ominous roll of thunder. A sombre cloud clung to the roof-tops. Beneath the listless trees of the Square, the air was no longer inert, but stifling.

Lightning crackled overhead . . . luckily the box was in the next street!

Her cheeks were flushed, her ideas seethed. At this stage she simply dared not face the implications of the situation.

"*If you disclaim the money, he still gets nothing.*"

It can't be true! she told herself. It's a nightmare—ironic, grotesque.

"*I propose in this way to effect the impossible.*"

It was a desperate predicament, and a deliberate one on the part of Mrs. Willoughby.

Marriage, Andra thought, and her heart drummed painfully, marriage? Was this what Mrs. Willoughby was now trying to bring about?

Yet whether Mrs. Willoughby died now (which God forbid) or later, Andra's own problem remained——

At all costs she must make her peace with Philip before he discovered that she was an heiress—and at his expense.

"*The more you think the matter over, the more convincing will the situation seem.*"

Was marriage the situation which she herself was now considering?

Well, if it were not a success—she could at least, as his wife, give him his own money.

But would Philip take it?

Any solution was beyond her. The events of the past two days had overwhelmed her. She could only trust——

As if in answer, above the street, there came a deafening crash of thunder.

Barely had she gained the telephone-box than the storm broke. Lightning flashed incessantly. Torrentially, rain deluged the small scarlet booth.

Shakily she inserted her coins.

With regrettable speed she achieved the Club . . . and the Head Porter, suavity itself.

Two minutes later she heard Philip's voice rasp in her ear——

"Well?"

Unsteadily she said: "Philip, I've unexpected news for you. Your Aunt is in London. On Sunday evenings I work at the Henrietta Nursing Home, and to my surprise I find she is a patient there. . . . No, no . . . I hope it is not grave. But she is going to have an operation at nine-thirty to-morrow morning. I think you should go to the Home right away, for even if she cannot see you to-night, they may give you further details. I left this to you. Yes, of course . . . I've told her I'll be at the Home early to-morrow morning, and will wait till the operation is safely over. Luckily I've a holiday from the Museum to-morrow. Perhaps Philip, we could meet then—at the Home? Yes, I'm still in town. No, no, please don't think of it. I'm on my way home now. I'm . . . I'm sorry about this morning, Philip. Perhaps to-morrow may be a better day, once Mrs. Willoughby is safely through."

Her knees felt treacherously weak, as she replaced the receiver. She could only hope that she sounded more convincing than she felt.

Outside the downpour had redoubled onslaught.

Already the street was deserted. A narrow side street, yet,

in the lamp-light, through the mysterious amplitude of space, the rain advanced as an army of spears . . . phalanx upon phalanx, endlessly assailing the box.

She would have to wait—imprisoned in this glass case, with her thoughts.

Only with Philip was she still cast into confusion. It was as if this relationship, long since ended, were still unfinished. He was the most effectual distraction she had ever known.

"*A notable personality whom you recently lost through death.*"

So great had been her self-deception, that when the Reporter made this announcement yesterday—of Philip's death, as she supposed—she had been almost as bewildered by her pain, as by the news.

Vacantly she faced the deluge now——

And for one instant the storm, dashing at her through the glass shelter, lit up like a lost landscape the unknown region of her own soul.

How accurate were his unforgivable words!

Nothing had so effectively hardened her against him as the fact that he had loved Gerda. Yet, oddly enough, this had in no way altered her affection for Gerda—although it had amounted to a death-sentence where he himself was concerned.

Jealousy had sealed her off.

But it was one thing to recognize this herself, and quite another freely to accept that he also knew it!

How slyly too she had sought to heighten her own importance by repeated withdrawal! She saw it all now, for she was still, and always had been, passionately in love with him.

Quite unsuitably she had promoted herself to a solitude for which she was not truly fitted. At the same time, if it were not Philip, it could be no one else now.

Stricken she continued to stare out. But no longer blindly.

Of what use had been the restoration of her whole being through Monsignor Caius' discipline, if single-mindedness existed for a self duped as to its very nature?

Through the streaming window, lightning forked again. Startled, she glanced upwards and saw that the rain no longer advanced like lances at the level, but was descending in an assault of shining arrows.

"The next arrows," Monsignor had warned, "may be from above——"

Those arrows, which in Scupoli's words, were suggestions for excessive spiritual work—work beyond one's ability . . . for love was the only power that was not suspect.

Monsignor's final word had been *Watch*.

Well . . . at last she was on the look-out. She prayed that it was not too late!

And in her urgency now to put wrong right, there surged such a vitality that every effort, each difficulty was then and there discounted. All at once, she seemed to have achieved a second-wind.

To make amends to Mrs. Willoughby and Philip——

No, no, she had done with the dutiful approach . . . to love and to rejoice with them!

Mercifully there was still time.

Thank God for to-morrow!

As suddenly as it had started, the rain stopped. As conclusively as a direct answer!

Surely a good augury!

Then, and then only, did she realize that she was soaked through. The door of the telephone-box, which earlier she had opened an inch for air, had flooded the booth.

The arrows had got her after all.

Monday Morning . . . nine o'clock

By eight-thirty a.m., they sat side by side on the chintz sofa, in the waiting-room of the Nursing Home.

Philip had barely spoken. He looked haggard and remote.

Andra's surging confidence of last night had ebbed at the very sight of him.

But she was still determined on her course. She must earn the strength to see further, if insight were to be constant. And this could only be done by deed, although she now quailed at the thought of taking initiative——

Never before had she realized how slippery chintz could be! Each time Philip moved in his silent impatience, she slid towards him——

Spasmodically she clutched the sofa end.

The window was wide open, the air washed clean by last night's rain. Early sunlight, motionless and temperate, gilded the faded, pleasant room.

Mrs. Willoughby had seen neither of them this morning, nor Philip last night. Privately, Andra thought this hard upon him, but he had acquiesced with a grace that surprised her.

Through the open window they had watched Doctor and Anaesthetist arrive—both on foot.

The Doctor came first, his pace slower than one would expect. His expression was preoccupied, and somewhat daunting to the unseen observers.

The Anaesthetist followed in five minutes. He ran lightly up the steps—but he was frowning, his lips compressed, very much the man of the moment.

Finally, by car, the Surgeon himself stepped out, clean-shaven, fresh-faced, alert. A man-servant carried in two large cases, as if Mr. Cuthbert were going on a journey of some length.

Mr. Cuthbert, empty-handed, advanced up the steps at a level pace—his features mercifully so calm that the anxious might almost hope that he were smiling.

Through the closed door of the waiting-room, a certain voiceless bustle could now be heard in the hall.

Twenty minutes later, the Doctor went quickly down the steps. They could not see his face. He turned to the right, like a man in a hurry to be gone——

Then it became as quiet outside, as within, for the Surgeon had earlier dismissed his car.

The postman passed; a boy on a bicycle; a woman with a dog on a lead—but these people had no reality. They came and went like figments.

Abruptly Philip said: "They told me as little as they could last night. How long will the operation take?"

"At least an hour . . . perhaps more."

"Ha!" he exclaimed.

"Philip," she said, almost fearfully, "did the Vaucluse relic come before you left?"

"Of course not . . . and never will now." He sounded almost indifferent, but she was not deceived.

"I see from to-day's *Clarion*," he continued, "that you are opening the Standish Club this afternoon. An exceptional occasion," he added soberly. "It is very good of you to spare us time this morning."

It was now or never. She swallowed, and exclaimed:

"Philip . . . I'm sorry for my unkindness since your return. I begin to realize that if one fails with one person, one fails with all."

He gave a short laugh. "A spontaneous reaction is all

that matters to me. So spare me your charity. I'd feel more at home with hate."

"No, no," she said hurriedly, "now you misunderstand! In the past, I was afraid of loving you too much. But I know now that I've been incapable of loving you as I ought . . . I see that at last. And I would . . . I would be very glad to begin again with you."

To her consternation, he turned round, affixed his eye-glass, and surveyed her as if she were some curious and not altogether desirable object——

Then, rising deliberately, he seated himself on a chair opposite, as if more distantly to investigate an unwelcome phenomenon.

Apprehensively, she continued to gaze at him, the morning light full on her guileless face, revealing its startled intent.

Crossing his legs at leisure, he regarded her formally.

"May I ask," he inquired, "if this is a full-dress declaration on your part? Are you, in fact, proposing to me?"

"Yes . . . no . . . yes," her face flushed painfully. "That is to say, I wondered if you were still of the same mind about me? I didn't think you'd take it quite like this——"

"This is so sudden!" retorted Riberac. "I believe that is the classic response to an unexpected proposal——" but for the first time in their history, his voice shook.

Andra leant forward, forgetful of all as she heard this tremor. She put out her hand——

He continued, however, to regard her with a ceremony that dumbfounded and confused her.

"Before I accept this offer," he said politely, "I must know what has altered your attitude to me."

Abashed, she dropped her gaze. "I feel now that it would be a good thing . . . that is to say——"

"Oh, you do, do you? Perhaps this electric change of soul has something to do with my Aunt?"

Her heart lost a beat. Terrified she faced him. "What do you mean?" She sounded almost defiant.

"Exactly what I say. Intuition has briefed me. It occurs to me now that last night, in your heart to heart talk, my Aunt may have broken the lamentable news that in the event of her death, I do not get a *sou*. Belatedly you are going to award me with your affection—in compensation."

"How can you!" she broke off, paling.

"Quite easily. Well, as I have already said: I shall consider your offer. Half a loaf is better than no bread—as beggars cannot be choosers!" his irony was elaborating itself.

"Philip, I never thought of myself as even half a loaf."

"I do not refer to you—but to the cheerless motive that inspired your change of heart. That's all I'm interested in at the moment—although it now occurs to me that my Aunt may also have confided in you how she is disposing of this money. Has she?"

Trembling, Andra replied: " Don't you think that question rather indelicate?"

"No, suitably direct—from an interested party!" he broke off. "How well you play your part!" he gibed.

Again she swallowed, started to speak, failed.

"As you hesitate to reply," he pursued, "perhaps I can answer for you? I now think it highly possible that you have recently heard that a large portion of the Orth money may sooner or later, be coming to *you*. Hence your anxiety to benefit me. For, my dear Andra, you are nothing if not benevolent. Benevolence might almost be described as your besetting sin—where I am concerned."

"*Philip*!" her protest was all but inaudible.

Unmoved, he continued: "I see my surmise is correct. In which case there can be no doubt of my answer. I very much regret, my dear Andra, that I cannot accept this offer of yours—kindly meant as it no doubt is!"

His sarcasm ran like acid through her.

Blenching, she turned aside: "At such a time that's unforgivable," she whispered. "I can never forget this."

Disagreeably he smiled: "It's at least a comfort to have made some impression at last on your self-sufficiency."

Rising, he left the room, and, for the rest of their vigil, spent the time pacing up and down on the pavement outside.

At eleven-thirty, Mr. Cuthbert came downstairs, and Riberac re-entered by the open front door.

The day was again assuming the heat-wave pressure of the week-end.

In the waiting-room, Mr. Cuthbert's appearance surprised both enquirers—

He was smiling, and, as dapperly dressed as on arrival. But now his skin was pale, his brow wet, and he looked like a man who has just done a heavy route march under the worst possible conditions.

"I am happy to tell you," he began, "that the obstruction was a calcified fibroid. There were some particularly trouble-some adhesions. But Mrs. Willoughby should do well now. These findings are, I admit, a great relief to me."

Dr. Riberac frowned. "What did you fear?" he challenged.

Equally explicit Mr. Cuthbert replied, "A carcinoma of course."

Fearfully, Andra said: "Do you think she guessed?"

Carefully Mr. Cuthbert considered this. "Her's was a condition that usually starts with vague abdominal pains. Patients sometimes know more than we think. It is part of the burden of intelligence, and Mrs. Willoughby is not only highly intelligent, she is, in the best sense, a superior person. Silence is often a notable feature of such. Your guess is as good as mine."

There was a brief pause in which Mrs. Willoughby's unrecorded surmise leapt to life like a juggling giant among them.

"When may we see her?" demanded Dr. Riberac.

Mr. Cuthbert smiled again. "She may not be conscious till about nine to-night—and will probably be quite un-interested in her anxious relatives! But I see no reason why you should not have a look at her round about ten to-night. In fact, before she had her anæsthetic to-day, she instructed me to present you both with a gilt-edged invitation to this effect!"

"Thank you," said Andra, almost voicelessly, "I'll be here in good time." Quickly she turned, and left the room.

For the fraction of a second Riberac hesitated.

Then maintaining his stance, he declared: "It was only by chance last night that we discovered my Aunt had this ordeal before her. I am appalled that she should have faced it alone."

Mr. Cuthbert shook his head. "Some people prefer it that way, you know. I admit that they're the exception. But women who have learnt to live alone can face almost any-thing, I find. As the French say: it gives one to think!"

"Ha!" exclaimed his interrogator glassily. Then: "How long will she have to remain here?"

"At least a fortnight—if all goes well. After that she deserves a first-rate holiday. She's been pretty seedy for some time, you know. Like Rome, this sort of thing doesn't build up over-night. And she and I," Mr. Cuthbert admitted with yet another drop running fleetly off his brow, "certainly covered some ground in that theatre to-day. In fact—it's been quite a morning!"

Monday Afternoon . . . five o'clock

Riberac sat alone in his Club bedroom, a dreary back-chamber, facing the wide well of another forbidding building, but which to-day certainly boasted the virtue of coolness, as the last of the afternoon panted forth its heat beyond those gaunt walls.

By the old-fashioned wash-stand, were two pails of water which on Saturday he had ordered to remain in readiness for the Vaucluse relic which had never come. Pails that remained a mystery to the Club staff—the water of which the chamber-maid, nevertheless, religiously changed night and morning. There was also a builder's dandy-brush, purchased on Saturday, which stood on his toilet-table, to the further astonishment of that good woman. In fact the floor-staff had already wagered that a horse was expected.

In the desultory silence of the empty room, aftermath seemed to prolong itself indefinitely.

Doggedly he decided that the Club itself had got him down. He reminded himself that he had never been able to determine whether its bedrooms were uncomfortable or not —so cunningly had an adroit housekeeper, coping with deterioration of stock and a conservative committee, managed to mix the Members' blessings with minor miseries: his present unsatisfactory armchair plausibly cancelled by an excellent bed; the shabby carpet, which looked dirty but was not, mitigated by some redoubtable mahogany furniture; the face-towels thread-bare around their impressive monogram, absolved by a whale of a bath-towel. And although the elevator over the way rendered life hideous each time

anyone but himself used it, the floor service itself was
satisfactory enough.

He was perhaps as well here, as anywhere—hell being
clearly now his lot. And having slept little on Sunday night,
present discomfort was gradually merging in growing
weariness.

He could still see Andra's keepsake face and hear her
timidly say: "I never thought of myself as even half a loaf."

Maddening creature! Yet it was by such remarks that
she managed, time and again, to bring him unseen to her
feet again.

It was just possible that had he not spent the night
reading those accursed Standish memoirs, he might have
been less bitter this morning.

The book had proved one of the worst shocks of this
deceptive Jubilee week-end.

With patronage he had first scanned the eulogies from
reviewers on the paper-jacket. Fulsome, he decided, was the
word for these. Standish, whom he knew to be a talented
sculptor, but no more, was hailed here as a writer of exceptional ability. The book, it was claimed, would hold
a unique place among memoirs. Not only was it a summation, instead of the usual dispersal of impressions, but the
peculiar quality of the artist's inspiration lent it a fascination
so personal that this became of individual interest. But the
charm of the book, like the bouquet of a summer's day was
beyond analysis. *Armature* was in fact a masterpiece.

Sceptically Riberac had begun to read . . .

In the small hours of the morning he had put it down—
for the second time in his life, shaken to the foundation.

Yet not by a marble statue, this time, in Cadogan Park.

Again he saw Andra and Standish on that ball-room floor
at Buxleigh-on-Sea . . . once more he noted their curious
physical resemblance. They were exactly the same type.

But they had not danced together like brother and sister. Instinctively he had known that then.

And now this book revealed that, in a very different way, Standish had been nearer than hands or feet. In the only way that counted. And for years——

As the afternoon slowly sweltered on, the traffic of the distant street rising and falling like some metallic tide, he had begun to read the damned thing again. A section this time that was not concerned with Andra——

Imperceptibly, some of his fever left him.

The opulence, beloved of Standish's outward eye, did not betray him where words were concerned. With words he seemed able to draw upon a wider experience, involving the whole man. Modesty disciplined this study of himself. It had invested his memoirs with a simplicity more truly Greek than any of his sculptures.

His reviewers had but done him justice.

Silently Riberac relinquished the book again.

He was more deeply moved by it than he dared admit.

He glanced at his watch.

Five o'clock at last! The opening of the Standish Club would be over—hours ago. She must be safely home again —on her own. Beloved wretch!

With a sigh of relief that, likewise, he dared not examine, he lifted the telephone-receiver.

"Head-Porter?"

"Yes, sir?"

"Has the evening paper come in yet?"

"On its way up now, sir."

At that moment, an unseen hand slid it beneath his door. Swiftly he picked it up.

There, on the front page, he found what he expected. Triumphant head-lines and a close-up of the face that the Sculptor had made famous.

La Pleureuse full of Smiles Opens the Standish Club, spanned the sheet. But in the smiling photograph there was a hint of bewilderment in the eyes.

Poor angel, he thought suddenly, what a day of strain!

The captions however, gave no indication of this. *Memorable occasion . . . distinguished gathering . . . Miss Andra Hood recalls with charm to a crowded assembly an unforgettable incident in Sir Amos Standish's life——*

Riberac's relentless eye flashed down the column.

An incident as fantastic as it was simple—and yet completely characteristic of the man as Riberac now knew . . . this story of the young student who, through night work and the need to support his sister, could only reach the Art School after 10.0 p.m. when it was officially closed. Yet night after night, Standish had done what he would not ask the night-janitor to do. He had broken the rule himself— entering the empty place, as a director, and, once in the basement, secretly opening the window there to the young man, where clay, tools, and the antique models for diploma work were available. The student's nightly period of study completed, Standish had seen him out of the window, bolted it, and himself departed by the main entrance as usual. And this sacrifice of time had continued for a year. If the janitor had suspected that the law was regularly broken, he had given no sign, except by a careful avoidance of the basement at midnight! And this same student, no longer young, no longer wedded to central London, would now be able to reach Sir Amos Standish's house, for delivery of a weekly course of Lectures, to similar students. He was, in fact, present this afternoon and had authorized this story, for he was none other than the eminent Paolo Baptista, winner of the Rome Grand Prix, and although now middle-aged, still an expert in basement window negotiation!

For the first time in days, Riberac smiled.

Amid enthusiastic applause La Pleureuse declared the Club open to all members by the front door! Wearing a summer-like ensemble in clove-carnation colour, Miss Hood's heart-shaped hat framed her suave beauty to perfection, and will no doubt sponsor a new fashion.

Probably one of her Venice dresses——

His smile faded.

The nightmare element in the day again enclosed him.

For the third time that afternoon he put a call through to the Nursing Home. His Aunt might now be conscious. Surgeons did not always know.

This time the voice appeared more resigned to his.

"Mrs. Willoughby is not round yet, Dr. Riberac. It is not to be expected. There had to be injections as well as the anæsthetic, you know."

"But how does she look?"

"As she should," the voice assured him. "Everything is quite in order."

A spurious confidence faded as soon as he laid the receiver down.

Sombrely he stared out at the remote patch of blue sky, from which colour was now draining with the diminishing day.

All along his Aunt must have known that where she was concerned, her money came first with him. What an insufferable affront! Yet all those years she had, impassively enough, put up with him!

And now that damned fortune meant less than nothing to him.

This was his nemesis.

Her recovery had become his one concern. No, if the truth were known, would always have come first. He had sacrificed Andra and himself for a mirage. He had not even known *himself.*

His Aunt's recovery must still remain in doubt (they could say what they liked) till she came round——

An ordeal that consumed him hourly.

Andra's problem and his own—everything had come to a standstill as the minutes trickled through a blocked sandglass.

Was it possible that this present, peculiar anguish of his was with others a commonplace?

Then, in the enormous dis-array of life, freedom must lie in evolving an ordered attitude to this agony, which he now found unbearable? And this, he next suspected, would only be secured at some prodigious cost—— Therefore, there must be, after all, a sense in which suffering could be regarded as *work*.

Was it conceivable that prayer was, then, the means by which this burden grew intelligible?

Certainly, he now found himself reduced to a state of almost speechless supplication.

That 12th century hymn once heard at Kew jingled again in mind.

> *O come, Thou Key of David, come . . .*
> *Make safe the way that leads on high,*
> *And close the path to misery.*

But so green was he in this unwelcome growth, this gnawing anxiety, that had he been one of those enabled to kneel, he would simply now have besought for something, anything to distract his mind until the worst was over——

In God's name, he would!

The telephone bell rang stridently.

He seized the receiver—and heard the Head Porter announce:

" Sir, an Inspector from the Post Office has just called with a parcel. He believes it to be the one you have been expecting since Saturday. It is in good order, but went in error first to Pimlico and then to Peckham, instead of Pall Mall—the writing of address leaving something to be desired."

Dazed, Riberac ejaculated, " *What*?"

"As the parcel is in good order, sir, and I have signed to this effect, the official has gone."

"But the package——"

"It is now on its way up to you—alone."

Hoarsely Riberac replied, "Oh it is, is it?"

He rang off with a laugh that the Head Porter regarded as abnormal.

Again Riberac stood in the centre of the torpid room, a man of unusual size and strength, but now stunned, inert. The instantaneous answer to his prayer amounted to a blow beneath the belt. He was completely winded by this benevolence.

Through the open window, a breath of air twitched the casement curtain—the first semblance of a breeze in days. But he neither saw nor felt. He merely waited.

The Vaucluse Angel was on its way up at last. And alone!

Two minutes later there was a peremptory knock on the door. An unmistakable summons. The second porter was taking no chances. This was an important occasion, and he knew it. The entire Club knew it—although the blinking Parcel, with its fancy labels, looked no better than a blasted football on the spree.

Dr. Riberac opened the door, gripped his treasure, and briefly said: "I may have to place the contents of this package in the Club safe shortly. Will there be space to accommodate it?"

"Certainly, sir. We'll clear a place at once." There had been nothing in the safe for days except Lord Kearsey's spare denture, and the second porter retired at once to report the latest.

With deliberate calm, Riberac laid the package on the toilet table.

Then, with calculated precision, he unrolled a large blue print and spread it on the bed. A diagram of measurements——

The Vaucluse Angel's skeleton.

Sheer affectation, of course, as Riberac knew this by heart.

Methodically, without any hurry, he next drew out a large photograph of the Panel itself.

Frowning, he considered this afresh, in an attempt to steady himself.

Like a thread, the crack dividing the first and second find ran across the Panel. Yet dynamically the Angel advanced to his own—the man outstretched on his bier. Or the monk upon his bed, as Riberac believed it to be—so closely did this structure resemble a Carmelite couch of trestles and boards. He still cherished the idea that the rigid form upon it might well be a self-portrait of the artist. Now, with Standish so recently in mind, he even toyed with the idea that the Angel's missing hand might be conveying to him some tool of his calling. The weighty turn of the Angel's forearm had always precluded, to him, the suggestion of a scroll; the Angel's ironical smile, the presentation of laurels.

Across the top of the Panel, there now ran the completed inscription: *O God, the Light of every heart that sees Thee*, with at the foot, *The Strength of every mind that seeks Thee*, while along the narrow couch of the monk, the once missing phrase was in its place, *The Life of every soul that loves Thee*.

The gift of the Angel alone was lacking, but might even now lie in this very room.

Swiftly Riberac scanned that heroic form again: the

blameless benediction of the raised right hand, the bland brow, the sightless eyes, the sardonic curve of those mediaeval lips. Even to a sceptic, this figure's divinity was embarrassingly apparent.

Riberac drew a deep breath, and removed his coat.

"Now for it!" he muttered.

Rapidly he cut off the string from Baxter's package. Dexterously, he undid the wrappings. Baxter had made a sound job of these. There was still hope that the relic might be undamaged.

In a matter of seconds, Riberac lifted out the wedge, but Mrs. Baxter's soiled green baize covering took much longer to dislodge. Her linen thread was compacted with the dirt of years, and Riberac grunted with satisfaction. This thick padding was the best protection that the relic could have had.

Her final stitches, however, proved to be the very devil—coated with grime that was now slippery as wax.

Finally, he folded back the rotting baize, and in both palms delicately held a thing like a shapeless but heavy boulder.

Against this putty-coloured mass, his own hands were, for the first time, arrestingly revealed—large, as befitted his frame, but spare and singularly spiritual . . . the bones, beautifully proportioned, and, in movement, supple, expressive. Hands that could as easily deal with a spade, an instrument, or a pen—in the catholic fashion of the monks of old.

Next—he drew up the low chair, then at once rejected it. This might prove a long business. Owing to his exceptional height, he would make better speed upon his knees.

Bending over the first pail, he plunged his hands with their precious burden into the waiting water.

Slowly, rhythmically he proceeded to knead the clay.

At the end of twenty minutes he had loosened the mass. Then with infinite care, he began to remove the clay, tirelessly dipping it, at every other moment, into the water.

By the end of a further laborious half hour, the bulk had gone.

As the authentic gray stone began to show, he recalled Andra's exclamation on first seeing the Panel:

"Why, it's a gray Angel!" and then the words she had quoted, "' *Drudgery, the gray Angel of success!* '"

Persuasively, persistently, his living hands continued to chafe the cold gray one.

Then slowly he reached for the other pail of water. And with this now before him, his tall back bent almost double, he started upon the most critical part of his task—softening, relaxing, mollifying the last tenacious grip of clay.

No patient ever received a more penetrating or solicitous massage than was now given this hidden hand.

On one point he was determined. There should be no examination, no truckling to curiosity till the imprisoned member was free. The occasion was too unnerving——

At the end of an hour and ten minutes, he held the Angel's hand in his.

With a sense of stupefaction, he stared at it, and continued to stare—the tears which for the first time in his life had painfully pricked his eyes in Cadogan Park on Friday, now starting freely to his lids.

Yet it was characteristic of him that his glance flashed first to the broken wrist.

Yes . . . it would fit well enough into its old socket. He knew those projections, and that hollow as if he'd designed them!

Holding his breath, he turned the heroic hand over——

It held a formidable stone key, about seven inches in length. By some providence the protruding wards were still undamaged. The terminal bore ornamentation—no, he was wrong! A Latin inscription gave this enrichment.

His heart beating faster, he stretched for the builder's dandy-brush, and smartly whisked the last of the clay from the close-set letters. Then, his magnifying glass adjusted, he translated with astonishment.

O, come Thou key of David, come.

Shaken, he laid the massive hand upon the table.

The identical invocation of the hymn sung at Kew had reached him again, but this time in its original 12th century setting!

He was bereft of all but wonder.

But so strange, so foreign was this emotion that he could not sustain it. Instead, an up-surging of hope came to his aid.

Urgently, but reverently he bent over the Angel's hand.

"You've been damned lucky to me all along," he muttered, "damned lucky. Now, for heaven's sake see the three of us through!"

It was perhaps less a petition than an order, but a prayer it nevertheless remained.

As the *Clarion* had already stated, Dr. Riberac had at last a clue.

The afternoon's celebrity, having earlier removed her hat and gloves, sat solitary in the kitchen, and began a light supper of sandwiches—found that she could not eat, and drank instead some water.

In the dim light of the chestnut tree, the clove carnation summer frock clung like a cloud to her, formless, vague. Her face was pale, her gaze withdrawn.

"No!" she cried suddenly, "it's gone on too long——"
In two minutes she had telephoned the Nursing Home.

"Sister, I'm sorry but——"

"That's all right, Miss Hood! We've had Dr. Riberac on the line almost hourly. You're a model of restraint in comparison! Mrs. Willoughby came round twenty minutes ago, and, I'm glad to say, seems fairly comfortable."

"Oh, thank God . . . thank God!"

"Yes, indeed . . . And she has already asked for both of you! But this doesn't mean that *we* want you here a minute before ten to-night. Matron telephoned Dr. Riberac at once to set his mind at rest. Unfortunately, he'd earlier gone out —so he hasn't heard yet. Probably he'll be ringing soon——"

To the moment, with shattering precision, the front bell pealed.

Smiling, Andra opened the door, and saw him dark against the golden blur of the evening—for once his forcible face gentle.

"Philip, she's safely through—twenty minutes ago. And has asked for both of us. Isn't it wonderful?"

Soberly he bent and kissed her—neither aware that he had done so.

Quite simply he followed her into the kitchen, and without a word spoken, without pausing to sit down, began to devour the last of her sandwiches.

Compassionately she watched, as she poured his coffee.

"Nothing since breakfast," he added hastily. "One hundred apologies."

In the green gloom of the room, they seated themselves at last—with a sigh that again neither noticed.

Spent as they were, their present peace seemed to both dream-like. For Riberac—so precarious it must be lightly snared.

"At the risk of appearing coquettish," he announced, "I am about to change my mind."

Helplessly Andra began to laugh. "You've made me very happy."

"The happiest woman in the world," he corrected. "What about San Francisco next, and a glimpse of the Moffats?"

Smiling, she nodded. "But Mrs. Willoughby must come too, Philip. It's essential now. A sea voyage would be the very thing."

"Confound it! This must be the first time on record that a man's been expected to take his Aunt on his honeymoon!"

"But you were born to make history, dearest! Besides I ought to warn you: already she's asked Major Treves to call."

"Major Treves . . . what the devil has that to do with our trip?"

"Everything, Dr. Riberac! Have you forgotten that Madame Franz Orth, if left alone, invariably marries?"

Amused, his eye gleamed. "In that case, I can still foresee personal benefit. Major Treves is, as far as I am concerned, the perfect uncle."

Trifling together in the warm dusk, he found it idyllic to watch her. All the colourless beauty of the statue was there, with the calm that carries its own shadows. No wonder the Sculptor had loved her, and that London had hailed her to-day.

"Just tell me this," he demanded. "Why did Standish never marry?"

For a moment she hesitated.

"In confidence he once told me. There was insanity in his family."

"Good God!" said Riberac, stricken, "good God . . ."

"And yet," she said slowly, "he was the sanest man I ever knew."

With compunction, in the attendant pause, Riberac heard for the first time the secret ticking of the kitchen clock—felt its neglected pulse race, then check, before it pursued its set course.

And it was he who started violently when again the front bell rang.

"Sit!" he commanded, "I'll settle this——"

Just as he used to do at Kew . . .

Frowning his disapproval, he opened the front door—his lack of cordiality instantly justified.

Inexplicably—there stood his pet aversion, hat in hand, pleasantly smiling. Burrowes of the *Clarion* in all his guile. Static behind those glasses . . . tenacious as a leech.

"Dr. Riberac!" said the Reporter winningly, "how d'you do? I didn't realize that you were a friend of Miss Hood's."

"Well, I am and I'm not. You've come at the worst possible time. That seems to be your fate and my misfortune. We can give you exactly ten minutes."

He prodded him towards the kitchen.

"Good evening, Miss Hood! None the worse for our afternoon, I hope? Dr. Riberac, this lady might have been opening Standish Clubs every day of her life—which brings me to my present mission. The suggestion of a permanent hostess there. Lord Fortdevon's idea. The Trustees have a proposal to make——"

"Too late," said Riberac grimly. "I've beaten his lordship by minutes—but a miss is as good as a mile."

"Then am I to understand?" hungrily Mr. Burrowes looked round.

"You are. And your astonishment is as nothing to mine. For years in my earnest, artless way I've believed myself to be in pursuit of a recluse. To-day I discover her to be the *Clarion's* top note, instead of my lost chord. The National Anthem, however, winds up all hubbub, and sends everyone home. You too I hope."

"Then there's no chance?"

"None. We're emigrating—in self-defence."

Hurriedly Andra intervened. "But please thank the Trustees for me, Mr. Burrowes. From the heart."

"Well, Dr. Riberac, it only remains to congratulate you, and to wish Miss Hood every happiness. Is this vital news by any chance public yet?"

"Public? How can it fail to be public when you butt in on my declaration?"

Sympathetically Mr. Burrowes clucked. Soothingly he said:

"But think of the time that this is bound to save you to-morrow!"

"*To-morrow?*" the word shot from Riberac.

"The Vaucluse Angel, of course. And a matter of public importance. Come, Dr. Riberac, you know that! But here you are to-night. What could be better—for all concerned? The *Clarion's* got one question—and one only. *Has the Vaucluse find been verified?*"

"This afternoon—at five o'clock. I have examined it myself. It is in excellent condition——" he hesitated for a second, "which I admit is the greatest possible relief."

Mr. Burrowes' glasses gleamed. He had already pulled out a paper pad.

Andra, her lashes wet, but wreathed in smiles, silently watched them both.

"Now, Dr. Riberac," said the Reporter softly, "you really must have a heart! Let me put it like this: I too am an excavator of sorts, and digging out information has its own difficulties. But this is a great—indeed, a unique occasion," he moistened his lips in anticipation: "*What has the Angel got in his hand?*"

"A key," said Dr. Riberac briefly. "Notably carved, as befits a masterpiece. But that is all I shall say of this particular object meantime."

"Then at least give us your final views on the Vaucluse Memorial itself."

Reflectively, Dr. Riberac frowned. "It is a purely personal belief, of course, that in the dying, or awakening man, we have a portrait of the unknown artist. But the irony of the Angel's smile now seems to suggest that beyond the present vision of the seer, there is a further mystery to be overcome . . . more effort . . . greater achievement."

"But the key in the Angel's hand?" persisted Mr. Burrowes, for once forgetting to pacify. "Hang it all, that's surely the solution?"

Dr. Riberac smiled. "The key is a great comfort. I have no doubt of that. Like any other clue it must prove most helpful—to the zealous inquirer. Yes, undoubtedly the searcher is on the right road."

"But you feel it will be a long one?"

"Not necessarily. It does not do to dogmatize on any quest. In the archaeological field (like your own to-night!) some important discoveries have been made with ease. The celebrated Giovanni Belzoni, for instance, excavated a valuable Tomb near Biban el Muluk when his walking stick suddenly sank by chance. Such cases are, of course, rare, and in Belzoni's own words he suffered atrocious persecution from malice, jealousy, envy throughout his many and curiously lucky researches. Difficulty certainly seems to be our usual element. But whatever the way turns out to be, and it may well differ in each case, I have no doubt of one thing——" Riberac paused.

The Reporter's pencil poised—attentively.

"That it will be supremely significant . . . even in the case of failure."

"And that's your last word on the Vaucluse Angel?"

"No. It's my last word on the man visited. Who am I to express a first, let alone a last word on any angel? Let the Vaucluse Angel speak for himself! In a short time the Public will be able to form its own conclusions. His hand will be restored to him. The key will be available for all— who have the insight *and* strength to use it."

"Just so!" said Mr. Burrowes appreciatively. "And now, Dr. Riberac, as I'm as good as gone, would it be an imposition to inquire your own plans? I refer, of course, to the forthcoming marriage? It isn't every day that the *Clarion* enjoys a double scoop. I feel rather like Belzoni with his walking stick! I hope you'll be indulgent."

Riberac rose. "My plans? Well, it may save trouble later if you get these into the paper's mortuary-file to-night! *To all reporters whom it may concern:* As from to-day, my address ceases to be care of the Vaucluse Angel—for despite the fact that she has sometimes proved the very devil in elusiveness, I intend to spend the rest of my life by the Angel, Islington. Bury me with her—anywhere you like. And forget me."

Smiling, they showed the young man out.

Side by side, indulgently, they watched him drive away. After the gloom of the chestnut tree at the back of the house, the golden summer evening in front was bathed in shadowless glory. From the small garden plot beside them, raised like a posy before the basement's sunken eye, a late bee hummed home in the heat. The silence vibrated for half a lifetime with its 'cello note.

Facing west together, the light benignly gilded their bare heads.

"Oh, Philip," she cried, "and it doesn't set till after nine, when we leave for the Home. We could walk to Caenwood first, if we go now. There's still some of the day left. Isn't that joyful—we've got a whole hour yet!"

"An hour!" he scoffed. "What are you raving about? We've got the rest of our lives together. Merciful heavens!" he stopped short, "this is the worst of my many crimes-I've made you thankful for trifles. This I'll never forgive myself!"

Shaking with laughter, she caught his hand, and drew the door behind them.

"Wait," he ordered in his peremptory way. "We've forgotten something."

Shouldering his way into the dusk of the deserted hall, he picked up the Standish book from the table there.

"Not that we can do it justice to-night," he added, "but we'll take him along with us, nevertheless. After all, my marble love, we owe him a great deal. Perhaps more than we guess . . ."

THE END